Jack O'Connell
Seattle
16 marzo 1984

THE GARDEN
OF
PERSEPHONE

THE GARDEN
OF
PERSEPHONE

CESAR J. ROTONDI

ST. MARTIN'S PRESS / NEW YORK

Copyright © 1982 by Cesar J. Rotondi
For information, write: St. Martin's Press,
175 Fifth Avenue, New York, N.Y. 10010
Manufactured in the United States of America

Library of Congress Cataloging in Publication Data

Rotondi, Cesar J.
   The garden of Persephone.

   1. Roger II, King of Sicily, d. 1154—Fiction.
2. Sicily—History—1016-1194—Fiction. I. Title.
PS3568.O872G3   813'.54   81-14608
ISBN 0-312-31682-8   AACR2

Design by Manuela Paul

10 9 8 7 6 5 4 3 2 1

First Edition

To Michele Amari

Many of the keener perspectives of medieval Sicily are due to the work of one man, Michele Amari of Palermo. About a century ago this Arabist scholar wrote his brilliant *History of the Muslims in Sicily,* a work as yet unpublished in English. To my knowledge, he was the first historian to consult the text of Hebrew, Arabic, and Greek scholars written during the Middle Ages, enabling us to have a broader view—and often a more disinterested one—than that supplied by the historian monks whose works are more readily accessible in the West.

O singer of Persephone!
In the dim meadows desolate
Dost thou remember Sicily?

Wilde, "Theocritus"

Contents

Introduction
Under Etna

For a land that has enjoyed its "day in the sun" so often, Sicily has a sadly restricted image for most of us. Shakespeare's audience may have been more familiar than we are with the role of Syracuse as the most wealthy and powerful state of the 4th century. Even less familiar, perhaps, is Sicily under the Normans, those brilliant rovers from Scandinavia who settled on the northeast coast of France and conquered England at approximately the same time they wrested Sicily from Arab domination. After a few generations of Norman rule, the Renaissance showed its first beginnings in Sicily. Dante paid tribute to the southern court of Emperor Frederick II, the redoubtable *Stupor Mundi,* where rose the first comprehensive body of written literature in the West. The sonnet form remains to remind us of it.

The soil for this blossoming of the arts was fertilized by Frederick's grandfather, Roger II, who figures prominently in this book. Under his enlightened rule, Sicily reached a peak of wealth and distinction, and significantly, Roger encouraged a society that was unique in melding disparate cultures. The Arab and the Jew shared their knowledge of medicine, the physical sciences, and the ancient Greek savants; the Byzantines lent their art and sophistication; the Normans gave their energy and talent for government. My protagonist, Julien, was one of the many Englishmen drawn to Sicily during this fascinating period.

Julien is fictitious, as are the members of his family, his early acquaintances, and his friend Aziz. Robert of Selby, Thomas Browne, and virtually all the other characters had careers substantially as I have tried to depict them. Italics identify direct quotes from Bernard of Clairvaux and others.

BOOK ONE

THE BAPTIZED SULTAN

Chapter I
BROTHER RALF

All night the wind had hurtled with the relentless vigor of an early, assertive spring. Bits of hail no larger than grains of sand needled the narrow, cloudy glass of his single window, and Julien knew they would taste of the sea. He looked out over the cloister glazed with a fresh, rough coat of ice that struggled to trap the feeble glints of dawn. It had been an interminable winter. He unfastened the brooch of his cloak and sat down on the three-legged stool.

His was a choice cell. Directly over the ovens of the warming room, it was also close to the stairs that led to the latrine. He paced the length of it a few times and then sank to his knees to pray that he might be freed of frivolous distractions—a short prayer.

Matins had lasted for almost three hours that morning and the chapel had only just begun to warm as they were leaving. Apart from the fact that the long services were boring, they also meant less time for study. Last week Julien had to reproach himself with penance for that thought, but now it no longer mattered. After yesterday's surprising news, he admitted he could do little more than tick off the hours until he could leave the monastery behind him. He fingered the open book on the table, testing the thick edge of parchment with his thumbnail, then snapped it shut irritably and rose to hang his cloak on a peg.

Yesterday, in the hour before vespers, a canon on pilgrimage had come with a message from his father, Nigel, delivered orally since his father did not write and nor, it appeared, did the canon. Julien was ordered to return to Yorkshire as quickly as possible. His kinsman Robert of Selby had petitioned for him, and Julien was to leave Durham Abbey and his studies to sail from England with him as soon as the weather permitted. Where were they going? The canon didn't know, or didn't remember if he had indeed been told, but Robert had already left his service in King Henry's exchequer and was with Nigel in Eastallerton, waiting for Julien's arrival.

Julien had seen Robert only once, years ago when he was still a child. He reckoned Robert was no more than a dozen years older than he, but his adventures and his successful career in the king's service were spoken of proudly in his family, and there was no relative Nigel admired more.

It was Robert's father who had led Nigel to the Crusade over thirty years before. Robert was said to be much like his father. He was certainly as strong and quite good looking; fair and taller than most of the others in the family. Julien himself was about five feet, five inches tall, taller than most of the Saxons on his mother's side, but he often wished he'd inherited the Norman stature of his father's relatives. Many of Julien's contemporaries mingled the blood of the conqueror with the conquered. The knights who followed King William from Normandy were urged to take Anglo-Saxon wives, often with the inducement of an heiress's estate. Julien's mother was a Saxon with just a strain of Danish blood, and her family's name was respected well beyond the bounds of Yorkshire.

Julien's toes were still numb from the chill of matins, and he bent to massage them. The pointed leather slippers were finer but not as warm as the ones which had been made from two rabbits trapped by his older brother, Godwin. When his cold feet seemed almost unbearable in the icy chapel, he would glance at Brother Edward, who had gone to matins barefoot that morning, as he was wont to when suffering from one of the knottier trials that plagued him. Now that Julien was preparing to leave, he was tempted to tell Brother Edward exactly what he thought of his penance. Better not to. Edward had signalled that he wanted to visit Julien's cell to speak to him later that morning, and Julien had nodded.

He sighed and continued rubbing. Quite a number of the monks were missing toes, and Julien supposed Edward could hardly wait until he too bore the same visible acknowledgment of his triumph over the flesh. The thought was loaded with seeds of sin, and he sank to his knees for a quick, expiatory prayer. He had only himself to blame for his disappointment, he reflected. How could he possibly have hoped to have his prayers for the future answered when he was still subject to so many importunate but trivial distractions?

Julien returned to the window and looked at the smoke that had started to issue from the louvers in the kitchen roof just to the side of the dormitory. The wind fanned the smoke into a gauzy, horizontal curtain that was quickly dispersed. At least, he thought, I'll be leaving gloomy Durham.

If he were to stay at Durham Abbey much longer, he was sure to be pressured into taking solemn vows. Prior Anselm had been quite firm on this point. Options were running out.

Prior Anselm had cold gray eyes that bulged like a lizard's, and he squinted until the pupils were thin wet slits when he spoke of the rewards of a vocation. Julien believed he knew exactly what Anselm had in mind. There would be a year, or maybe even two or three, of his subdiaconate spent on the Holy Island. Then Anselm might actually want him to be a deacon there. Lindisfarne! Julien shuddered and rubbed the places on his arms that had started to prickle against the rough wool of his robe. The ground there, he had been told, often thawed by June. Late June.

"Precisely." He could hear Anselm assenting in his dry, rustling voice. Lindisfarne was a discipline, of course—a discipline particularly appropriate for clerks who seemed to value their intellectual exercises more dearly than the spiritual ones offered by Durham Abbey.

Julien knew his character had been closely observed by his superiors in recent months, and Prior Anselm's comments were the most critical. Only Brother Ralf could be depended upon to appreciate his absorption with temporal knowledge. On the other hand, Ralf could hardly defend what the others considered Julien's excessive concern for his physical comfort.

There was more to it than that, but Julien knew it was wrong to think about it. If only anyone but Prior Anselm had been chosen for his confessor! At first when Julien confided the lapses in his not remarkable conduct, Prior Anselm rarely expressed anything but an overwhelming longing to return to the private meditations of his cell. Having already catalogued all possible misdemeanors, Anselm found it convenient to apportion guilt for them equally to all who came to him. But Julien found him an avid listener the night he decided it would be best to mention that he did indeed occasionally slip his hand under his shirt at night to get some relief from the hungry incubus that plagued all the younger inmates. From then on, he heard footsteps outside his door more times than usual, and there appeared to be increased surveillance of his private hours.

There was often an eye at the peephole of the younger clerks' cells. It was a peephole quite large enough to admit a ray of light that fell precisely on the center of the straw mattress. Not much was thought of these casual nocturnal surveys, but Julien was sure he recognized Anselm's shuffling steps more often.

When did Anselm find time to sleep? he asked himself. He had heard that some saints never needed sleep and wondered if Anselm might already be destined for sainthood. Northumberland had contributed more than its share of saints to the calendar, and not a few of them had been abbots of Durham.

Bede, whose sainthood was further distinguished by the title The Venerable, was buried at Durham, and Julien genuinely did venerate him, as he did the scholarly St. Cuthbert, whose tomb was there as well. But Julien often wondered about Oswald, Swithbert, Benedict Biscop, Aidan, Ethelwold, Wilfrid—and so many others that the recitation of their names seemed to drone on forever during Mass. He recognized that it was a sin of pride that made him revere Bede more highly than the others, and he quickly mumbled a prayer for forgiveness.

A scratching sound at the door told him that Edward was there, and Julien rose to ask him in. Edward was still barefoot. He stepped in and gave Julien the kiss of peace. "We're going to miss you, Julien. I know we didn't always get along too well, but I think of you often and always remember you in my prayers."

Julien thanked him with a curt nod. It occurred to him at just that moment that perhaps Edward was better inured to the cold by reason of the fat that enveloped him. It was easy to forget how fat he was, because when one thought of Edward, the first recollection was of his color. He is surely the pinkest man anyone has ever seen, Julien thought. It's all that pink fat that keeps the cold out. That's why he can bathe in cold water.

"Do you mind my coming to see you for a private farewell?" Edward said. His eyes were sweeping across the room, which was as bare as his own except for a shelf with a dozen books on it suspended over the desk. "By the beard of the virgin Wilgefortis, why do you need all those books?"

Although his question was posed good-naturedly, it struck a raw nerve in Julien. "We don't all have the same intellectual standards," he said icily, then instantly regretted his patronizing tone. He knew that Edward was perfectly content with a life of self-examination, and he had long ago decided to avoid a head-on confrontation with him. "I'm sorry. It's very kind of you to seek me out on my last day."

"Don't mention it. I have some information for you about your kinsman Robert of Selby."

"Yes?" Julien instantly perked up.

"Have you ever spoken to Father Cuthbert, the one who runs the bishops' mint?"

"I know who he is, but I've never said much to him."

"Then, you probably don't know that he trained with Robert of Selby before accepting his post here. They were both in the king's exchequer in London. He knows him well."

"And what does he say of him?"

"That you should be pleased that he asked your father to let you join him. He has a great career ahead of him, and the kind of opportunity he can offer you doesn't appear very often."

Julien sighed. "I suppose so, though I do wish my father had consulted my wishes before committing me."

"What did you want instead? I know you were set against taking your solemn vows."

Julien looked at Edward levelly. "You know how I feel about Abelard. I'd have given anything to study with him in Brittany. Imagine being able to spend time with the most daring thinker of our day!"

Edward pursed his lips. "He may be daring all right, but you won't find many here who agree with his ideas save you and Brother Ralf. All that humanist business may be very well for foreigners, but here in England, you'd best stick to revealed knowledge."

Julien rolled his eyes in exasperation. "But don't you see what's happening here? In the old days, when Bede was abbot, they used to write books. Now you're happy copying them and making them prettier and more graceful."

Edward looked at him loftily. "Our illuminations are considered as elegant as any produced anywhere."

"That's just what I mean. Oh, let's change the subject. Tell me about Cuthbert. Did he have anything else to say about Robert? Does he know where we're likely to be going?"

"Well, he can only guess, but he gossiped about Robert's reputation."

"I know about that. He's the most respected man in my family."

"No, not that, you goose," Edward giggled. "Didn't you know he's got a string of bastards between York and London that was the talk of the court?"

"So, what of it? Does Cuthbert know anything I don't?"

"He thinks you'll be going to Aquitaine."

"Aquitaine? Whatever for?" Julien's eyes widened, but the prospect didn't displease him.

"Well, Robert has such a taste for high living. If you were to choose a place for the finest wines, plenty of good music and poetry, and the most available women, it would be Aquitaine, wouldn't it?"

"Yes, I suppose so," Julien said thoughtfully. "I love the idea of travel. Have you ever been to London?"

"No, have you?"

"No, but my brother Godwin went a few times on his knight's service. He tells such wonderful stories. They have cookhouses on the banks of the Thames with the most savory meats and honeycakes, and there are fine French wines to be sampled too. Last time he went he was even daring enough to incise his mark on a corner of the great Tower."

"Are the women as fine and beautiful as they say?" Edward had opened his narrow blue eyes wider than Julien had ever seen them.

"I suppose so, but Godwin's really not very good at describing such matters. He always ends up describing things as he imagines them."

"Oh, come now. Didn't he ever . . . you know?"

"Once when he was drunk he told me so, but he was pretty blurry. All I could make of it was that he had a go at a ha' penny upright."

It took them a moment to realize that someone was standing in the doorway Julien had left open. They both blushed at the sight of Prior Anselm's ashen face smoldering with indignation. "How dare you disobey one of our most essential rules?" he hissed. "Julien, you know what the penalty is for entertaining a peer in your room."

"He was taking his leave of me," Julien stammered, "and anyway the door was open."

"It wouldn't have remained open much longer!" Anselm seemed to be pushing the words out from between his teeth. "I heard enough of your conversation to know where it would have led. Evil thoughts to evil words to evil acts."

Julien knelt. "Please give me penance, then, for the foul thought I expressed, but that was the extent of my evil intent." He remained with his head bent.

Anselm looked at Edward, who was trembling in the doorway. "Leave us. I'll give no punishment now." Edward hastily blessed himself and fled. "Get up, Julien. I want a word with you." Julien rose and faced the prior but kept his head meekly bent.

"I respect the choice your father made for you, but it is still my duty to see if there is a possibility of a vocation in the Church which has been overlooked by you."

"I don't believe so," Julien replied quickly.

"It's not what *you* believe. Let *me* be the judge of whether or not God has chosen you. The ways of the Almighty are strange, and it wouldn't be the first time his grace fell upon one of the most grievous of sinners. Remember how vice-ridden St. Augustine was."

"Yes, Your Grace."

"It's my belief you're just bored. You think too much of travel. Couldn't you have waited until after the first year of your subdiaconate? You know I always promised you a pilgrimage to the shrine of your choice."

Julien mustered his courage. "I believe I *am* bored."

Something about his reply disturbed Anselm and his features knotted.

"You need discipline. I pray it's not too late. Will you come to my office this evening? I wish to leave a few last thoughts with you at that time." He turned and shuffled silently out.

Julien sat on his stool again and wiped his brow in relief. He was bored, all right. The thought of going on with rounds of study and prayer until death claimed him was appalling. Here he was, eighteen since last St. Sebastian's Day, and, with the exception of an occasional visit to one of the neighboring monasteries to hear a lecturer, the only times he left Durham were when he was allowed to join the hunting parties to search out red deer in the bishop's forest.

Prior Anselm's promise of a pilgrimage set Julien's thoughts roaming. The prospect of such a trip often occupied much of the time assigned for meditation. He yearned to go to Mount Gargano in Italy to visit the shrine of St. Michael built on the spot where the saint first showed himself in Europe, a favorite with the Normans, perhaps because they saw in St. Michael's upraised sword an echo of their own destiny.

Julien decided he would think of his trip with Robert of Selby as a sort of pilgrimage. Even if it wasn't the undertaking of his choice, the years of discipline at the monastery helped to numb his disappointment. And Robert had travelled to every corner of the kingdom, even to Normandy.

The door to Julien's cell opened and interrupted his woolgathering. "Do I disturb your prayers?"

"Come in, Brother Ralf. I was hoping you would find a few minutes for me before lauds." Julien rose and embraced his tutor warmly.

Ralf was not yet forty, but he looked years older. His large frame carried little flesh on it and he was pale, but his eyes were often unexpectedly merry in an otherwise ascetic face. His hands were broad and rough, more those of a farmer than a scholar. Instead of the monk's tonsure, Ralf's hair was clipped to a short stubble which grew unevenly over badly healed scars that covered his scalp. He appeared graver than usual. "Are you still so disappointed?"

Julien took one of Ralf's hands in his own smaller ones. It was warm and dry, and he enjoyed the strength he felt in it.

"I've been thinking of nothing else for the last two nights. I don't believe I've slept more than two hours since I got the news. But how kind of you to come to me. I've tried to see you several times, but you were always with someone."

"I know. But tell me, are you truly disappointed, Julien?"

"Of course I am. Not that I regret leaving here, except for leaving you. It's because I thought my father understood how much Brittany means to me. He has always indulged me in the past. I know he had no other plans for me when I spoke to him or he would have mentioned them. It could have been the money, I don't know. But I'm afraid there's nothing I can do about it now. He's made a decision, and I must abide by his judgment."

"Yes, it appears you have no choice. Tell me, you don't think he might have decided against Brittany because he heard something about Abelard that prejudiced him? Has Anselm been in touch with your father lately?"

The question caught Julien by surprise and he hesitated before answering. "Anselm? Oh, I doubt it. I'm sure he'd like to push me into my vows, but I never seriously spoke to him about wanting to study with Abelard. He knows I'm interested, of course, but I doubt that he'd take the trouble. He's not even that concerned."

"Did it ever occur to you that it might be because of me?" His tone was bitter.

"You? But why? You're the finest teacher here. Everyone knows that."

"Thank you, but Anselm doesn't trust me or my beliefs. I have to be very careful of what I teach. You're the only student I've had full confidence in. Can you imagine my discussing some of the things we talk about with the others?"

"I'm grateful, but you'll have other students far brighter than I. If I've done well, it's because of the special attention you've always given me. I explained to my father that the reason I'm so anxious to study with Abelard is because you've acquainted me with his teachings and because I'd go to him on your recommendation."

"It's a pity I never met your father. I should have spoken to him."

"I wish you had. He knows about the years you spent with Abelard, and he's certainly pleased with the education you've given me. As a matter of fact, one day the canon from St. Crispin visited our house while I was there, and my father asked him to question me so he could see how my education was progressing. I steered the canon towards a discussion on the source of responsibility in human actions, and my father soon seemed satisfied that I was better educated than he."

Ralf was frowning. "I'm still suspicious of Anselm. I don't think he's above warning your father against encouraging your interest in Abelard. To Anselm, and many like him, Abelard remains foremost a seducer and betrayer."

Julien's excitement was mounting. "I had no idea you felt so strongly about Anselm. The one time I allowed myself to complain to you about the way he punished me for my sin of vanity, you didn't even answer me."

Ralf gripped his shoulder. "You're no longer my pupil, Julien. I think of you as my friend now, my ally." He fixed his eyes firmly on Julien, and they were softer than Julien had ever remembered them. "Do you really believe I didn't care? Remember when you were ill for a month because that swine made you spend the night naked on a wet stone floor? Weren't you aware the abbot was informed of it? If I had told your father about it, he'd have taken his sword to the old whoreson."

Julien started to laugh. "I should have guessed."

"You're a man now. You know I have to enforce discipline, and not least on myself. Don't think it's been easy to prepare myself for your leaving. It hurt when I told you months ago that I had nothing more to teach you. I don't even have any more Greek texts here, and I have no idea when they will honor my requests for some. No, *I'm* the one who is truly disappointed. I know how much further you could go with Abelard. You can't imagine what a thrilling experience it would be for you."

"If it's at all possible, I'll try to continue studying him. Perhaps it will be easier to find new books where I'm going."

"I hope so. But there's something else I felt constrained never to tell you before. It is Abelard who could use *you* right now. The monks of St. Gildas de Ruys never welcomed Abelard as their abbot. You see, he was truly revolted by them—not simply by their vices and wanton ways, but by their slovenly thinking habits. Vices are easy to conceal, but not bad reasoning. Last winter they actually tried to kill him; I suspect they'll try again."

"Murder? Abelard? I can't believe it!" Julien dropped to the stool and cupped his head in his hands.

"It's true. All of Cluny has been in an uproar about it, but they won't commit themselves to helping Abelard—no matter how much they sympathize with his attempts to clean up the abbey. They're afraid it might appear as if they're accepting his teachings."

Julien moaned and shook his head. "It's awful."

"A man born before his time must expect it. But he's in great danger now, and he needs men around him who are his champions. He detests violence, yet he can't escape it." Ralf fingered the largest of the welts on his scalp. "As if the old days in Paris weren't bad enough!"

Julien smashed his fist into his hand. "Maybe it isn't too late for my father to change his mind. Perhaps if you were to explain to him how important it is, not just to me, but because the ideas are important . . ."

"No, Julien. It would be presumptuous of me to try to alter his decision now. If I haven't failed you, your education will continue wherever you are. Robert of Selby is a brilliant man. Keep your eyes and ears open. . . . You will learn more from him than you ever did from me. If he's leaving King

Henry's service after his rapid advancement, you can be sure this new endeavor of his is an attractive one."

"But will it be attractive to me? Brother Edward said he suspected I'd be going with him as a clerk to the court of Aquitaine."

"Why Aquitaine? What's there for you, Julien?"

"Well, you've heard Robert has a reputation for high living, and Edward said that if he were leaving England, it would be for a place with the best wine. They say the court there . . ."

Ralf shook his head impatiently. "What little Edward knows of Robert of Selby is through hearsay, which is absolutely meaningless. Still, I don't say it's not possible."

"I suppose I might enjoy Aquitaine. The music is supposed to be wonderful, and they say the women are . . ."

"Forget all that nonsense. If you can learn from your new position, then stay there. If not, then get out." He paused a moment, then smiled. "I'm sorry. I forget your age sometimes. Of course you'll want to enjoy yourself too. I hope you do, and I'm confident you won't neglect the important things. Julien, I'm truly unhappy about losing you, but I like to think we may see each other again one day. Paths do cross. Even though you're not of my flesh, I feel there's much of me in your creation."

"Of course we'll see each other again, Ralf. Do you think I could ever forget you? I promise to come back, first chance I get."

"You ninny. What makes you think I'll be here? I'm going to Brittany just as soon as I can. Oh, they made a little fuss when I asked permission to leave, but frankly I believe they're just as glad to be rid of me. No, now that you're leaving, nothing could induce me to stay. You should have guessed, Julien. I hope to be with Abelard late this summer, and I pray I can be of some use to him."

"How I envy you! Tell me, when was it you last saw or heard from him?"

Ralf's face turned grim. "He's never communicated with me since I left and came here, the same year you did. I still remember you, you know, with your brother's cloak dragging the ground behind you, and those wide child's eyes . . . so frightened. Frightened. I didn't know you had just lost your mother. I was frightened too. I was still having nightmares, awful ones. I left France because I couldn't bear to— I just lacked the strength."

"Ah, it was 1118." Julien's voice was a whisper.

Ralf nodded. "Yes. I was there when Canon Fulbert had Abelard castrated. I saw. I was beaten bloody and unconscious, but they kept reviving me to make me watch. I suppose I'm lucky I still have *my* balls. Not that I have much use for the ugly things." A corner of his mouth turned up in a crooked smile and he clapped Julien's shoulder. "We mustn't lose contact with each other, Julien. Wherever you are, you can always reach me through Abelard. I plan never to leave him again for as long as either of us lives. And if God wills it, you too will see him one day."

"I will. I must. If he speaks as well as he writes . . ."

"*I* think he does, but from what I hear, it is the Cistercian Bernard who has crowds kissing his hem and fainting at his feet."

"They say he's irresistible.

"No one—not even Abelard—can match the Abbot of Clairvaux's skill in appealing to the emotions. But—to the *emotions,* Julien. . . . By the way, do you know of Bernard's latest triumph? The town of Foigny was being plagued by flies, so Bernard excommunicated them—and they vanished!" He paused and shook his head. "No, Abelard hasn't cured lepers, produced visions, or cast out flies. His is the miracle of stirring men's ideas, perhaps the most difficult miracle of all. He shakes the earth with pure reason, the companion of his faith, and I'm confident that this marriage of faith and reason will one day triumph. Now, let this be our goodbye."

"I hear footstps. Must be time for lauds. Will you go with me?"

"Why not? I always enjoy seeing Anselm's face when we enter a room together."

Chapter II
THE OLD CRUSADER

It was over fifty miles to his father's house but Julien hoped to be there in no more than three days. Since Durham lay on the historic attack route between Scotland and England, the roads were wide and well maintained, second only to the king's high roads in England. At Stockton-on-Tees, twenty miles south, there was a great manor house belonging to the bishop of Durham where Julien could spend the night and leave his horse.

The horse the abbey had loaned him for his leavetaking was far superior to the old jades offered him when he was going home on holiday, and Julien arrived much earlier than he'd expected to.

The manor house was large and warm, built from a double thickness of timber. The staff remembered him well and seemed pleased to see him. Julien joined them at their prayers and at dinner, and spent an hour giving them the latest gossip of Durham. He was growing drowsy from the sleeplessness of the last nights and was grateful when his hosts tactfully decided to retire early. Such luxury. He pulled a pallet close to the fire, grateful that he didn't have to share the hall tonight with any other traveller, and was soon fast asleep.

He rose before any of the others and repacked his few belongings. He carried only two knee-length shirts, some toilet articles, a few personal souvenirs, and his sheepskin blanket. He rearranged these until the pack was tight and neat before he was satisfied. The refectory wasn't yet set up for serving, so he went directly to the kitchen to be fed. He ate a huge breakfast of a stew made from beans and peas, then bread and cheese with a large wooden bowl of cider. When he was leaving, the fat cook pinched Julien's cheeks until they hurt, patted his bottom, and stuffed his purse with oatcakes. He was obliged then to go to matins before leaving, but happily they took only two hours.

He had been walking for just a short time, enjoying the sharp spring morning and greeting all the travellers he passed on the road, trying to make conversation where he could. It was an honest pleasure to be able to speak English again. At Durham he spoke only Latin except for his many conversations in Greek with Brother Ralf. At home with his family, they spoke only Norman French. Although the English language was unpolished and inexact, he enjoyed it nonetheless, and found it particularly diverting to listen to the workers on his father's farm combine the crude Anglo-Saxon words they knew with the smattering of French they'd picked up from their lord's household.

Julien found himself overtaken by an ox cart filled with salmon. The driver greeted him warily. "Do you have any money?"

"Five pennies," Julien answered, wondering when he'd ever before seen such large, perfectly black teeth, "but I expect I shall need them before I get home."

"By the milk of St. Martina, I have to get this salmon all the way to York, and I don't know if I'll have enough to pay the tolls."

"But I thought salmon went free on this road unless it was salted."

"Aye, it's supposed to, but I've been stopped before to pay tolls. Thieves they are. I could take them to a court of justice if I had the time, but this salmon isn't getting any fresher, or hadn't you noticed?"

"I noticed," said Julien. "When do you think you'll get to York?"

"Four or five days. There's a poor stretch of road ahead. It's been a wet spring through these parts."

"Let me ride with you an hour or so," Julien proposed, "and I'll give you a delicious oatcake cooked by a pretty wife with the roundest hips you ever saw."

Julien left the cart no more than ten minutes later when he realized the increasingly offensive smell was not entirely from the salmon. They had come to a bog enriched by a dozen trickles from the thawing hills, and the ooze covered the wheels almost to the axles. Julien's progress, slowed by the mud, was still faster than the cart's, and he was exhilarated by a bracing breeze heavy with the scents of spring.

Flocks of sheep and cattle were being driven to market in both directions and they slowed Julien down but didn't alter his high spirits. When he stopped to munch an oatcake or buy cider from a farmer's roadside stand, there was always someone to exchange a few words with about the weather, the road, or local gossip. The villagers seemed rather more cheerful than usual, and Julien guessed the tax collectors weren't as demanding this season.

He arrived at Northallerton a little later than he'd hoped. It was just after vespers, but he was made welcome and given some barley bread and hard cheese, which he was able to wash down with a bowl of thin, sour beer. They appeared to be observing the Lenten fast somewhat more rigorously than the clergy at Stockton did.

He'd no sooner finished his meal than it was time for compline, the last of the canonical hours, and he had to fight to stay awake during the monotonous drone of the prayers. He stumbled back to the hall and started to make preparations for sleep. The straw mattresses were torn and it looked like small creatures had already started to nest in them, so he undid his pack and spread his sheepskin blanket near the fire and pulled his cloak about him.

Falling asleep immediately, he was soon awakened by the arrival of other guests. Two monks let themselves in and dragged mattresses to the side of the fire opposite Julien. Before they retired, they knelt and prayed, and Julien was lulled to sleep again by the monotonous murmur. He was awakened again shortly after by the fulminous snore of one of the monks. Julien's eyes opened and then widened at the roar that shattered from the man's lips. His stare turned to the other monk as he wondered if sleep had come to him yet. Instead, the monk rose quietly and went to one of the bundles stowed in a corner. He withdrew a long object and held it appraisingly in his hand a moment. The fire was still bright enough to cast an eerie, elongated shadow of the man's figure across the wall. Julien watched him slip out of his shirt and sink to his knees, still clutching the object in his hand. The monk raised his arm and there was a swish, a stinging thwack, and a suppressed gasp. Julien shuddered and pressed his eyes tightly shut again.

*   *   *   *   *

The last night Julien had spent at Durham Abbey Prior Anselm had asked him to come to his study directly after compline. Anselm did not say much that Julien hadn't heard before. He started with his customary lecture, reasonably expanded for the occasion, on the vanity of Julien's person. Julien had gone to the bathhouse right after vespers and Anselm was able to comment, quite accurately, on the extraordinary amount of water that was used and the excessive temperature to which it had been heated. A basin of cold water, he was firmly reminded, was judged more appropriate for a man his age. Bodily humors that were clearly already too thick and hot should be chilled instead of warmed further. Cold water also reduced the disposition to remain naked. Julien was offered the example set by many of his fellow students with more determined morals who were able to wash without ever exposing their bodies or touching them.

There was also the matter of his grooming. Julien seemed to take extraordinary pride in his hair. Was it the color that made him so proud? It was, indeed, a rich dark red. He was advised to wear it shorter, never to wash it, and never ever to look at it in the glass.

Julien had been seen examining his face in the mirror after he shaved. Never, never must he do so again. Shaving was to be done quickly, focussing the eyes only on that part of the skin the razor touched, and then the face was to be quickly rinsed after the mirror was put away.

Far more disturbing to Anselm was Julien's preoccupation with books. Since he had already committed his sacramentary to memory it was not necessary or advisable for him to search further. Hours set aside for study were better spent reflecting on the knowledge already revealed to him through the word of God. Everything else was superficial, and if Julien would only keep these rules with him when he was out in the world he would never have the Devil for a companion.

Before dismissing Julien, Anselm lowered his voice to a whisper. "I want to make you a parting gift, something that will help you to reach the level of spirituality I believe is inside you, but which you continue to shun. You will find it in your cell. Use it, and I pray it will help you find the peace of spirit all Christians must work for. *Work* for, do you hear, Julien? Now God bless you, my son, and Godspeed."

Julien thanked his prior in as humble a voice as he could manage and offered him the kiss of peace. Anselm turned his head and said nothing more.

There was a bulky package wrapped in sackcloth on his mattress. He unfolded it gingerly to find a leather whip with nine thongs studded with nails. Not a very imaginative gift, even for Prior Anselm. Then he felt another smaller object, half hidden in the folds of sackcloth. He held it up curiously but was at a loss to identify it. It was a metal cylinder several inches long and open at one end, attached to a strap. He examined it more closely and saw that the cylinder was hinged. He fumbled for a moment and finally pried it open. The walls were encrusted with tiny, sharp needles. He was still puzzled and snapped it shut again. Then he remembered something Brother Edward had spoken of over a year ago. Of course! This must be "the monk's bride." Its use was permitted only to clerics who complained of being unusually harassed by incubi. Once fitted and then secured around the hips it was guaranteed to discourage arousal. He studied it a few moments longer and then slipped the bride and the whip under his mattress and left them there.

The monk was still laboring his flesh with the whip when Julien felt himself slipping off to sleep again. At least, he thought to himself, he looks too old to need the bride. He slept fitfully until awakened for matins. The monk he guessed was the flagellant appeared not to have slept at all. His eyes were imbedded in sooty rings, and his lips, crusted with white, hardly moved when he spoke.

The monks were travelling in the same direction as Julien, but when they accepted a ride on a cart full of eels and herring, Julien pleaded he needed to walk to help him meditate. He soon outdistanced them. By midday, however, he fell by the roadside, exhausted.

A girl about fifteen years old, with wide hips filling out her full kirtle, and a cheerful, freckled face, came past him with two buckets on a pole over her shoulders. She smiled invitingly.

"Good morning, pretty. Do you know where I can be fed?" he asked.

"I don't know if there would be anything fine enough for a gentleman like yourself," she answered pertly. "You do look like you could do with a bit of milk though." She put down her load and brought him one of the buckets.

He drank thirstily and then sank back on his elbows. "I'd better leave you some to make your cheese. Would you like a halfpenny?"

Her eyes twinkled. "That's a good deal more than the milk is worth."

"How about finding me some food, then?" he asked. He was pleased to find her so friendly as he suddenly felt famished.

"We've already had our midday meal," she answered, "but I might be able to find some oat porridge." She started to rock her shoulders back and forth. "Were you joking or will you really give me a halfpenny?"

Julien looked approvingly at the way her breasts fought her gown as she twisted her body. "I said I would, didn't I? Where's your cottage?"

"Just a few minutes away, but I could never take you there. I get a stick taken to my legs every time they find me talking with a lad. I'll just tell my mother there's an old priest lying by the road, and maybe she'll let me bring you a bowl of porridge. I won't be gone long." She picked up her milk and went down the road, turning often to glance at him.

Julien stretched out and tried to nap while he waited for her to return. If Prior Anselm knew what I was thinking right now, he thought, he'd have me exorcized for forty days and forty nights. He was awakened by her a half hour later. She had washed her face and tied a bit of cloth around her hair. The wool shift, which came just above her knees, was cinched now with a girdle that revealed her ample body more clearly.

"There was no more porridge, but our hens had something for you." She reached into her purse and took out four eggs, still warm.

Julien cracked and greedily swallowed them. "Are you sure you have nothing else for me?" he said archly.

"I'm sorry. That's all there was. Can I have my halfpenny anyway?"

"Of course you may, but first I want to be sure you're not hiding anything from me. Don't you have a little tidbit tucked away somewhere?" He leaned forward and raised his hand towards her bodice.

"Where would I hide anything?" she laughed, but she didn't move away.

Julien's hand reached out teasingly, and she drew back quickly, still smiling.

"Oh, so it's pinch and tickle, is it?" she said. "Well, you may get your slap and giggle first."

"I had a feeling you knew the same country games I did. Don't be shy, my dear. It's a long time since I saw a girl as pretty as you. I just wondered if you felt as good as you looked."

"I'll wager I do, but I've no time to waste with saucy boys." She paused and pursed her lips. "Can I have my halfpenny now?"

Julien took a halfpenny from his purse. "Come and get it."

"So that's how it is, is it?" She reached for the coin cautiously, and he stretched his free hand forward.

"Come now, I'm a good girl, I am."

"You certainly are, lovey. That's what I said to myself the moment I saw you."

"Look lad, if it's a bit of tit you're after, I can take you to our cow."

"Fine. Is she near a pile of hay?"

"Cheeky!" She snatched the coin from his hand just as he moved forward swiftly and tumbled her onto her back. He was stretched over her in a flash, fumbling for her skirt and trying to kiss her.

"All right, just one kiss. But mind your hands."

He thrust his tongue between her lips and had just reached inside her bodice when her knee came up sharply into his groin. She rolled free and raced a few yards away.

"I should've known," she panted. "You can't trust a redhead with gat teeth. And full of the Devil too. I'm sure I felt one of his horns. Well, you'll not be giving *me* a green gown for your halfpenny, sir." She wriggled her girdle into another position and placed her hands on her hips. "Not that I don't think you're fair enough. Better'n most of the lads around here, even with that ugly split between your front teeth. Never mind, I've got to go churn butter." She started down the road.

"No, wait. I'll behave. I promise. Please don't go." He started to his feet.

The girl raced across the meadow, and then when she felt she'd gone far enough not to be overtaken easily, she stopped and raised her skirt to her waist. "Was it an oyster you were wanting for your meal, lad?" She screamed with laughter and ran back towards her cottage.

Julien shouldered his pack and continued his walk in good humor. The day was the warmest of the year, and just ahead he could see the first spring gentian poking through the meadow. "New life, new world, new me," he said aloud joyously.

When he'd gone another mile or so, he saw a familiar figure coming towards him on horseback. The man waved and shouted his name. There was no mistaking his brother Godwin's voice. Godwin was now the eldest since Harold was killed in a campaign against the French three years earlier. Godwin was more than half a foot taller than Julien, with the same dark red hair and blue eyes, but his fair skin had been tanned and seasoned and carried the nicks of old scars. Everything about him bespoke a life far different from Julien's. He beamed his pleasure at seeing his brother.

"Godwin, how wonderful to see you. I thought you'd still be away at service."

He reined up beside Julien. "They let us go sooner than expected. It looks like we're headed for more peaceful times." Godwin was a candidate for knighthood now, and the eventual heir to his father's estate. He was naturally well equipped to be a knight—as strong as a bull, yet agile enough to move his horse through the most intricate maneuvers. His style with the lance and sword was not particularly graceful, but his arms were powerful enough to guarantee a creditable showing on the battlefield.

"I knew I'd find you on the road." Godwin dismounted and smothered his brother in a rough hug. "By St. Gudula's gloves, I think we've another grown man in the family. Let me have a look at you. No, not bad for the runt of the litter." He reached into his saddlebag and took out a leather flask. "I think you could use a drink."

Julien tilted his head back and took a long swallow. He was instantly convulsed with a fit of coughing and spewed out most of the drink. "St. Perpetua's cow! What in hell was that?"

Godwin roared his appreciation at Julien's language. "Bravo! I knew they'd never make a mealy-mouthed monk out of you. Here, try another swig. It's much easier the second time around. Go on. I brought it back from Normandy. They make it out of apples, so it can't be too different from cider. Drink up."

"I'll wait for some beer. Godwin, what happened to your teeth? I'm sure you had more the last time I saw you."

Godwin's laughter was aggressive but ingenuous. He stuck a finger in the gap left by his two missing front teeth.

"Did you lose them in battle?"

"Battle?" He roared even louder. "Hell, no. I lost them in a ball game. Battle is child's play compared to the way they play ball in Normandy. They've got some roaring boys down there."

They mounted Godwin's horse, which was two hands taller than the horses Julien was accustomed to at the abbey.

"What about father, Godwin? How is he?"

"Very tired. But I'll wager he perks up when he sees you. I think he's very pleased about this new business with Robert. Are you sure you won't have another swig?"

"Have you any idea where Robert is planning to take me? I've been told nothing about any of this yet."

"Robert's probably at the house right now. He's staying at Bishop Thrugar's manor, but he comes to see us every day. I think I ought to let *him* tell you about it. You know I'm no good at getting things straight. Speak up now, or this will all be gone." He drained the flask noisily.

"Godwin, if you weren't twice my size I'd beat you bloody."

"I don't know all that much about it either. I heard some of what he told father, but I never pay too much attention when those two are talking. There's some Norman lord in Italy, and he's very rich, but it seems they're mostly heathen in those parts, except for the Normans of course."

Julien couldn't conceal his disappointment. The last thing he expected was service with some Norman adventurer in the south. "Who is this Norman? Do you remember his name?"

"Let me think. Yes, Hauteville. Roger de Hauteville."

"But that's the Guiscard's family, then."

"That's right. I think Robert did say he was the Guiscard's nephew. Big family. Best fighters in the south." Robert de Hauteville, the skilled warrior and technician in battle, was known to everyone as the Guiscard, or the Fox. Although he was now dead, his career was rivalled by none.

"Why would father want me to join the Normans in Italy? I'm not a mercenary." Julien's hopes for a career seemed dashed.

"They need all sorts of men. This Roger is far and away the biggest lord in the south now. He simply took his fief and forced the pope to accept it on his terms."

"Yes, I know something about him. He's been made a duke now. But he just finished making war on the pope. What kind of life is that going to be for someone like me?"

"Don't fret. Robert expects you'll all make your fortunes there."

"All? Who else is going with us?"

"It appears there's been quite a number of chaps headed for those parts. Robert has someone else with him now, a Thomas Browne, lad about my age or maybe a bit older. He's a kinsman of Robert's, but you'd never guess there's any Norman blood in him. Still, he seems right enough. Never make a soldier, though."

"I can't imagine what father's thinking of. Does he expect me to land a fief in Italy? Godwin, what am I going to do?"

"There, there now. Robert says the court is full of surprises. Roger keeps a harem like all the heathen rulers."

Julien's eyes widened. "A harem? But how can he if he's truly a Christian?"

"Come off it, boy. You'll love it. Now perk up." He jabbed his brother's ribs so hard Julien almost fell off the horse. "We're planning a celebration tonight. Ediwa's come home for it too."

Julien's sister Ediwa had just taken her vows the year before and was helping to found a new Cistercian monastery for women in Yorkshire. She and her sister nuns were still housed in huts, and subject to unusually strict vows as anchoresses of this relatively new and rigid order.

"She's happy with her vocation, is she?" Julien grew even more serious at the thought of his sister.

"Happy? Now there's a strange word for Ediwa. I'd say she's going at this vocation of hers as if the future of the Cross rests on her shoulders. You know how she can be." He shuddered. "She'll be an abbess one day, I'll wager. And a good thing too! She'd have made one hell of a shrewish wife. Can't you pity the poor fool who'd fancy bedding her?"

Julien ignored his brother's levity. "I respect her vocation. It's a sincere one, but it's a dark life she'll make of it. I can't help but feel the order she's chosen is too severe for anyone as impressionable as she is." He remained silent the rest of the way home while Godwin prattled on about horses and falcons and the cockfight pit recently installed in the village.

Julien perked up only when the manor house, a long timber building with a thatched roof, appeared around the bend. He was proud of his home, the largest for many miles, larger than the manors of the other landowners in the area. Not until you reached the baron's stone castle did you meet a more imposing building.

Nigel's estates comprised almost a hundred acres, one-third of which made up the home farm. The rest was divided between villeins and tenant farmers. The organization of the estate and its divisions seemed arbitrary and chaotic to Julien, who was accustomed to the efficiently managed farms controlled by the bishop of Durham. Some of Nigel's tenants held no more than an acre of land, others up to four or five.

Nigel kept only the most rudimentary accounts, most of them unwritten. He was wont to bargain with his tenants for work done on his farm or for other goods and services, assessing them more highly when he was called upon by his lord for extraordinary taxes or services, and relaxing his demands when he was not pressed.

The household was a modest one, but its maintenance seemed increasingly expensive. Fortunately Ediwa required no dowry, but there was still an endowment to be made yearly to her order. There had once been another daughter, Fressenda. She was lovely, and Nigel favored her greatly above his other daughter. As soon as she was of age he arranged an auspicious marriage for her with an impoverished but attractive baron of Saxon stock in Kent. But her dowry had been ruinous, and although she died when delivered of her first child less than a year later, there was no possibility of its restitution.

Nigel had another son named Geoffrey, a year younger than Godwin. Right after Harold's death, Geoffrey's body began to show red marks that scaled and itched and would not heal. No one in the household mentioned his affliction, praying it would leave him, but word of his unpleasant condition spread, and one day three priests came to the manor house to examine him. They questioned Geoffrey regarding his morals, his acceptance of God and renunciation of the Devil, his success or lack of it in combatting temptations of the flesh, and his family history. The examination concluded, they withdrew to confer. When they returned, they declared him unclean. At a ritual patterned after the funeral ceremony, they cast three handfuls of dirt on his head, excommunicating him from society.

Then, according to the local laws borrowed from Scotland, they sent for a surgeon (really a barber), and while two assistants held him down, Geoffrey was castrated. This was customary for persons having leprosy, madness, epilepsy, gout, or any other serious illness believed to be passed from father to son. Nigel was powerless to interfere, although he recalled an uncle of his who had similar symptoms which eventually healed and only occasionally returned in milder attacks.

Once officially diagnosed a leper by the priests, there were few options open to Geoffrey. Nigel sent him to a lazar house which had a reputation for sympathetic treatment, and every year he sent ten shillings at Christmas, another five at Easter, and two on Lady Day to the monks who cared for him.

Now that Godwin was approaching knighthood, there was new armor to be bought, new clothes, and dozens of incidental expenses. When Nigel had been knighted, it was a much simpler matter. If you owned a horse and knew how to use a sword, your liege lord invested you with knighthood in a simple, contractual ceremony and you fought for him. Later, if you were lucky, he gave you some land as a fief—in Nigel's case by the favorite expedient of arranging a marriage to one of the native English and conferring land which would have been dispossessed by the Normans in any event.

It seemed to Nigel that there was some new folderol added to the ceremony every year. The richer English families seemed to be imitating some of the foppish habits of Louis the Fat's knights. It was already fashionable to spend a night's vigil in church with a Mass said for you. There was a ritual bath too, and more and more costly robes were considered essential, in addition to the precious armor, which had recently started to include leg armor as a necessity. Some of the fops were even spending a fortune on robes to caparison their horses with, and coats of arms were becoming important enough to invent where they didn't yet exist, so that they could decorate their shields, clothing, equipment, and everything in sight. It was a far cry from the days Nigel remembered when a knight was looked on as little more than a serving man by his lord. He was glad Godwin was as intolerant as he of what he felt was effeminate nonsense.

Nigel lost most of his interest in women after his wife, Godiva, died. He was never sure at first whether she had welcomed the match, but he

wooed her with gentle ways, and she liked his rough good looks. They grew
to love each other quite a good deal, and he mourned her deeply. Godwin
used to urge Nigel to take another wife, at least to help him with the household affairs, but Nigel would share his chamber with no other. He still felt
sexual longings, and on these occasions he would visit a widow on the estate
who would quietly follow him to her mattress and allow him to use her, but
they spoke hardly at all, and he never demonstrated any interest or affection
for her once out of her hut. The only way he would acknowledge one of
these visits was to see to it that a rabbit or a bit of game was sent to her the
next day.

It was only natural that Nigel showed more affection to Julien than he
did to any of his other children. Julien had the small, slight build of the
Saxon, his mother's same round, blue eyes and crisp, burnished hair. One
would hardly guess he was Godwin's brother, except for the hair. Julien rode
well, and his muscles were well knit, but he never developed much skill at
the popular competitive sports.

Their arrival was heralded by the hysterical barking of dogs that surrounded the horse and made him rear. There were a greyhound, two red-
and-white spotted Bretons, two shaggy boarhounds, and two enormous black
mastiffs. Julien was instantly knocked to the ground when he dismounted
and the dogs were reluctant to let him enter the house.

Julien was surprised to see how drawn his father looked. His body, still
robust, seemed to move more slowly, and the skin around his rounded cheek-
bones lacked its usual high color. His arms trembled as he held them out to
embrace his son. Julien cradled his father's head protectively. Now that he
was at the point of leaving him, he felt a quickening of compassion for the
tired old soldier. They both wept freely, and even Godwin was moist-eyed.

"Where is Ediwa?"

"She's at her devotions. She'll be out before dinner. Sit down and have a
drink, my boy. I have a keg of Scottish aqua vitae that I've been saving for
something special. It may be a long while before you taste the likes of it
again."

The steward handed around wooden bowls half filled with a dark
brown liquid. It was more pungent and smokier than any Julien had ever
tasted.

"I can't drink the whole bowl, father. I'm not used to it." Still, he much
preferred it to the raw, acrid drink Godwin had given him. This smelled
almost like fine smoked bacon. "I thought I'd find Robert of Selby here."

"He was, earlier. I believe he wanted to let me have you all to myself."

They chatted awhile, before either Julien or his father made any reference to his future.

"What do you know of Sicily?" Nigel asked.

"We don't hear too much about it at Durham. The Normans there seem a less noble lot than our English Normans. I know that the Hautevilles had been a family of mercenaries at one time and that the pope conferred Sicily on them as a reward for recovering it from the heathens. Was that part of the Crusade, father?"

"Not really. They didn't go down there with the Cross, but what you say is mostly true. The Guiscard and his brother, Roger, owned Sicily together, while the Guiscard also had fiefs all over the south of Italy. Then the Guiscard ceded Sicily to Roger as count, while he remained overlord. Yes, they are a roughish lot, but they're shrewd too, and I can understand Robert's enthusiasm."

Julien was following his father's words intently. "And the present Roger, the count's son . . . he's now a duke because he just took over all the Guiscard's lands when the Guiscard's grandson died. He sounds greedy."

"Nothing wrong with trying to keep it all in the family. That land, Apulia especially, is full of cutthroat barons and knights who are always at each other. Those southern Italians are even worse than the English barons that keep giving Henry trouble with their dirty private wars. The Normans who went down and just took their fiefs recently are the worst, but then there are Lombards, Greeks, and God knows what all as well. Sounds a proper mess to me."

"But father . . . " Julien's voice had turned petulant. "This Duke Roger has been at war with the pope. There's the matter of my conscience."

"What if he has? The rift's been mended, at least for now. The pope still hates Roger, but in the interests of peace, he was forced to recognize his claim last August. With all those petty barons raising a storm, right on his doorstep so to speak, he realized Roger was the only man strong enough to keep the peace. And he's doing so. Roger isn't a man to brook any nonsense from his lords. He seems fair enough with those who show loyalty, but for the last months he's been teaching a hard lesson to all who dare challenge him. He's a tough man."

"We heard such terrible things about him at Durham—burning churches, slaughtering whole towns. Father, do you really think I'm . . ."

"That's talk, son. You'll learn soon enough what men are like in the world outside Durham. Roger's claims seem just. Robert's been talking about little else to me." He paused a moment to drain his cup of whiskey. "I suppose he has been harsh in punishing some of those towns, but Robert swears the reports are exaggerated, and an oath of fealty has to stand for something. Look, I can't tell you any more about it. Robert will answer all your questions when he sees you, and I don't know how many more times I can stand to listen to his stories of Roger. He hasn't shut his mouth since he's been here. Let's have another cup of this. An excellent stimulant for the appetite."

"But father, what do you suppose he wants with *me?* I don't see where I could fit into this man's campaigns. I'm no fighter."

Nigel patted his son's hand. "This Roger is an able administrator, as was his father. Robert thinks he's the rising star in Europe. It's men with brains he's after now. This Thomas Browne seems to be much like you, a sort of bookish chap, and Robert's got his head swimming."

"All right, father, I have nothing else to say until I speak with him. Godwin, you finish my drink, will you? I think I'll go fetch Ediwa. I can smell dinner."

Julien entered Ediwa's room and closed the door quietly behind him. There was only one slender candle giving a feeble light. Ediwa gave no answer when he called her name, and then he saw her figure, prostrate on the floor, her arms extended stiffly from her torso and her entire body rigid. He went to the chest to get some more candles and kept lighting them until the room was well illuminated. Ediwa did not stir for several moments, then groaned and rose slowly to face him, glaring. He went to her to embrace her, but she shrank from him and turned her head away. He repeated the gesture and then shrank back himself when he saw the filthy hair shirt she was wearing. He plucked a fold at the shoulder and examined it. A glance was enough.

"Lice," he exclaimed aloud. "Ediwa!"

"Forgive me for not rising at once, brother. I sometimes receive a high degree of exaltation during my meditations."

"Exaltation! Yes, I see." He looked at her pityingly. "Do you want me to bring you some water to wash?"

"No thank you, I have some here. Why are you looking at me that way? You come from a monastery. Is it so unusual to see someone engaging in discipline?"

"I'm sorry. But the lice."

"To arm against the allurements of pleasure and the wiles of the Devil." Her voice was almost a chant.

"Ah yes, the Cistercians. Those are St. Bernard's exact words, aren't they?

She looked at him coldly. "You don't approve?"

"Let me answer your quote with another. 'The suffering of hermits and martyrs is all in vain, for God is an easy and amiable God who delights not in such things.' "

"Sacrilege!"

"No, Abelard."

"I should have guessed. Julien, promise me, for the sake of your soul, that you'll find yourself an honest confessor when you get to Sicily. They must have some uncorrupted priests there, and I won't rest until I know you have the firm, spiritual guidance you need."

Her eyes were shining, but in the candlelight the blue in them was lost and he became aware of the dark hollows that surrounded them. She had a welted rash, fiery against her translucently white skin, which covered her chin and most of her throat and proceeded below the hair shirt.

Julien fought the revulsion that rose in him as he looked at her. What a pity she was the one given that ugly crop of carrot-red hair. Any of the boys might have suffered it, but it's no wonder she was such an unlikely candidate for marriage . . . with that hair and that dead-white skin that's always erupting in pimples! And it's been years since I've seen her smile.

"Very well. I promise, Ediwa. I will look carefully until I find someone who can offer the spiritual counsel I need."

"I love you, but I don't trust you, Julien. I can only hope my prayers for you will be answered. And now, please leave me so that I can wash and change. Your father wants this to be a festive evening, and it is our duty to him to see that it is."

There was venison, woodcock, and grouse for dinner, all Julien's favorite dishes, as well as peas, beans, barley porridge, and stewed onions. They sliced off large chunks of the meat with their knives and placed them on the thick trenchers of bread which served as dining plates. Pieces of this bread were broken off during the meal and dipped in the serving bowls to mop up the juices. At the end the serving boy brought them a dish of fat eels in lard, greeted with cries of pleasure. The dogs ate with them, devouring all the bones and passing from person to person to be slipped tidbits and to allow fingers to be wiped on their fur.

Nigel tried to recite a poem he used to know about King Arthur's court, only he had forgotten most of the words, but they stayed on at the table and chewed little sour apples and drank wine sweetened with honey. Godwin, very drunk, fell off the dining bench at last, and the two serving boys were called to carry him to his room.

After he was gone, Nigel kept glancing irritably at Ediwa until she caught his meaning and announced she was late for her prayers. She alone had eaten scarcely anything, but had tried bravely to be part of the festivities, asking polite questions from time to time and pursing her thin lips only when conversation took a turn she didn't approve of. Only once had she threatened to leave the table and that was when Godwin tried to bet Julien that his tits were twice as large as hers.

Nigel gripped Julien's arm when they were alone and the serving boys had cleared the table of everything except their bowls and a pitcher of whiskey. "Julien, I know you must be tired from your journey, but I'd be pleased if you'd stay up with me awhile. There are so many things I'd like to talk to you about. I couldn't when you were a boy, and now, it looks as if I'll have you such a short time as a man."

"I'm not at all tired, father," Julien lied. "I'm always up at this hour and even later."

"Good. I want to clear the air first about one thing. Are you angry with me because I didn't let you go off to study with that Abelard?"

Julien flushed. "Angry with you? No, I'm sure you know what's best. But you can't know how much it meant to me."

Nigel nodded. "I'm not mean, son. I know you've asked me for very little, and last Christmas I almost said very well, go to him. Perhaps it was a mistake. At one time I thought it was natural for you to become a priest— yes, and maybe a teacher too. I knew for certain I didn't want you to be a soldier. I promised your mother that, may Holy Mary keep her to her bosom, and it was surely my strongest wish. Perhaps you feel I should have considered your happiness first."

Julian started to protest, but Nigel silenced him with a finger to his lips. "I suppose I am selfish about you, but I believed it was your happiness I was considering. What if you did continue your studies, whether with Abelard or with anyone else? You'd probably take solemn vows, and I believe I know you well enough now to say I think you'd be happier with a wife. It would certainly make me happy to know that you shared some of the joy I had with your mother. What do you say?"

"I don't think much about marriage, but I admit I like women well enough."

Nigel smiled. "Good. Godwin will no doubt provide me with more than my share of grandchildren, but I confess it's yours I fancy seeing one day. I feel you'll have a fine career, and now I can also hope that you'll be richly happy. To me, that means a loving wife and family."

"You've already made me very happy, father."

Nigel leaned towards him entreatingly. "Then, make me certain I've made the right choice for you. When Robert came with his proposal, it was totally unexpected. He has great charm, that man, and he's quite a talker. You'll soon see why it's hard to refuse him anything. He's entirely convinced there's more opportunity for an Englishman in Sicily than there is anywhere else in the world. Anyway, he guarantees your future, and that's good enough for me."

"Then, it will be more than good enough for me too." Julien's resignation seemed firmer.

"I see I have a dutiful son. If you disagree with me, don't be afraid to say so. There were other reasons for my choice too, Julien. But you must be ready to humor an old man, and try not to find my fancies too strange. Before I start, be a good lad and fill my cup. Yours too. This is the finest aqua vitae I've had in a long time."

Julien measured whiskey into each bowl and then filled his own to the brim with water.

"As I was saying . . . the first time I heard of Sicily, apart from knowing that Normans had gone down there and were doing well for themselves, was when I was on the Crusade. We were bitter about the Sicilians then, and our priests hated them—for what we thought was a good reason. Roger, the great count and father of the duke you're going to serve, ruled Sicily in those days and had received several honors from the Church. Urban had given him countless blessings and favors for reclaiming Sicily from heathen rule, and how did he repay him? Disgracefully, we believed. Roger was the only prince in Christendom, the only one, mind you, who never sent one blessed soldier on the Crusade. No, and never contributed a brass farthing either."

Julien seemed bewildered. "How could a Christian lord refuse those of his knights who wished to join the Crusade?"

"He never let the Crusade be preached on the island. There were no recruiters. Some say Count Roger was a heathen himself, although Robert doubts it. After he restored Christianity to Sicily, he built dozens of monasteries and new churches. But his lands were filled with Muslims, you see, and he was using them everywhere in his government and in his army. They understood how to run things, and he needed them more than he needed the pope.

"Now his son, this Duke Roger, they say he's even more taken with infidel ways than his father was. Duke Roger keeps a harem right in the palace, and he lets his people worship as they please." Nigel eyed his son then and started to laugh. "I can tell from that look on your face you're beginning to be interested. . . . Well, Roger's court is full of Muslims and

Greeks, and they say there are more languages spoken in his land than anywhere else in the world."

Julien had been listening so eagerly he took a longer swallow of his whiskey than he meant, and even though it was watered, tears ran to his eyes. "Yes, now I remember. Brother Ralf told me they were translating so many Greek philosophers into Latin."

"I wouldn't know about that, son, but I want you to understand this. I don't care if Godwin wants to go to war against the Saracens one day. I'd rather he didn't, but I accept it. I believe there *will* be another Crusade, you know. It's only a matter of time; nothing was really concluded by mine. One day soon some saint will decide it's time to go back and fight the heathens again. There'll always be some Christians who won't be happy until every Jew and Saracen lies dead, and when they're all gone, they'll no doubt start on each other. That's not what I want for you."

"Father, I've already told you how little taste I have for battle, so it's easy to promise you I won't go."

"I truly believe Heaven never intended you to. Julien, do you know why you were given your name?"

"I never thought about it. It's a good Norman name."

"You celebrate it on March 16th, don't you?"

"Yes, St. Julien of Antioch's day." He wondered what his father was getting at.

"But there are other Juliens."

"I think I know most of them. There was St. Julien Sabas the Hermit, St. Julien the Martyr Priest of Terracina, St. Julien the Gouty of Alexandria, St. Julien the Jew of Toledo, St. Julien the Hospitaler, and . . ."

"Stop right there." He brought the flat of his hand down hard on the table. "We've no need of the others. Now! Tell me what you know of the life of St. Julien the Hospitaler."

Julien looked at his father oddly. "All right, but won't you tell me why?"

Nigel pressed a forefinger at Julien's chest. "First tell me what *you* know."

"Very well." In the course of his education, Julien had committed to memory the recorded lives of some three hundred saints, and he scarcely faltered as he recited the story of St. Julien the Hospitaler. "St. Julien was of a noble family, but the dates of his life are uncertain. In the forest one day, he received a prediction that he would murder his parents. I always thought that part of his story was very ancient Greek. Anyway, to avoid doing so he left home and travelled the world, and he became very rich and honored. Then he married a beautiful princess, and his happiness seemed complete. Years later, he left his wife to go off on a journey of some kind, and while he was away an old couple came to his door and asked his wife of him. It was his aged parents, who had never given up their search for him. His wife bade them welcome and gave them to eat and drink. Then, as a mark of respect, she offered them her marriage bed to rest in. St. Julien came home unexpectedly during the night and went directly to his bed, expecting to find his wife in it. Instead he saw two figures lying side by side and then saw one of them was bearded. Enraged by what he believed was the discovery of his wife's infidelity, he took his dagger and killed them both on the spot and that's the way the prophecy was fulfilled." He paused to see if his father had any comment, but Nigel merely nodded for him to continue. "Afterwards he was half mad with grief, so he abandoned his wife and his palace. He gave away all his riches and decided to dedicate the rest of his life to serving the poor. He lived miserably in a primitive hut and clothed himself in rags. There was a river near his hut and he used to ferry travellers across, refusing all pay, or even thanks. Then one day he ferried a hideous leper who asked him for his hospitality. Julien took him at once to his hut and gave him all he had to eat and drink. Next the leper asked for Julien's bed, which was just as quickly given. Then he complained of the cold and asked Julien to disrobe and lie next to him so that he might be warmed by the heat of his body. Julien did as he was asked. The leper shivered, saying he was still cold, and asked Julien to embrace him. When their bodies were pressed together the leper took him in his arms and carried him straight to Heaven, for it was Christ himself that Julien had entertained. It's a beautiful story, father."

Nigel's eyes had filled with tears as he listened to his son. "I like it too. The story as you related it is as I learned it too, except that you omitted the early part of St. Julien's life. It's his earlier years that interest me more. The prophesy delivered in the forest was given by a stag who wasn't simply making a prediction but was cursing him. This is how it all began. . . .

"When Julien was a small boy, he was gifted and beloved. He lived in a great stone castle, where his parents lavished all manner of luxuries on him. One day at church, he saw a mouse during Mass and was filled with an unaccountable hatred for it. He saw it every Sunday, and his hatred for it grew deeper, until one day he trapped it and killed it with a stick. A drop of its blood fell on him and wouldn't be washed off. From that day on he took joy in killing small animals. He would shoot birds in the garden and delight to see their little bodies rain down on him. Then, when he approached manhood, his father judged that it was time for Julien to learn the art of venery. He quickly excelled in the sport of hunting far beyond any of the other youths of the land. He had the fastest horses, the fiercest dogs, the most savage falcons. With these he would go into the forest and kill with his axe and spear, slaughtering wild bulls and boars fearlessly, but also all the rabbits, squirrels, and deer that crossed his path. He was killing not for sport or food, but for the thrill of letting blood." Nigel paused and Julien saw that his lips were quivering. "It was one day after he had killed a mountain of animals that he drew an arrow and shot a hind suckling her fawn. While he was revelling in the lust of this dreadful act, a stag larger than any he had ever seen, charged him. He shot an arrow into its forehead, but the stag wouldn't fall. The sky turned red, and the stag, which could have killed him then, stopped in its tracks and delivered its curse. You see, everyone knows of the miraculous end of St. Julien, but few know that part of his story. It has never been popular with the Normans, and it is even less so in times of war. The sin of St. Julien is the sin of bloodlust."

"I find it very touching, father, but disturbing too. What made you tell me this now?"

"To tell you that you were named in honor of St. Julien the Hospitaler because I had hoped that in some way, through you, I could help expiate my most grievous sin. Yes, St. Julien's sin. Will you swear an oath to me that you will never shed blood except in the strictest demands of self-defense?"

"I swear it, father, on my blessed mother."

"I can't ask this of Godwin because I have no right to. He has a duty of service that I, because of my own oath, could never interfere with. I would have asked Geoffrey as well had he not been visited with that dreadful disease. His leprosy didn't come from *his* sin, Julien, but from mine. It was God's judgment that one of my sons should carry on his body the foul manifestation of my own fall. Pray that your oath may help me with my penance. Only through you now do I hope to gain the intercession of St. Julien that may one day allow me to join your mother in Paradise."

"Oh my dear father, I never knew you to be so troubled. I beg you not to carry the sins of battle on your conscience. Surely the Church has long ago absolved you . . . even before you went into battle. You were only following orders, as all men do under arms. And your cause was a holy one. You had the Cross."

Nigel wiped a tear that had formed, then looked at his son gravely before he spoke again. "Let me tell you what it was really like, son. To begin with, there was no possibility of maintaining discipline with a body of men as large as we were on the Crusade. And these weren't armies of soldiers. There were priests, starving peasants, cutthroats, madmen, all sorts of poor, misguided souls who were looking for an easy entrance to Heaven. Those of us who had any experience in battle were far outnumbered. People took their families with them and even carried their sick and dying.

"My group started out well enough. Baron Drogo had assembled a dozen knights and a hundred foot soldiers, and we went first to Normandy to join Count Mauger, who was assembling a Norman army that was first class in every way. But after our first hundred miles of march, we found we were already far outnumbered by the ragtag of every village we passed through. They came from everywhere, and we had no idea what to do with them, much less how to feed them. We weren't carrying enough provisions for ourselves. Soldiers can usually feed off the lands they march through, but you can't care for thousands of extra mouths when that land is so poor it can't feed the people who live on it. I suppose we still looked better fed than the villagers, which is why they joined us. There were riots, confusion, people dying of disease and starvation all along the way."

Julien was hanging on his father's words, and he regretted that he hadn't been able to know him better.

"Anyway, we were encamped not very far from Constantinople and already tired of the whole mess. A certain Norman named Reynald led a number of us on an expedition to find fresh food, and I was with them. We arrived at a village where we saw these men wearing turbans and other outlandish articles of dress. Very dark they were, swarthier than any men I'd ever seen. They hailed us in a friendly enough fashion and we saw they appeared to be unarmed, but Reynald was sure it was a trick. We believed him. They were so foreign, so different from us! We fell on them and didn't stop killing until every man, woman, and child in the village was lying in its blood. Then, when we started to loot their homes, we found they all had crucifixes on their altars. How were we to know they were Christians?" Nigel shook his head sadly and swallowed back tears.

"Our priests tried to comfort us, reassuring us these people would have looked like Saracens to any civilized man. The empress of the Byzantines, Anna, wrote about it, and later there was a minor scandal when her words were circulated. If you ever come across her writings, my son, please believe me when I tell you she exaggerates. We behaved like beasts, it's true, but she says that children were spitted and roasted. If that were so, I can only say I never saw it."

Julien rose and started to embrace his father. "My poor father. I had no idea you carried such a burden."

Nigel motioned him to be seated again. "Our stay in Constantinople was a disaster. The Byzantines were supposed to be our allies, but I think if we had stayed any longer we'd have massacred each other before we ever saw a Saracen. And I'll never trust a Greek again. Two-faced and tricky. We never knew what secret plans they were making with the Turks behind our backs. It's true they're good soldiers. They have discipline and they're clever tacticians, but they're also damned effeminate. They like to lead the battle until the first blood flows and then let the mercenaries do all the work. I believe it's all that bathing that weakens them, plus the rich food. And they have other habits it's just as well you didn't know about.

"As you can guess, they didn't like us very much, either. They made no secret of the fact they thought us all barbarians. Their emperor went so far as to say he preferred the Muslims, at least for their table manners. It was a relief for all sides when we left.

"You look a bit green about the gills, lad. Pour us another drink, and don't be so stingy with yourself this time. These are tales that may make you glad you had a little something to help you sleep."

Julien obeyed his father, though he wondered how much more he could consume before it overpowered him. Their bowls replenished, Nigel continued.

"When we reached the outskirts of Jerusalem we heard Peter the Hermit speak at the Mount of Olives. Dear God, what a golden tongue that man had. He made our mission sound so beautiful. I had been sick in body and soul since the slaughter of those villagers, but his words made us forget our sins, the sickness, the heat, and all the frightful filth around us. We could believe again that God was truly with us, and nothing mattered except the divine promise that inspired our cause. I was still just a soldier, remember. Even though I was disgusted by what I had done, it's all I was ever trained for, and now this wonderful man made me feel it was all right."

Julien was spellbound. Something in the old crusader's voice and the distant look in his eye alerted him that he was hearing something his father had told no man before. "In June of 1099 we marched on Jerusalem. For forty days we laid siege to the city, but as usual, everything was disorganized and it took us longer than it should have to get our war machines assembled, although we Normans were certainly doing a good deal better than the others. What a strange time that was! The deeply religious among us were in a frenzy, and not a day went by without reports of new visions and miracles. Many of us believed the end of the world was at hand or that Jesus himself would join us at the gates of Jerusalem. The truth of it is, we were all going a little crazy from the summer heat.

"Peter the Hermit kept baptizing anyone he could in the river Jordan, where our Savior was baptized, and the mania grew even among the most disciplined of us. Hundreds were gathering palms and singing psalms, believing that the holiness of our cause would let us walk right through the gates.

"The attack finally came. The native Christians of Jerusalem had already either left the city or been thrown out because, as you can guess, in Jerusalem they too were having problems feeding their people during the siege. A few of these Christians joined us, but most of them ran as far away as they could. There were about ten thousand of us, all crusading armies combined, and inside Jerusalem the Saracens and Jews must have numbered at least forty thousand, although some people say as many as seventy.

"The fighting was fierce, and as it mounted, a kind of madness swept over the men. Only soldiers can know what I mean. A group of my companions caught me up, and we headed for the Great Mosque known as Solomon's Temple because we were told the greatest number of Saracen troops was fighting there."

Nigel paused and drained his cup, signalling Julien for another. His voice was hoarse as he resumed his story. "What followed was the greatest massacre in the history of the world. Those aren't just my words, Julien. Ten thousand people lay dead around the Great Mosque alone. All the Jews were herded together and put in the synagogue, and then the building was set afire. At the end of the day's fighting, those of us in the mosque were wading through gore that came over our ankles. When it was all over, I remember dragging my legs through piles of mutilated bodies in the darkness, looking for a way out of the mosque. I must have passed out. Some of our soldiers found me the next day, still unconscious on a sea of entrails and dismembered corpses. No one in the city escaped. There was a mountain of dead bodies outside the Holy Sepulcher, and the priests were standing on it, weeping in ecstasy, blessing our soldiers and offering prayers of thanks for our great victory. Our great victory." His voice cracked and he was weeping freely now, but he brushed Julien's arm away when he tried to embrace him.

"I didn't get well for a long time. I returned to England at once, but my fever lasted for six months, and it was over a year more before either my health or my sanity was restored to me. When I was well enough, I wedded your mother, and through her saintly care I've been able to put some of the nightmare behind me. Enough to go on living.

"My hopes are all with you now, Julien. Once I'm able to believe that your good life has helped me expiate my sin, I will have the courage to die. I do believe in God and I do love Him. What I cannot believe is that He watched that scene in Jerusalem and did not turn from man in disgust."

The door to Ediwa's room opened, and she came towards them in her long black robe with the hood covering her hair and most of her face. Her voice was firm. "I heard you, father. Listen to me. I shall pray that your conscience be no longer troubled. You need have no fear. Your place next to mother in Paradise is assured. You suffered in the name of the Cross, and even though you did not die in the Holy Land, you are still guaranteed a martyr's place in Heaven."

Nigel drew back his arm as if to strike her, but Julien quickly put himself between them. "Go back to your room," he told his sister. "You had no business listening. This was my father's counsel to me alone."

Ediwa backed towards her room with her head bowed. "I'll pray for you too, Julien. I pity you greatly. Remember what I said. Find yourself a good confessor. It is faith, not reason, that will save your soul. I pray it is not already lost."

Chapter III
ROBERT OF SELBY

"I'm a cleric too, you know, same as the two of you, although I dare say it's not likely any one of us will ever say a Mass. We have that in common, as well as our blood, but the main difference between me and you is that I'm not educated. No, it's true. I can read little more than my prayers, and God knows it's not often I glance at them. That didn't sound like a boast, I trust? I respect education, and I'll tug my forelock to the lowest clerk in my command if he has a gift for letters. Our good King Henry taught me that. Come lads, let's drink a toast to him, shall we?"

Julien smiled feebly and held his bowl out to Robert for another round of whiskey. The drink had already made him lightheaded, but that was preferable to the queasiness brought on by his first sea voyage. Thomas, seated beside him and looking perfectly miserable, had responded even less well to the tossing of the small boat. The tiny cabin shared by the three of them was still acrid with the smell of his sickness, a smell made no more bearable by the smoked mutton and salted fish that filled the adjoining hold.

While their ship was not as large as most that plied the lane from Scarborough to Normandy, all other scheduled craft had been reserved for cargo that had accumulated over the last months waiting for navigable weather. They considered themselves lucky to have secured passage, even though the frail two-master creaked with every wind and there was a constant accumulation of sea water beneath their bunks.

Thomas and Julien were perfectly content to huddle beneath their sheepskin blankets and allow Robert to do all the talking. For weeks they had looked forward to his briefing them on their coming adventure, but Robert had seemed a little diffident about intruding on their last days with their parents.

No matter. They'd be sharing each other's company for months, and Julien admitted to himself he could ask for no more congenial a companion than Robert seemed. He'd been instantly flattered by Robert's open acceptance of him as a peer rather than as a green youth of no experience in the world. If only his other companion were as friendly or as sanguine about his expectations. Perhaps it was only his illness.

Julien glanced apprehensively at Thomas again. Thomas's skin seemed blotchy, and his high forehead glistened and diffused the light from the determined flickers of the three candle ends in the cabin. His tongue would dart out occasionally and try to moisten his lips, but they remained dry and cracked.

By contrast, Robert looked dramatically healthy. He was one of those men, Julien decided, whose skin never loses its ruddiness and whose eyes never dull. Although he too had a sheepskin blanket over his shoulders, Robert's shirt was opened halfway to his waist, and Julien could see a thick mat of dark blond hair that looked more like animal fur. It proceeded down his arms and curled across the massive span of wrist and knuckle that gripped its wooden bowl of whiskey as if the bowl were childsize. His face and head were covered by the same luxuriant fur, but the beard separated sharply at his chin to reveal a deep cleft there.

He must be no more than thirty, Julien thought, but he handles himself like a man who's always been in command. He addressed himself to Robert after watching him down a generous swallow of whiskey. "We've heard so many wild tales about this land we're going to. I suppose we'll just have to see for ourselves what's true and what's false, but in the meantime we've been so anxious to have you tell us whatever you know of it."

Robert grinned amiably. "I'll do my best. Duke Roger and I have been corresponding for well over a year now, and I'm sure it's already plain to you how far this mission has caught my fancy.

"I think you should know something about the country itself first. I hope you lads don't think I'm taking you off to some dim corner of the world where we'll scratch for our livings. Oh no, let me set you straight on that."

He reached into his pack for a parchment map and unrolled it across their knees. It was not particularly detailed, but it indicated areas to the south and east of which the two younger men had only the vaguest knowledge.

Robert put his palm down firmly on the lower portion of the map. "The most fertile and richest part of our world has always been the Mediterranean, and Sicily's the key to it. Before the Normans took over, there were three great powers ruling the Mediterranean and none of them belonged to the West." His finger traced an arc across the vellum. "You both know about Byzantium, of course, but then there was the caliphate here at Cairo, and the caliphate centered at Cordova." He paused and smiled at the two bewildered youths. "I've had to do a lot of brushing up on history and geography since I started correspondence with Roger. Anyway, the Normans were the first westerners to dare set up their court in this territory since ancient Rome, and they're holding it. So you see, men, we're not just running off to join a band of uncouth freebooters."

Julien caught Robert's enthusiasm and held his cup high, then tossed off a much larger swallow than he was accustomed too. He was seized with a coughing fit and was instantly aware of Thomas's contemptuous glance, but Robert merely leaned forward and refilled his cup before continuing.

"Now about the man we're going to serve. Duke Roger was born in Sicily of Count Roger de Hauteville and an Italian mother, and he grew up in a court with more foreign languages and strange customs than you'll find anywhere else in Christendom. His father died when Roger was only a boy of twelve or so, but he had fine tutors, and Roger's surely more learned than any ruler in Europe. By the way, his mother, Adelaide of Savona, appears to have been a proper, good regent in her own way—I mean, considering she's a woman and an Italian at that."

Thomas shifted uneasily on his stool and struggled to speak. "His teachers. We were taught they were heathens."

Julien was surprised to hear him speak. He seemed to be suffering so.

Robert nodded. "I suppose some of them were. I admit I find some of Roger's ideas sound a bit heretical, but don't pay any attention to those stories going about that he's a heathen himself. I swear to you he's a devout Christian. I know he's had his troubles with the Church, perhaps more than other rulers, but there's no truth to the stories of his lapse from faith.

"I believe it's his courting all these Arab philosophers and scientists that makes the popes uneasy. But what's he to do? He's got all these Arabs and Jews living right there in his kingdom. He can't get rid of them, so he does the best he can. As nearly as I can tell, Muslims and Jews are forbidden to own Christian slaves; oh, and they pay an extra tax of some kind. He doesn't deny his court is full of them, so I guess he enjoys them. They're supposed to be very learned."

Thomas's eyes were glowing unhealthily, but he struggled to speak again. "You know that's not proper learning, Robert. I'm certain you were taught the same as Julien and I that knowledge must edify the soul and carry with it the reflection of God's truth to be true knowledge."

Julien started to answer, but a glance from Robert silenced him. "Yes, I was taught that, but since Roger's involved me with all these new ideas, I've come to wonder if there's some value to other kinds of knowledge too. I suspected you'd disagree, Thomas, but Julien already told me he believes God can reveal himself to some extent outside scripture, the incarnation, and the Church. That's your Abelard, Julien; am I correct?"

Julien nodded, pleased to have Robert recall their earlier chats, but he was apprehensive about the uneasiness he saw in Thomas.

"I'm not sure I can go along with you, Julien, when you say the pagan philosophers were superior to the Christian fathers and Jews, but I do agree they're important enough for learned men to consider. . . .

"I wish you wouldn't look so upset, Thomas. We'll be together for quite a while, so you'd best be a bit more tolerant of your companions' talk."

Thomas's jaws were flexing oddly. "It's not just the ancients, Robert. You're talking about Muslims, and our fathers just finished fighting them. The enemies of Christ! How can you say you accept Christ and still give an ear to those who would overthrow His kingdom?" His body was shaking.

"I'm glad you brought that up," Robert said. "I told Roger right off, in my first letter to him, that I wasn't sure I'd care to rub elbows with the ignorant heathens, much as I was grateful for his interest in me. His answer got back to me fast. Very arch he was. He begged me to be patient with his ignorant heathens and then asked me how large the library was at the monastery I was schooled in. I counted a hundred or so books on the wall of the cloister and a few more that the monks kept in their cells, but I didn't get his meaning at first. You probably had somewhat more at Durham, Julien, but let me continue. He went on to let me know that his librarian at Palermo was the great grandson of one of the librarians at Cordova who helped assemble a library of four hundred thousand books a hundred years ago under the caliphate. He's a sly one, that Roger. He said that with this man's help he'd make every effort to lift his Muslim population out of their ignorance. I was told, right enough. Now, I'm prepared to let them stick to their side of the road if they don't crowd me on mine, and I hope you lads will do the same. We've got to keep an open mind. After all, we're making ourselves subjects of the same lord, and that appears to be the way he wants it."

"I don't believe we'll have any trouble there," Julien answered. "Will we, Thomas?" He looked at his companion doubtfully but Thomas pursed his lips instead of answering. "What started this correspondence between you and Duke Roger in the first place?" he asked Robert.

"It would be immodest of me to answer that," Robert said, grinning. "Or didn't you know I'm said to have some talent as an administrator? Anyway, I hope not to disappoint him. I hope none of us will."

Thomas shifted in his seat and looked away.

"You, Thomas," Robert went on, "you're as good a man as I know for organizing details and seeing a job through. I'd consider any man lucky to have you with him."

Thomas's lips soundlessly formed a word of thanks, and Robert turned to Julien. "I can't say I've any real idea of what Roger's likely to want with you, my friend, but he appears to have been intrigued by my description of you. I checked your record very thoroughly, and it amused me to see that Roger was as attracted by the somewhat unpleasant observations your prior made as he was by your friendlier critics."

"I hope you didn't flatter me too much," Julien said. "I'm really not trained to do anything useful."

"Not at all. I believe you're as quick as any man need be, and if your ideas are a little wild, well, Roger has probably heard even wilder ones. I suspect if anyone knows how to bring out the best in you, it will be he."

"I trust you're right," Julien answered. "One thing I do know, I was ready for a change after those years at the monastery. I was fed up with pretty nearly everything—except some of my studies."

"Well, one thing I can promise you. Whatever we're assigned and wherever we go, we'll be living well. Roger isn't tightfisted, and he knows I've a taste for comfort. Don't misunderstand; I wouldn't want you to think I was persuaded only with promises of money, but the country is rich, richer by far than other lands."

"Has he conquered so much?" Thomas asked.

"He has, but that's not the measure of his wealth. He's more committed to trade and industry than other rulers. Sicily controls the passage of traffic between East and West, and he's profiting from it. Then in addition, the Sicilians are manufacturing great varieties of stuff—paper, for example, which even in the exchequer I've seen only half a dozen times in my life. They're producing and dyeing silks, trading in hides and cotton as well as foodstuffs, and the Muslims refine a product, *shukar* they call it, which sounds like a substitute for honey. Roger seems to think it has great commercial possibilities. And Sicily has every mineral imaginable in its mines. Yes, the people are getting rich, and we'll be part of it."

"I've no objection to being rich," Julien said, "but I hope there's more to our career than a commercial venture."

Robert shook his head slowly. "Men, if I didn't think this was the most exciting adventure anyone could ask for, I never would have urged your families so strongly to have you join me. Do you think I had nothing to lose? This year I settled all my lands and goods on my children. Every penny. I'm not married, thank the Lord, but I had enough spare time on my hands while at the monastery to sire three healthy children and one more since in London. No, with prospects like ours, I'd welcome the opportunity to provide for another four brats, or forty, if need be. Let it never be said that I'm one of those men who complain that his mace is too heavily taxed—Not when I consider the service it's seen." He winked broadly at Julien. "May your mace be put to as heavy use in Palermo."

"Do you think we'll be living in Palermo, then?" Julien asked.

"If we're lucky. But Roger's lands are now so vast that their administration is much more complicated and it's possible we may have to do service in one of the mainland cities. Of course it would be really wonderful if we could live in the palace in Palermo. The city has a quarter of a million people, and one out of every ten lives in the palace. Imagine!

"I don't know if we'll ever get to see it, but the women are quartered in one entire wing of the palace called the harem, complete with eunuchs to watch over them. Sounds like the saucy tales we've heard of Baghdad, doesn't it?"

Thomas interrupted his talk with a paroxysm of coughing.

"Am I embarrassing you, Thomas?"

Thomas's cough eventually subsided to a wheeze and sputter, and he answered with some difficulty. "My father never allowed suggestive conversation at home," he said.

"Well, I suggest you try to get used to it, my friend, because I'm not likely to change, and while I respect your father's high moral standards, I'm just as glad he's not with us."

Julien could not repress a snicker.

"As for you, Julien, you'd best learn to control that wicked glint in your eye. As a matter of fact, I think there's something I'd best speak to you about now. The customs of Palermo in regard to women are very different from ours. It's the Muslims again, I don't doubt. I suggest you be very careful about flirting lest you find yourselves joining the unfortunates who guard them. There are plenty of slave women available to meet your needs when they arise, as it were, but it would be wise to consider any other women forbidden. I hope you'll find there are many exceptions to this rule once we get there, but I insist on your discretion."

"You may count on it," Julien said somewhat unconvincingly as Thomas looked at him, smoldering with contempt.

"You're probably wondering what we'll be eating down there, I suppose," Robert went on. "We'll no doubt miss honest English cooking for a while, but the food is said to be quite good once you get used to it. They have dishes from Cathay we've never heard of and all manner of strange-looking fruits and vegetables from Africa, Persia, and everywhere in the East. Their wheat is fine, but I'm told they like to muck up their dishes with all sorts of herbs and spices and garden plants. You've doubtless heard some stories of the weird foods our Crusaders were forced to eat in the Holy Land. But at least I have it on good authority that their wines are fabulous." He took a cue from this and poured another measure of whiskey into their bowls.

"The climate will be rather warm for you after England, though one thing sounds most pleasant to me. . . . Their houses are built with a courtyard and gardens for private entertainment, and the palace is filled with flowery pavilions and fountains with small lakes around them. I personally never believed English winters couldn't be improved on. How about that, lads?"

Julien took another long swallow of whiskey, and this time it went down so smoothly he couldn't resist flashing a triumphant look at poor Thomas.

"Now, I'd say we're off to a good start," Robert went on. "I'd like to get all the way to the Norman coast with this ship, to Honfleur, perhaps. From there it shouldn't be hard to get a Norman ship headed down the French coast. Our next destination will be Rochefort, or as close to it as we can get. I'm not sure they're ready to welcome Normans in their harbor yet, but we may be lucky. We're stopping there on our first commission for Roger, and it should be a pleasant one. We're to go on foot through the south of Aquitaine towards the Mediterranean coast. Our destination is Narbonne in the duchy of Gallia, just a bit west of Marseilles. Roger wants a firsthand report on Narbonne's administration because the city has some interesting parallels to Palermo's. Narbonne had been conquered many times, but when Charlemagne took it over, he found the Saracens in command, with the Jews who so often follow them in charge of the port's trade. It looked like a good arrangement, so after he got rid of the Saracens, he divided Narbonne into three lordships—one for the bishop, one for his Frankish overlord, and one for the Jews—and that's the way it's been functioning ever since. Interesting?"

Robert ignored Thomas's perfectly blank expression. "In Palermo, because of the many races and religions, Roger has allowed the chief races to administer their own courts of justice except where there's a conflict with the interest of the duchy. We're to stay in Narbonne just long enough to see how the system there has been working after nearly four hundred years. Then Julien can write up everything we saw on the next leg of our voyage.

"From Narbonne there are Pisan ships going to Naples and Salerno, and from either of those ports it's an easy matter to take one of Roger's ships directly to Sicily. I can promise you we'll be in Palermo in time for Michaelmas at the cathedral. That's less than five months from now. I think it's time for another toast . . . to the girls we left behind."

Chapter IV
THOMAS BROWNE

Narbonne
St. Swithun's Day

Dear father,

Blessings and salutations from your most miserable and disconsolate Thomas. The months that have passed since I was at your side, sheltered at the hearth of a God-fearing family, seem like years. Dear father, was it really so necessary that I leave England? You know I would never dream of questioning your judgment for fear you may think me ungrateful after all the care and comfort you have lavished on your undeserving son. But it has already gone too far for me to keep silent any longer. I ask myself a thousand times a day, how well could my noble father have known his kinsman Robert when he agreed to contract me into service in another land?

Truth is, you were deceived, dear father. You are blameless, of course. How could you possibly have guessed that this man, respected as he is in good English society, could be a drunkard, womanizer, and heretic, totally unworthy of your trust. You will remember, please, that from the beginning I was never sure I liked him. When I think of the love and effort you spent on me, nurturing my soul for so many years, guiding me to be a servant of almighty God . . . and then to come to this! It breaks my heart to tell you that you have handed me over to a demented pagan who has already begun my corruption in preparation for the service I am to render to a lord of the heathens who appears to be every bit as far away from the sight of God as are his subjects. I tell you this, not by way of reproach, but in the hope that it may not yet be too late. Be advised, my fate is doomed unless your prayers can save me, for I believe the fiend will never release me from my contract. Go speak to the priests of our church, I beg you. Implore them to pray, to say Masses for me, to invoke the saints and all the unhappy souls in Purgatory to intercede for my soul in its present dark passage.

And how could you have been expected to estimate the character of my other companion? This Julien Fitz Nigel, however comely and innocent his appearance, has been abysmally corrupted by monks in the service of the Devil. He speaks too glibly, well coached as he is in Satan's own dialect by, I doubt not, the Prince of Evil himself. I grow dumb when he insists on discourse, and my faith loses its force when he confronts me with his diabolical logic. If you only knew how I loathe that evil smile of triumph he assumes when he believes he is winning me over to the forces of darkness. Help me.

The first leg of our journey seemed innocent enough. The winds that met our sails were fortuitous, and I had only the vaguest forebodings of the dire events that lay ahead. Not until we set foot in Aquitaine did I see the plot against my salvation. The saints have powers of protection that are ineluctable in England and Normandy, but once away from these blessed lands, I am at the mercy of the monster Robert.

Instead of heading directly south by southeast as planned, Robert insisted on crossing the river Garonne because he had heard there were interesting towns on the western bank where we could spend a few pleasant hours. Our journey had been swift, and we arrived weeks ahead of schedule, so I could advance no argument. Father, what that evil man conceived of was—and I use his words—"a wine-tasting tour."

For weeks we went from town to town—three days in Pauillac, four in St. Julien, four more in Margaux, and so forth. As you know, I have never been fond of wine. I found these wines sour and little attractive, but Robert and Julien spent evening after evening in carousal, and our observance of the canonical hours was ignored completely. Yes, mine too. It's hard to leave your companions in a foreign country, however much you know that in not doing so you invite the Devil. My only defense is that I often tried to moderate their outrageous appetites.

But this was only the first step in their campaign to endanger my soul. Never mind that we passed Whitsunday, Trinity Sunday, and Corpus Christi in the most meager observation of those solemn holy days. Robert led us further south, and there they plied me with a wine so golden it seemed to have trapped the sun. Sweet it was, and of an incredibly delicious flavor that lulled me and lowered my guard against Satan. I was able to keep pace now with their riotous imbibing, so that the next day I was quite sick, but by dusk I was able to join them once again. This wine, whose manufacture is surely overseen by Lucifer, although so sweet, is made without honey, and the natives call it sauternes. We stayed in the area a few more days, and Robert insisted it was for my pleasure we did so. Then he had us cross the Garonne again, and we traced and retraced our footsteps for weeks, going from place to place until it seemed we could have floated to Narbonne on the river of wines we consumed. Father, when it is the Devil himself who hands you a cup of the grape, it is your virtue he seeks.

I must continue, though shame flames my cheeks. Robert sought and found drinking companions along the way. I mean women, father. They looked decent at first, but after a while you could see they were not the sort you and I would welcome into our home. After Julien and I used to fall asleep from the effects of the wine, I know Robert used them. It didn't surprise me much, because he had already confessed to his many sins of the flesh, but I had no idea how insatiable he was, nor what lay ahead for me.

We finally arrived at Narbonne, a month later than need have been. I found the city unspeakably revolting. I don't like the smells of the waterfront; the seamen looked like cutthroats, many of them so swarthy they didn't seem human. I wondered if it might not be the Devil's own mark upon them, but one of the priests at Narbonne laughed when I asked him about it, so I suppose it isn't so. I had already asked Robert and Julien, but I knew their answers are not to be trusted. They make fun of me, father. Outwardly they seem kind and companionable, but it's all part of the scheme to include me in their satanic mischief and so damn me. Yes, they laugh at me.

Actually I saw very little of them after we reached Narbonne. They were busy investigating everything they could about the city. I stayed with them at first, but let them go about their evil affairs without me after I found out they intended to visit the house of a Jew. Imagine! When they were gone, I reported their errand to the priest there who had become my friend. Can you believe he told me a number of his parishioners were Jews? This is a strange country. And if Duke Roger sent them to the house of a Jew on his commission, do you not think it is Roger himself directing all these evil machinations? I must fight to keep my faith from being subverted. That alone is left to me, as you will soon see. I am wary. I have armed myself with rosaries, roods, scapulars, and relics. I bless you anew for the relic you gave me on departing; the blessed finger of St. Swithelbert never leaves my body.

It is with trembling hands that I write you of the next step in my corruption. Be forbearing, I pray you. We spent yesterday making preparations to leave Narbonne. When it was clear we were as well organized as possible, Robert insisted on celebrating. I knew it would be exceptionally riotous. Still, I could not refuse to join them without incurring their ill will. Father, I remind you how for twenty-six years I have striven to keep myself pure. Now this poor clay is so sullied I ache for penance.

There was, predictably, a great deal of wine consumed, and towards the end of the evening Julien fell asleep—or rather, fell into his accustomed stupor, this time with his face smothered in the fat bosom of a drunken cotquean who was quite as insensible as he. Oddly my eyelids weren't even heavy.

I soon became aware of a certain woman, not the usual slut Robert finds to consort with, but a virtuous-looking, modest girl whose face might have passed for that of a saint. And very clean too. When she took me to her chamber, I still didn't dream she was a tool of Satan. I went with her only because I had grown hungry and she had promised me a slice of hare pie. How can one tell? She cast a spell on me that not only drove away all thoughts of sleep but inflamed my senses! I lay with her. Yes, and without the slightest hesitation! When it was over, I tried to excuse myself to my conscience by saying I had been enchanted by something in the wine. But I know that could not be so, because I slept afterwards . . . and when I awakened I lay with her again—and this time the enchantment was greater, so I know it was truly the Devil within me who had assumed control.

Pray for me, father, I beseech you. You didn't raise your son to be a drunkard and whoremonger. My virtue is utterly lost, because even now, when I think of her— Oh father, you would be so ashamed to know what I am thinking. Alas, where is innocence? Can virtue ever be recovered?

I'll write you next from Sicily. I must close. There is just enough time to entrust this to a sailor headed for holy England. Pray for me, father, pray for me. I fear that once I find myself in the land where so many stand against Christ, I may not have the strength to resist Lucifer further. And father, you really should have told me more about it.

Your obedient, loving, and undeserving son,
Thomas

Chapter V
THE DOCTOR

The sun seemed to mock the breeze. It was at least twenty degrees warmer than any summer day they had ever known, and they marvelled that the ship's crew should appear so unconcerned by it. Robert and Julien wore only their knee-length shirts and had rolled the sleeves to the shoulder, but the shirts were woolen and had chafed their damp skin almost raw. Julien especially regretted that he had hesitated to buy cooler clothing while they were in Narbonne. Robert had bought himself a light cotton shirt, but had given it to Thomas when he started to complain of being unwell. Julien's shirt felt abrasive and stiff with salt.

They had been anchored outside Salerno for over an hour, waiting for the small boat that would carry them to shore, and the restless rocking combined with the unaccustomed heat was making them sick. The view of the city was nonetheless spectacular enough to keep them at the boat's rail. Salerno's ancient castle could be seen far above the glistening flat roofs of the city, and they judged it as impressive as any they had known.

Aggravating the queasiness of their stomachs was the fear, occasioned by an overheard remark, that the authorities might not permit them to disembark at Salerno. Their captain had made it clear that he debated whether or not to leave them at the first port that would have them as soon as he noticed Thomas's condition. It had started almost as soon as they left Narbonne, and Thomas had not come up from his berth since the fourth day out. He had become, quite simply, disgusting, and it was all Julien could do to feed him and try to comfort him as best he could. Robert had grown solemn and spoke little, but after they were ten days at sea, he had a violent row with the ship's captain about the facilities available. The three Englishmen were the only passengers on the voyage and so had been charged outrageously, but at least they had private cabins. After Robert's quarrel with the captain, they'd become unpopular with the Pisan crew, and the lowliest deck hand thought nothing of holding his nostrils every time he passed one of them.

Julien had been still only a boy when his brother Geoffrey was taken away to the lazar house, and he could remember only faintly how Geoffrey's body had looked, but there was an unpleasant similarity to Thomas's condition. The red eruptions that seemed at first no more than a light rash soon became covered with white scales that itched and were sore. A few days later open scabs formed, and his appearance was hideous. Thomas was quick to notice Julien's revulsion and refused to speak to him any longer, about his illness or anything else.

They could see boats now a hundred yards away, and the sailors were running about, following the orders barked at them by the toothless, hairy ship's officer, who looked like an ape as he sprang from one deck to another between commands, scratching his body with long, curved arms.

As the boats drew closer, Julien saw that they were manned by nut-dark men whose bodies were naked except for a shame cloth drawn between their legs and fastened around the hips. Some wore turbans; others simply knotted kerchiefs around their heads.

Robert and Julien went below and lifted Thomas off his bunk. They drew his cloak around him and carried him to the rail where the first boatmen were already clambering up the ship's ladder. A copper-colored man wearing a gold hoop in one ear approached them grinning, and made signs asking if it was they who wished to go ashore. As soon as they nodded, he took Thomas from them and effortlessly slung him over one shoulder and went over the side with him. Julien and Robert picked up their packs and clumsily followed down the ladder. Strong hands gripped their waists as they reached the waterline and swung them into the boat. They hastened to pick Thomas up and prop him up between them to make his appearance more unexceptional. Julien couldn't control a prickle of revulsion as Thomas's bare arm slid out from the cloak and made contact with him. "Tell me, Robert," Julien said, attempting nonchalance, "do you think we gave them enough time to make ready for our arrival?" But the sailors had already stopped being concerned with them and were ferrying them briskly through the choppy waters.

As they neared the shore, two dolphins appeared off the port side and started to sport with them. Julien's spirits lifted at once. Perhaps, he thought, it wasn't as bad as they feared, despite Thomas's woebegone appearance.

The seamen smiled good-naturedly at all three of them, also pleased by the omen.

At the dock they were greeted by a robust Muslim whose face was dominated by a bristling flourish of moustache. His ample frame was swaddled in layers of gauze that hung slightly below the knee, and under these robes he wore loose trousers. They struck Julien as extremely effeminate, and he wondered if the man might be one of the eunuchs he'd heard of, although weren't eunuchs beardless? The Muslim roared a command to his aides to tether the boat and assist the voyagers ashore, in a vigorous tone that put Julien's doubts to rest.

The official inquired politely in excellent Latin as to the nature of their business in Salerno. They could see him take note of Thomas's condition, but he didn't mention it. Robert formally unrolled the *licet* forwarded to him by Roger. It was far more elaborate than the customary "safe conduct" supplied to travellers, in that it invested the bearers with privileges barely secondary to those due a vice-regent.

The official sucked in his breath and bowed very low after glancing at the document. "My name is Ali ibn Athir, first officer of the Salerno *diwan*. You may rely on my eagerness to assist you in every way. When I saw your companion, I believed you had come to Salerno for a consultation at the University. This man needs medical attention at once."

Thomas had been propped on a bench by the official's aides and looked even a shade worse than he had on shipboard. Robert was relieved by the Muslim's considerateness. "If you could arrange to help us get him to a doctor . . . Is it possible?"

"The medical school's a short distance away. One of my men has already gone to arrange for transportation. Be assured he'll be well taken care of."

"Excuse me, sir," ventured Julien, "but I didn't understand what department you said you belonged to."

"Ah, the diwan. You Normans pronounce it douane. All the ports in the duke's realm continue the Muslim practice of having diwan officers to collect taxes on all merchandise imported and exported, and to prevent illicit materials or unwanted persons from entering. We take great pride in our office." He bowed again.

"Has there been news of our duke?" Robert asked.

"There's good news. His campaign against the rebellious barons goes well. And we heard only this week that Admiral George of Antioch has had a full triumph in Bari. After two months the rebels in the city surrendered to his siege and have sworn their loyalty again. They would be wise to keep their vows, *akbar u Allah*! Our duke has already moved on to Troina, where the faithless will have a taste of his Muslim guards' steel before this month is out. Do you gentlemen plan to stay long in Salerno?"

"It was our intention to go at once to Sicily," Robert replied, "but perhaps it isn't so urgent since Duke Roger is still occupied here."

"Never fear. He'll make short work of the rebels. We had a minor insurrection in Salerno too, earlier this month, but it was a simple matter to stop it. Roger doesn't lack for troublemakers in his realm. Ah, the chair is here. No, no. Don't disturb yourselves. My men will take care of him. Present your credentials when you get to the dispensary, and all his needs will be seen to in a manner befitting a friend of Duke Roger's. If I can be of further help, please call on me. *Akbar u Allah*." He salaamed and returned to his office in a long, low building that was built out over the water.

Because the city came right to the waterfront, they quickly found themselves on one of the main avenues, an alameda leading directly to the medical school.

Thomas rode in a sedan chair carried on poles by two muscular, fair-skinned Italians while Julien and Robert walked beside them. Surprised to hear the sedan carriers speak Greek to each other, Julien welcomed the opportunity to practice. He asked the litter bearer nearest him what he kept in the little cloth bag he wore around his neck.

"Garlic," the man answered. "It's excellent protection." He forked his fingers and then quickly rubbed his crotch.

Julien knitted his brows but kept silent.

The complex of buildings that made up the school and clinic was larger than any city Julien had ever seen. As the oldest medical school in Europe, it attracted lecturers and scholars from all over the world, especially from the Mediterranean and Near East. Julien couldn't help staring at the first truly black men he'd ever seen—far darker than he imagined them. Most wore turbans, but when he saw a bareheaded black approach him, he couldn't help slowing his wonder at the man's tight curls. The black smiled good-naturedly when he caught Julien's stare and bowed in greeting. Julien was startled to see a crucifix he wore around his neck freed by the movement. The black laughed and returned it inside his shirt.

"Don't be surprised at anything you see from now on," Robert told him. "There are Christian settlements throughout the African coast, remember. Think of Simon's apostolate in Egypt. The Muslims there appear to tolerate them well, as they do in the Holy Land. You can't know anything about a man's religion from the way he's dressed."

"So my father taught me," Julien said reflectively.

The sedan stopped at the entrance to a dispensary, and two subordinates in white shirts hurried out to escort Thomas in, while a more grandly robed clerk came forward at a leisurely pace to inspect their documents. He too was visibly impressed. They were led into an antechamber where Thomas was already being undressed above his protestations. They examined his sores, prodded and poked once or twice, and then proceeded to wash their hands from a basin and pitcher on the table.

They conferred briefly in Arabic, and then the clerk told Robert, "I am sure the master will want to see him. His lecture ends in a few minutes, and he will be told of your arrival. If you would like to stay with your companion till he arrives, please follow us to the wards."

Thomas was carried through a succession of whitewashed corridors until they arrived at a large, airy room with half a dozen linen-covered mattresses raised off the floor on a wooden platform. There were no other occupants, despite the size of the room.

"There is a bench here for you," one of the interns said. "Please make yourself comfortable. You will not have long to wait."

In no more than ten minutes the interns returned with three slightly older associates, and followed by a small, reedy man whose extravagance of curly white beard covered his chest to the waist. He wore only a simple white robe, and his turban was less elaborate than others they had seen on persons of high office. Robert and Julien bowed to him, but Thomas's eyes roved like those of a terrified horse, and his lips had pulled back from his teeth in a grimace.

"I am Doctor Astruc," the old gentleman announced. His voice wheezed as though his lungs were filled with dead leaves. He could not have weighed more than ninety pounds.

The Englishmen introduced themselves; then Robert provided information on Thomas's condition. "At first it seemed a surfeit of dry red humors that were accumulating at the surface, but then moist white humors appeared to take the ascendancy."

Dr. Astruc was already inspecting one of the lesions. "Please spare me your medical jargon." He addressed himself to Thomas. "Have you ever had a rash like this before? Other skin disturbances?"

Thomas's face turned grayer, and he began to mumble a prayer.

Julien interposed haltingly. "He hasn't spoken in days, sir, but we've been with him these last months and he did tell us he had experienced a rash in the past, and some itching, but it was much less pronounced. It troubled him more often while he was at school."

"Before examinations?"

Thomas nodded his head feebly.

"Well, I see you can understand me. Tell me, have you ever had a sore on your penis?"

Thomas howled at this and burst into sobs.

"Answer me. I'm a doctor, not your judge."

Thomas started to sputter with anger and embarrassment. He finally subsided a bit and shook his head.

"No? Do you examine yourself regularly?"

Thomas glared but nodded.

"Do you consort often with prostitutes or other loose women?"

Thomas began to bawl so loudly that Julien moved forward to comfort him. "Sir, it is my belief that my friend was a virgin until a few weeks ago."

"I see. I have to eliminate various possibilities, you understand." I think we can rule out the great pox for the moment, although it seems it is appearing alarmingly often in the north countries."

Thomas propped himself on an elbow and struggled to speak. "It is a curse," he croaked. "God's moral judgment for my most grievous sin."

"Is that what you believe it is?" There was no suggestion of irony in the doctor's voice.

Thomas clutched Robert's hand and brought it to his mouth, kissing it passionately. "Robert, I beg of you. You are my kinsman. Don't let them put me in a lazar house. Not in this cursed foreign country. I implore you in the name of the blood we share to see to it that I return to England. At least there, if I am cast out from society, it will be on my own dear, native soil."

"You're not going to a lazar house," the doctor said firmly. "I'm not certain yet I can cure you, but there is certainly no question of a lazar house. To be quite frank, we know very little about skin eruptions, but there are a few things I can try."

"Offer your prayers for me, doctor."

"Of course I will, if it pleases you, but you may not think very much of them. I am a Jew."

Thomas had fainted, and one of the young doctors brought a clean cloth which he moistened and put to Thomas's lips. Thomas opened his eyes abruptly. "Robert, please take me out of here. Oh my dear God, have I really offended you so much?"

Robert's voice showed his concern. "Doctor, are you quite certain he—"

"I'm satisfied he doesn't have leprosy and doubt he has the pox. I can promise you he will receive no better treatment anywhere than what is available here. My teacher was an Egyptian who was considered the finest doctor for these ailments, and he had a remarkable degree of success with the treatment I plan for your friend."

Thomas's eyes narrowed. "Did you say an Egyptian? What treatment? No, Robert, don't let him. I'll have none of his devil's tricks used on me. He's a Jew, Robert. He admitted it."

"I know no devil's tricks. Do you believe God made the sun evil?"

Thomas continued to look at him fearfully but said nothing.

The doctor smiled. "To begin with, you must spend a good deal of time in the sun. Only a few minutes at first until we can increase the treatment to several hours a day. You see, much of your cure will be quite pleasant. Then there are poultices which will be applied several times a day. You and your friends are free to examine them. They will be mostly river mud, ground papyrus, and common herbs ground together. We don't dispense miracles here, although I do invite you to pray for one if you wish. It's been my experience that prayers do a great deal of good when employed together with our treatment. Meantime, I must ask your patience for the next few weeks. I don't expect results much sooner."

"A few weeks!" Robert winced. "But doctor, we have a schedule. Weren't you told we have business with Duke Roger?"

"So I hear. But Duke Roger is himself on important business not far from here. Come now, Salerno isn't such a bad place. We'll do our best to make you comfortable. Actually, I believe you would be wise to wait here until Roger arrives. He's certain to visit his mainland capital before returning to Palermo."

"But what if he's detained a great deal longer?"

"Then you'd have to wait that much longer in any case. I doubt he'd want you with him while he's subduing the rebels. And isn't it far better that I do all I can to make your friend presentable to his duke? The longer you wait, the better his chances of a cure."

Robert was still hesitant. "You won't cut him or do anything radical without discussing it first with us?"

Dr. Astruc drew himself up stiffly, and his voice sharpened. "Sir, I told you I was a Jew. Our religion forbids treating the human body with anything less than the maximum respect. Doctors who employ bloodletting or enter the body with knives in any way are butchers. No Jew or Muslim would perform such an abomination, I assure you." His manner carried such authority it seemed pointless to question him further.

Dr. Astruc's body relaxed, and he spoke more softly now. "Your papers are most impressive, I'm told. You can be sure your friend will be accorded the most privileged attention here. It is to my honor that Roger is as proud as we are of the reputation our school enjoys. You can be sure we would do nothing to risk our good name."

Thomas signalled feebly to Robert. "I want a priest, please."

Dr. Astruc patted his hand. "You shall have one right away. I consider it an indispensable part of your cure. We have many priests on our staff, but I expect Father Louis will be the one most disposed to counsel you. He shares the opinion that in maladies which manifest themselves primarily in the skin, the link between body and soul is most evident. I recommend that you be shriven daily and receive communion every morning. Now, gentlemen, if you will excuse me, I have other patients to see."

"Doctor," Julien faltered, "may I have a word with you please?"

"Do you have an eruption somewhere you'd like me to look at?"

"No, it's about my brother, doctor."

"Oh, you have a brother in Salerno?"

"I'm afraid he's in England."

"Then, I can be of no service to you."

"I just want to ask you something. Some years ago my brother was sent to a lazar house—"

"—and you want to know if I think he was truly a leper." Doctor Astruc's eyes softened. "Thank you for your confidence in me, my son. I know that when these maladies strike, the family suffers along with the patient. What comfort can I possibly offer you? There's no way you could send him to me however much you wanted to, and without seeing him I'd be a charlatan to venture an opinion. But I can tell you from experience, it would not surprise me if his illness were incorrectly diagnosed. I visited a lazar house in France once, where almost certainly half the patients had the great pox and the other half I couldn't be sure of.

"But does that really make you feel any better? I don't wish to sound cruel, but I believe you'd best forget him. Troubles will come to you without searching them out, so make the most of the joys which are possible to you. Sadly they will pass more quickly than your woes."

Astruc turned to Robert. "I will leave word every few days of our patient's progress, but if I can be of service, please don't hesitate to call on me." He gave a signal, and two of the interns helped Thomas to his feet so they could escort him to his room. Thomas seemed almost capable of walking unassisted now.

"Be sure to visit him often—every day if you like. It will hasten his cure.

I believe it would be best if you would leave him now, however. Father Louis will want to be alone with him. Your documents will assure you a cordial reception at the castle, and your hosts there will help you find all you need to know about Salerno. Shalom."

Robert and Julien decided to walk to the castle, although the road was a steep one and they had to pause often to catch their breath.

"Robert, have you ever seen a Jew in England?"

Robert laughed. "You can be sure of it. With my habits I've had to visit the moneylenders often enough. But I always paid back every penny I owed. Do you mean you've never seen one before?"

"You know I've seen very little beyond Durham."

"Oh, but not even Josce of York? Surely you've seen the house he built, the first stone house in York?"

"I've heard my father mention it. Is it a castle?"

"No, not at all. It's right in the center of the city. I thought everyone in Yorkshire knew it. You know, in York the Jews live right alongside the Christians, but in London they have their own quarter of the city and aren't permitted to live anywhere else. Many of Josce's neighbors thought that building a stone house was an affectation, but that wasn't it at all. The old Jew built it for his protection and nothing else. Not just against thieves, you understand. Some people have nasty ways of welshing on their debts."

"I see. But this doctor though . . ."

"Wasn't what you expected. Took me by surprise too. But I can promise you he wouldn't be so highly placed at the school if he didn't merit it. Quite a place, this. It's a pity they don't get more Englishmen studying here. They all looked quite foreign, didn't they?"

"Yes, I hope Thomas doesn't mind too much. How long do you think we'll have to stay here?"

Robert shrugged. "Let's not concern ourselves too greatly about it. Salerno should give us a good idea of what we can expect in Palermo, and I'm looking forward to our first night on land." Julien agreed readily, and they resumed their hike.

"One other thing, my boy. I suggest we go to the market first thing tomorrow. These cotton robes I see on everyone look a sight more comfortable than what we're wearing, and take no offense, but you're beginning to smell like a rutting billy goat."

Chapter VI
THE BAPTIZED SULTAN

"The duke is coming." The fat chatelain interrupted all conversation in the hall with his news.

The aristocratic Lombards, the earliest residents of the castle, usually scorned Pandulf's indecorous outbursts, but they turned to him this morning with interest. Those whose loyalty to Duke Roger was questionable turned pale; others seemed stirred, albeit mainly by curiosity; a few actually cheered.

The company of Salerno's ancient castle was gathered around a trestle table in the center of the hall, enjoying the coolness retained by the two-foot thick stone slabs. Servants with buckets of water sponged the walls all day so that the slow evaporation on the saturated stone would help make light of the oppressive heat. It was almost time for the midday meal, and the nobles were drinking cups of white wine diluted with a great deal of water.

On the right were seated the Lombards and Italians of the old guard, most of them still resentful of the new claims made by Duke Roger on the castle after he had restored it to them little more than a year ago.

On the left were the Lombards of unquestioned loyalty, a few Normans, and a number of Italians and Greeks with bureaucratic posts. This was the new guard installed by Duke Roger when he reclaimed the castle. Then there was Pandulf, the fat chatelain, who claimed to be seventy, but his age appeared less a disadvantage in discharging the duties of managing such an enormous household than did his oppressive weight. Still, he remained surprisingly spry. His was a sentimental appointment since he was not personally known to Roger, but his family had been linked to the Hautevilles since the early days, when Roger's uncle, the Guiscard, had taken for his second wife a Salernitan named Sigelgaita, a member of the most powerful of the Lombard families ruling in the south. It was Pandulf's mother who had been lady-in-waiting to Sigelgaita after she became the Guiscard's duchess.

Pandulf was hoarse with excitement, his rosy cheeks now almost purple. "He'll be with us tomorrow. Peace has been restored to all Apulia and Campania. Praise be to God and His favored on earth. Come men, let's drink a victory toast to our conquering hero. Sebastiano, go fetch the new cask of Vesuvio. We'll drink to our duke in liquid gold."

The English visitors had even more cause for celebration. For the last week Thomas Browne had been visiting his friends at the castle for several hours a day, and he had just been judged well enough to leave the hospital. His face shone with strength and good health, and only the faintest trace of the last persistent lesion was visible below his throat. The three friends rose to join the others in a toast and were followed with only a trace of reluctance by the party on the right of the table.

"Here. Pass this around. You've never had a better wine. It actually sparkles on the tongue." The chatelain's excitement had made him discard his customary obsequiousness to the lords. "Do you know what it is to see a Norman conqueror return in triumph? Ah, I see some of you remember all too well."

A young Italian baron stretched back lazily and sneered. "Perhaps you're thinking of the Goths. I don't recall seeing you around during any triumphal returns, much less during any battles."

Pandulf shrugged. "I was always unfit for military service."

"You mean you were too fat to sit a horse." The other lords joined the baron in laughter.

"As you will, as you will, but I did see the Guiscard once. I was still a boy, helping my father with the grape harvest, when the great Guiscard came here, back in 1077. What a day that was! Lady Sigelgaita's brother, Gisulf, had been resisting stubbornly and we'd been starving under a siege for months. The only creatures who were well fed were the rats, and the corpses were piling up in every square. The castle held out the longest, thanks to its height above the city, but we knew it couldn't last. That Gisulf nearly got us all killed, but after all, his family had held the city for over three hundred years and it was hard for him to see their time had ended. Even Sigelgaita, loving sister though she was, had no sympathy for him, and not just because of her love for the Guiscard."

He drained his cup of wine and held it out to the serving man for another. "If you could have seen those Normans coming into the city . . . exhausted, but still riding tall and straight on their horses; the Guiscard's beard torn and matted with the gore of battle, his armor stained with the blood of a hundred men. And beautiful Sigelgaita! She looked every inch a queen with that horned helmet and a lance held proudly in that mighty arm. Tired as she was, she treated us to her battle cry as she rode up to the gate. You must know of her battle cry? It saved the day at the battle of Durazzo. My mother was there with her that day. The English were attacking us fiercely, and some of our men had started to fall back."

He turned to the three Englishmen. "Oh yes, there were plenty of English. After the battle of Hastings, many of them left to join the Byzantines as mercenaries. There wasn't much left for them at home, if you'll forgive my saying so. Anyway, there they were, all experienced soldiers, these English, swinging those bloody two-headed axes at our cavalry and pushing ahead, no matter how many of them fell. It looked like the day would be theirs until Sigelgaita rushed forward and shouted at her troops. *"How far will you flee? Stand, and quit you like men!"* They still didn't stop, so she took after them at full gallop and drove them back to battle with her long spear, uttering that bloodcurdling cry of hers. I tell you, there weren't many soldiers that could stand up to that cry of Sigelgaita's."

The rest of the company didn't think much of Pandulf's stories, and it appeared the three Englishmen were the only audience left to him. Pandulf signalled to have their cups refilled with the new wine, then embraced them each in turn, spilling wine on himself but not caring.

"And you, Thomas. You should be thrilled to be out of hospital. Drink up, drink up. Is something wrong with your wine?"

Thomas smiled and took a light sip of his cup. "I drink gladly to our great duke. Forgive me if I do so in sips, but if I'm to have a master on earth I prefer that it not be wine." He looked warmly at his two companions and gripped Julien's wrist affectionately. "I have more to celebrate than any of us. No one could have convinced me a month ago that I would enjoy a place today among the living."

Robert laughed appreciatively. "This truly is a great day, Thomas. You can't imagine how happy we are to see you your old self again. No, I believe it's much better than that. You're a more enjoyable companion than I ever knew you to be. Don't you agree, Julien?"

"Yes, and I too am very happy for you, Thomas."

Robert tilted his head back and drained his wine. "What say we go to the city gates to welcome Roger tomorrow instead of waiting for him here?"

"Oh no, please don't," Pandulf said. "I want his entrance to the castle to be as grand as his entrance to the city. I've been waiting so long for this day." He turned to the group at the right of the table. "We'll give him no more reason to regret Salerno, eh good sirs?"

A few of the older men smiled wanly, but no one answered. "I see your hearts may not be fully with him yet. Well, just wait till he gets here. The blood of the Guiscard flows in that man's veins. Fear not, you'll soon see what stuff a Norman hero is made of."

"Do you know Roger well?" Julien asked.

"As well as I do my own family—except that I haven't actually met him. I did see him when he was a boy, back in 1111 it was, shortly before he was knighted and took the government from his mother, Adelaide, God bless her bones. He was sixteen or so, and as fine-looking a young man as you could hope to see. Then I glimpsed him again the next year when he saw his mother off to Jerusalem to marry King Baldwin, but not since. What a sad day that was. And what a sad journey for that poor, sainted woman."

"Why sad?" Julien asked. "I seem to recall that she married Baldwin. Or didn't she?"

"Oh, she did indeed. Went to him with nine ships loaded with treasure . . . more gold and jewels than that penniless wretch Baldwin had ever seen. It didn't take him long to go through it. That rotter owed money to anyone he could swindle or steal from. Then four or five years later, when he'd wrung everything he could out of Adelaide, he suddenly remembered an earlier wife he'd neglected to mention. The pope, Paschal II it was then, divorced them with never a word of reproach to Baldwin, and Adelaide went back to Sicily with a broken heart. The poor woman felt so shamed. She died soon after."

"Wouldn't you say she went into the marriage a bit incautiously?" Julien asked. "How could she not know he was married?"

"Incautious perhaps, but how was she to know? There was no first wife to be seen, no one in the Church stopped it, and no one outside Jerusalem cared. Baldwin wanted sons as well as money, and Adelaide was a good breeder, having given her first husband two sons in the short time they were married. But she wasn't stupid. When she made the marriage contract, she made Baldwin promise the Kingdom of Jerusalem to Roger if there should be no issue between them."

"And there wasn't," Julien said. "So Roger must still have a claim on the kingdom."

"Baldwin died a year after Adelaide, and his cousin was made king on the grounds that the contract was as invalid as the marriage. Besides, Roger was still young, and in no position to claim a foreign kingdom. But you can be sure he hasn't forgotten, though. He kept his grudge against Pope Paschal, and never let that old man forget he was the instrument of his mother's divorce. But then, that's probably the least of his problems with the popes."

"I daresay there's not much love between the throne of St. Peter and Sicily," Robert said wryly.

"It's understandable," said Pandulf. "The last thing the Holy Father wants is a powerful ruler just below Peter's lands. And you might say the same for the Holy Roman Emperor and all the other crowned heads. There's many a wary eye on Roger, now that he's announced his intention to fulfill the Guiscard's dream by uniting all the lands of the south in one strong government.

"Forgive me, gentlemen, I do have work to do. The ducal chambers must be readied and preparations made for Heaven knows how many." He bustled away, clapping his hands for his servitors and shouting commands as they approached.

Robert turned to his companions. "Let's stretch our legs, shall we? There's a loggia upstairs where we can talk." He was unquestionably pleased with the turn of events. "Our timing couldn't be better. Roger will be under the same roof with us tomorrow, and I suspect that as soon as he's rested, we shall all be off for Sicily. Thomas, are you certain you're well enough to travel? You never looked better, but are you sure?"

"They told me at the hospital I was, and frankly, I can't wait to get back to work again."

"That's wonderful," said Julien. "You must be very grateful to your doctor."

"Of course I am. And no less grateful to my priest. I can't decide which of them is more responsible for my cure. Never have I had a more sympathetic counselor than Father Louis. He would place his stool right behind the head of my bed and listen quietly to my confession, rarely saying anything until I had finished. He was a great comfort to me, and yet, at first he gave me things to meditate on that troubled me a good deal. Only later did I begin to feel cleansed and worthy again."

"He appears to be no less a doctor, then," Robert said.

"Oh, but Father Louis is a doctor, as well as a priest. Both he and Astruc are magisters at the school. It's an amazing place. Not all of the scholars there are of the same mind, you know. Fifty years ago Constantine the African was the great influence at Salerno, and it was he who introduced Muslim medicine to Italy. But since Constantine, there have been many new influences. They're speaking about humanism now."

"I'm impressed," Robert said.

"I believe the south really agrees with me. The first week in hospital I hated it every time they carried me out into the sunlight. Now I dread the idea of winter. And the fresh fruit and vegetables! I don't think I could ever live without them again. To be truthful, though, I still entertain some doubts as to Roger's character. The stories I heard at the hospital!"

"I would assume so. But then there are those who would look on *you* with misgivings too because of your Norman blood."

"Yes, I daresay there are still some who end their evening prayers with

'From the terror of the northmen, dear God, protect us.' But you know as well as I, that for all that fat chatelain's song of praise for the Guiscard, he really was a bandit, albeit a clever and interesting one. I just don't know anymore. So many of my old ideas have changed. It embarrasses me now to think how dreadfully rude I was to Dr. Astruc my first week in the hospital. When he dismissed me yesterday, I told him I would always remember him in my prayers, and he thanked me. Can you imagine!"

"That you actually said you'd pray for him or that he thanked you?"

"No, don't joke about it, Julien. I really meant it. I bless him and pray for him every night. Do you think it's a sin to bless a Jew?"

"Blessings can only please God. You know, Thomas, I feel we're closer friends now than before you took ill. Isn't that so?"

"You know it is. We'd best go back and take our places at table. They must be starting to serve. After our meal will you go with me to the market? I'd like to get some new clothes, some fresh cottons like yours to wear for Roger's arrival. They look comfortable. What time do you think he'll get here?"

"He shouldn't be more than a day behind his scouts. In the morning sometime, I should guess."

The castle was in a hubbub from dawn on the next day. Citizens had been recruited for scrubbing, airing, and decorating the halls and chambers with garlands and bouquets of fresh flowers. Perfumes permeated every corner, and merchants crowded the corridors delivering robes and jewels to the noble families. At eleven word arrived that Roger had entered the gates of Salerno and was even now circling the cathedral, presenting himself to his subjects.

At high noon the procession headed towards the castle. The chatelain had put on a heavily embroidered, bright green woolen cloak over his white robes, and he would have been miserable in the midday heat were his enthusiasm not so all-consuming. He wore a massive gold chain around his neck with a gold key dangling from it to symbolize his position, while around his waist he carried a ring of iron keys as large as a man's head that made his girdle sag and caused him to wriggle every so often to adjust it.

"I can't think of anything more exciting than seeing Duke Roger again after so many years." Pandulf addressed himself exclusively to the three Englishmen now, since every time he'd opened his mouth that morning the Lombards would roll their eyes and assume exaggerated displays of boredom. "He must be exactly like his uncle," he continued. "How well I recall the

Guiscard, riding like a god on his horse, his short, blond hair gleaming like gold even when he was an old man. I can see him now, holding his helmet in the crook of his bridle arm while he spun his broadsword over his head and bellowed his cry of victory. Ah, the Normans are destined to inherit the earth."

"Do you really think so?" Robert asked coldly, irritated by the man's fawning. "I suspect they may one day be its conquerors, but isn't it to be the meek who inherit it?"

Pandulf looked at him oddly and blushed. "No offense. Wait, I think I can see him. Yes, that must be his golden hair flashing in the sun. Oh no. It can't be."

The chatelain remained mute as the procession filed into the castle courtyard, headed by a platoon of tall black men carrying lances. They were barefoot, and naked except for voluminous scarlet trousers. Following them were a hundred horsemen, Saracens in full armor with the spiked helmets favored in the East. They were all bearded, impassive, and steely; their eyes focussed unwaveringly ahead. Behind these were a dozen eunuchs on white geldings, wearing brilliantly colored silk robes that floated behind them. They were tossing yellow roses to right and left from twin, gilt saddlebaskets.

There was an interval of twenty yards between Roger and his escort. Four cheetahs linked with gold chains attached to his horse's bridle loped before him, and four naked boys of ten or so, with huge turbans dwarfing their heads, marched beside his horse. Roger wore a turban of gold cloth from which an egg-sized ruby dangled over his forehead. His robes were white silk trimmed with gold and were spread out to cover the sides and tail of his horse. On his right wrist he carried a Scythian tercelet, the most elegant white falcon Julien had ever seen.

Roger's complexion was dark, not particularly tanned, but of a strong Mediterranean cast. His nose was long and generously shaped, and his bushy black beard, trimmed to a spade, was oiled and exquisitely curled. He smiled amiably but vaguely at the crowds that lined the path, while behind him two blacks were majestically tossing handfuls of cakes and sweets to the scrambling children.

"What do you think, Julien?" whispered Thomas.

"I've never seen anything like it. He certainy doesn't look like a Norman, does he? And the troops . . . there's not a westerner to be seen."

Roger's cortege took positions around the courtyard while he dismounted at the castle entrance, aided by the naked children. Pandulf pulled

himself together and ran to greet him. "Welcome, Duke Roger. Your subjects . . ."

Roger stayed him with a toss of the hand. "No speeches please. I will
take some wine, though. Will you see to it that suitable quarters are found
for my personal guards? My army's encamped south of the city, but I doubt
I'll be seeing them again for a while."

The chatelain was staring goggle-eyed at two of the seminaked blacks
who had produced ostrich fans on slender, golden poles and were already
wafting them around their master. "Of course, of course. Rest assured, Your
Grace. I have refreshments waiting for you inside, and wine for your guards
too."

"No wine for them; their religion forbids it. Just show them where they
may prepare their own refreshments. It's been a warm journey. I trust you'll
have no difficulty making them all comfortable."

"At once, at once, Your Grace."

"Where is Robert of Selby? Is he here?"

Robert stepped forward smartly and bowed. "Your Grace."

"Robert! You can't imagine how much I've looked forward to this
meeting. And this must be Thomas, and you're Julien, no doubt." He
chuckled softly as he nodded to them.

Thomas and Julien stepped forward and mumbled politely as they
bowed.

"Give me a chance to change into something simpler, and then we must
dine together. I'm eager to talk with all three of you. You must forgive me
for keeping you waiting so long in Salerno, but I was concluding some
important business. In an hour, then?"

He turned to the chatelain. "You sir, Pandulf, is it not? I must say you
bear little resemblance to that charming woman who bore you. I shall want
some food prepared. Yes, I'm sure you've already arranged everything—and
I hope that my good loyal noblemen here will enjoy the feast—but would you
be kind enough to see that my cooks are escorted to your kitchens? They are
familiar with my tastes and will prepare everything I need. Thank you."

Four of the eunuchs stepped forward and gazed down icily at Pandulf, a
shadow of a sneer on their lips. Julien realized he was gaping and snapped his
jaws shut. They were long legged and lean, but there was a softness about
them, a roundness at the shoulder and hip that, together with the conspicuous
absence of facial hair, marked them as not quite men.

Roger took off his turban and shook out his hair. It was richly black in
its dressing of perfumed oils, and he wore it quite long, in the Byzantine

fashion. He addressed Pandulf again, who was staring in disbelief. "Can't we go in now? It's a bit warm to be standing around, you know."

The chatelain jerked as if stung and led the way in, his legs paddling furiously.

"Not exactly what he had in mind, I daresay," Robert remarked, and the three Englishmen broke into laughter. Immediately those of Roger's guards within earshot tensed and gripped their lances more firmly. Julien noted their wariness. Robert saw it too, and addressed the guards directly. "No offense to our duke intended by that, men. It's just that our fat friend was expecting a blond Viking." The guards did not move, but the tension lessened.

Household stewards appeared and proceeded to direct the various groups to their quarters. Billeting them would not be a strain on the castle's resources. Since the soldiers carried their own bedding, three or four times their number could have been accommodated, and the kitchens could easily feed as many.

Julien and his companions reentered the castle and decided to find some wine to pass the time with while they waited for their interview with Roger. The stewards had cleared all the casks away and seemed flustered. "A fine thing," one said. "What kind of soldiers are these that drink tea? It isn't natural." He directed them to a pantry off the dining hall, where they found some of the wine reserved for the Lombard nobles.

"You can see why his enemies in the Church call him 'the baptized sultan,' can't you?" said Robert. "Still I don't believe it's affected. He was brought up in Palermo at a time when the city was still overwhelmingly Muslim. I don't know, though. If that's what Palermo is going to be like, I'm not sure I'd want to have my children growing up with . . . You know what I mean. It just doesn't seem manly to me; and those eunuchs make my scalp prickle."

When they were led into Roger's chamber, he was reclining on piles of silk cushions, and the floors were thickly carpeted with exquisite Persian rugs. There were fragrant wisps of smoke emerging from pierced brass burners in each corner of the room. Roger had changed into a loose, sea-blue robe with a border of turquoise and emeralds at the throat and was fondling one of the cheetahs stretched beside him with its paws in his lap. The other cats were attentively watching the eunuchs who were readying their meal.

"Come sit by me. Conrad won't bother you."

The trio gingerly settled on the furthest of the cushions he offered, trying to maintain a respectful distance from the great cat.

"I don't suppose any of you has ever hunted with cheetah. Perhaps you'll have a chance to one day. It takes over three years to train them, but they give a certain zest to the sport. I always try to get a bit of hunting in while I'm in Apulia, but it's hopeless after the warm weather sets in."

One of the cheetahs that had been sniffing around the eunuchs ambled over and began to show an interest in Julien's ankles.

"Down, Frederick. He won't hurt you," Roger said, smiling, "but it's best not to forget that even at their tamest, they're still wild beasts. You might scratch his forehead if you wish. He likes that. Yes, he seems to have taken a fancy to you."

Julien tried to conceal his excitement. He was thrilled by these giant cats the moment he saw them, and wondered if he might ever have the courage to touch one. He moved to Frederick's ear, and the cheetah's tongue rolled out and splashed itself across his cheek. "I've made a new friend. By the way, I greatly admired your falcon."

"Thank you. It was a gift from my kinsman, Coloman of Hungary. He's married to my cousin Busilla, although it was really my sister whose hand he was after." He turned his gaze on the falcon, now hooded, which was fastened to a perch nearby with gold jesses. "You must be sure to visit the falcon mews as soon as you get to Sicily. As a matter of fact, I'll give you each a gift of a falcon on our return. Let's see . . . for you, Robert, a fine tercelet from the Caucausus. And Thomas, I believe you would enjoy a German gyrfalcon, and for you, Julien, an aristocratic saker from Babylon might please you well."

"Thank you, Your Grace," said Robert. "You're most generous. I know Pandulf has seen to all your needs, but if there is anything I or my companions might do . . ."

Roger waved his hand airily. "Poor Pandulf. I'm afraid I'm a disappointment to him, but I suppose I should be used to that by now. I've had to live so much of my life in the shadow of my father and uncles. There were twelve of them, imagine! And every one a hero on the battlefield, or so their chroniclers would have us believe. You know, I'm actually rather tall for a Sicilian, as tall as most Normans at any rate, but people are always reminding me that my relatives were taller and handsomer, and oh yes, blond, blond, blond. Everytime a description of me appears in the German countries, they never fail to comment on my blondness. I suppose they're afraid *not* to describe me as a blond, because no one would believe them. And it's really hard for me to believe that my uncles William the Iron Arm or Drogo were even faintly good looking, but once these stories get started . . ."

Julien was grateful for Roger's easy manner. The three of them settled into their cushions more comfortably and waited for Roger to continue, not certain yet how much of the conversation it would be polite for them to assume.

Roger didn't mind carrying the conversation along. "Are you aware the four of us have a great deal in common? My grandfather Tancred was only a poor knight . . . poorer by far than he knew when he found himself with sixteen living children to support. What a relief it must have been when the eldest of them left for Italy to start their careers. The castle was never big enough for all of them. Perhaps your families have told you of that part of Normandy. It's just outside Coutances, probably less than a day's journey to your fathers' villages. I used to think I'd enjoy seeing it one day, but now my sights are in other directions."

Julien imagined the reaction a visit from Roger with his entourage would produce in Normandy among the rough townspeople there, and smiled.

"Ah, I see our food is ready," Roger observed aloud.

The Englishmen looked around them to see where a table might have been set up for their dining, but instead the eunuchs carried small tabourets to each of them and set them at their sides. Three more black men arrived carrying a basin, pitcher, and hand towels of rough linen. The Englishmen watched carefully as water was poured for Roger to wash his hands, and then followed his example when their turn came.

"Muslims are forever washing," Roger said. "There are five ritual ablutions a day. You'll get used to it."

A series of small silver bowls was placed before each of them with the ingredients of the first course. Again they watched Roger closely to see how he twirled the stew with his fingers, added a pinch of cracked wheat, then brought it swiftly to his mouth and used his thumb to flip the food forward. They ate and found it delicious.

"You don't mind if I continue while we eat, do you? I was telling you about my uncles," Roger said. "It didn't take long for the first of them who arrived in Apulia to find there was a good living to be made in the south as mercenaries. The lords were constantly fighting each other, and even if they weren't, one could always find some excuse for sweeping down on a village and looting it. They sent for their brothers quick enough—there was always one coming of age every year or two—and soon they were all here and had begun to settle on their own fiefs. They soon came to realize, though, that the fiefs weren't worth anything unless you could hold on to them, and with the Lombards and Greeks constantly squabbling, there wasn't much chance of that. For one thing, there were plenty of other Normans around too, and all swords were for hire, even against their own countrymen when it suited them."

Julien was fascinated by Roger's discourse but no less by the man's grace at table. He had never seen a man speak and eat at the same time without feeling obliged to quickly avert his eyes towards his own food. It gave him pleasure to note the graceful position of Roger's body and the ease with which he fed himself. His appetite was hearty, but he satisfied it with a delicacy other men might summon in consuming no more than a walnut.

Roger would pause only briefly in speaking, passing his eyes from one to the other to see if he could read a contradiction or a question before continuing.

"The Guiscard was the clever one, as usual. He realized it was time to bring order to the south. This meant uniting the territories under one strong man with one strong set of laws. He almost made it too. If he'd lived another few years he'd surely have united all of southern Italy with Sicily, and perhaps even the Byzantine Empire."

"That's no small ambition, even for the Guiscard," Robert said.

"Ambitious, yes, but also realistic, and necessary. There must be one law or anarchy. So I plan to finish what the Guiscard started. Oh, I know I'm not the soldier he was, but after a certain point it takes more than force of arms. Perhaps the lessons I got from my father, the youngest son, were more valuable than the Guiscard's. In these southern lands diplomacy is more effective than war. To keep these barons in line with no more than force of arms, I'd need a standing army in every corner of the duchy at all times—no one is strong enough for that. What do you think, Robert?"

"We're greatly impressed by what we've seen and all you've told us, Your Grace." Robert's face was expressionless.

Roger sighed. "Don't be so stiff. I can get answers like that from anyone at my court. I see I need to clear the air. I'm going to suggest that you call me Roger, in private only, of course. I assure you no one knows better than I how to impress with rank and the trappings of station when I feel it's advisable to do so. Informality saves time, and when I want an answer I don't like to wait for it. Agreed? I include you, Thomas, and Julien, in my invitation.

"Now, have some fruit and tea. You'll find it's a refreshing end to the meal; and for digestion's sake, let's talk of lighter things. I want to know how you've been enjoying Salerno. Thomas, I heard you were not well when you arrived. I assume you were impressed by the facilities at the medical school?"

"The school deserves every bit of its reputation," Thomas answered. "I had despaired of ever being well again."

He smiled and turned to Robert and Julien. "I trust you profited from the time spent waiting for Thomas's recovery by acquainting yourself with this part of the duchy."

"Most certainly," Robert answered. "You have a young bishop here named Romuald with a keen interest in politics, and his acquaintanceship has been most rewarding. I might add he is entirely in your camp."

"I know Romuald very well. I plan to make him archbishop, but don't tell him so yet. I see you look surprised. Have you forgotten that Pope Urban II gave my father hereditary rights of investiture?"

"No," said Robert. "It just seemed odd to be reminded of your power after your agreeably informal conversation. Rights of investiture were still such a thorn in King Henry's side."

"Yes, a prick from the papal rose, as it were. Julien, tell me of your impressions."

"One day we took horses and rode to Amalfi," Julien said. "I've always wanted to go there. My school was very close to Scotland and I wanted to see the tomb of St. Andrew, the patron of the Scots there. The cathedral was certainly beautiful, but I was also surprised to see how developed the countryside is and how prosperous."

"It is, it is. And were you told that just a year ago no traveller could have dared that journey without an armed guard? I don't exaggerate. You've no idea how things get out of hand when the barons take over. And I hate to admit it, but the Norman knights who settled here are still the most restless and criminal unless they're treated to a taste of ducal justice."

"Yes. Even the Lombards of the Independent Party admit that things are far more orderly now."

"Ah yes, the independents. If there were only those to contend with. Did you meet many of the commune-ists while you were here?"

"Quite a few," Julien answered. "But all this talk of communes has confused us. Some of them appear to be papists, and some pro-Byzantine, and then some protest their loyalty to you. We didn't know what to make of them."

Roger nodded. "I'm not surprised. There were communes, or free cities, in south Italy even before the first Normans arrived. Some communes were granted their charter by the popes and some by the Byzantines. But to whoever granted the charter, the important thing was that the commune be strong enough to hold off invasion from the neighboring barons until help arrived. Amalfi and Salerno are communes under my law and will be given even more liberties when I feel it's safe to do so."

"But they told us you have communes in Sicily too," Julien said, "where there is little or no pressure to create them."

"I bow to expediency," Roger answered. "My Muslims are thriving, and as you know, there are few restrictions placed on them. But many, mostly agricultural workers, have started to leave. I suppose it's hardest on them in any country, but there is a growing feeling among the lower-class Muslims that they'd be happier transferring to Muslim countries. Fortunately, my officials and the members of my court have no such inclinations, but I have to find replacements for these emigrants. The logical place to attract new people from was the mainland—and the best way was with a charter. Since the movement started on the mainland, it's no surprise that it should be the fashionable politics of the Lombard cities, but it's doubtful the emperor will allow it to go much further. Communes are anathema to imperialists."

"This is fascinating!" Julien said. "Can you tell me why we don't have a commune movement in England and France?"

"That's simple. The French and English live in the countryside. In Italy even the peasants live in cities and travel every day to work in the fields. Citizens living in towns are more likely to band together to satisfy their mutual needs. And then, apart from the agricultural workers, Italy has many more cities that are fattened on commerce and industry and feel rich enough to demand independence. When you're out among the people, keep your eyes and ears open. There's much for you to learn."

"Oh, but we have," Julien answered. "Robert's had us going to meetings nearly every night, investigating all the factions we could uncover."

"It's kept us busy," Robert added. "Julien has done an excellent job of writing reports for you on all we've seen, both here and in Narbonne."

"Good. I'm told you write well."

"Thank you, Your Grace . . . Roger. I've been told that all your records are kept in Latin, Greek, and Arabic. I regret that I know no Arabic, but I've written what I have in Latin and Greek for the convenience of your court."

"Well done. I plan for us to spend as much time as possible in each other's company in the coming weeks. You'll sail to Palermo on my ship, of course. Once I'm at court, it will be considerably more difficult for us to spend time together, so let's make the most of our journey. I hope that by the time we reach Sicily, I shall know exactly how to make the best use of your talents."

"We're grateful for your confidence," Robert said.

"It's not misplaced. If Henry had already been king of England I'm sure my father would have been as quick to adopt his exchequer and system of travelling justiciars. Now, with your help I intend to use those tools as efficiently as ever they were in England. Better, because I'll brook no interference from vassal lords, and thank God, I have no brothers, as poor Henry does, whose ambitions need to be curbed."

"Hear, hear!" Robert squirmed delightedly at these words.

"I admire Henry a great deal, you may be sure of it, but I can't understand why, with an efficient exchequer such as his, he still depends so on meeting the needs of his treasury by going with cap in hand to all his vassals. He should learn to take a note or two from my douane. Let him collect money from international trade instead of taxing every peasant who sells an onion at market. And England would do well to concentrate on building a merchant fleet as I have . . . yes, and an aggressive navy too. We're rich, Robert, and we're going to be a good deal richer. That means the three of you, too."

"We've nothing against that," said Thomas.

"Good. I know you're all God-fearing Christians, but you must know you can do more good on earth when you can pay for it. By the way, I hope you haven't lacked female companionship while you've been here. I assume you knew Pandulf could be relied upon to help you find anything you wished."

"He has been most hospitable," Robert replied, "but I confess we've not thought too much about women with all the other wonders crowding for our attention."

"A commendable attitude, but a pity. I was prepared to hear you rave about our southern women. No matter. There's Sicily ahead of you. Don't let me grow too sentimental. It's my custom to spend an hour or two with my concubines after dining, but regrettably, I can't always take my harem with me when I'm off on a campaign. Today I'll just take a nap. Can you be at my disposal this afternoon?"

"Of course." Robert bowed as though preparing to withdraw.

"No, don't leave just yet. I wasn't dismissing you. I'm enjoying our talk, even though I am doing most of it. I have a few light responsibilities this afternoon that I'd like you to join me for. The Salernitans would be scandalized if I didn't visit the cathedral my first day here. I like the cathedral well enough since it meant so much to the Guiscard, but these official visits are a bore. I suppose you've seen that old battle-axe Sigelgaita's tomb there?"

"Yes, we admired it, and Pope Gregory the Seventh's as well."

"Ah well, that's another matter. Although of course I shall have to pay my respects to his bones as well."

"I seem to detect a lack of enthusiasm towards Gregory," Robert said.

"Come now, it's hardly a secret. The popes are no great friends of Sicily. We can bully them into treaties, but they'd gladly see us crushed."

"But Gregory!" Robert countered. "Surely he had every reason to be grateful to the Guiscard after he went to Rome to save the papacy for him."

"Yes, and slaughtered half the city to do so. No, Gregory wasn't grateful. He'd already excommunicated the Guiscard once, and probably hated him for his help. Not that it bothered the Guiscard. Bans are as easily lifted as laid. Gregory had one goal above all others—to make the Church supreme and infallible in temporal matters. God knows, the Church needed reform, but the popes have taken entirely too much on themselves.

"As far as their reforms within the Church go, you do agree they've been largely successful. In Sicily too, we may assume?" Robert asked.

"Of course in Sicily too. I've scarcely a priest in the whole island who dares to live openly with his wife."

Robert smiled. "If that's the principal measure of their reform, I wonder what real comfort it can give the guardians of doctrine."

"I couldn't care less what they choose to allow or not allow among themselves. It's when the pope uses his position as a religious leader to insist that all worldly power is subject to his authority . . . well, come now! We know that's all rot. If they intend to fight for power on earth, they'd best be prepared to fight for it the same as any soldier, instead of hiding behind their tiaras and using excommunication as a weapon."

Julien's eyes were dancing. "I can't believe I'm hearing this."

Roger nodded. "Gregory is guaranteed to go down in history as a saint, not for his virtues, but because the Church is doing such a thorough job of milking people's emotions with that touching scene at Canossa. Every child is told of the Emperor Henry humbling himself, bareheaded and barefoot in the snow before all-holy Gregory. Such a melting submission, with Gregory sweetly forgiving him. Nonsense! Gregory's earlier conduct was not at all what I would expect from a spiritual leader."

Thomas seemed startled by this. "But I believe all agree Gregory led a morally blameless life."

"Morally blameless? Oh, forget about sex. I'd rather have a whoremaster I could trust as pope than some mealy-mouthed celibate who wouldn't hesitate to stick a knife in your back. No, I was thinking of Gregory's ungodly ambition. And his cruelty. Yes, I know they call *me* cruel, but do you know what happened before Henry humbled himself at Canossa? Let me tell you. I'm no great admirer of the emperor, but at least he conducted himself like a man. When things looked dark for him, he sent his envoys to Gregory to see if they could negotiate a truce. It's exactly what I'd have done. But Gregory decided to teach Henry how secure his position as pope was, so he had all the envoys castrated and sent back to Henry unmanned for his answer. Now if any Christian ruler ever did a thing like that, he'd be accused of the most severe breach of international relations, and rightly so."

"I wasn't aware of the incident," Robert said. "Since I feel firmly attached to my balls I've no sympathy at all for that form of reprisal. And yet we see you surrounded by eunuchs in your court."

"The eunuchs aren't of my doing. I've never castrated a man. Never! Of course the Arabs do. So do other easterners. I agree it's cruel and barbaric, but their reasons for doing it aren't easy for a westerner to understand. You think of castration as punishment for adultery or sexual vice, but many of the castrations performed in the East are done to an enemy beaten in battle, or to his children. I don't deny there's great cruelty in the Levant."

"But can't you do something to stop it?" Julien asked.

"Castration is illegal in my duchy and it's punished severely if it's done outside warfare, but I can't change their conduct in battle. It would be taken for weakness. And you must remember, I was born a Sicilian. It isn't so strange or shocking to me."

The Englishmen remained silent, but Roger could see they were still disturbed by what he'd told them.

"When a Christian soldier sacks a town, we know he loots and rapes and that doesn't shock us. We also know that if he wants to humiliate his enemy, he forces him to watch while he rapes his wife and daughters. That's a bit more disturbing, but it's familiar, isn't it? Now when a Muslim wants to humiliate his enemy, he forces the women to watch while he rapes the man and his sons. I suppose you could say that's one of the main differences in the cultures."

Julien was wide-eyed. "What about your eunuchs? Were they all castrated in battle?"

"Some of them. But you still have a good deal to learn about our eunuchs. Arabs and Greeks have a taste for boys. . . . Don't make such a face; I don't care for them, either. You'll find that a number of the eunuchs at my court were introduced there as the lovers of some of my ministers. Quite a number of pretty boys are sold for that purpose in the East. Castration extends their period of adolescence, and I suppose there are other subtle attractions. Make no judgments until you've seen a good deal more of them. The kitchens, the maintenance of my household, and of course the harem, are all in the care of eunuchs, and there are eunuchs with posts in my douane, in the navy, in the mint, and even on my campaign board. I admit they sometimes show a tendency to become involved in petty squabbles, and I've seen them behave maliciously, but they can outperform most men in positions demanding secrecy. Perhaps because they don't have as many distractions as we do."

"I like to feel," Robert said, "that I perform better after I've indulged myself to satisfaction in those distractions. No matter. With your permission we'll leave now and let you rest. But first one question."

"How soon do we leave for Sicily? Soon. My wife is Spanish, a race of people not noted for their infinite patience, and I'm anxious to see that superior woman as soon as possible. We have to wait here a day or two for my sons Roger and Tancred to join us. I believe you'll enjoy meeting them. They've acquitted themselves well in their first taste of my affairs, and I allowed them to spend a few days amusing themselves. I see no reason why we can't leave within the week. Good day, my friends. In two hours then?"

Chapter VII

CEFALU

Both air and water were stagnant and the ships hovered listlessly between them, their irresolute bobbing made perceptible only by a flash of sunlight dancing across the feeble splash of water at the bows. "So much for Apulian astrologers," Roger muttered irritably.

"Your Sicilian astrologers offered the same date for departure." Roger was reminded of this by a handsome eunuch who was chafing his master's wrists with cloths dipped in cool water scented with bergamot.

"They're all alike. I should never trust them when they give me those obscure predictions. Why can't they just tell me I should leave on the first of the month if I want to arrive in less than three weeks?"

Julien was seated cross-legged a few feet from Roger making entries in his journal, but there was little to report except the tedium. He had caught Roger's impatient mood and tried to limit his conversation, despite the eagerness with which he welcomed their daily talks. "Exactly what did your astrologers say?" he asked.

Roger scowled. "That if we left when we did, it would fit the pattern of my destiny and the journey's events would enhance my memory for all time. Sounds like an irresistible time to leave, doesn't it? There was a Neapolitan who said we should leave sooner if we wanted to arrive sooner, but I thought he was just being simple."

"Still, the Apulian astrologers predicted your victory with perfect accuracy." The eunuch's voice was deliberately soothing.

"I'll let you in on a secret, Hadim. One reason I always use the Apulian astrologers when I'm campaigning on the mainland is that I know my enemies are using them too, and I can always predict exactly when the fools will strike and where. That's the chief virtue of astrologers in battle. In peace . . . well, see for yourself. We've scarcely moved in a week."

"The captain wouldn't answer my questions this morning," Julien said. "Did he tell you anything? Surely this calm can't last much longer."

"He'd be guessing if he did. These are strange waters. All the seas around Sicily are unpredictable. Scylla and Charybdis, the whirlpool and the rock, lie in the Straits of Messina. The coast between Catania and Taormina is still called the Beach of the Cyclops. Circe's island isn't far, and the Sirens sang their songs here. When you've sailed these seas as often as I have, those myths will all be completely believable to you."

"It's certainly eerie enough. I can almost imagine a magical sea monster rising from the water right now and—"

"Stop that," snapped Roger. "I don't value surprises on sea voyages, and I told you anything is possible here."

A sudden spurt of wind rocked the boat and then as quickly subsided, spilling the water from Hadim's basin over Roger's robe.

"What did I tell you!" Roger said. "No trace of a breeze for days and then a burst of wind that can almost knock a man over."

It was still early afternoon, but the water was as dark as it had been at sunset, its oily surface reflective and offering no hint of depth. They hadn't seen a fish sporting all day, and even the insects that appeared when they were no closer than this to shore were nowhere to be seen.

Thomas and Robert came up from below decks. "Does that mean the calm's ended?" Thomas asked. "My head was knocked against the hull by that one."

"I have a feeling we'll be moving soon," said Robert. "The navigator told me we're about fifteen miles south by southwest of Alicudi. We could be in Sicily in no more than an hour or two with a decent wind."

"Alicudi?" Julien asked.

"One of the Lipari islands," Roger answered. "You probably know them as the Aeolian islands. They took their name from Aeolus, king of the winds, whose home is said to be here. I would guess King Aeolus is looking on us with disfavor."

"Jealous, no doubt," Robert said, "since you've taken his islands."

The surface of the water was ruffled by a fresh breeze that skimmed quickly south towards the Sicilian shore. The ship rocked sharply, then calmed again. A minute later the sun turned white, then gray, and then a darker gray, as if a series of veils passed over its surface. The temperature dropped suddenly and prickled the skin on Julien's arms. The seamen started scurrying about the decks, preparing for the storm that seemed imminent.

They heard the wind sighing a long way off before it reached them, and the first gust carried with it a fine grit that powdered the deck with a red coat of sand. It stung their eyes and seemed to clog the pores of their skin. This was a hot wind, warmer by twenty degrees than the cool air that had surrounded them minutes before.

"Sirocco!" The word travelled from one end of the ship to the other. The dread sirocco was the hot wind that moved north from the Sahara, carrying with it the red sands of the desert. During the times of the sirocco, people's tempers were so unpredictably affected that the Sicilian courts traditionally weighed the sirocco as a mitigating circumstance when trying crimes of passion.

While they were still bewildered by the first parching blast of the sirocco, they saw a new menace moving implacably towards them from the north. A murky curtain of rain that went from sea to sky grew darker and closer every minute. The seamen were now scampering furiously, lashing down everything movable, and the captain himself came to ask the passengers to go below decks and secure themselves as best they could.

Only a quarter of an hour after they had been completely becalmed, the ship was being tossed around like flotsam. In the ship's cabins it sounded like the deck was being overrun by marauding beasts intent on smashing everything at hand. The main mast went with a wrenching shriek, and the ship started to spin like a coin. They were in water above their ankles, and even the breath they drew was salty and moist.

The sailors alternated their hopeless task of bailing out the water with repairing damages that seemed to multiply as fast as they were detected.

Roger appeared extraordinarily calm, and he dismissed the attentions of his eunuchs. "We're at the mercy of God," he declared. "Men. All of you. Join me in prayer." He dropped to his knees and bowed his head a moment silently, then raised it again angrily. "Stop what you're doing there. It can't help us. Join me in prayer, I say. All we can do now is consign ourselves to the mercy of the Lord. Muslims, pray to your Allah while we beseech our God. One of our prayers may reach Him."

The entire ship's company started to pray, some to themselves, but most of them loudly. The Greeks bowed deeply with their arms extended behind them and rocked to and fro. The Muslims, on their knees, dipped their heads into the water as they lowered themselves in rhythm to their chants. The westerners clutched their hands and invoked the intercession of every saint in Heaven. Julien tried to concentrate on his prayers, but although he was goaded by fear no less than the others, the spectacle and the babble of many languages excited him, and he experienced a perverse thrill.

It was now nearly dark and still the ship was being tossed from one churning wave to another. The water in the cabin was above their waists as they knelt, and the creaking of every seam added to the din of the prayers. Some of the seamen were growing hysterical, tearing their hair out and lacerating their bodies with their nails.

There was a horrendous crash, and one whole side of the ship gave way. Before he could grasp what was happening to him, Julien felt himself lifted up and then sucked into the maw of the sea. He was churned in the froth like a beetle for what seemed an eternity, gulping air frantically every time he felt his face freed of the sea. The water was in such commotion, it didn't seem possible for anything to sink in it. His foot was dashed against a rock, and he realized that he must be somewhere near shore. He started flailing his arms more energetically, but it was purposeless in that swirl of sea. Then his feet touched bottom, and he started to wade to dry land. Some others had reached the beach before he did and lay on the sand, whether conscious or not he was unable to tell.

He struggled to a mound of grassy dune and lay there a long time before he was strong enough to rouse himself and take stock of the situation. The carcass of their ship was beached on rocks not fifty yards from shore, but he could see nothing of the other ships that had accompanied them. The sky had grown lighter, and with the passing of the storm, there was a tranquil twilight. Some of the men stumbled along the beach now, while others still dragged themselves in from the water. It was a miracle. Without trying to account for all the ship's company, it seemed they must all be here, survivors of the completely splintered vessel.

He found Robert dressing a bruise on Thomas's cheek. They were otherwise unhurt and cheerful. They didn't have to search long for Roger. They found him half a mile down the beach, splinting Hadim's broken arm. The eunuch was ashen and in severe pain, but he managed to smile when he saw them approach. Roger's face was flushed, and he fervently embraced them each in turn.

"It was not God's design that we perish," he said simply. "Join me in a prayer of thanks, won't you?" They dropped to their knees and prayed silently for several minutes. When Roger rose, there were the marks of dried tears on his cheeks. "I promised God that if He granted us our lives I would build a church on the spot of our salvation that would be the wonder of the Christian world for all time. Thomas, find out the name of this place and come back as soon as you know where we are."

"I know where we are," said Robert. "One of the seamen near me was helped by a fisherman who said we're at Cefalu."

Several fishermen were running along the beach, stopping to investigate the survivors and chattering excitedly in Arabic. Others were going for more help.

"I know it well," Roger said. "Cefalu." He pronounced the word reverently as his eyes scanned the coastline, probing the deepening shadows. "Yes, there's the mountain. It's named Cefalu, from the Greek word *cephalos,* because it looks like the head of a giant rising from the earth." Julien felt that in the dim light it could well have looked like anything, but he kept silent. It was clear Roger was greatly moved.

"Listen, Thomas, I'm giving you your first commission. I want you to make plans to build a truly great church here. Magnificent, but not too large, because I want the mountain it stands against to be no less monumental. But be sure to hire the finest mosaicists from Byzantium, the most skillful Arab stone carvers, the most brilliant Norman architects. Build it there . . . at the foot of Cefalu, nestled against the giant's jaw. This will be my gift to God, and I enjoin you all to see to it when I die that my bones be laid to rest there. It is more than just my wish; I express it as a sacred vow."

Villagers were arriving with litters for the injured and jars of hot tea. They started up the beach to look for the captain and were greeted by cheers from all the seamen they passed. There were shouts of joy and prayers of praise to God, and Roger was weeping again by the time they reached the captain. He was genuinely cheerful as he announced to Roger that all but two of his seamen and one of Roger's guards had survived. There was no news as yet of the other ships. Among the survivors there were a number of broken limbs, and the captain himself had lost two teeth, but they accounted themselves under Heaven's direct care.

It was only a few minutes' walk to the village of Cefalu. The fishermen's houses were all whitewashed cottages of baked earth with the entrances painted bright blue. There were several more imposing buildings of stone at the heart of town, and the three Englishmen were escorted to the house of the local imam. He greeted them by prostrating himself and kissing Roger's feet. His family had already been moved to other quarters, and he placed his house, which was ample, entirely at their disposal.

Julien, Robert, and Thomas were to share the same room, a pleasantly austere one which belonged to the imam's eldest son. The walls had been freshly plastered, and over the bed was a palm print in the same bright blue on the doors. They were told it commemorated the palm of Fatima, the prophet's daughter, who would protect them while they were guests of the house. Julien felt oddly thrilled by these words, as if he'd entered a forbidden world where he was beyond the range of his own familiar Pantheon. It occurred to him that Thomas might have refused to sleep here two months ago, but his companions seemed as pleased as he by their surroundings.

Mattresses of cotton cloth stuffed with combed wool were brought in to supplement the beds already there, and then servants started to arrive with baskets of flowers and fresh fruit, nuts, and candied pastries. Roger seemed pleased with their accommodations and left them to go to his own apartment.

The variety of fruit was bewildering to the Englishmen, many of them unfamiliar even after their experiences in Salerno. Julien bit into a pomegranate, and they all laughed at the face he made. One of the servants peeled prickly pears for them, and they settled down to taste the delightful new foods in earnest. The basket of dates stuffed with almonds was finished so fast a servant had to be sent for another.

Thomas was feeling merry. "I must say, after today I no longer have any doubts about the sincerity of Roger's religious beliefs."

"Don't you feel too," asked Julien, "that the Muslim prayers must've been heard as clearly as ours?"

"It's hard to doubt it," Robert said. "Now, have you two thought of visiting town tonight and getting our first taste of Sicily? It occurred to me, but I confess I'm still a bit sore— Listen. What's that?" Through the evening hush they heard the wailing chant of the muezzin, picked up and echoed by another muezzin in a further part of town, and then by still another.

"It's their call to prayer," said Thomas, "like for our canonical hours."

"It's very beautiful," said Julien. "Shall we begin our vespers?"

As they finished their prayer, they became aware of another presence in the room.

Robert rose from his knees. "Roger! Should you go about unattended?"

Roger had changed to a long, white cotton robe like the ones they were wearing. "Never mind that. It's a relief to get away from my staff occasionally. I have some things I want to say to you, and they are for no one else's ears."

"We're greatly honored," Julien said as he arranged some cushions for him. "I was sure you'd be resting after today."

Roger took a handful of dates and munched them thoughtfully for a moment before he spoke. "I told you I had great plans for all of you. I think I can tell you now what they are."

The Englishmen curbed their curiosity and kept silent while Roger munched another few dates. "Robert, for the next months, or perhaps even a year, I will see to it that you're made familiar with every department of my government. You will sit in all my councils and I will personally undertake your training. When we both feel you're ready, I want you to return to Salerno as my subchancellor. Are you aware of what that position involves?"

"It's a great honor, and I thank you for it."

"In my government's organization the chancellor is second only to the admiral. As subchancellor you will become familiar with all the chancellor's duties. My chancellor Guerin is an excellent man, but aged, and he will undertake your training from then on. I mean, you understand, that he will train you to succeed him. My admiral, who is also the emir of emirs, is effectively in charge of my seat at the head of the curia when I am away, but on the mainland the chancellor is my direct viceroy."

Robert smiled. "I see you used the word viceroy. Am I to assume, then, that my suspicions are correct?"

"Suspicions, you say? Could you have doubted it? My realm is as rich as any kingdom in Europe and greater in size than most. Of course I intend to be king. It's merely a matter of time."

"But what of the pope?" asked Julien. "If he hesitated to have you a duke, isn't it unlikely he'll confirm you as king?"

"I fought for my dukedom. I'll fight harder for a kingdom. I've already begun to put pressure on Honorius. He's furious, of course, but he'll find he can't afford *not* to instate me.

"And now, as for you, Thomas, I've already given you your first assignment; next I must give you the powers to act in my behalf. You'll be introduced to my curia at once. After a reasonable length of time, you'll be invested as a *kaid*. It's an Arabic title and carries with it responsibilities and high honors. You'll work primarily with my treasury and my mint, but I urge you to give your finest efforts to the building of the church here. In time it will be made a cathedral, a fitting monument for my— I'll say it, my kingdom."

Thomas bent forward and kissed Roger's hand. "My king, I thank you."

Roger turned to Julien and assumed a wry smile. "Julien, Julien, Julien. Your future is more of a problem to me. Your intelligence belies your youth, and I honestly respect it, but you aren't seasoned enough yet to take on duties as weighty as those assigned to your comrades. If I gave you a title, it would be meaningless; and if I introduced you as a member of my curia, your associates would respect neither of us."

"I wasn't expecting a title, Roger. I would be happy with a post where I could continue to learn."

"We're all learning, Julien. You won't be offended, will you, if I say that I find you diverting? I don't accept your ideas, but I believe they give a balance to my own point of view that could prove valuable. This Abelard of yours, for example, would find much to disapprove of in my conduct, and yet you aren't the only one in my court who admires him greatly. No, I don't discourage innovative points of view just because I can't accept them."

Julien looked miserable. "But I too wish to be useful. I can't justify my being here just to discuss Abelard with members of your court."

"Who said you wouldn't be useful? You'll have plenty of work. I can't afford to support dreamers who don't produce. How would you like to occupy yourself in the chancellery?"

Julien bowed his head. "I will go wherever you wish, Roger, but I'm afraid a clerk's duties would dull me. Do I speak too frankly?"

"It's a habit of yours I hope won't become too irritating. No, silly boy, I have enough clerks. I was thinking of you as a special secretary. God knows, most of our court's business is dreary, and I can't promise you won't often be bored, but then I am too. I want you to be privy to all my councils from the start. When the occasion presents itself, I'll try to use you as imaginatively as I can, but I'm not yet sure how that will be. To begin with, I'd like to have you around me. Trust me, then, for whatever interesting assignments and honors may come to you later."

"You've honored me greatly already, Roger. I'm most pleased."

"Good. I expect the three of you to live in the palace. If you choose to have families and establish your own households elsewhere, you won't lack the means to do so when the time comes. I myself keep several small palaces outside the city, but the palace of Palermo is the center of our lives, whether we live there or not.

"You'll find there are many advantages to sharing my roof. When you eventually return to Salerno, Robert, you'll have my suite at the castle, as well as offices in the city. Thomas, we'll make arrangements for you tomorrow for the time you'll spend in Cefalu. Now, have you all had your bruises seen to? You look fit enough."

"Fit enough to travel, if that's what you mean," Julien said.

"Fine. I'm impatient to get back. My wife has expected me long before now, and I can't wait to have her at my side again. Does it surprise you to find me a doting husband? Ah, but I am. My Elvira has all my love. No other woman shares a place in my heart."

"I see." Robert dropped his eyes, and there was an uncomfortable silence.

Roger laughed heartily. "My harem, is that it? Oh, you English! You're so infected with French notions of romance. I use my harem the way other men go gaming. It's far less compromising than having a mistress or favorite. You'll soon become familiar with Mediterranean ways, and I expect you'll find a lot more in my character to give you pause than my dalliance."

"We weren't critical, Roger," Robert explained. "It's just that a harem . . . well, it's such a commitment."

"Forget it. Now, I'm told there's a small galley in Cefalu which can accommodate me and a few of my staff. I plan to leave on it at noon tomorrow. If you insist, I could find room on it for you, but I'd rather you went on foot. It isn't far, and it's an excellent opportunity to acquaint yourself with the country. The road between Cefalu and Palermo is a good one, not more than two days' journey, travelling at your ease.

"More importantly, it will allow me to prepare the way for you at the palace, though I doubt anyone will raise a charge of favoritism on account of your Norman blood. I've made very few appointments from among my Norman nobles and you'll soon see why. They're worse than the Lombards when it comes to feuding."

Roger was interrupted by a knock on the door. "That must be Hadim. I asked him to come here if there was any news."

The servant's broken arm was now in a clean cotton sling, but he looked otherwise unruffled by the day's events. He bowed low to Roger and nodded shyly to the others. "Your Grace, one of our convoy has put into the harbor and has word of the others. We lost one more ship, but most of the men were saved."

Roger crossed himself. "Lord have mercy on their souls. Still, it could have been much worse. And my cheetahs, Hadim?"

"All safe, master. They're on the ship in the harbor now and, apart from nervousness, appear to be well. They will not eat but take quantities of water, and will no doubt be restored to themselves when back at the palace."

"WeH done, Hadim. Wait for me and I'll go back with you." He turned to the Englishmen. "It looks like I'll be returning on one of my own ships, after all. But I'd still rather you followed later. Amuse yourselves along the way, and if it takes you three days instead of two, it will be just as well. Pleasant dreams, and when we meet again in Palermo, don't take my reserve for coldness or think you've fallen from my favor. I'm forced by policy to function quite differently at court. I've a reputation as a tough duke, and I'm going to be an even tougher king."

The three Englishmen remained silent a moment after Roger's dramatic departure. Robert spoke first. "Well, what do you think?"

Thomas smiled. "He's a man who knows his star is rising. It should be interesting to see how high it goes and how far it can carry us with it."

Julien remained thoughtful, almost troubled. He recognized how far he'd been seduced by Roger's charming posturing more than by his promises, but a good deal remained to be answered. There was something mercurial about the duke's temperament that disturbed him. The ease and generosity with which he dispensed his favors was certainly attractive, but there was a hint of darkness to the personality, a suggestion of deep emotions that could make him capable of heaven knew what excesses. I'm half Norman as he is, thought Julien, but he might as well have come from another world. Perhaps it's that I've never met a man who revealed his passions so freely. At the monastery there were whispers against the pope, but I never dreamed I'd hear a man speak out against papal authority so openly. Not even Abelard. Then there's the matter of his eunuchs. He seems almost to approve of them. Even Robert admits they make his flesh creep. And such ambition. Of course he wanted to see Roger king, but there was something awesome in the man's juggernaut determination. Well, there was no sense allowing his friends to sense his brooding mood. "I suppose a man who shows that much concern for the welfare of his cheetahs can't be all bad," he said aloud.

Chapter VIII
PALERMO

The three Englishmen set out early in the morning to see what they could of their first Sicilian city. Never had they known a countryside as fertile as Cefalu's, nor as rich in its variety of crops. The fields were covered with vineyards and orchards, and scattered with markets, where farmers were joined by merchants and importers of goods from Europe and the East. Julien and his friends quickly realized that Cefalu was not the quiet village of their earlier impression, but an active metropolis, controlled in size but cosmopolitan, diversified, and prosperous.

As Palermo lay only forty miles away, they decided to spend the entire day in Cefalu. They strolled about, more like a trio of excited students, delighting in the abundance of unknown fruits and vegetables and making conversation where they could with the natives. Thomas seemed particularly delighted with the discovery of a peach. "And I love their name for it," he said. "*Persica*. The fruit of Persia. Have you ever tasted anything more delicious?"

"The Romans knew them," Julien said loftily. "Horace. Robert, do you think it would be rude if I asked someone why there aren't more women about? The only ones I've noticed are fat and veiled, except for a few slaves old enough to be my grandmother."

"I can't see why they'd be offended," Robert said. "Most of the men in this market appear to be Christian, at least from their dress." In fact, the evening before, it had seemed that Cefalu was predominantly Muslim, but they soon realized it was because the Muslims were mainly engaged in fishing and had their cottages closer to the shore. Christians, mostly farmers, were actually more numerous.

Julien saw a fellow about his own age selling cups of prickly pear juice who smiled as they drew closer, and returned his smile. "Tell me, why is it we see so few young women at market?"

The young man broke into a laugh. "You wouldn't know a young woman when you saw her," he answered. "They all wear padding under their clothes in public to resemble their mothers as much as possible and so avoid the possibility of insult." He cocked his head to the side and winked. "Do you want to get laid? There's a man with a red turban at the corner who can take you to a clean house."

"No, no," Julien protested. "I was just wondering." He gave the youth some coins and they drank juice which was refreshing despite its intense sweetness.

Towards the end of the day, they returned to the beach to find a fisherman willing to take them as far as Termini, halfway to Palermo.

It was difficult for Thomas and Robert to understand the Sicilian speech, but not for Julien, as their dialect was closer to Latin and spoken with a soft Greek cadence and intonation. Almost all the people seemed to speak Arabic as well, only the Normans and Lombards of unmixed blood resisting.

The ship left at midnight, and favorable winds carried them to Termini by the first rays of dawn. The voyagers had not slept more than an hour or two, but they were wide awake and eager to explore the city, which was already coming to life. The fisherman offered them a breakfast of raw sea urchins plucked from the rocks along the grottos stretching from the harbor. Julien looked at the spiky, dark mass suspiciously, and when the fisherman split one open, he was revolted by the soupy brown lumps inside. Robert brought it to his lips without hesitation and declared it delicious so they all fell to.

The boat had let them off at the mouth of a river that was still swelling with the tide. Termini was in an unparalleled position, straddling the sea and encircling the bay with its fortifications. The domes of the mosques outlined against the yet unwarmed sky identified the Muslim quarter.

Within the city a good deal of traffic centered around a massive building in the Greek style and faced with polished marble, which proved to house a thermal spring supplying a bathhouse of enormous size. Puzzled at first, they recalled Roger's reference to the ritual ablutions of the Muslims. Robert stopped two merchants wearing white turbans. "Excuse me sirs, but we wondered if there was some kind of public entertainment going on at the bathhouse."

The shorter of the two, plump and rosy as fresh fruit, thought a moment before he spoke, while his companion merely shrugged. "Entertainment? Why no, I don't think so, except for whatever diversion people may find in bathing."

"You mean all those people are going in there only to bathe? A full bath underwater?" he asked incredulously. He had assumed all ritual washing was no more elaborate than the washing of hands before their meal with Roger.

"Certainly to bathe," the taller man said. He was as grave as his friend was merry. "We meet at this hour and do it daily."

"Daily?" Robert seemed genuinely astonished. "My word! You must have very different constitutions from ours. That much total immersion would do no end of harm to Christian bodies."

Even the taller man joined his friend in laughter at that. "It hasn't hurt our Christian bodies," the plump one answered, and they walked on with Robert still scratching his head in amazement.

He turned to his companions. "What say, men, shall we give it a go?"

They paid a small fee to the gatekeeper, and a slave ushered them to a dressing room where they disrobed. The slave carefully folded and took away their clothes, indicating another room they should enter. It was cool and dimly lit, since the sun had not yet reached any strength. In the center was a wooden tub of water just long enough for a man and surrounded by four marble benches.

Robert looked at the tub, wondering what all the fuss was about, when a man of about Julien's age entered the room. He was smaller than Julien and wiry, his muscles cleanly defined beneath his dark skin and his hair neatly shaped to his head in short black curls. He introduced himself as Tahir, recently from Persia, and asked if they wished the standard bath or preferred the complete cleansing.

"By all means, the full treatment," Robert said.

Julien's body was rinsed and then lathered again with a soap strongly scented with bergamot and jasmine. Then Tahir took a handful of straw and proceeded to scrub Julien's body with it until his skin was chafed bright red. The water that ran off him now was a great deal clearer. After his final rinsing, Julien waited until at last they all stood there bright pink and glowing and in high spirits. Tahir now led them on.

In addition to the changing room and the massage room there was a cold water room, and then a hot water room, which was fed by the famous thermal spring at one end and had a conduit for the water to run off at the other. Then there was a sweating room, where water was ladled onto hot rocks to produce steam, and finally a resting room. It was in the resting room that Tahir said he would look for them to give them their final rubdown with scented oils. There were already several dozen men ringing the sides of the cold water pool.

"Where do the women bathe?" Robert asked.

"The baths are open to them on certain days only. Each bathhouse has its own arrangements, but most often there are two days for women. I recommend you stay in each room no longer than it takes to eat a simple meal. Enjoy yourselves. I'll be waiting for you." He bowed and returned to the massage room.

The sequence of baths was alternately invigorating and then soothing, and any trace of fatigue felt earlier was soon erased. They left the resting room reluctantly when Tahir came to take them to be oiled.

"Are there many baths like this in Palermo?" Julien asked the Persian.

"None. Termini's thermal spring is unique. It cures aching bones in the aged and speeds the production of male essence. We have pilgrims from everywhere who come for the water's miraculous cures. Others drink of it to ensure long life, and there's no question it enhances the performance of all sexual acts."

"*All* sexual acts?" Julien said, puzzled. He decided to ask Robert more about that later. "What a pity there are none in Palermo."

"Oh, but there's no lack of baths there," Tahir said. "It's just that they are not furnished by thermal springs like ours. You'll find a great variety, for there are many tastes that must be catered to. Greeks and Arabs each have their own style of bath; then there are those which cater to specialized tastes."

Robert gave Tahir a handsome tip, and they thanked him before leaving. Hungry again after their bath, they bought some prepared foods from a roadside vendor and spread them out under an orange tree for a picnic. There was fresh soft cheese, three kinds of olives, and a dish made of flour, eggs, and fresh basil baked into a high, round cake and dressed in oil. With it they drank generously of a light, unwatered white wine which made them sleepy. Robert signalled to their roadside restaurateur, who was also showing signs of sleepiness. He'd been standing nearby, shifting from foot to foot to indicate it was time to close up shop.

"Is there some place nearby where we can find lodging?" Robert asked him.

The man seemed relieved that Robert wasn't going to order still more wine. "Yes indeed. Stay on this road till you reach the other side of town; you'll see warehouses where they let rooms—long, low buildings at the edge of the market."

Robert paid him, then the three of them walked slowly and somewhat unsteadily towards the warehouses. The buildings were exactly as they had been described, and they entered the largest of these to inquire about a room. On the ground floor were stored fresh produce, tanned hides, and woolen fabrics. On the second floor were offices and rooms which could be rented to travellers. They chose a large, airy one and tried to sleep despite the market hubbub which kept them awake until half an hour later, when the sounds vanished abruptly and all was as quiet as if the market had never existed. It seemed the entire town had gone to sleep. They heard the muezzin's call piercing the tranquillity, and then all was silent again.

When they awakened it was cooler, and they left quickly when they discovered they had slept much longer than they'd planned. There was still a good deal of the city left to explore.

The market's business had resumed its brisk pace, and they found the bustle cheerful.

"Do you notice how people nod as if they recognize us?" Robert said.

Julien agreed. "They must be used to strangers. I can't guess who lives here and who's a visitor."

"As a matter of fact," Thomas added, "I stopped noticing who might be Christian and who a Muslim. But I've had enough of markets for now. Why don't we walk along the beach and return when it's time for another meal?"

"An excellent idea," Robert said. "But not too long a walk, please. My appetite's back already."

The beach was rocky, and they found walking difficult until they removed their slippers and waded in the shallow water. They came upon an area where mussels were cultivated on nets of ropes tended by boys and young men who went about their work unashamedly naked. A small boy approached them and offered them mussels no larger than a thumbnail, which he insisted they taste.

Accepting them, Robert dipped into his purse for a coin, which the boy took and put into his mouth, pushing it between his lip and jaw for safekeeping. Robert laughed and asked, "Do you keep anything else in your purse?" The boy evoked an even heartier laugh when, from the other side of his mouth, he pulled out an amulet of carved ivory.

The Englishmen returned to the city as the afternoon air cooled, in search of an interesting place to dine. Many of the townhouses had outdoor hearths built next to their entrances, and in the market areas these were often the kitchens for restaurants.

"I like these open kitchens," Thomas said. "There's something reassuring about seeing what goes into your food."

"I wonder if I'd have enjoyed some of these dishes quite so much if I'd seen what went in them," Julian answered. "By the way, I noticed this cookshop when we passed this morning." He indicated one of the kitchens that had tables and benches invitingly set up in the shade. "They serve those bristly things we thought were hogfood when we saw them displayed. Would you be brave enough to try some?"

The fragrance coming towards them encouraged an enthusiastic assent from his comrades. They seated themselves, and an Arab with a paunch which did credit to his house's reputation approached them at once.

"We've never eaten these," said Robert, pointing to a heap of artichokes nearby. "Do you think we'll like them?"

"*Carcioffi?* If they serve food in Heaven, then *carcioffi* will head the menu," their genial host reassured them. "Not only are they delicious, but they're guaranteed to make your member stand harder and stronger and give you more frequent service."

"A double portion," Robert said. "I knew it was a formidable food the moment I saw it."

A generous bowl of artichokes was brought to the table, steaming under a dressing of hot olive oil and garlic. The restaurateur delayed their attack only by insisting on instructing them in the proper technique for eating them, but they were devoured soon after, and another bowl was brought, then another. Their host joined them at the table and let them know he was impressed by their appreciation of his cooking.

"When you feel you've had enough of those," he said, "you might be interested in walking to the main square. There's a special entertainment scheduled for this evening that might amuse you. I'd go myself if I could. Some eastern dancers arrived only this morning with a full orchestra. They'll be performing at twilight."

"Dancers! What a marvellous idea!" Robert perked up. "I think we have time for another cup of wine first."

Arriving at the plaza, they found townspeople sitting cross-legged in a semicircle, waiting for the entertainment to begin. Vendors were selling hard little balls of fried dough covered with honey and studded with bits of dried fruit. Water sellers were there too, with tiny circles of mirror and bright pompons sewn into their clothing, selling cups of water flavored with jasmine and sugar.

The musicians arrived before the dancers and took their positions, some standing, others squatting. There were six of them, and it was apparent from the number of instruments they brought with them that their skills were varied. There were several flutes and whistles, two bagpipes, a set of three goatskin-covered drums which were struck with the heel of the hand and fingertips, a metal kettle attached to its leather baton—plus sticks, bells, cymbals, gongs, hollow gourds, and castanets.

"They look ready to begin," Julien said, "although I can't imagine what unearthly sort of music they're planning to give us with that odd assortment of junk."

They started with a short overture featuring a jew's-harp, and then a small boy went around with a bowl to collect coins, nuts, fruit, or whatever was offered. The audience grew noisier for a while and then the din ebbed dramatically when a drum roll announced the entrance of the two dancers.

The dancers snaked their way to the center of the clearing and raised their tambourines above their heads, rattling a noisy fanfare. The Englishmen looked at each other wonderingly. The dancers were heavily veiled and robed, and beneath their full garments, they wore corsets padded thickly at the bosom and hips that not only disguised their bodies but greatly amplified their girth. All that could be seen of the dancers was two inches of kohl around their eyes, and their hands and feet, the palms and soles stained red with henna.

There were no women in the audience, and from the excitement of the men, it was apparent this was to be a highly erotic dance. The music joined in, one instrument at a time, as the dancers' hips began to undulate, softly at first, then mounting into spasmodic, almost jerky movements magnified by the shifting of the padded corsets. Their arms described sinuous patterns in the floating layers of multicolored veil, while their feet hardly moved at all but beat lightly to the strange rhythms. They gyrated furiously at the finale, then collapsed into heaps of untidy laundry while the flutist mounted a screeching crescendo and the audience cheered its approval.

Julien turned to a turbanned man on his left. "I'd have appreciated the dance more if I could've seen more flesh and less of all that bedding around them."

"Is that so?" the man replied. "I myself have never cared for boys."

Julien wondered if Robert knew but decided he'd better not ask. They returned to the warehouse as darkness fell, and a servant brought them sweet wine and seeded biscuits. They ate every last one and slept like ticks.

The next morning they decided to go straight to the Palermo road, but first they breakfasted on grape juice and milk curds. The morning air was cool, and they were soon well out of the city; but the road was still so heavily trafficked they thought it must be a continuation of the market. There were more people going to Palermo than coming from it at this hour, and many of the men and women were carrying loads of food and even furniture on their heads to take to the metropolitan markets. All along the way there were stands where refreshments could be purchased, so the trip took on the air of a holiday picnic.

Towards evening they arrived at a town they were told was called Qasr Sad, and a roadside sign told them they were one parasang from Palermo.

Julien had to ask a number of people before he was told that a parasang was a Persian unit of distance equal to about four miles. Since there was still time and this town looked so different from Termini and Cefalu, they decided to spend the night there and arrive in Palermo fresh the next day.

At the edge of town was a castle which had been built in antiquity, its austere walls rising right from the shore. Questioning one of the guards, they were told that since the time of Muslim domination, it had been a home for pious Muslims and continued so under the Normans. A ponderous steel door barred the entrance, but the gatekeeper let them in, telling them to inquire inside for further information. The steward who greeted them at the office seemed embarrassed by their request to tour the castle, and even more by their inquiry for lodging. He explained that the entire second floor was a mosque which they were forbidden by law to enter. However, encouraged by the group's friendliness, he offered to take them to the corridor outside and allow them to look through the door if they would respect its holiness. They quickly agreed, and the steward led them up a staircase brilliantly lighted from pierced brass lanterns that drenched the stone with patterns.

The mosque was three times the size of Julien's parish church, with forty enormous lanterns of brass and multicolored glass panes, more magnificent than any display of lighting they had ever seen. It was oblong in form, with gracefully elongated arches, and on the floor there were clean mats artfully arranged in intricate designs. The steward apologized for not allowing them inside, but offered to show them where they might spend the night.

Around the mosque was a gallery which encircled the entire second story of the castle, and at the foot of its rear staircase was a pool of sweet water with a decorative fountain plinking delicately into the pool. The apartments seemed all well laid out, and each had its own imposing belvedere. Their host explained that this was traditionally a hostel for Muslims, since many pilgrims of high station visited the cemetery at Qasr Sad, but that so long as the customs were respected, the Englishmen would be most welcome.

Robert was offered the largest apartment with the richest rugs on the floor and a majestic view of the sea and coast. Julien and Thomas had rooms that were sparser in their furnishing but afforded equally glorious vistas from the windows. Once established, it was hard for them to believe how hungry they had grown again. They followed their host's recommendation and went to a nearby inn, where they dined on roast kid with white onions, a salad of baby octopus with red onions, celery, and red and green pepper rings, a flat baked bread covered with olive oil and herbs, and some pungent goat cheeses. However much he missed England, Julien decided he wasn't likely to starve to death.

Only a mile away the next morning, they came to another castle greatly resembling the one in which they had spent the night. The Castle of Galfar had a famous fountain in it from which issued the sweetest water they had ever tasted, and there were throngs of people there taking it away in pitchers and amphorae.

Setting out again after the refreshing recess, they found the road to Palermo even busier and the buildings that lined it much larger. They paused at one very impressive structure and asked the doorman if they might inspect the grounds. They were eventually ushered to an interior office, where they were presented to a Byzantine bishop with a beard so bushy it looked thorny. He bowed to them gravely and invited Robert to speak.

"Excellency, it isn't empty curiosity that brings us to your door. We're going to be citizens of Sicily serving Duke Roger and would like to know more about the palaces we see here. They seem to be too large for residences and too far from the city to be government offices."

The bishop was obviously flattered by their interest. "I welcome you in the name of God and of the duke we serve. What you see in this suburb are all hospitals, monasteries, and homes for the aged and incurable. Most of these institutions for public care have been here for hundreds of years."

"Then, this institution was founded when Constantinople ruled here?" Robert asked.

"Exactly. We are a hospital. The Muslims saw no reason to change the way we operated, so we've continued as we always have. They built more of their own institutions in this same area, and now Duke Roger sees to it that we are well supported and has even increased the number of public care centers. Would you like me to show you our wards?"

"We unfortunately do not have that much time," Robert answered. "But if we could see just one, that would be sufficient."

"Take some refreshment first; then I'll arrange for your conduct anywhere you wish."

They accepted fruit juice and were then taken to a spacious room in which twelve beds had been positioned with plenty of space between them. Eastern nuns were the nurses in attendance, and slave women were busily scrubbing the halls. Robert thanked the bishop and left a generous sum of money as a donation. After a brief prayer in the chapel, the three men took leave for Palermo.

The road grew broader and smoother as they approached the city, and the travellers were surprised at a glimpse of the palace as it rose abruptly over the steep walls surrounding it.

Their pace quickened as they approached the gate, which was large enough to admit eight men abreast. Two Norman soldiers armed with swords stepped forward. "Halt. Are your papers in order?"

Robert nodded and fumbled in his purse for the *licet.*

"That's all right, sir. There are some formalities to be met before you can enter the city. Be good enough to follow this man." He signalled another soldier waiting in the guardhouse within the gate who saluted them crisply and led them away. He directed them past a bewildering succession of plazas, then three more stone arches and iron gates, a ducal courtyard, and gardens with lofty buildings on either side.

The Englishmen murmured their awe to each other, but their escort showed no interest in their comments, pausing to address them only when they had arrived at the office of the commissar. He turned and smiled at them. He was no more than fifteen and spoke in an affected, schoolboy Latin. "Please feel welcome. Someone will be with you directly."

Robert felt he would have found the young man patronizing were his tone and manner not so engagingly ingenuous. "Isn't it an exciting place?" the youth said eagerly. "I've been here six months, and I'm still dazzled."

Julien smiled agreeably. "Yes, dazzled."

"I've never before seen a city built on such a grand scale," Robert said.

The boy pointed to a hall in a wide courtyard surrounded by gardens and flanked by arcades. It occupied the entire length of the courtyard, and every five yards or so there was another belvedere from which hung flowering vines of bougainvillea and hibiscus. "That's where Duke Roger dines with his court. And all around there are offices for magistrates and other public officials."

A door onto the courtyard flung open and the commissar waddled forward to greet them, swaying between two young servants who were holding the train of his voluminous gown. He was old, but florid and robust, and Julien was surprised when he addressed them in fluent Norman French. Robert produced their papers, and the commissar smiled broadly. "Only one more formality, please," he beamed. "I know you have recently been with our esteemed duke, but during the time since you left him, did you hear of any fresh news that you could report? I trust it was a pleasant journey, but it is our unfailing rule to inquire of all travellers for news."

They regretted they had no news for him, but it appeared the question was indeed a formality.

"Would you like one of my men to escort you to the palace? No? Do you see that covered arcade just ahead? It is used by Roger to go from the palace to his cathedral. If you follow it to the right, you will arrive at an entrance where you will be met by palace guards."

Leaving his office building they saw two Sicilians seated near the gate whom they assumed to be Christians from their dress. "Pilgrims, watch out what you're carrying," one called out, "lest you be surprised by one of the excise men."

Robert smiled and turned out the palms of his hands to indicate they were carrying nothing which might be subject to duties.

"You see. Mind your own business," the other Sicilian said to the one who had spoken. "Why do you make them feel they have something to fear?" He addressed Robert then. "If, on the other hand, you should happen to have first-class jewels you were interested in disposing of, I could lead you to the finest merchant in Palermo who would give you the best price for them."

"I daresay Roger's famous douane isn't as foolproof as he thinks it is," Robert whispered.

A good deal of Palermo was visible from the courtyard since the city lay on a gentle slope away from the palace. The buildings were made of stone cut in the Arabic style called *kaddan.* They had seen a good deal of it between Qasr Sad and Palermo, and recognized it too in the newer buildings erected by Roger and his father.

The palace guards seemed to know who they were and quickly ushered them through the iron gate into a spacious atrium filled with date palms and flowering shrubs. The openness of the area was a surprise. The palace had seemed so massive and solid, almost ominously so, from the outside that the discovery of light and flowers within it charmed and surprised. An obsequious Greek came out and informed the Englishmen that they could be escorted to their apartments whenever they wished, so the friends agreed to meet again in the atrium just before dinnertime.

The sound of light laughter broke out, and looking up they saw a crowd of at least twenty women enter the atrium from a broad staircase leading down from a balcony above. They were all wearing robes and veils in the

Muslim fashion, and yet they chattered more loudly than the Muslim women they had observed previously, and seemed somehow different. As the women passed them on their way to the gate, they looked at the strangers with no attempt to disguise their interest, and their veils presented no barrier to the frank welcome delivered by their eyes.

Julien froze in astonishment. He had never seen so many enticing women all at once. Their robes were silk and in every color imaginable, all richly embroidered with gold. Their slippers were delicately fashioned of heavy gold embroidery, and these women wore jewels everywhere. Ankles, wrists, and collars were weighted down with gold chains and jewels, and there were all manner of ornaments in their headdresses and at their ears. The veils they wore were soft and just sufficiently transparent to hint at the beauty of the face that lay behind their flutter.

"These women," asked Robert, "are they of the harem?"

"All women are of the harem," one of the aides replied. "The harem simply means the place where the women live. But these are not Muslim women. These are Christian women on their way to church."

The men found this information startling. Thomas was gaping at them openly. "But their clothes," he said. "Christian women don't dress that way."

"They are fashionable women," the guide replied, "and it is Muslim women who set the fashion in Palermo. Christian women almost always go about veiled if they are of a better class, and they've learned the diabolical art of painting their faces from the Muslim women too."

"They are so fragrant," said Julien. "They smell better than soap and bathhouse oils."

"It's perfume," the guide laughed. "They've learned to use even more perfume than the Muslim women do. A fortune in rare oils and perfumes is washed down the palace sewers every day."

Standing by the gate now, the women were flirting quite openly and whispering among themselves until one of the older women spoke sharply and they moved out.

"Never in my life have I smelled anything so heavenly," said Julien. "It makes me dizzy. Do they all smell like that?"

"The ones who can afford to do, as, alas, do some who can't."

The friends nodded their departure again, and Julien was led up two sweeping flights of marble stairs and through a maze of corridors that made him wonder how he would ever find his way back by himself. They passed more veiled women, eunuchs, blacks, orientals, and foreigners of such varied appearance and unfamiliar dress that Julien's head was reeling by the time his guide indicated they had arrived at his new apartment.

Standing in the doorway was a man of Julien's age wearing an earring with an emerald the size of a small acorn clasped in the gold. A cluster of gold chains glittered around his neck, and from each was suspended an amulet: a coral *figa*, an ivory horn, a turquoise eye, and a bloodstone dagger. Julien looked at the man more closely. His eyes were lightly outlined in kohl and his lips seemed unnaturally red and moist. Julien was embarrassed and didn't know if he had been taken to the wrong apartment, but the young man greeted him by name.

"Welcome, Julien. My name is Manuel. I'm here to help you find whatever you may need for your comfort. If you have time now, we should start by furnishing your room. I can take you to the warehouse and help you find suitable pieces."

Julien noticed that Manuel was nearly as fragrant as the women he had passed. He started to speak but felt awkward and found himself stammering.

"Is something wrong?" Manuel's voice was cool but not unfriendly.

"No, no. I—"

"What is it? You can be frank with me."

"I'm sorry. To tell you the truth, I've never seen a man painted before. You see, the eunuchs attending Roger were—"

"Eunuchs! Indeed!" Manuel snapped. "I'm not a eunuch, I'm a page, and I'm as fully equipped as you are." He saw Julien's expression change from awkwardness to acute embarrassment, and his voice softened. "It's all right. I suppose this is your first time away from home. They said you were a Norman, but you don't look like one."

"Yes, I'm an Anglo-Norman," Julien answered, grateful for the chance to produce a simple statement. "You're not a Sicilian, though, are you?"

"I certainly am. My parents were from Constantinople, as is the lord I serve, a most distinguished gentleman of impeccable taste. He brought me here and trained me when I was eleven. Now I'm frequently called upon to help new arrivals become acquainted with the palace and ease them into our style of living and customs. A minister of social protocol, if you will. By the way, I should tell you that Roger must certainly be impressed with you. This is one of the most pleasant apartments available. Wouldn't you like to look around before we select your furniture?"

He led Julien in and showed him a room about sixteen yards square with a small chamber in the rear for sleeping. The windows looked out on a garden ringed by a colonnade with fountains half hidden by flowers. The walls were newly whitewashed and unadorned, but the arched ceiling was elaborately tesserated with designs of flowers and vines, and beasts Julien couldn't identify. "Those are tigers, those are camels, those are lions, and those are antelopes," he was told. Julien decided he must find out more about these fantastic creatures.

Manuel led him to a window and showed him where a previous tenant had scratched a rough map onto the sill indicating the way to the dining hall, to the chancellery, to the various gates, to the locations of the privy and bath.

"I suggest you don't wander around too much by yourself at first," Manuel advised. "You might accidentally find yourself in the harem, and then no matter how much Roger likes you, you could wind up suited for guard duty there."

Julien paled. "Is that really so?"

Manuel laughed. "Don't give it a thought. I always tease new arrivals about the harem, because they all seem so fascinated by it. There's no great mystery, and if you were to get lost and find yourself near the harem, you'd be stopped by one of the eunuchs before you got into trouble."

"Yes, but we were told that all the women are restricted to the harem—or all Muslim women, anyway—and yet I know some of the women I saw in the halls were certainly Muslims."

"Yes, they probably were. As a rule, all women, whether Muslim or Christian, live in the harem, but some of the married women prefer to live with their husbands in this wing. The slaves see to all the household duties, so you'll find these women free to spend their days in the harem visiting and chatting with their friends. Concubines and slaves, however, are often severely restricted to their quarters. You're likely to glimpse one only when she's being escorted by a eunuch to her master's apartment. Older women are generally freer to come and go, but since there are such diverse backgrounds here, even among the Muslims, there are very few hard and fast rules. The only absolute is that no men are allowed in the Muslim women's quarters."

"Then, where am I going to meet women? I mean, younger ones."

Manuel's eyes glinted cunningly. "You should visit the Tiraz, the palace workshop. The women who work there are all Jewish, and most of them are quite good looking. They are all free to make love with you if they like you. I have my mistress there."

Julien looked at him in amazement. "You have a mistress?"

"Certainly. My lord likes me to have women. I mean, anyone can tumble a eunuch, can't they, but if your taste is for young men, then you want them to behave like young men."

Julien found his glibness confusing. "Tell me more about these women of the Tiraz. Are they slaves?"

"Oh no, they're highly skilled free workers and greatly prized by Roger. You'd have to go to the Jews of Thebes to find needleworkers in the same class. I don't know when the tradition of their lovemaking started, but the Muslim noblemen used to sleep with them the same way before the Normans came. The Jews of the city, however, consider them unclean and won't have anything to do with them. I don't understand Jews. Perhaps you'd like to pay a visit to the Tiraz right now? We still have time to choose furniture. Besides, I've just about decided what you should have."

"Can we? I think I'd like that." Julien admitted to himself he could make no criticism of Manuel's manners; nonetheless he hoped that Thomas or Robert wouldn't see them together.

On their way down they passed two tall eunuchs with elegant Semitic features and golden skin. They detained Manuel a moment to ask directions, and Julien studied them closely. They were dressed in sumptuous robes and carried themselves with every mark of good breeding, but he noticed that unlike other eunuchs he had seen, they wore no jewelry except for a long gold tube encrusted with jewels thrust into their turbans.

"What were those long gold straws in their turbans?" he asked Manuel after the eunuchs left. "I've never seen jewelry like it. Rather jaunty."

Manuel laughed wickedly. "Those two were clean sweeps," he said.

Julien's face went blank.

"Clean sweeps," Manuel repeated. "Some of the eunuchs just have their balls cut off, but a number of them have their pricks taken too. That's a clean sweep. They use the gold tubes you saw to pee through. I must warn you, however, to never mention it in their presence; they're terribly sensitive about it. No one ever sees a eunuch pee. As a matter of fact, be careful of your speech around eunuchs. Avoid words with double meanings that could offend them, because if a eunuch is angry with you, he'll never forget."

Julien couldn't be sure Manuel wasn't still teasing. "You mean, they stick those tubes into themselves to pee? I don't believe it. We had eunuchs at the monastery, and they never had to do anything like that."

"They weren't clean sweeps, then. Your monastery eunuchs were probably self-inflicted eunuchs. Frankly I'm more revolted by *them* than you are by these."

"I'm not defending them. They justify themselves with words from

Matthew: 'There have been eunuchs who have made themselves so for the Kingdom of Heaven. He that is able to receive it, let him receive it.' I never thought much about eunuchs or the differences between them."

"Well there's a great deal of difference. Most of your clergy make themselves eunuchs by tying a cord around their balls to cut off circulation until the balls wither. There were probably a lot more of those than you knew of, since when it's done after puberty there's no change in the voice or facial hair. The two you saw had it done before puberty, judging from their lack of beard. Everything is taken off with a curved knife after the thighs and belly are bound tightly to avoid hemorrhage. Then a needle is inserted into the orifice, which is then packed with wet paper and bound. No water can be taken for three days because urination is impossible during this period. At the end of the third day the needle is removed, and if the subject is lucky, a scar will have formed around the wound and there's a fountain of piss. From then on, though, he can pee only by inserting the tube. Oh, speaking of peeing, you're fortunate to have the privy just a few yards from your room. Don't worry, you won't smell it; it's flushed with water into the sewers, same as the bath."

Julien's bewilderment made him hesitate. "Is there only one bath for everyone?"

"Of course not. Perhaps you'd like to inspect the one you'll be using? Would you like to bathe now?"

"No, no. I'll find it myself when I need it." He was suddenly struck with the idea that Manuel might want to bathe with him; he could never undress in front of him, although nakedness had never caused him to be self-conscious at the monastery, even when he was with students about whom stories were whispered.

They reached the Tiraz, and Manuel led Julien into the main workroom, where three hundred women were seated at tables working on silks that were heavier and richer than any he'd ever seen. He murmured his astonishment at the extraordinary colors.

"Yes," Manuel agreed. "We have quite a textile industry. Our dyers are unquestionably the best in the world. Jews control just about all textiles in Sicily, from weaving and dyeing to the fashioning of garments, and a great deal of the selling of them too."

Three Tiraz women nearest them turned to look at the youths and smiled broadly. A few nodded to Manuel but continued their work. They were heavily painted and had the same sooty eyes that Julien wondered if he could ever become accustomed to. Their palms were stained with henna, as were their long nails. They all seemed to possess brunette complexions, but many had hair that had been bleached to various shades of red and blond. They wore simple smocks which revealed generally ample bosoms, and their hips were wide and fleshy, reflecting their sedentary occupation.

"The dark-haired woman working on the purple silk seems to like you," Manuel said. "Do you fancy her?"

"I certainly do," Julien answered quickly, before he had looked closely and seen that she was far flabbier than he liked. "Yes, I must keep her in mind," he added. "She looks like she'd be good."

Manuel smiled slyly. "If you'd like to have her tonight, I'm sure I can arrange it."

Julien colored. "No thanks. I prefer to do my own courting."

"You're a virgin, aren't you?" Manuel said suddenly.

"Of course not!" he sputtered.

"That's too bad. I could probably get you anything in the palace if you were still a virgin, and I mean anything," Manuel said insinuatingly.

"You're already going to too much trouble in my behalf," Julien said coldly.

"I suppose I should apologize, but there's something about you that makes teasing you irresistible. You must understand, Sicilian men get their experience earlier than you northerners. A boy is a prize here, you know." He took Julien by the arm. "Come, there's something here I think may interest you."

He led Julien to another section of the workroom where half a dozen women appeared to be working with extraordinary diligence on sections of a dark red silk with gold thread. Julien studied the stencilled design and saw that it depicted animals similar to the ones on the ceiling of his room— "Tigers attacking camels."

"Yes, but can you guess what this magnificent garment is to be?"

"I agree it certainly is magnificent."

"It won't be ready for a year or two yet, but it's a ceremonial cape suitable for a coronation." He paused. "You can guess whose. The artisans say it will be the grandest cape ever seen."

Julien's eyes kept going from the cape to the almost fully revealed bosom of a voluptuous brunette who seemed to be bending lower than the others over her work. She saw him and cocked her head prettily as she smiled.

Manuel was amused. "You seem to be making a great number of conquests, Julien. I think we'd better go on to the warehouses now, before someone drops a stitch. Before we leave the Tiraz, are you sure you wouldn't like me to arrange something? I don't mind acting as the groom of your chamber. We could take two of these women to your rooms and inaugurate your new quarters with a party. What do you say?"

"No, thank you," he said sharply.

The procession of new sights, unfamiliar situations, and exotic people began to fatigue him, and Julien was relieved when they arrived at the warehouse and found it empty except for the slaves working there quietly. The warehouse was just outside the palace, but attached to it by a covered arcade. The first room was sixty feet long and piled with wooden furniture of every description, most of it finely finished and polished. He found the choice intimidating.

"I need very little—a stool, a writing table, something to sleep on."

"Come now, what if you're called upon to entertain in your quarters? This isn't a monastery, you know."

"I live very simply."

"Nonsense. What would they say about me if it were known I let you furnish your room like a cell? To begin with, you must have a divan. Your station calls for it." Manuel noted the blank look that seemed to creep over Julien's face periodically. "It's a kind of bench covered with cushions for seating your guests."

Julien's curiosity was sharper than his modest appraisal of his needs, and he settled for the divan. Then Manuel chose two carved chests of scented wood from Persia, a desk twice as long as the one he had at the monastery, three walnut faldstools, an assortment of leather hassocks, two low dam-ascene tables, and a small ivory-and-camphorwood coffer for personal be-longings. Julien protested the coffer was much too fine, but Manuel insisted on it.

Next they went into another room for bedding, linens, and cushions. Julien chose a plump linen mattress stuffed with combed wool and framed on a low platform of wood, while Manuel selected a dozen and a half pillows in brilliantly colored silks, some of them embroidered in precious metals.

"Now you must have some rugs," Manuel announced.

"Rugs?" He had seen rugs only a dozen times in his life. "Does my station here entitle me to rugs too?"

"Well, they won't be the best, but they'll be quite good."

Manuel led Julien to a loft with a loggia along one end that was filled with rugs in neat piles as high as his head. Manuel pulled one down and offered Julien a corner to inspect, showing him how to scratch the underside with his thumbnail to check the density of the threads.

"I favor Anatolian designs, but our best selection at the moment is from Armenia and Turkey. There are several nice Persians too, although I think they're being overdone since Duchess Elvira started using nothing else."

Julien sensed another presence in the storeroom and turned in time to see two figures moving quietly towards the exit. Manuel turned and called to one of them. "Claire. I didn't see you in here. Hold on a minute."

The girl turned and stood there uncertainly, her eyes flickering between the men and the door. She was unveiled, and Julien decided at first glance that she was, quite simply, the loveliest and most exciting woman he had ever seen. Her figure was slight compared to other women, but there was no lack of sensuousness in her lithe body. She was dark-haired, and her eyes, free of any cosmetic, had longer, thicker lashes than Julien had ever dreamed of. He stepped forward and saluted her.

"Introduce us please, Manuel." Julien's voice was not as firm as he would have wished.

"Will you please stop looking at me," she said testily. Her eyes dropped, and her fingers started plucking at the border of her girdle.

"I beg your pardon, but you can hardly blame me for looking." He was certain he'd never seen brows so perfectly arched.

"Claire, this is Julien Fitz Nigel," Manuel said formally. "He arrived only today and will be working closely with our duke."

"Tell him to stop looking at me. The boy has no manners."

"But I tugged my forelock," Julien said. "What more do you want?"

"Tug your forelock indeed! Country manners! Stop looking, I say. How dare you!" She dropped her head further and averted her eyes.

Julien decided she was about sixteen, although he had heard women matured much earlier in the south and she might actually be as young as fourteen. "I mean no disrespect, but it's not easy to take my eyes off you. If this were England, I daresay you'd be angry if I didn't give you a second look."

"Damn!" She forked the fingers of her right hand and thrust them at him. "I'll have to keep my veil on if this is the sort of impudence I must put up with. And in my own home too! Where were you brought up, boy? Don't you know it's unforgivable to stare at a woman that way? I don't suppose I can expect *you* to correct his manners, Manuel."

"How can you criticize my manners when you keep calling me boy?" Julien answered sharply. "I'm at least two years older than you, if not three. Where were *you* brought up?"

She turned her eyes directly on him and thrust her fingers out again. "In a place where men are taught how to behave towards ladies."

Manuel made no attempt to hide his amusement but decided he'd best intercede. "Come now, Claire. You're being too dramatic. There's plenty of time for him to learn palace protocol."

"A fine example you set for him!" She glared at Manuel. "I don't know which of you is worse, but I was told redheads often have the evil eye." She thrust her forked fingers towards Julien again, but less forcefully.

"Julien, let me explain, or she'll keep making a fuss. Claire, you see, is a maiden and obviously of good family." Manuel's tone was only slightly mocking. "She's the only daughter of Baron Serlo, who died in battle for Roger. You must understand, it's not customary to stare at a woman as openly as you do, unless she's a woman of no reputation, like the Tiraz workers. If it were noticed, it might lessen her chances for a good marriage. Assuming, of course, she could find someone willing to put up with her bad temper."

Claire scowled at Manuel. "The Tiraz workers, eh?" she sneered. "I suppose you're already had him down there so you could both lick your chops over all that spoiled meat. Did you find him a nice fat hen with too much jasmine scent?"

Julien decided if she were truly offended, she'd have gone by now, so he pressed for an advantage. "I beg your pardon. I truly meant no disrespect. I thought as long as you weren't wearing a veil I might as well look. It's a long time since I've seen such a pretty girl."

Claire wasn't yet mollified. "It's stupid to wear one while I'm working, and the men I see here are all respectful and would never stare."

"If you understood my reasons for staring, you might even feel flattered."

"Flattered! You make me feel naked." She blushed then at her own boldness.

Julien was encouraged. "Will it be better if I turn my head away like this when I talk to you?"

"Yes, I suppose that's better," she answered softly.

"But I can still see you . . . and have the same thoughts."

"It's still more respectful. By the way, why don't you have a beard? I thought all barbarians had beards."

"For the same reason you don't wear a veil. I don't care to."

"Oh dear, perhaps you're a eunuch."

"Step closer and I'll let you find out," he said boldly.

"There! You're being rude again." Her hand had raised briefly as if to slap him, when she noticed her servant, who had been standing quietly by, look at her apprehensively. She lowered it quickly.

"Come, Jordan," she said to her servant. "We'll finish our inventory another time. Good day. And Manuel, remember what I said. You would be kind to teach him better manners."

"I'm sure I'd learn them faster if you were my teacher," Julien said. "Come to my apartment tonight and I promise to be a good student."

"If my father were only alive! Manuel, are you going to allow him to insult me this way?"

"Claire, my dear, my orders are to show him every consideration. Just be thankful you weren't asked to do the same."

"You're hateful, both of you. If Roger thinks so much of him, I'll bet it's because he bewitched him. I knew there was something unnatural about him the minute I saw him. Just look at that ugly red hair!" She made one more thrust with her fingers and pushed her servant out of the room before her.

"Do you always make such a devastating impression on girls?" Manuel smirked.

"Are all your girls so outspoken? I'd say she needs taming." Julien felt his eyes sting with shame, and he decided he was liking Manuel less and less.

"She's just spoiled. She needs a husband to take a stick to her; then she'll learn how to behave."

"I know just the stick I'd like to take to her, right enough—but I do pity the man she weds. She's sure to make him miserable."

"Yes, she's impossible, but it's not all her fault. You see, her father was off fighting most of the time, and the poor girl had no uncles or brothers to beat her. Never fear, Roger will see to it she's married within the year. She sets a very bad example for the other women."

"What's she doing working here if she comes from a noble family?"

"She insists on it. When she took over this part of the warehouse, it was over her mother's objections. The girl may be headstrong, but she's also clever. She has this place so well organized I can find anything I need without looking—last year it was hopeless."

"There's just the two of them, then—she and her mother?" Julien's voice lost its anger and became thoughtful.

"Yes, they keep a handsome apartment in the Greek wing of the harem, which is more free, quite different from the Muslim harem. The baroness is from Taranto and is one of those old line Greeks from Italy's heel. She's a grand lady, a relative of the old catapan of Bari, and she still thinks she married beneath her station no matter how many honors Roger heaped on her husband. You'll find we Byzantines can be snobs, but then it *is* the older culture, and the refining element here."

"But it's the Arab culture that's dominant, isn't it?"

"The Arabs? My dear boy, what have the Arabs ever done? They carry the traditions of other cultures and they preserve learning, but what have they ever developed by themselves? Medicine? The sciences? Look closely and you'll see they learned it all from the Greeks and Egyptians—except for a little mathematics, perhaps. Credit them rather with the intelligence to recognize superior attainments in others and use them. They love to boast about the intellectual standards of Cordova, but the texts, my dear, are mostly Greek."

Put off by Manuel's haughtiness, Julien decided it would be pointless to argue with him. "Tell me more about the Greek women here. Are they all as beautiful as Claire? However repulsive I found her personality, it would be hard to imagine anyone more exquisite."

"Oh, she's a beauty, all right. She has those famous Taranto eyes, just like her mother's. But take my advice and stick to the women of the Tiraz or the whorehouses, until you're more familiar with our ways. It's much safer, and Claire was quite right, you know. If you pass a woman who is unveiled, and particularly a maiden, you must bow your head and never look at her directly or you could seriously compromise her. If she initiates a flirtation, or if you know she's a tart, it's quite different, of course. You'll find the women will let you know soon enough when a more direct glance is welcomed."

"Do you think I'll be able to see her again?"

"How should I know? I don't even have any idea where you'll be working."

"I must see her. I want to convince her that I'm not as crude as she thinks."

"She was just being silly. You're not crude at all, and for a foreigner, quite clean."

Julien felt himself blush. "We bathed yesterday." He had noticed that everyone he'd seen, including the servants, looked freshly scrubbed.

"No offense, but how often did you bathe in England?"

"Very often." He knew his answer sounded defensive.

"I'm not criticizing you, Julien. I'm just trying to acquaint you with some of our traditions so you'll be more comfortable. Here at the palace most of us bathe every day. We also wash our hands before dining, our bottoms after the privy, and our privates before making love."

Julien tried unsuccessfully to hide his consternation. "But doesn't that much bathing . . ."

"Make you weak? No, nor sick. If you're going to be a member of court, you'll make yourself more agreeable to those around you if you follow court practices. After you've been here awhile, when you travel through the city it will be very apparent to you who does or doesn't observe these habits."

"I appreciate your telling me this, but if the men here are all so much cleaner, why do I see them constantly pawing at their crotches? I mean, anyone can pick up a flea or a louse now and again, but from the way they're always going at their balls, you'd think everyone here has nothing but crabs. I never see them scratch anywhere else."

Manuel was amused. "Yes, I do it myself. I've heard some explanations for part of it. The Jews, the Greeks, and the Arabs always swore by their manhood, and they'd touch their balls to attest to the truth of what they said. The Arabs still do. If you compel a Muslim to take an oath, don't be surprised if he lifts his shirt and holds his prick in his fist to be convincing.

"There are superstitions as well," Manuel continued. "If you pass a corpse or if a funeral goes by, you must touch your balls. If you see a male hunchback it's all right, because he's lucky, but if you see a female hunchback be sure to touch your balls before she sees you. And if you're too late, you must form a *figa* with your left hand by thrusting your thumb between your index and middle fingers and jab it at her three times while you clutch your balls with your right hand. If you see a freak of nature or a particularly repulsive beggar, touch your balls. If you see your neighbor's house burn or his cow grow sick, touch your balls. Besides, it feels good. Any other questions?"

Julien was laughing openly after he decided Manuel wasn't such a bad sort after all. "I think you Sicilians just enjoy playing with yourselves."

"And why not?"

"Indeed." His voice sobered somewhat. "I can assume, then, that Claire bathes every day?"

"I'm certain of it, and she probably rinses her thighs as often as the Muslims do." He lifted his eyebrows saucily. "I recommend it. It's really a matter of politeness, when you think about it."

Julien felt a warmth suffusing his groin at the thought of Claire's personal ablutions. "At what hour is it best to bathe?"

"Any time. Most of us do it before dinner, or before sex. Suit yourself, just as long as you do it. We have a saying in Sicily: 'When northerners or peasants mate, they yoke like beasts.' When you get to know us better, you'll have a better idea of what we mean. Don't worry, I think you'll get along very well here. If you'd care to go back to your apartment now, I'll see to it that your furnishings are delivered, and I'll be up in an hour or so to see they're all arranged properly."

Chapter IX
AT HOME

Julien had been lying awake for half an hour, soothed by the distant chorus of bird song and plashing water that reached his room. He had slept soundly, his senses intoxicated by the fragrance of his linen mattress and his brain exhausted by the rapid assault of unfamiliar images. When he had dined with Robert and Thomas last evening, they could scarcely communicate, so overwhelmed were they. Robert said he had been promised an interview with Roger after dinner, and Julien wondered if it might be his turn to speak with Roger today. He still had only the vaguest idea of what his duties were to be, and yet, if his position carried with it the rewards of so much luxury, he would be foolish to complain.

His thoughts turned to Claire and lingered there again as they often had that morning. He closed his eyes and tried to re-create her face exactly. Her eyes and lashes were unforgettable, but the shape of her nose was a little uncertain, and although he distinctly remembered the evenness of her teeth, he wasn't sure how full her lips were, nor how wide. He realized his re-creation of her face was an academic exercise because his mind's eye wandered perversely to explore the hidden parts of her body, and his own flesh responded throbbingly to what it found there.

There was a knock on the door, and he jumped up and looked for something to cover himself with. His visitors let themselves in unceremoniously just as he was recalling he had left all his clothes in the next room. He placed his hands in front of himself in an ineffectual attempt at modesty and nodded sheepishly at three servants who lined up formally before him, smiling and bowing. The first had a basin of warm water and some towels, the second had a tray with tea, pistachio nuts, and sesame seedcakes, and the third held his arm up proudly to exhibit a magnificent falcon. Julien recognized it as the Babylonian saker that Roger had promised him. Roger had remembered him, then. He said something cheerful to the servants and went inside to find his shirt.

"Where can I keep this falcon?" he asked. He wasn't sure whether he was expected to keep it in his room.

"I will return it to the falconry mews," the servant answered. "It is already fully trained. You are free to visit the mews any time you wish. This bird is exclusively for your pleasure and hunting."

Julien worried the ruff just under the bird's hood, and the falcon drew itself up stiffly. "Please convey my thanks to Duke Roger. I'm very pleased."

"I'm sorry sir, but I've never addressed the duke. You'll have to do so yourself. I was sent here by the head falconer."

The man who carried the tea tray spoke next. "Breakfast will be served in the common room in half an hour. Your friends plan to meet you there, and afterwards you will be expected at the chancellery."

When they had gone Julien pulled his shirt off again and sipped some tea, then dipped one of the towels in the water and washed himself thoughtfully. "I'm likely to grow soft with all this fancy living," he said to himself. He knelt and prayed until it was time to go down to breakfast. It was a prayer of thanksgiving, but he prayed too that his soul not be corrupted by all the pleasures around him. He suspected some severe trials of his spirit were in the offing.

Breakfast was lighter and more hurried than he expected. The others dining were mostly young bachelors, or men who had not yet established a household in their living quarters at the palace, and they seemed more eager to be off to the day's duties than to linger. Robert, too, seemed impatient to be off.

"Chancellor Guerin and Admiral George are seeing me this morning," he announced. "It will be a small, private council without Roger, and then I shall be leaving with Guerin for a while, to Salerno I expect. I don't know when I'll be seeing you again."

Julien was genuinely disturbed. They had been at each other's sides for so many months now, and he needed his support in this still overwhelmingly foreign environment.

"You'll still be here, won't you, Thomas?"

"Just for a short while. I'm to study architecture for the next few months, and then I start interviewing artists and craftsmen before returning to Cefalu. I doubt we'll be seeing much of each other, but we'll both probably be too busy to notice."

"I hope so," said Julien. "I'm to report to the chancellery this morning but still haven't the faintest idea what to expect."

"Roger will be sending for you soon," Robert said. "At least he said so when I saw him last night."

"What did you talk about? Can you tell us?" Thomas asked.

"Women mostly," Robert answered. "He's extraordinarily considerate.

And generous. One of the eunuchs brought a beauty to my rooms last night. An Ethiopian she was, from Harar. The eunuch told me the women of Harar are considered the most beautiful anywhere. She was proud as a princess, with skin like dark honey. I think I may buy one when I'm more settled in. How about you two? Have you seen anything you liked yet?"

"I met a Lombard girl I found interesting," said Thomas. "She's the daughter of the building commissioner, and he was already hinting she might be a suitable match for me. A quiet and lovely girl, very well bred, with wide blue eyes and dark hair. I couldn't get her out of my thoughts all night. She's not twelve yet, but I'm in no hurry. And you, Julien?"

Julien described the women of the Tiraz, exaggerating their beauty, and then decided not to mention Claire. After all, there was no point telling them he'd been impressed by her, when the girl had behaved so wretchedly towards him. He couldn't even be sure she might not try to embarrass him if they were all to meet one day.

"Well, it looks like we're off to a good start, men," Robert said. The three of them embraced firmly and separated.

It was a short walk to the chancellery, a building which would have been imposing were it not dwarfed by its surrounding administrative offices. Roger had no meeting with his curia today and it was not known if he would make an appearance. Julien hesitated in the corridor outside, trying to decide how he should present himself for the most advantageous impression. He finally admitted to himself that he felt intimidated by his lack of experience and tried to pray for guidance while he paced the corridor.

He saw a familiar figure about twenty yards away. Even though she was veiled today, he couldn't be mistaken about those eyes, those perfectly formed brows. Claire was approaching him slowly, leading a boy about three years old by the hand. If she recognized Julien earlier, she gave no sign of it until she was directly before him. Julien's hand went fumbling towards his forehead for an obeisance.

"Good morning," she said. Her voice was at least neutral. "I'm told I was very rude to you yesterday."

"You weren't, but I'd rather you be rude to me than not notice me."

She seemed momentarily flustered. "My mother explained that a newcomer should be treated as a guest and allowances made for unusual behavior until he has had time to adjust to new ways. But you did look at me so very peculiarly. As a matter of fact—"

"I can't help it. Perhaps you can adjust, too, to the way I look at you, for I swear I don't know how to change it, and there's nothing I'd like better than to spend the rest of my life looking."

"Prettily said, but my mother told me I didn't have to trust you, so I won't. You're doing it again, you know. That look."

"It's stronger than I am. And no one's watching."

"I'm glad I wore a veil." She raised her hand to her bosom and kept it there as a modest gesture, then was startled to feel her heartbeat thundering through the cloth.

Julien stepped closer. "You must allow me to know you better. I'd like to change that unfortunate first impression you had of me. I want nothing better than your respect."

She smiled at that. "Somehow I don't believe that's all you have in mind." She saw men approaching and gestured quickly with her eyes that he had best disguise his gaze in front of strangers.

He caught her signal and placed his hand on the boy's head and teased a curl with his finger. "Is this lucky little fellow a relative?"

"No, this is Ahmad, the son of Aziz al Madih. I take care of him sometimes. He's a good companion for me, my protector. I'm just taking him to see his father for a moment before the day's work begins."

"Let me help you find him."

"You don't need to. He's standing right there behind you. Aziz, this is Julien Fitz Nigel, who just arrived from England. I've no doubt you'll be seeing more of him since Roger looks kindly on him, or so I'm told."

Julien studied the man standing near him who nodded and reached his arms to his child. Little Ahmad kissed his father courteously on each cheek and withdrew shyly to Claire's skirts again. Aziz was several inches shorter than Julien, with slender arms and a prominent paunch. He looked about fifty, with a neatly curled gray beard and his hair cropped close to his ears. He was simply dressed and was one of the few people Julien had seen since he arrived who wore no jewelry.

Aziz fondled his child's head and turned his attention to Julien. "We've been expecting you. If you like, I'll go in with you and introduce you to some of the people you'll be working with." His smile was relaxed and gently reassuring.

"You're very kind."

"Aziz is a mathematician," Claire said, "as well as a poet, and a very good father."

"My experience as a father appears to exceed all other talents," Aziz said, laughing. "Ahmad is the youngest of my twenty-six children, and all are living and well, praise Allah."

Julien was taken aback somewhat by the unfamiliar invocation, but Claire appeared not to notice. Aziz's perception was acute, and he said to Julien good-naturedly, "You haven't known many of my faith, I take it?"

"No, I can't say I have," said Julien, wondering how Claire and Aziz could appear to be on such easy, familiar terms.

"You'll meet many more," Aziz said, "and I hope we will be friends. Outside, people tend to live in their own communities, but here in the palace . . . well, we are all under one roof, aren't we? I won't claim there are not many who hate people of a different faith, but in our immediate circle, you will find that Muslims and polytheists tolerate each other quite well."

"Polytheists!" Julien exclaimed indignantly.

"Don't take offense," Claire intervened. "The Jews and Arabs do not conceive of Jesus and God the Father as one, and then they're confused by what they see as worship of all the saints. It's not intended as an insult, the way we use the word infidel, for instance."

"I apologize if I've offended you," Aziz said. He took Julien's wrist gently in his left hand while he salaamed by touching his breast, lips, and forehead with his right.

"It's all right," Julien said. He had to admit he was drawn to Aziz, and if Claire seemed to be well acquainted with him, he thought it might be a good idea if they became friends.

Claire was already starting away with Ahmad. "Wait," he called. "When will I see you again?"

"I don't know, but it's inevitable we will," she said. "After all, we share the same roof."

"Come inside," Aziz said. "There are many people for you to meet, and I believe someone said he had a message for you from Brittany."

"Brittany!" He felt the blood rush to his face.

Julien mumbled his way through dozens of introductions, trying hard to suppress his eagerness to receive his message. He was introduced at last to a Greek clerk named Dmitri who had taken the message. He fumbled among his papers a good while before producing a note he had written to himself.

"It was a week ago," he said, referring to his notes. "A pilgrim priest from your country came by on his way to Jerusalem. He had been in Brittany, and a monk there named Brother Ralf asked him to tell you that he was with Peter Abelard."

"Is that all?" Julien asked in dismay. "Wasn't there a personal message for me?"

"The old pilgrim is gone now, but I'm sure that's the extent of the message."

"Thank you," Julien said drily. "Would you be kind enough to let me know when you hear of someone who is headed towards Brittany so I can send a message back?"

"There's no need to wait," Dmitri answered. "Leave your note with me and I'll find someone to give it to. There's no trouble finding travellers for most places."

"Very well," said Julien. "The message is for Brother Ralf, to be found with Peter Abelard in Brittany, and the message is that I, Julien, am with Roger and that he can write me at the palace. Thank you."

Aziz continued with him on his rounds, explaining the duties of most of the associates of the chancellery. "Do you know this Abelard?" he asked. "He has many friends at this court."

"No, I've never met him, but he is my teacher nonetheless. I would enjoy speaking with those here who knew him. But now, have you any idea where I am to work, and at what?"

"A place has been made for you here in the chancellery, but if you like, I have a large study I could share with you. You might find it more comfortable and quieter."

Julien looked at him steadily. "I would like that very much. But what of my duties? Will I be able to perform them as well there?"

"I expect most of your duties will be performed in Roger's presence or with the curia. Think of my studio as a quiet place for study. If your duties are such that it would be unsuitable, you can always leave."

"I accept with gratitude. This means, I suppose, that we shall be together a great deal."

"Presumably. Do you have some objection?"

"Not at all. I was just wondering if I could take advantage of your generosity by asking another favor of you."

Aziz turned his palms towards Julien and bowed slightly.

"I know how busy you must be, but do you think you could possibly teach me Arabic?"

Aziz's eyes widened, and a smile spread slowly across his face. "You really want to learn Arabic! I'm delighted, but it's not easy, you know. There's another alphabet, and it's written from right to left."

"Alphabets aren't difficult for me. I learned Greek. If you find me stupid or you get bored, you could find me another teacher, but I really want to learn, and I know it will be useful to me."

"Allah is great. We already have many polytheists—Excuse me . . . I mean Christians—here who speak Arabic and write it well, but they are

Sicilians. I've never heard of a foreigner—and an Englishman at that!—who wanted to learn. Of course I'll teach you. I promise to have you reciting the Koran within the year."

"Is that necessary?" Julien said hesitantly.

"Don't worry. I won't try to convert you. Roger doesn't approve. He even discourages Muslims from becoming Christians. I'm sure he'll be pleased if you learn Arabic though. And as long as it appears we'll be spending a good deal of time in each other's company, there's something else I'd like to teach you."

"Yes?"

"Would you like to learn chess? It's one of our most popular diversions."

"By all means. I think I've heard of it somewhere."

"Good. Shall I show you our study now?"

"Yes, please. And if you don't mind my asking—" Julien hesitated and felt his skin coloring. "How did you come to know Claire?"

"Yes, she is lovely, isn't she?" Aziz smiled slyly. "Several of my children were her playmates in one of the harem nurseries. She was virtually adopted by them, but now my daughter Fatima, who was her closest friend, is preparing to marry in a month and will go to Seville with her husband. I think she grieves more over leaving Claire than leaving us. And you saw how Claire has all but stolen Ahmad from us. He adores her."

"Did I hear correctly that you have twenty-four children? How did you manage to sire such a large family?"

"There are twenty-six, and it's a wonder I don't have more. My appetite is a healthy one; may it continue so until my death, with the grace of Allah."

"My compliments. But please tell me more about Claire, since you're such close friends. Are there many suitors for her? She looks about the right age to marry."

Aziz raised his hands to his temples. "Suitors? Only Allah knows how many. Do you think you're the only man with eyes in his head? Even two of my sons are mad to marry her, but of course it's out of the question. Yes, she's caught the eye of many a young lord who thought he could tame her, but her mother always manages to raise objections to the match. In truth, I believe it's Claire who objects and gets her mother to voice it."

"I suppose that can happen when there's not a father about to make decisions."

"Roger keeps in touch. He's bound to choose a husband for her soon. I think he's hesitated to do so until now because he knows she's capable of making the man's life miserable before he masters her. I find her much too headstrong for a woman. I love her dearly, but I thank Allah daily that he has not cursed me with such a daughter."

The study was handsomer and more spacious than Julien expected. A servant moved a desk in for him at once, and he spent the rest of the day in an enthusiastic exploration of the Greek texts that were part of Aziz's personal library. Then before Julien returned to his apartment, Aziz took him to the palace library, where he grew almost feverish at the sight of more books than he could ever hope to read in a dozen lifetimes.

For the next two weeks all Julien could think of was his new course of study. He would make an appearance every morning at the chancellery to see if there was any word or assignment from Roger, but he was told by Dmitri only that Roger knew he was involved with independent study and that he approved. A few days later he received a copy of Ptolemy's works inscribed to him by Roger, but with no additional message.

Julien saw Claire almost every day for a moment or two when she brought Ahmad to pay his respects to his father. It seemed to him that her attitude was a bit softer, but she kept her reserve guardedly, even when Aziz was not present. He felt there was something far more intimate in the anger she had shown him at first, but she withdrew before he was able to make more headway.

One day Julien saw her at a distance with a tall, dignified woman whom he assumed to be her mother. They were both unveiled, but Claire gave him no encouragement to draw closer, and when he started to approach them, she took her mother's arm and hurried her away without another glance at him.

He had mastered some simple phrases of Arabic by now, enough for the most basic conversing, but learning the script required long, tedious exercises that wearied him. Aziz came to him one morning when he was robustly cursing the page of undecipherable wriggles that he had been given. "Julien, why don't we have a bit of a holiday today? You've been working very hard, and I know that you've seen nothing of Palermo yet. Why don't we go out on the town? I know some amusing places to eat, and then later this afternoon you might enjoy accompanying me to my bathhouse."

Julien welcomed the idea. His studies had kept him from investigating the city as much as he would have liked, but he was determined to discipline himself severely, at least until he had a specific assignment from Roger.

"We have some foods in Palermo that you won't find anywhere else in the West, not even in Cordova." Aziz was evidently looking forward to the outing as much as Julien was. "I hope your appetite is good today."

They went first to the old quarter below the palace, but Julien had managed to venture that far by himself, so they moved on a few hundred yards north to the Jewish quarter. The market was the busiest he'd ever seen, with stalls crammed with food, household goods, and clothing choking every street.

They stopped at a street kitchen and ordered artichokes which had been pounded flat with a mallet and then deep fried in olive oil. "These are called *carcioffi a la Giudia,*" Aziz told him. "*Carcioffi* is now part of the Sicilian dialect, but it is an Arabic word. They've started to eat them on the mainland too. *A la Giudia,* as you must know, simply means Jewish style. They cook them well."

"It was one of the first foods I tasted in Sicily, but I never had them prepared this way," Julien said. "They smell wonderful." The artichokes arrived crisp and sizzling and resembling a faded, pressed rose of enormous size. Julien immediately wanted to order several more, but Aziz persuaded him to save his appetite.

"Now that I've learned some Arabic," Julien said, "I find it interesting that so many Arabic words have entered the Italian language. The words for butter, warehouse, shirt, alembic, toll, and zenith, for example."

"You forgot to mention the most important one," Aziz answered. "Since you've learned some Arab mathematics too, I'm sure you appreciate the value of zero."

Julien was thoughtful a moment. "Yes. I'd almost forgotten how much the concept of zero changed my attitude towards mathematics. Now I can't imagine how northerners can solve problems using Roman numerals." He shook his head. "The next time a Greek tells me the Arabs have contributed nothing of their own to the world, I'll have a quicker answer."

"Yes, I've heard that from Greeks on occasion. But we're even more critical of them, however much we admire their ancients. They're clever all right, but decadent and effete.

"I have a special treat for you now," said Aziz. "I'm taking you to a place where they serve a dish I've never seen outside of Palermo. The Arabs call it *itriyah*; and the Sicilians, *vermicelli di tria,* or the little worms of tria."

"No thank you," said Julien. "This sounds like another of the Arab delicacies I can live without. Two nights ago it was roasted sheep's eyes."

"No, no. They're not really worms. They're a little like the Cathay noodles you've eaten here, but they're made differently. It's made from the hardest wheat, without eggs, and dried before cooking. I have a passion for it."

Aziz led Julien to a row of tables set into an arcade off the shopping street and shaded with striped canopies. Bowls of pasta were brought to them almost at once, the noodles steaming and coated with a sauce of garlicky olive oil studded with capers and sprinkled with basil and parsley.

"I was served a dish with capers in Salerno," Julien said, "and I tried to send it back because I thought they were rat turds." Aziz roared with laughter.

They washed their fingers from the pitchers of water on the table, then ate with relish. When Julien finished, he pronounced it the best food he had eaten in his life.

"We've eaten too much," said Aziz, patting his paunch appreciatively. "Now we must find some fresh fennel to finish our meal. Its digestive qualities are essential after *itriyah*. And then if you will indulge me, I should like to treat you to my bathhouse. A short walk, a vigorous massage with your bath, perhaps a nap afterwards and you'll be in great shape. Pity we can't do this every day."

They found their fennel and walked to the edge of the old quarter closest to the sea. On the way they refreshed themselves with a slice of the deep red melon, which Aziz told him was a staple of the poorer classes and did not often make an appearance on finer tables. Julien found it as good as any food he'd tried.

When they passed a teahouse, Julien's nostrils caught a scent that was by now familiar to him. "They are smoking hashish," Aziz explained. "It is a great comfort to many of our people, as is chewing *qat*, but I don't recommend you try it. It appears to have an unpredictable effect on westerners."

"But if your foods agree with me so well, maybe the hashish will too," Julien argued.

"Perhaps one day. But I'd rather you tried it at home. Mine, if you like, or I can send you some pastries cooked with it. The ones with ginger preserves are best, and they're readily available."

The bathhouse was set back from the street, with lemon and bergamot trees sentried before the entrance and two carved fountains on either side splashing their coolness across borders of flowering jasmine.

Aziz was greeted warmly by the attendant in the entrance room. "Welcome, Aziz. Ishkar has been waiting for you." He nodded and then bowed to Julien. "You do us honor by bringing a friend. Does he have any preference?"

"My friend is new to Sicily. I leave it to you to choose someone suitable. One with good, strong hands I should think." He turned to Julien. "They have the best masseurs in Sicily. The clients are almost all Arab, but everyone is welcome."

They took seats while the bathkeeper went to summon the masseurs.

"I've been coming to Ishkar for months," said Aziz. "He's actually twenty-five, I'm told, but you'd never guess he was a day over fourteen."

"He's a eunuch?" Julien began to feel uneasy.

"Oh yes, they all are here. Ishkar is one of those beautiful Assyrians. I think he must have been altered when he was still only ten or so. Ah, here we are."

The bathkeeper conducted two masseurs into the room. Julien stared goggle-eyed, and then almost choked in his effort to suffocate his laughter. The two eunuchs stood quietly and gave no notice of Julien's rudeness.

"I'm very sorry," Julien said at last, but he addressed the bathkeeper and not the eunuchs.

"Don't mention it," said the bathkeeper. "I admit they're very amusing to see together."

Aziz had already gone over to speak with Ishkar, and Julien saw him fondle the youth's cheek in greeting him.

Ishkar was about Julien's height and very slender. Although his hair was dark, his skin was extremely white and soft. Both eunuchs were completely naked, and Ishkar had the undeveloped penis of a child. The other eunuch was more than a foot taller, with muscle definition incised deeply into his torso, and arms powerful enough to strangle a bull. He was endowed with a giant's penis that seemed absurdly large next to Ishkar's thimble.

"Rom is a Nubian," said the bathkeeper. "Will he be satisfactory?"

"Certainly," said Julien, unwilling to offend his host, but feeling a bit intimidated by the towering black man.

"Take a nap when you're through," said Aziz, "and I'll have you awakened when I'm ready. I always take a long time."

"Aren't you coming with me?" Julien asked, trying to conceal his apprehension.

"Oh, no. I engaged us private rooms." Aziz laughed lightly. Don't worry, you'll be quite comfortable." He handed the bathkeeper some money, and the eunuchs stepped forward to lead their customers to the massage rooms.

Julien was still ill at ease as Rom insisted on helping him undress but decided this was something he would have to get used to. He noticed that Rom wore an ivory crucifix on a gold chain. "I see you're a Christian," he said. "I saw another black Christian once, in Salerno."

"My people are from Dongola," Rom said proudly. "We were Christianized six hundred years ago, long before half of Europe, and even under the Muslims we have kept our religion." He paused to bless himself. Julien was silent but felt more comfortable.

"The friend you came with is a most respected man. I believe you are fortunate in his friendship." Rom's voice was reassuring.

"Yes, I agree. I gather you see him often."

"I don't. He comes for Ishkar."

A disquieting thought crossed Julien's mind again, but he stretched out on the stone bench and tried to relax. "I went to a thermal bath last month in Termini. The waters were very soothing and the massage excellent."

Rom nodded and continued to sponge down Julien's body. He produced a bar of scented soap and started to work up a lather, kneading it into his skin. Julien jerked to his elbows in alarm as Rom's hands moved towards his groin. "Don't. I can do that part myself."

Rom paused and looked at him impassively, then handed him the soap and stepped back. "Whatever you wish, sir."

Julien found he was just as embarrassed to touch himself with Rom watching as he was at the idea of Rom handling him. He thought for a moment of asking him to turn away or even to leave, then decided he was making a fool of himself. "I'm sorry, I'm terribly ticklish. Very well, go ahead." He shut his eyes and clenched his jaw until Rom finished and started to rinse him.

"We don't have baths like this in England."

Rom merely nodded.

Julien thought of Rom's entrance and regretted his lack of poise. He was afraid his rudeness must have been insulting. "I'm sorry I laughed when you walked in with Ishkar. Poor chap . . ." He stopped short, remembering that Rom was a eunuch too.

"You don't need to apologize. It's happened before."

"Yes, but you see . . . in England— What I mean is I've never seen—"

"It's perfectly understandable. We're used to it here. The palace eunuchs are sensitive about that sort of thing, but we can't afford to be."

"I see," Julien said gratefully. "You're an educated man, aren't you?"

"In certain areas. But I've had more occasion to contemplate my state and other persons' reactions to it. You reacted normally."

"I felt I was rude. Thank you for not thinking so."

Rom was silent a moment.

"Then you did think I was rude. Please speak frankly to me."

"Your feelings are confused and you're not certain why." Rom smiled.

Julien admitted this was so. "I think I was more revolted by Ishkar, although I felt sorry for him too."

"Men don't often know what they feel about us, but somewhere there's a secret knowledge which all men carry. Our pagan fathers made many of their gods eunuchs, but they continued to be gods. You might even say it was necessary in order for them to be gods, just as it was necessary for the priests to sacrifice their manhood before they could officiate."

"I see what you mean, the priests of Cybele, the Dionysian rites."

"Yes, those come to mind first. But think of the number of castrated gods there were. Attis and Osiris, Bacchus and Dionysus, Uranus, Cronus, and Saturn, all with their cults of castrated priests."

"You're exceptionally knowledgeable."

"I'm not an intellectual, but I'm not a fool either. These are facts that are known to the dullest eunuchs. Some of us find consolation in them. I was telling you that the castrated priests became a matter of concern to the heads of state. It became outlawed in Egypt and circumcision was offered as a symbolic substitution."

"I'm relieved to find that you can speak about it so freely as well as so eloquently. But I can see that you had the cut when you were already a man—you have the dignity of a full prick. I felt so sorry for Ishkar."

"Don't. And don't feel sorry for me either. It's actually much easier on the eunuchs who have it done while they're still children. I had already known women before they cut mine off."

Julien felt embarrassed again and was silent.

"I don't mind answering your questions, although many of us do. And so many of us lie. I've spoken to northerners before, and the first question they usually want answered is whether we can fuck. I was grateful that you were more original."

"But I thought it, of course. The minute I saw you, or even when I saw the first eunuchs in Salerno, I wondered it. That's only natural, isn't it?"

"It must be. Very well, I'll answer the question for you. Those with mature pricks like mine can get hard, but fucking is a miserable experience. The eunuchs with immature pricks can satisfy a woman in other ways, and many of them are very skillful. Some of us lose the urge and even the capacity after a few years, but there are those of us who function for a long time."

"But all the eunuchs that guard the harem. If they are still capable of some things, why are they used?"

"Speak to any eunuch of the harem and he will deny any capacity for sex, but the wise man will choose only clean sweeps, and ugly ones at that, to guard his women."

Julien grew thoughtful. "If you knew women before you were cut, you must miss making love."

"No, no. I said it was miserable. For those of us in whom the urge persists, it can be horrible. To experience joy truly, there must be a release from joy. There is no hope of that for us. All the eunuchs I've known in the service of women are irritable and often sickly. And if they are owned by a cruel woman. . . . Let me tell you, I had a friend, also from Dongola, who was sold to service a woman. She used to get frantic, driving him further and further and getting into such a frenzy that she used to tear his flesh with her nails and bite whole chunks of flesh out of his chest before she was satisfied. But she never thought of what it was like for him, pushing himself on and on with no hope of release. He killed himself, as you can guess."

Rom was now pouring a perfumed oil on Julien's body and smoothing it into his skin. "That's a strong scent. I don't think I like it." He suddenly felt a fresh repugnance to the smells of the bathhouse, to Rom's touch, and to everything he'd listened to.

"I'll wash it off later and there will be only the slightest hint of it, but it's good for toning your muscles." The action of his hands was vigorous but occasionally almost caressing, and Julien allowed himself for just an instant to relax and respond to their sensuality. He caught himself and tensed again, then directed Rom into more neutral conversation. "Have you worked here long?"

"A few years. It's considered a choice place to work. In another few years I should have enough saved to buy my freedom and go back to Africa and marry."

"You'll marry? But you said it was unpleasant."

Rom shrugged. "As a free man I should have a wife. I might even afford two or three."

"But you're a Christian."

"What difference does it make if they're not bearing my children? In my country a man has as many wives as he wishes or can afford in spite of the Church. With so many eunuchs there is no lack of women, and you can't expect their fathers to care for them all their lives."

"And Ishkar. Will he buy his freedom too?"

"It's more likely someone like Aziz will fall in love with him and pay my master a huge price for him. Assyrians and Persians are very popular with the Arabs. The Greeks, on the other hand, tend to like other Greeks or blonds."

"Oh." Julien was openly demonstrating his embarrassment. "Then Aziz— But he has twenty-six children."

Rom looked at him curiously. "Well, you can see he enjoys making love, then, can't you? How could he not like Ishkar? Ishkar is very beautiful."

"I don't see things that way." Julien was clearly uncomfortable.

"Clients don't come to me for the same service Ishkar gives, if that's what you're thinking. I don't attract boy-lovers the same way. Look at my body." He flexed a bicep and sucked his middle in sharply. "I have to be religious in my calisthenics or I would go soft like the others."

"I didn't think so," said Julien, sighing his relief.

Rom's tongue moistened his lips slowly. Then he smiled and lifted one of Julien's hands. He folded down the thumb and little finger, clasped the three center fingers together and placed them in his mouth.

Julien pulled back from the pressure of the man's lips as if he'd been burned. "No. Don't!"

"As you wish. I'll leave you now so you can rest."

"No, get me my clothes. I'm leaving. Tell Aziz I went back to the palace."

Rom bowed very low, went for Julien's clothes and bowed very low again. There was nothing left to say.

When Julien arrived at the palace, he practically raced to his room, trying to avoid the eunuchs he passed in the corridors. He stretched out on his bed, but sleep was crowded out by the troubling images that clung to him. He couldn't recall a more bewildering day. It wasn't until he fastened on the recollection that Aziz had been kinder to him than any man he'd met since his tutor Ralf that he was at last able to fall asleep.

He awakened an hour later sweaty and trembling, his sleep shattered by the vision of an enormous black man who grew larger and larger and leaned over him, his thick lips warm and wet as they opened and then closed over his head to suffocate him. He continued to lie in bed for another hour, waiting for his brain to lose its numbness so he could sort things out further. He heard a knock at the door and rose to answer it, realizing it was dark now and he had slept through the evening meal.

There was a eunuch from Roger's household at the door, a smooth Greek with an impassive face. "His Grace wishes to see you at once." He glanced at Julien coolly. "If you'd like a moment to wash your face and smooth your hair, I'll wait."

Julien dipped into the basin on his linen chest while the eunuch picked up a towel and held it for him. "I thought the reception rooms were closed at this hour."

"They are. Duke Roger will receive you in his apartment. His study is just off the Pisan tower."

Minutes later Julien was ushered into what was surely the most beautiful room he had ever seen. It was not a great deal larger than his own room, except that the ceilings were loftier and beautifully curved into arches. In the center stood a round table of multicolored petrified woods that glistened like jewels. The walls were tiled in exquisite mosaics that followed the curved walls and niches. Griffins and lions were carved in medallions at the ceiling, while swans and herons curved their necks on the side walls. It was the main wall directly ahead that fascinated Julien the most with its fanciful arrangement of citrus trees and palms separating leopards and peacocks, while in the panel above them centaurs arched their bows. Ornamental friezes of rosettes and straying garlands wove their way everywhere, and yet the overall effect was one of simplicity.

Julien stood studying the enchanting designs when he felt a small hand like a child's slip into his. He started, then leaped back in consternation when he saw a white gibbon offering its friendship. Glistening hair swept from its long arms in threads of pale gold frosted with white, and while he found the small ape charming, he was still alarmed by it.

"Oh, did Otto find you first?"

Roger strode in dressed informally in a simple, low-cut robe of pale turquoise trimmed with a narrow band of gold embroidery. On his shoulder he carried a brilliant green parrot that preened and flurried its wings when it saw Julien. "He's well behaved, but if he disturbs you I'll send him away."

"Not at all. He was certainly friendly to me."

"My pets seem to like you. This is Pepin, my jungle parrot," he said, stroking its neck. "If you wish you can feed him some pistachios later, but we really mustn't put off our talk any longer. It's entirely my fault we haven't had it sooner, but I was told you lost no time in occupying yourself as soon as you arrived. You're studying Arabic." He indicated a seat with a wave of his hand and sat too.

Julien adopted a more formal tone than he had since their first meeting. "Yes, Your Grace. Should I have requested your permission first?"

"There was no conflict with your other duties since I hadn't yet given you any. No, I'm pleased. I want you to become a Sicilian, and it's a good first step." He paused and looked at Julien intently. "You're finding some of the customs here very strange, aren't you?"

"I was at Durham Abbey only seven months ago, sir. There couldn't be a stronger contrast. Excuse me, but did you ask me that because you've spoken with Aziz?"

"Yes, I have. He's a valuable friend, Julien, and an entirely respectable man, honored no less by me than by my court."

"I honor him too, Roger. I will apologize to him tomorrow for leaving him at the baths that way. I was confused, I'm afraid, and behaved childishly."

"You upset him a great deal. He had no intention of leading you into a situation you found distasteful."

"I certainly didn't mean to offend him. Actually, I realized later that I could just have had a massage and that would have been the end of it if I hadn't asked so many impertinent questions. Aziz is my friend."

"Good. He also tells me you've met Claire."

Julien winced as if stung. "Yes, I find her most attractive."

"Granted, but she's not for you. Claire must have a husband much older than herself with a good deal more experience of women than you have, or she will lead a miserable life and make her husband even more so."

"But why? I beg your pardon, I didn't mean to sound contradictory."

"Then don't. You don't know enough of woman's place yet, Julien. Paradise was lost to man because he let his wife lead him. Believe me, I'm very fond of Claire, but she could become another Eve if she isn't ruled by a strong man. When it's time for you to marry, I promise I'll help you find a suitable woman."

"I'm not thinking of marriage yet."

"That's very intelligent of you, but perhaps it's time you had a woman. Aziz and I discussed it, and he tells me he's delighted by your powers of concentration, but that occasionally he feels your sense of purpose would be increased if there were less sexual pressure on you. I understand you're celibate."

The blood blazed to Julien's cheeks. "What's wrong with celibacy?"

"Nothing . . . for those who choose it."

"I admit I think about women a good deal. Probably too much. I find it hard to tame my flesh."

"It's much healthier to have a woman tame it for you. You'll see what a difference it makes. I'd like to make you a gift."

"A woman?"

"Well, I'm certainly not going to part with my gibbon. Of course a woman."

"No. Thank you, no. I prefer to find my own."

"And you will, too. But when you do it will be much to your advantage to be experienced. The idea of two virgins in bed is appalling. Disgusting."

"I didn't mean a bride—a woman to make love to."

"Don't exasperate me. I'm sending you a woman who will teach you. Before you can be a predator, you should know what it is to be the prey. If you'd grown up in Sicily, I wouldn't have to talk to you this way."

Julien looked at him in amazement. "I don't want to be the prey."

"Be quiet, you puppy. There's an incredible Circassian who's been here only a few months. When my chief eunuch found her in the market at Crete, he came to me raving about her. When he examined her to check her virginity, he said he could hardly get his finger inside. How does that sound to you, eh? I found her positively delightful, and since then she's been trained by the eunuchs of my harem to give pleasure as an art. Her name is Ula, and I give her to you with the ducal seal of approval."

Julien hung his head and was silent.

"What? You ungrateful wretch. Do you have the effrontery to refuse my gift? You'd best learn now that's not possible. Go and take her. I promise you, tomorrow you'll seek me out to kiss my hand in gratitude. Go, but be sure to come to me tomorrow evening at the same hour."

"Thank you, Roger. I'm not ungrateful for your attention. May I have one question answered please before I go?"

"Very well."

"About my work. Can you tell me . . ."

Roger flung his arm towards the door impatiently, disturbing the parrot who squawked complainingly. "Tomorrow."

When Julien returned to his apartment, there were candles lighted in every corner . . . and a woman stretched out on the cushions who he thought for a moment was Claire. She rose when he came in and he saw that she was about the same size as Claire and had the same dark hair and fair skin, but this woman was more voluptuous; no older than Claire but far more a woman. Her hair hung in velvety ropes well below her hips in the back, and she wore a sheer robe of the palest pink silk fastened at the waist with a girdle embroidered with white- and salmon-colored coral. Her eyes carried only a sharp outline of kohl, and he couldn't be sure whether the faint blush of color at her lips and cheeks had been painted there.

Julien had never seen as much jewelry on one person. A chain was fitted around her brow from which were suspended silver talismans alternated with turquoise and coral. One of her necklaces was made of amber beads as large as quail eggs. There were also earrings, hairpins, ankle and wrist bracelets and a dozen rings. Attached to many of these were twists of wadded cotton saturated with the aphrodisiac scents of amber, musk, and sandalwood.

She approached him unselfconsciously and fastened her mouth on his.

Julien moved back, saying, "You don't have to do this, you know." But his pulse was racing, and he didn't pull away for a long time.

She shook her head when she was freed, to indicate she didn't understand his Latin. He addressed her next in Greek, in Sicilian, with phrases of Arabic and then a few Germanic words that he had learned from a monk at Durham, but she continued to shake her head.

"I don't know a single word of Circassian. Does this mean I won't be able to speak with you?" he said woefully as she struggled to raise his shirt over his head. She smiled when he was undressed and pressed her warmness to him. "Don't you speak anything besides Circassian?" he moaned.

She unfastened her girdle and urged him towards the bedroom. Julien followed her meekly, then lay on the mattress, his leg crossed to conceal himself, and half shut his eyes as she slipped out of her robe.

"The candles," he said. "Don't you want to put out the candles?" He gestured towards the three candles sputtering on a chest and started to rise to extinguish them, but stopped when he saw her advancing slowly towards him, cupping her breasts as an offering. He sank back as she knelt down beside him. Her hands reached out to stroke his face just as his groped clumsily towards her breasts, and he surrendered to her with a guttural cry.

Chapter X
DECLARATIONS

Aziz shook Julien's shoulder firmly to rouse him. "My friend, it's so unlike you to fall asleep in the middle of your studies."

Julien raised his head from the desk and stared at Aziz blankly. He was hollow-eyed and his skin was as lusterless as travertine. "Was I asleep?"

"You were, indeed. Are you bored yet with taking advice from a more experienced if not a wiser man?"

Julien shrugged. "This was a very difficult text."

"Yes, I know. May I speak frankly to you, Julien? For the first week or so after Ula came to you, you had a spring to your step and your eyes were clear. There were the obvious benefits of a well-regulated sex life, and I was happy for you. But now, either you're unwell or you're overdoing it. Which is it?"

Julien continued to stare at his friend dully for a moment before he answered. "It's not my fault. She keeps insisting. Every night she thinks up new ways. I suppose she's trying to please me."

"But aren't you able to indicate to her when you're satisfied?"

"I guess not. I don't think she's very happy with me. What's worse, she sometimes behaves as if she's sure I hate her, and I don't. If only I could make conversation with her. It's maddening not to be understood. I've tried to teach her some simple Latin and Sicilian, but she won't learn. She resents it. I'm much more frustrated now than I was before I had a woman."

Aziz raised his head as if sniffing the air which was his way of indicating that a new thought had occurred to him. "You know so little of women, Julien, and practically nothing of harem women. Don't think me rude for asking, but what sort of presents have you given her?"

"Presents? I haven't given her anything. Why? She seems to have tremendous quantities of jewelry, and she's always beautifully dressed. I thought I'd wait till the Epiphany and then give her a fine gift. The holidays are only a short time away."

"Oh Julien, Julien. Sometimes I worry lest you think my interest in you is too personal, but someone must teach you what's expected of you. Have you any idea what women in the harem do all day?"

"The usual things, I suppose."

Aziz's smile was only slightly scornful. "They have nothing whatever to do except wait for their master's call. Servants do all the rest. The married women spend some time whipping up new desserts to tempt their husbands with, or trying some new recipe they hear is a guaranteed aphrodisiac. But the rest of the time, they're all idle, free to visit each other, to gossip, and to show off their finery."

"But who would Ula gossip with? She can't speak anything but Circassian."

"All right. Assuming there are no other Circassians in the harem, although I'm sure there must be, she still sees other women. What do you think they do when they visit each other?"

"How would I know? It sounds to me like they would have absolutely nothing to talk about."

"By the standards of a man's world, that is so. But she needs to display her status. Remember, she was a concubine of Duke Roger. After Roger passed her on to an Englishman, whom none of her friends have ever seen or known anything about, certain questions must surely come up. Did Roger reject her? Is she now in disgrace? Is she being punished by being handed down to the first penniless rascal Roger could think of? Imagine how she must feel when she returns from your bed in the morning without a token to show her friends, so they'll know she has a man of substance and that she pleases him."

"Oh, now I *am* embarrassed. I'll buy her something at once."

"You must buy her lots of gifts. Women like it, and Sicilians are used to it. She's been draining your body because she feels she hasn't pleased you yet. Start by giving her a small piece of jewelry, and then a couple of days later a pretty veil, then perhaps some perfume. You'll find that she'll soon be convinced she's pleasing you and will stop pressing herself on you when you appear to be satisfied. Great Allah, I'm sure it has been a terrible strain on both of you."

"I'll go shopping today. But I know so little about women's things. My taste doesn't run to perfumes and jewels."

"Leave it to me. I'll have some suitable things selected for her."

"I'm truly grateful, Aziz. It just never occurred to me."

"She'll also need spending money. Among other things, it's customary to tip the guard who brings her to you."

"I've already tipped him."

"But she must too. It's very important. If you had three women, for example, they would all be bribing the guard outrageously to make sure he'd be inclined in their favor. It's not uncommon, you know, to have a guard bring a woman other than the one asked for and then claim the woman requested was ill."

"St. David's leeks, what a system!"

"It has its critics, but it works."

Julien rose from his desk to splash water on his face, then returned to his studies.

If Roger had noticed how tired Julien appeared lately, he had made no mention of it. Julien was summoned every day now to Roger's council chamber, to listen to the day's business and take notes. It took only a few hours from his afternoons and evenings and left the mornings free for his Arabic lessons. These were progressing to Aziz's satisfaction, but Julien had expected to go faster. He was now able to make conversation without much faltering, and the Muslims he attempted to converse with were delighted by his efforts. He discovered too that Aziz's sponsorship did a great deal to enhance his acceptance at court.

All in all, Julien felt his life was a promising one, and his disappointment of less than a year ago now seemed ill-founded.

Ula was far from what he envisioned when he first dreamed of having a lover, but he had to acknowledge her beauty and her skill, and if she seemed unconcerned with any way to be agreeable to him outside their bed he would have to accept that. Wouldn't Robert think him foolish not to just enjoy the situation! But the instant he entered the studio later that afternoon he saw this fragile peace of mind shattered. Claire was with Aziz, standing by his desk and examining a pile of silks and glittering objects. She turned an expressionless face towards him while he struggled far less successfully to maintain his composure. If Aziz noticed Julien's discomfiture, he paid it no mind.

"Julien, you must thank Claire for doing such a fine job of shopping for you. She spent only half the money I gave her and brought back enough treasures to turn the head of a sultan's favorite."

Julien avoided her eyes while he stammered his thanks.

"Come take a look," Aziz continued. "These scarves are beautifully embroidered with silver. She bought twelve of them, all in different colors. Now, be sure not to give them to Ula all at once, or you'll spoil her. One a day at the most. As a matter of fact, you must be sure to skip a day occasionally, or she'll be too upset if the presents stop."

"Aziz, how could you! Claire is the last person I would have—"

"But you told me how much Ula resembles Claire; you said they had the same size and coloring. It's always a simple matter for a woman to choose things that suit herself. And you must admit no one has taste as fine as Claire's. Haven't you seen how lovely she always looks?" If Aziz was mocking him with his last question, his voice gave no sign of it.

"Yes, I've seen," Julien answered, his bitterness undisguised.

"If there's something here you don't like, tell me now," Claire said brusquely. "I can exchange it."

"I'm sure everything is perfect," Julien said quietly.

Aziz was determinedly cheerful. "Claire, why don't you try this shawl on and show Julien how splendid it is?"

Claire demurred briefly, then slipped it over her shoulders. "Yes, it is beautiful, isn't it?"

Julien dared to look into her eyes and felt his blood flowing warm again. "I want you to have it. Please take it."

"I wouldn't dream of it. I bought it for your lady love."

"She's not my lady love." Julien blushed. "I want you to have it."

"Call her anything you wish, then. It was bought for her, and I don't wear gifts bought as a reward for the favors she does you."

"Come, Claire," Aziz interposed. "Don't be difficult. Take the scarf. Julien wants you to know he's grateful for the kindness you showed in shopping for him."

"What do you mean, for him? I did it for you. I wouldn't raise my little finger for that . . . that lecher." Julien's color changed abruptly from smoldering red to ashen gray, and he felt speech was impossible to him.

"Claire," Aziz chided. "It's neither seemly nor becoming for you to speak that way. It isn't your place to have an opinion of men's habits. You wouldn't dream of criticizing me, would you?"

"That's different. You're a Sicilian. He has no business taking up certain of our customs before he's even settled here. You can tell he has a very corrupt nature. I suspected it the minute I saw him."

"That's still no concern of yours. Or are you trying to make it so?"

"Aziz, I respect you as if you were my father, but you men always take each other's sides."

"Save your respect for the man unfortunate enough to take you as wife."

Julien suddenly found his tongue. "Claire. Your respect means more to me than that of any woman I have known."

Claire looked at him wonderingly, and now it was her turn to blush and avoid his eyes.

Aziz faced him sternly. "This is no time for such a declaration. I think you're both behaving like children."

Claire had tilted her hear curiously. "Do you really mean what you just said? My respect means that much to you?"

"More than you could dream."

Aziz broke in almost angrily. "Julien, you've gone much too far. If there is anything else you wish to say on this subject, I can tell you whom you must speak to. This is all my fault. What a fool I was not to have seen it sooner, in both of you."

"What do you mean?" Claire said, but she asked it almost as if she were questioning herself.

"We've all said enough. Thank you for your help, Claire. I see now I was wrong to have asked this favor of you, but it's too late now. You'd best go back to your mother's apartment at once.

"No, please stay." Julien implored. "I need so much to talk to you."

Claire seemed oddly perturbed. "No, Aziz is right. I must go."

"Then, when can I see you again? Please, I must."

"Goodbye, Julien. I hope she likes the presents." Her voice carried no hint of sarcasm.

"I don't care anything about her, Claire. She was a gift to me."

"A gift!" Her voice resumed its earlier scorn. "Goodbye, then."

Julien turned to his tutor passionately as soon as she left them. "Aziz, I must talk to you."

Aziz sighed. "Is it possible you don't know how far you've overstepped yourself? Surely there were bounds of decorum to guide a young man in his behavior towards a maiden in England."

"I don't care. I love her."

"Roger would never agree to the match. And take my word for it, my boy, you would certainly regret such a marriage. You simply aren't old enough for her."

"I'll have no other wife. I'll never marry, then. Never!"

"Fine. That's the first sensible thing you've said today. Why don't you make yourself as comfortable as possible with the relationship you already enjoy? There's nothing wrong with Ula."

"Nothing wrong with her? When I can't even speak to her? Everytime I try to say something to her, she just grabs my prick to see if it's hard enough to use yet."

"Consider yourself fortunate. If you ever had to listen to what most Muslim wives call conversation, you'd know you're among the blessed."

Julien's exasperation was increasing. "I just don't understand. I'm ready to accept practically everything else about this crazy country. In some ways it's more wonderful than any society I could dream of, and yet, with women it's made so difficult. It's all wrong, Aziz."

"If you're part of the society, then you must accept it. The hand cannot rebel against the arm."

"Accept?" Julien's eyes were flashing now. "Look, I accept the fact that you can leave your women and go running to sleep with your boy any time you have a free afternoon. I've even gotten used to all those freaks without balls running around the palace and those pages with made-up faces, but why can't we have more normal relationships with women? It's you Muslims. You've turned everyone here—Normans, Greeks, everyone—into one race, the Sicilians, where women don't exist except for the pleasure of men. It's unnatural."

"You think the Christians here are any better? Or any closer to your nice English ways? Perhaps you admire the new French chivalric idea of love? To adore a woman but never dream of sleeping with her? Is that more realistic? More natural?"

"I don't care. I just want to be me," he groaned. "Oh, Aziz, I don't mean to hurt your feelings. I know you're very good to your wife and that she's as happy as any woman I've known. It's just that we Christians see women differently."

"Of course you do. Listen, have you ever heard the expression, 'You shall know a people by their gods'? Well, take a good look at the patron saints of Palermo. Do you remember when I took you to the crossroads that mark the center of the city?"

"Yes, *i quattro cantoni*. The four corners."

"Very well. And at each corner you Christians have a statue, a graven image in defiance of the sensibilities of the Muslims who live in all the buildings surrounding them and abhor statues. I have good reason for bringing them up. May I go on?"

Julien hunched his shoulders and nodded.

"The histories I am going to relate to you may not be as well known to an Englishman as those of your northern saints, but you can verify them by going to any hagiology.

"In one corner we have Saint Nympha. Of the four she is the least interesting to me, but she was a native Palermitan and might be expected to look after the interests of her city. She fled to Italy in the 4th century and was put to death at Porto after some relatively uninteresting torture. Fairly boring, no?

"But at the next corner we have Saint Christina. She came from a pagan Roman family, and when she broke up her family's golden images and sold them to help the poor, her father beat her and cast her into a lake with a stone tied around her head. She managed to escape but was caught and brought before a magistrate who felt she should be severely reprimanded for going against her father's wishes. First her tongue was cut out. Then she had to overcome a test of serpents, which she withstood, presumably with the help of her god, although it strikes me he was notably slow in getting around to helping her at all. She then spent the next five days in a burning furnace from which she emerged unharmed. The magistrate, who was by now understandably exasperated, finally did her in by having her shot through with arrows. Her principal relics are here at Palermo, where the faithful may meditate on her virtues as they gaze on them."

"I've seen them." Julien fought to conceal his amusement.

"Next we have Saint Agatha, whose birthplace is so hotly disputed by both Palermo and Catania that blood has been shed in the argument more than once. She came from a rich and illustrious family and decided early in life that no man should ever have her. Self-made eunuchs can be females too, you see. She was able to withstand countless assaults on her purity, but eventually she attracted the lustful attentions of the consul Quintian, who was angered by her steadfast refusals. He had her abducted and handed over to a local brothel run by a woman named Aphrodisia . . ."

"Oh you *must* be making this part up," Julien protested. "Aphrodisia indeed!"

"I am not making this up; again it's all in your Church records . . . Aphrodisia and her six wanton daughters," Aziz insisted. "Despite all the wicked stratagems of these seven practiced whores, Agatha retained her virtue. Quintian, now thoroughly irritated, had her beaten and taken to prison. There she was stretched on the rack and her sides were torn with iron hooks while she was burned with blazing torches. She apparently suffered all this quite cheerfully, which further enraged Quintian, so he ordered them to crush her breasts and cut them off. This unhappy event is still commemorated on her feast day, when all the nuns in Sicily are kept busy baking cup-shaped cakes topped off with cherries. You know that women who suffer afflictions in their breasts pray to Agatha for relief."

Julien grinned. He remembered the cakes well and had been told of the association with Agatha's breasts but never gave it further thought.

"Well, Agatha persisted in living after this last grim desecration, so she was remanded to prison and kept without food or medical care for an astonishingly long time. Eventually Quintian succeeded in dispatching her only through the resourceful expedient of rolling her naked over live coals mixed with potsherds."

Cracking at Aziz's stonefaced delivery, Julien yielded to a paroxysm of laughter. Aziz raised a hand and paused a moment until Julien regained control. "The last of our Sicilian goddesses is Saint Oliva, and her unfortunate circumstances are blamed on the Muslims. It may seem odd to you, but she is greatly venerated by the Muslims of Tunis who are convinced that anyone who speaks ill of her is certain to be visited with calamity.

"Anyway, Oliva was a beautiful Christian maiden of thirteen when the Saracens arrived in Palermo. They kidnapped her and carried her off to Tunis, where because of her distinctive lineage, she was permitted to live in a cave as a recluse. Word got around that she was effecting miraculous cures, and then later that she was also effecting conversions to Christianity along with the cures, which of course wouldn't do. She was shut up in a dungeon without light or food; they don't tell us for how long, except that her jailers became understandably impatient with her persistence at survival. She was next scourged until her flesh was cut to the bone, then extended on the rack and torn with the iron comb. I presume I needn't describe that instrument.

Her virtue was still undaunted so they stretched her on the rack again and tried to set fire to her with torches. It is said the torchbearers were all converted on the spot when the torches fell miraculously from their hands, but in any case the stubborn virgin continued to live until her now thoroughly dismayed persecutors had her beheaded.

"Now, do these stories tell you anything about the Christians of Palermo? These are the saints who are invoked daily in the prayers of the faithful and their martyrdoms recounted over and over to the children of the city. Don't you find the local taste in saints a little bizarre? We Muslims can be as cruel as any men in war, and perhaps even in our daily life, but we don't confuse cruelty with our religion.

"Our women are sheltered, yes, and denied many freedoms that Christian women enjoy, but they are protected too. I'm going to see my wife now. Think, if you will, about the women of Sicily, but make no mistakes about a good Muslim's responsibilities to them."

Julien wiped his eyes. "You've made your point."

Julien was grateful to be left alone. Aziz meant well, he knew, and he valued his friend's perspectives, but there were still some things he was sure he could never adjust to. If he had met Claire in England, where his position was not as secure as the one he enjoyed now in Roger's court, there was no reason to believe his suit would not be heard with greater favor. Here, it seemed Claire's future was to be decided by whim, and his bid for a place in it not even to be heard.

He was roused from his brooding by a page announcing that he was to report to Roger's private chamber at once. The urgency in the page's voice alerted him that Roger did not expect to be kept waiting.

Julien was surprised to find Roger alone, pacing the chamber with Pepin the parrot balanced precariously on his shoulder. "Sit, Julien. I have an important letter for you to write."

Julien sensed from Roger's intentness that some extraordinary affair of state had come up. He assembled some writing materials on the desk and waited for Roger to dictate.

"No, I want you to compose it, then bring it to me for my signature. The subject is one demanding secrecy. No, by God, I can't do this by letter. Is Robert still in Salerno?"

"As far as I know, sir."

"Are you free to travel? Nothing urgent pending?"

"I can leave whenever you say. Is the message for Robert?"

"No. Robert is to deliver it. As a matter of fact, you both will. I must send Robert because anyone with a rank below subchancellor wouldn't do, but no one is more familiar with the argument of my cause than you are."

"Then, if I understand you correctly, sir, this must relate to the matter discussed at your private meeting with the curia last Friday. Your uncle Henry's plan?"

"Exactly. I want you and Robert to go to Pope Honorius to arrange for His Holiness to meet with me in Benevento no later than three months from now. The pope isn't getting any younger, and I can no longer ignore the reports of his failing health. We must act at once if I'm to be made king by him."

"How much of your proposal are we permitted to disclose to him to get him to meet with you?"

"All of it. The man's no fool. I could have gotten him to give me the crown when he acknowledged my dukedom if he hadn't been so afraid of the emperor. He knows well that without my strong hand in the south there's no chance of peace. It's urgent that we act now. If Honorius were to die, there's no telling how long our suit might take with a new pope."

"I can leave tomorrow if you wish, and join Robert by Christmas. We'll be in Rome as early as weather and fate permit."

"Tell Robert to take plenty of money. It's the one thing they understand in Rome. No expense must be spared to have my case heard. And won. Tomorrow is not too soon for you to leave. I still have a lot to go over with you, so we'll spend the morning together while I give you a short review of Vatican politics. You'll carry with you the names of all the cardinals we believe we may rely on for support, the names of those we know we can buy, and those who are our enemies."

"I'll try to commit them to memory. It may not be wise to have such information in writing."

"If you believe you can memorize them in such a short time, so much the better. I'm pleased to see you're learning your lessons in politics well. No one here is to know of your mission, not even Aziz. Is there anyone you particularly wish to take leave of?"

"Yes sir, there is." Julien's face brightened.

"Of course, the Circassian. Well, that's no problem. Spend the night with her as usual, and before you leave we can always have her brought to you for an hour."

"No sir, it isn't Ula I was thinking of. It's someone I have no claim on, and I don't even know how she feels about me. May I take leave of Claire?"

"Claire!" Roger stretched to his full height and glowered down at Julien a moment before he spoke. "Out of the question. I plan to marry Claire to a natural son of my cousin Bohemund, the Prince of Antioch."

Julien hung his head. "I had no idea. When was it arranged?"

"I haven't done anything about it yet. She's still young, and I've been too busy. Are you really serious about her?"

"I can't imagine being happy without her."

"Nonsense. Those are feelings which should be mistrusted unless they come after years of marriage. No, Claire is not for you. She's a ward of the state since her father died, and her marriage has to be arranged as judiciously as possible for maximum benefit to the state."

Julien remained silent.

"What's wrong with Ula? I'm told you've been humping like demons. You've had her no more than three weeks and you're already acting like a sick calf about another woman. Would you like someone else? I can't imagine a better lay than Ula, but when you return I'll give you your pick of a dozen of the most beautiful slaves in Sicily."

"No, Roger. It wasn't my intention to fall in love with Claire, but the fact is I have, and I don't want another woman. I find I love her beyond all comprehension."

Roger stormed at these last words. "One more silly phrase like that and I'm going to send all those drooling troubadours at court packing back to Provence. I've never heard such nonsense. It's gotten so every young man has to believe he's in love before his nose is even dry."

"Forgive me, Roger, and please don't blame the troubadours. I never listen to those silly songs. I just find I can't get Claire out of my mind. It's beginning to affect all I do."

"In that case, it's just as well you're leaving. I'm sure you'll see things differently after you've been away a few months. Why, you're not even twenty yet."

"It may be more than a few months. Can't I have your permission to say goodbye to her? Even for just a few minutes."

"What madness! Do you want to compromise her?" Roger sighed in resignation. "Very well, Julien, but her mother will have to be present, or I absolutely forbid it. I'll arrange it for just before you leave, but remember, you are seeing her to say goodbye—and *just* that!"

Julien jumped to his feet and kissed Roger's hand. "My king."

"See to it that you're here directly after matins. Good night, my boy."

Julien startled a procession of eunuchs in the corridor by leaping and kicking his heels in joy on his way back to his chamber. It had been an incredibly full day, but even with its trials and setbacks he had reason to feel jubilant. Rome and a weighty commission from Roger were ahead of him, and even if he had been given no hope in his suit for Claire's hand, he felt too sanguine to believe she could be denied to him for long. For one thing, he had noticed the softening of her expression when she left him, and through the myopic eye of memory, it was already magnified into a look that held promise.

The gifts for Ula were piled on one of his chests and he selected a pair of red quartz earrings, a bottle of mimosa perfume, some embroidered ribbons, and a near-transparent veil. They seemed adequate for tonight's gift. He decided he would arrange to have the other things brought to her after he left, and then he expected he would be able to find something pretty in Rome to bring her for his return gift, perhaps even for his parting gift if his meeting tomorrow with Claire advanced any hope. He had no sooner put the rest of the gifts in the chest when Ula was ushered into the room by a eunuch who waited until a nod from Julien dismissed him.

Ula spotted the gifts he had laid aside for her almost before she had greeted him, and her eyes brimmed with pleasure. She took Julien's hand and covered it with kisses, then skipped to the chest to try on her gifts. Julien thought the earrings were certainly not as fine as many she owned, but she acted as if they were great treasures. When he complimented her on how well they looked, she understood him readily and seemed pleased. Another compliment and she started to lead him to the bed.

"Oh no," Julien told her. "I must rest tonight. I have important business tomorrow." This message was lost on her, so he sighed in exasperation and returned to sign language to try to communicate his wishes. She nodded at last but insisted on helping him undress, then blew out the candles and lay on the floor at the side of his bed.

"Do you mean to spend the night there?" he asked, irritated at the thought of rising and lighting the candles so he could indicate to her that she'd be more comfortable on the divan. He considered sending for a eunuch to have her escorted back to the harem but remembered it might be considered a serious insult to do so, and he had no intention of hurting her feelings.

While he was still debating his course of action, he became aware of the onset of his customary nocturnal erection and was glad the candles were extinguished. He shut his eyes more tightly, but in a moment he felt her hand on him and knew that his noble intentions were doomed.

"What a beast I am," he said aloud and pulled her into the bed.

Chapter XI
PIERLEONI

The treacherous rains of February had all but swamped the Via Appia just north of Velletri, and now Robert and Julien found themselves unable to go any further. They were less than twenty miles from Rome, but the ancient paving stones were invisible under a foot of mud that lay like jelly and sucked at the horses' hooves.

Robert's customarily easygoing nature had not been in evidence for weeks, and now Julien, too, found himself sulking more than he liked. Two days earlier Robert had told him testily that he was bored to sobs hearing the same tiresome stories of Claire, and that if her name was brought up once more he would make Julien's mouth too painful for speech.

The journey hadn't been an easy one. Reports of Honorius' failing health reached them with increasing frequency, and yet they were committed to several stopovers for reasons of considerable importance.

The abbey of Monte Cassino was directly on their route, and it was essential that they stop there to make a bid for the abbot's support. Abbot Seniorectus was warm but tactfully reserved, and a week of Robert's most earnest persuasion resulted in little more than an assurance of the abbot's prayers for Roger's continued good health. The abbots were traditional friends of the Hautevilles, but the climate was mercurial and the abbot himself had no tenure of office. Julien thought the outcome of their visit was as positive as circumstances would allow, but Robert's patience was steeply diminished lately, and he was dejected not to be able to send a message to Roger assuring him of Seniorectus's unqualified support.

Ten days at Benevento were even more equivocal in their result. The Guiscard's conquest had not endeared the Hautevilles to the townspeople, and there was no city in the south where the spirit of the commune was stronger.

Robert and Julien were humiliated by being asked to wait a week for an audience with the heads of the communal party, and Rolpoto, the most prominent of the commune leaders, was openly hostile. It was entirely unnecessary for Robert to hint of Roger's regal intentions. The Hauteville ambitions were more certain to the Beneventans than they were to most Sicilians. Still, the city was the gateway to Roger's kingdom from Europe, and a significant outpost between the south and the Vatican.

The odor of stagnant mud was becoming increasingly unpleasant now that the rain had stopped, and Julien longed to exercise his legs and breathe cleaner air. The improvised tent he was huddled in was no more than a tarpaulin slung across the branches of bushes, but at least it was on high ground, and the water that coursed from the hills was diverted by a barrier of rocks. He preferred this to Robert's shelter, a lean-to kept by peasants for a shady resting place when they worked the nearby fields. Robert was sharing his cramped space with their two horses and a pack mule, and Julien was sure he was still cursing the weather, the mud, and every soul hapless enough to live between Salerno and Rome.

He decided he'd best tell Robert he was going for a walk should Robert miss him and become further irritated. An extraordinary hush told him something was wrong before he reached the shelter. He quickened his step, and as he clambered down the turn which brought the front of the lean-to into view, he shouted Robert's name. When there was no answer he tried to run and tumbled most of the way.

Robert was lying face downward and the horses were gone. The sturdily wrapped bundles that had been fastened on the pack mule were on the ground, and it appeared the attackers had been frightened off before they had a chance to pilfer their belongings.

At least Robert was alive. He had been clubbed on the head and stabbed in the arm, but Julien bandaged the wound after first sterilizing it with the *grappa* they kept in their medical kit for such emergencies. The *grappa* was also used by them as a lamp fuel, and Robert occasionally drank some after a heavy meal, but the idea revolted Julien.

Robert was conscious but incoherent. When he started to make sense after Julien's simple ministrations, all he could do was curse the pope for not making the entrance to Rome safer for travellers. They had been stopped once before below Monte Cassino by a trio of apparent cutthroats, but they fled the instant Robert defiantly flashed Roger's ducal seal before them.

Julien knew he would have to retrace his steps to Velletri to get help. It was only about four miles back, but when they had passed through it earlier that morning, they found no one there who understood more than a few words of any language other than Etruscan.

But did he dare leave Robert alone until he returned? He was sure the robbers would return to finish their job. He heard a sound from down the road and unsheathed his dagger, then looked out cautiously. There was a small caravan coming towards him with a cardinal in an ermine cape over his scarlet robes reclining on a litter borne by eight men, and two of his retinue were leading the stolen horses. Julien rushed out to greet them and make himself known as the owner of the stolen horses and try to get help for Robert.

"I have heard of Robert of Selby," the cardinal said. "I am Cardinal Conti of Rome, and I'd be delighted if you would join my party. Robert can ride with me in the litter, and I don't believe you'll have any more difficulty with your horses after the next mile or two. The road becomes quite good."

"How did you get the horses back?" Julien asked.

"With ease. The thieves surrendered and confessed as soon as they were stopped by my men. Then they were happy to tell me where you were in return for my absolution, so we sent them to their graves secure in the promise of Paradise. Lift him in gently, men. Don't worry about your friend, Julien; there's plenty of room for both of us. Would you like to walk alongside us until it's safe to ride?"

"Thank you. I can't tell you how happy I am you came along. We're most anxious to get to Rome. I believe Robert's all right now, but he gave me quite a turn."

"Of course. I'm surprised there aren't more people on the road, even with this foul weather. I expected half of Italy to be making this trip now that the word is out that our Spiritual Father will soon join his Maker."

"Honorius is still alive, then?"

"He was three days ago. I hope to get there in time to receive a last blessing from him, and to assist, of course, in the new election."

"Yes, I'm sure you do."

Cardinal Conti was a very young man, Julien thought, to be a cardinal. He was handsome and patrician-looking, his appearance more suited to a young military officer than to a churchman, despite a slight portliness around the middle and a sensuous floridity to his complexion. He couldn't be more affable, it seemed, as he rearranged pillows to make Robert comfortable. "And you, Julien, what do you do for Roger, or are you Robert's aide?"

Julien decided to be prudent. "I'm Robert's aide."

"Excellent. Look, the road's really quite all right through here. Why don't you ride alongside my litter for a while. I'm afraid I'm a bit of a chatterer, and I fear it would be cruel to inflict myself on Robert so soon after his unpleasant experience."

"With pleasure. When were you last in Rome, cardinal?"

"Only a week ago, and I would never have left were it not for an emergency. As you can guess, there is a good deal of campaigning to be done there at the moment. Have you ever heard of Cardinal Peter? Peter Pierleoni?"

"I think I've heard the name," Julien said calmly. Roger had spent the better part of an afternoon discussing him at their last meeting, and it was a name he wasn't likely to forget.

"Peter is my uncle," Cardinal Conti said, "and it appears to be God's will that he follow Honorius as our new pope."

"Is it that certain, then?"

"I've taken an informal poll of the cardinals I could reach. He has a clear majority, but there will be problems nonetheless. The Pierleoni family is extremely popular in Rome, as well as with the majority of cardinals in the curia, but my uncle has more than his share of enemies too. The Abbot of Cluny is certain to oppose him, and the Cistercian Bernard hates him perhaps even more."

"Is there a reason?"

"How many would you like? Peter Pierleoni was a student of that other Peter, Abelard, and you know how unremitting Bernard has been in his determination to discredit Abelard and all his friends."

"A student of Abelard's! How wonderful. I think of Abelard as my teacher too, even though I've never met him."

"I'm pleased. I had a feeling that anyone in the company of the illustrious Robert of Selby would be worthy of my confidences. Abelard isn't the only reason for Bernard's enmity, though. Among other things, they feel we're too rich. I could give you lots more reasons, but you'll no doubt hear the rest of them when you get to Rome."

"Does Abelard support Pierleoni? I would assume so."

"We can't be certain yet, since we don't know who my uncle's opposition will be. Abelard isn't likely to be attracted to the idea of a rich pope, but actually my uncle is a very simple man, and philosophically he and Abelard have a great deal in common. I don't deny he's been more than willing to spend the family money to get himself elected, but so would anyone else. That's politics. And you can't imagine how ridiculously his enemies are behaving. You know how Rome is full of antique stone lions? Well, since the stone lion, *pier leone,* is a reminder to the people of my uncle's popularity, his enemies are trying to destroy all the stone lions. Such petty nonsense, really. By the way, where will you stay in Rome? Do you have friends there?"

"I don't believe Robert's given it much thought yet."

"It's all decided, then. You'll stay with me. I'll inform Robert as soon as he comes to."

Robert raised his head groggily. "You're very kind, but don't you think we might restrict each other's activities?"

"Oh, you heard! In my palace? Don't give it a thought. You'll have the keys to Rome, and privacy too when you want it. And, I might add, you'll find the atmosphere a bit warmer and friendlier than you might elsewhere. I'm speaking of your professional role, naturally. Not everyone is as kindly disposed to the Sicilian cause as my uncle and I, and I assure you, we are."

"For purely unselfish reasons, of course."

"As unselfish as Roger's or yours, I promise you. It's settled, then?"

Julien rode ahead to allow Cardinal Conti to continue his conversation with Robert privately, which he felt they were both anxious to do. He had his own thoughts to carry him. The closer they got to Rome the more excited he became. And now to learn that Pierleoni was a former student of Abelard's! He looked forward all the more eagerly to meeting him now.

By the time they arrived at the city gates the next morning, Robert felt strong enough to walk a few steps, and they were all feeling rather merry. Conti and Robert certainly seemed to have cemented their friendship after their long talks, and Conti expressed over and over again his wish to have them learn to love Rome as he did.

When they entered the city it was through the gate of St. Sebastian, and Julien was crestfallen at his first glimpse of the city he'd dreamed of so often. They went down a broad boulevard badly in need of repair and through a park that looked utterly abandoned by man.

"This part isn't very pretty, is it?" Cardinal Conti agreed. "I live in the southeastern part of Rome; we should be arriving there fairly soon. You'll have plenty of time for sightseeing later."

Julien left the escort for a while to ride ahead so that he might better explore the area they were passing through, but the pasture was so filled with rubble he was afraid of laming his horse and returned to Conti's side for the rest of the journey.

By the time they arrived at his villa, Cardinal Conti seemed exhausted but no less anxious to make his guests welcome. He entered his home shouting orders to his staff for his friends' needs. Robert was put to bed at once, and a physician sent for to check the progress of his healing wound. The doctor reassured them that in a day or two Robert would have forgotten he'd ever been scratched. He seemed a bit puzzled when Julien spoke of sterilizing the wound with *grappa,* but nodded his gray beard anyway and left to have a drink with the cardinal.

The cardinal's palace was splendid, Julien thought, and entirely different from the luxurious buildings of Palermo. The rooms were larger, and they used color in precious marble inlays rather than in mosaic, which he found impressive.

Robert admitted he was tired and was almost relieved when Julien asked if he'd mind being alone for a while. Julien couldn't wait to sample the sights of Rome, and he felt this might be his best chance to explore the city by himself. Conti showed him how he must fasten his purse underneath his girdle to thwart the notorious purse snatchers, and sent him on his way with blessings.

Julien stopped at the gate to ask the chamberlain for directions to the Tiber and to St. Peter's and was pleased to learn that the Tiber was only a hundred yards away and that he need only follow the river upstream for a mile to reach the environs of St. Peter's.

It was warm for mid-February, he thought. At least as warm as Palermo might be, except that he'd seen no trees in blossom yet, and he knew Mount Pellegrino would be all pink icing by now.

The people and surroundings changed greatly as soon as he started to walk north along the river bank. Gone now were the handsome villas set off from each other by trees and gardens with the sharp punctuation of the campanili, the brick bell towers of Rome that thrust themselves up from the horizon. Instead, the buildings that lined the Tiber were primitively built of mud smoothed over with plaster and roofed with thatch. He saw wine sellers with their carts and wineskins, but little other commercial traffic except for what he soon recognized was a teeming traffic in women.

He found himself staring at these women, the first he'd seen in a while. Their low-cut robes were startling to him after even half a year in the south. These women were painted too, but much differently from Sicilian women. They wore no veils, of course, and there was much less silk and color in their costume, but their lips and cheeks were often dyed so red he found it garish, and the skin of their faces seemed unnaturally pale, almost deathlike to him. Hair was tinted and swept into extravagant coiffures that couldn't hide the fact that it was often quite dirty. Their glances were more open. He tried smiling at them, but their expressions remained unchanged. The men, on the other hand, appeared to be looking at him suspiciously, or at best appraisingly, except for the priests who wore the same half-inquisitive but neutral expressions as the women. While they did not appear to be as motley as the Sicilians, he noticed there was an occasional black among the passersby and no lack of northerners.

It was twilight now, and torches were being lighted outside these shabby riverbank buildings. Julien could see preparations being made for the evening's commerce. Women stood in doorways or could be seen moving about through open windows, and his curiosity brought him closer.

Although Julien was walking along the path directly in front of the doorways, the women did not call out to him or otherwise invite his attention except by occasionally striking a pose that might be thought of as seductive.

As soon as he went a few yards further, Julien realized why they weren't more enterprising. Men and ragged boys appeared from nowhere and surrounded him, demanding that he allow them to escort him to the most beautiful, the hottest, the largest breasted, the most talented, the tightest pussy, the youngest, the most versatile, the most deep-throated, the most experienced, the cheapest, the cleanest woman in Rome. His progress was slowed down and even halted a few times, and more than once while he was most distracted by their insistence, he felt a hand under his cloak searching for his purse.

As he approached the Vatican, the whorehouses became a bit more substantial looking and the whores a lot cleaner. Now he would occasionally see boys among the whores, some of them as young as eight or nine, with their cheeks painted as fiercely as the women's and with their robes hiked up above the hips from behind to expose their buttocks. He began to walk more quickly, and he developed some skill at pushing the panders away with his elbow when they got too close. He realized that when he walked briskly they no longer persisted in trying to secure him as a client, but his curiosity often bested his prudence. The whores' clients began to appear more frequently now, and he could see they were mostly from the lower classes of Romans and the poorest pilgrims.

He judged he must be getting closer to St. Peter's and crossed an ancient Roman bridge that was clogged with goats and pigs coming from the day's market. Following the busiest street, he soon found himself within view of the basilica. It was nowhere near as large as he had expected, although its grandeur was heightened by the open space of the square around it. And he'd never seen a busier place!

The avenue was lined with booths selling rosaries, icons, scapulars, relics, crucifixes, every conceivable object of veneration, including reproductions of St. Veronica's veil, currently the most popular relic in St. Peter's treasury.

When he reached the corner, he saw a cart filled high with bleached bones and human skulls. He stopped in front of it, incredulous, and was collared at once by the vendor. "Blessed relics for sale, sir. All of them the bones of virgin martyrs. Uncovered just last year in a hidden catacomb outside the city. A martyr's burial place it was, all of them killed at the evil Emperor Diocletian's orders. You can even see where some of them was tortured and had their bones broke. Make a wonderful gift, sir."

"I don't think so," said Julien, not trying to hide his repugnance.

"All of them first class and guaranteed by Bishop Vitale. I got his paper with the Vatican seal on it right here, see. Only this morning a woman came and told me of a miraculous cure from a thigh bone she had bought from me last Friday. She rubbed it on her daughter's withered legs and the girl walked for the first time. I can see you're a man of taste, sir. How about this skull. From the size of it the girl couldn't have been more than twelve when she was killed. You couldn't ask for a better souvenir of Rome."

He walked on slowly, still fascinated despite his distaste and unable to take his stare from the array of objects that lined the street.

"I can let you have a finger bone real cheap, if it's a bargain you're looking for," the vendor called after him. "Real cheap. There were ten on most bodies."

A hag with matted hair streaming over her face pushed a beaker of water under his nose. "Drink this for a copper, young man, and you'll never be sick another day in your life. It's water that St. Felicity, the barefoot virgin, bathed in."

Julien drew back sharply and knocked her hand accidentally.

"You made me spill some," the crone screamed. "Now you'll have to pay for it just the same."

Julien looked at her exasperatedly and wondered if he should undo his girdle to find his purse, when a well-dressed stranger intervened.

"Go on, you filthy old trollop; you'd do better to wash in that muck yourself." He turned to Julien and said, a shade unctuously, "You shouldn't let these people take advantage of you. I can see you are a gentleman, but you must be firmer with them or they might trick you out of your money. You've no idea what unscrupulous people lie about to prey on the likes of us."

"Thank you. I was just about to send her packing."

"Allow me to introduce myself. My name is Guido, connoisseur and collector of art objects. Are you on your way to St. Peter's too?"

Julien nodded silently, not offering much encouragement.

"You must allow me to accompany you. These people are less likely to try to take advantage of us if they see us together. What did you say your name was?" The man put his face close enough for Julien to mark the foulness of his breath.

"My name is Edward," Julien lied.

"An Englishman! I knew it the instant I saw you. I've always said our English pilgrims are the most devout. And honest. You don't meet many honest men in Rome these days. I'd say we were truly lucky to have found one another. I'm on my way to St. Peter's to pray for guidance. I have a difficult choice to make, but I feel that as usual I can trust myself to be guided by prayer."

"No doubt."

"Ah me, when troubles come, they come in torrents. I come from a good family, like yourself, but a series of calamities has beset us. My father died last St. Michael's Day, never giving us a hint of the debts he had incurred through a lifetime of gaming and dicing with unscrupulous men. Now my dear sister is to marry, and she threatens to kill herself if I can't provide her dowry. I can do it, of course, but it means selling one of my family's last remaining treasures, and I might add, the most fabulous relic in all Christendom."

"I see."

"If you only knew how it pains me to part with it, particularly since the archbishop who has been trying to buy it from me is a notorious sinner and I cannot be sure but that he mayn't use this treasure in some evil, desecrating way. How I wish I could sell it to a simpler man, who could give it the honest veneration it deserves."

"No doubt you'll find one." Julien found himself tolerantly amused.

"It's not as easy as you think. Why, if the thieves around St. Peter's knew I had it on my person, they wouldn't hesitate to cut my throat for it. Edward, are you listening to me?"

"Yes, yes. Of course."

"But you haven't even asked me what it is!" Guido looked as if he were ready to burst into tears. "The holiest relic in the world, and you don't even care."

"All right, what is it?"

Guido clasped his hands as if in prayer and lowered his eyes. "When our good Lord was resurrected and ascended into Heaven, what sacred relic did he leave on earth for the faithful?"

"Apart from His Word, you mean? His shroud?"

"No, something far more personal. And I don't mean the fingernail parings, milk teeth, and dropped hairs you can buy from half these carts. I'm talking about something really important."

"I confess I can't guess, since our Lord ascended *in toto*."

"His foreskin, my boy, His foreskin!" The man halted Julien by stepping in front of him and then drawing back as if in awe, searching Julien's face for an appropriate reaction. He was not disappointed.

"Jesus Christ!"

"That's right, no one else. His foreskin, the only part of the divine corpus to remain on earth. You no doubt know its early history. It had been lost for many years, but appeared miraculously in a dream to St. Helen, your countrywoman, who was so good at finding things. This was right after her celebrated discovery of the true cross. She traced the foreskin and found it on a rock, just as it had appeared to her in the dream, and immediately had her son, the Emperor Constantine, found a church for her on the spot where it lay. The foreskin was given the reverence due it, and was responsible for untold miracles, until one day it was stolen. It reappeared and was stolen again many times before it was at last tracked down to infidel hands. My father, a very devout man, found it when he was away on the Crusade and returned it to Christendom. You can imagine how it grieves me to part with it. Would you like to have a look at it?"

"No," said Julien, then quickly, "Yes."

"Come into the doorway here, away from this scum." Guido drew a small object from his purse and handed it to Julien. It was a round box about two inches in diameter and half again as high, almost completely covered with a wax papal seal from which hung two limp yellow ribbons.

"Well, it looks like it has Vatican approval," said Julien, "but how do I know what's inside?"

"I told you, Our Lord's foreskin. How much will you give me for it?"

"How do I know it is? This only says that its authenticity is guaranteed by the Holy Curia, but it doesn't say what it is."

"Well, by the throat of St. Blaise, man, don't you trust the Holy Curia? You don't expect those cardinals to come out and say there's a bit of holy prick in this box, do you?"

"I think I'll go to St. Peter's another day. They're waiting for me at my friend's house, and I don't want to cause them too much concern." He handed the reliquary back to the man and started to retrace his steps.

"Wait. I don't want much. My sister doesn't need a large dowry. She's marrying a nobody, the son of a village priest."

Julien insisted he really should hurry back. He heard Guido's voice call after him. "You'll regret this later. You'll never find one for a price as low as mine. You think they grow on trees?"

Julien slowed his pace when he felt he was out of Guido's sight. It seemed to him that Rome grew busier after dark. Even in Palermo there were never anywhere near this many people about at this hour. In Messina, however, he'd been told there were sinister areas that kept active until dawn.

From St. Peter's to the river and as far as he could see, torches lighted the streets and plazas. Dancers, jugglers, snake charmers, and acrobats in costumes proclaimed their diverse origins in every square, and mountebanks on platforms and wagons exhorted the mob to purchase charms, relics, and potions.

Only when he crossed the Tiber and took the road south a short distance from the river bank did the circus seem to fade. The villas, half hidden by trees, presented uniformly blank marble faces, but he could see sentries silhouetted in the torchlight guarding the more imposing mansions. The streets were still far from deserted, however. He passed many large parties of men apparently going to or from a celebration, from the sound of their frolicking. Sometimes they were accompanied by women who appeared to be upper class but were as unreservedly merry as the men, something he never saw in Palermo.

On a dark avenue before a particularly reserved villa, he heard the snarling sounds of what he assumed at first to be a dogfight, and then he realized there were wolves several yards below him. He stopped in his tracks and counted four of them before he wondered where he should seek shelter. Two guards stepped out of the darkness armed with long spears and went towards the fighting wolves. There were excited yips and growls before the wolves were finally dispersed.

"Don't worry," one of the guards said to him. "They're around these parts every night scavenging for food, but they'll hardly ever attack a man."

A few minutes later he passed a sumptuous litter carried ceremoniously by six men of impressive size, as well matched as a fine team of horses. Although the curtains were drawn around the chaise, the silk stirred, and he caught a glimpse of a handsome woman reclining on her side, her hair piled high in masses of blond curls studded with jewels. Her eyes were rolled upwards in sensuous contemplation while her hand caressed the diamonds at her throat. He stared after the litter and a hawk-nosed man came up to him eagerly.

"That was La Assoluta, the favorite of two cardinals and a prince."

"I shouldn't wonder. She's extraordinary."

"A legend, my boy, a legend. She is already the subject of a hundred poems, and the songs to her beauty have been translated into five languages. If you'd like to meet her, I can arrange an introduction, and for a remarkably reasonable sum, considering the demand. No results guaranteed; she's not a whore, you understand, but she might look favorably on a handsome man like yourself, particularly if he were distinguished."

"You mean, distinguished by great wealth?"

"What would a poor man want with La Assoluta? Only a man of breeding and means could appreciate her conversation, her musical talent, her exceptional social graces."

"How much would an introduction cost me?" Julien was impressed by the tout's unique presentation.

"Two gold bezants. Not for me, you understand. Her major-domo is a very wealthy eunuch. He would never transmit a request for an introduction for less than a bezant. And then her maid has to be tipped, her footman too, and there are endless little expenses."

"Two bezants! And I thought one gold bezant was enough to sleep with the finest whore in Christendom."

"I told you she wasn't a whore. You must never use that word for our Roman courtesans. My error, sir. I mistook you for a man of more experience. Good night, sir."

Julien felt the pangs of another hunger now and made directly for Cardinal Conti's palace. Ushered into the central chamber, he found Cardinal Conti, with one arm around Robert's shoulder, proposing a toast to the company of two bishops, a cardinal, and two middle-aged Roman matrons whose features and bearing marked them as patrician. Julien was welcomed unceremoniously, introduced to the other guests, and seated at Conti's left before a platter of cold meat and vegetables.

The bishop and cardinal were solemn men who maintained a pious distance from the conversation at table, but the women intrigued Julien at once. Octavia, the elder of the two, scanned him expertly and with such precision that she left Julien with the feeling there was nothing about him she didn't now know. Massima, her companion, was less direct in her assessment, but her eyes were flinty and bright with wit.

"My dear boy," Conti said, "you are in luck. I have a prized invitation for you. We dine tomorrow at midday with Tullia, the most gracious hostess in Rome, and I might add, a great friend of mine."

Julien was thrilled at the prospect of meeting an important lady. "I am flattered, Your Eminence. What is the occasion, if there is one?"

"There are several. Tomorrow is St. Valentine's Day, you will remember, and I was prepared to have a quiet meal with the lovely Tullia, but then my uncle heard of your arrival and asked her to arrange a larger reception so that he might meet the two of you. You'll find Peter completely charming, I promise you."

"It will be an honor. And how very kind of the Lady Tullia to be so accommodating."

The two ladies smiled at each other, and Octavia said acidly, "Tullia is nothing if not accommodating."

"Don't be unkind, Octavia," Conti answered her. "You are a witness to her generosity no less than her wit."

Octavia bowed her head deferentially. "I admire her of course. There are few women who could capture the ear of the future pope as easily as his nephew's fork."

"You employ your tongue skillfully, Octavia, as so many of us know, including, I should imagine, Tullia. I can promise you a delightful afternoon, gentlemen. My hostess's villa is only a few minutes' walk from here. We can meet in this hall at noon and proceed together. Now Julien, you must tell us what you thought of Rome. How did you like St. Peter's?"

"I didn't quite get there. Today must have been a local holiday of some sort. There was a circus extending all around St. Peter's in every direction."

"Hardly a holiday. It's actually quieter tonight since the faithful are allegedly all at their prayers for the pope's recovery. This is Rome, I'm afraid. Did you meet anyone interesting or see anything exceptional?"

"Everything I saw was exceptional to me, and a number of people did speak to me. One man in particular seemed anxious to sell me a relic I thought was unusual."

"Let us guess," the woman named Massima said. "He was selling vials of the Virgin's milk."

"No, no, this is February," Octavia interrupted. "The big relic this month is St. Dorothy's dried apples and roses."

Julien hadn't expected such a direct challenge. "I'm afraid it's something best not mentioned in front of ladies."

"Not more martyr's balls," guessed Octavia. "They're too boring."

"You're getting warm," Julien admitted.

"Were you able to see what it was you were offered," asked Conti, "or was it hidden in a monstrance or reliquary?"

"He showed me the box. It definitely had a Vatican seal on it with yellow ribbons pressed into the wax, and it looked authentic to me, but it couldn't be opened for inspection."

"Another foreskin of the Lord, I should imagine," the cardinal ventured.

"That's right!" Julien gasped. "How did you know?"

"We tend to find it tiresome, Julien, but we're all in a position to know what's in vogue in relics here. How much did he want for it?"

"He didn't say. He asked me to make an offer."

"Then, perhaps you should have, if it had the Vatican seal. It might have been a good one."

"A good one! What's a good one?"

"Their price keeps rising on the market. At last count, there were at least twelve foreskins of Jesus that had been authenticated as genuine by the Vatican at one time or another. If this was one of them, it could have been quite valuable."

"Twelve?"

"Possibly more. The popes all have their favorites, you know. Well, never mind. Chances are it was from someone much less distinguished. St. John the Baptist's is the only other one that's really worth much. The asking price was two bezants last month."

"Two bezants. That's what some man asked me for an introduction to a lady I saw going by in a litter."

"Indeed," said Massima. "And who was this . . . lady?"

"He said her name was La Assoluta. She was quite beautiful."

"Beautiful? That poxy cow!" snorted Octavia.

"Well, she does have a certain presence," said Conti. "One might say an aura. I don't share your contempt for her. Tullia doesn't think much of her either, for that matter, but in Tullia's case I can make allowances for rivalry, even though La Assoluta has been far outdistanced."

"Your uncle should hear you!" snapped Octavia. "Don't you know La Assoluta has become a Frangipani tart?"

"I didn't know it was general knowledge," the cardinal smiled. "In that case, Julien, you did well not to accept the invitation. Now that she's involved with that family within one year's time she'll be happy to take on the entire imperial army for two bezants."

"Draft animals included," Massima added tartly.

"Enough of her," said Octavia. "Conti, I thought you asked us here to play dice as well as meet your illustrious guests, and my wine glass hasn't been filled for the last fifteen minutes."

Conti bowed. "I always wait for you to call the game, my dear. But only one hour, and then I must leave you for some rest. I have a day ahead of me that will put all my resources to the test."

Julien left the party when Conti did, grateful for a night's rest in a luxurious bed after the weeks he'd spent on the road. They had been drinking a sweet wine with a light sparkle to it, and he thought he felt sleep overtake him before his head had quite settled onto the scented pillow.

It was not yet dawn when Julien was awakened by a candle shining in his face. Robert of Selby held a finger to his lips and sat beside Julien. "Forgive this conspiratorial interview, Julien, but they've organized my day so fully I don't know when I'll be able to see you alone again."

"I know. I hope you didn't mind my going off by myself this afternoon."

"It was just as well. Listen to me. Things are moving rapidly. The pope can't live much longer, and every court in Europe has its ambassadors here to witness the campaign for the papacy. There's no question that Pierleoni is anxious to enlist Roger's support. This entertainment tomorrow at Tullia's is intended to win us to his camp, and also the English."

"The English are invited too?"

"Yes. King Henry is an old friend of Pierleoni's from the days when Peter was the papal legate to Henry's court. So far Emperor Lothair seems unwilling to commit himself, and the French . . . well, the Abbot of Cluny, doesn't trust his great popularity with the aristocrats of Rome, much less the commoners."

"Still, that's just one abbot. What about his king, Louis the Fat?"

"He'll listen to his prelates. Did you know Bernard is here?"

"No, I hadn't heard. Well, if Pierleoni was a student of Abelard's, we can be sure Bernard will have no love for him."

"You can depend on it. And then there's that one other thing that doesn't sit well with Bernard."

"What's that?"

"Pierleoni comes from a Jewish family."

Julien sat upright in bed. "How could that be possible?"

"It's true. They make no secret of it, but they don't bring it up either. His grandfather converted to Christianity, and it seems likely he did so as much for his family's political ambitions as for his faith. Pierleoni's education in the Church is faultless, and no one dares question his devotion to Christ, but I'm afraid that to the French he is still a Jew."

"As was Christ. And perhaps as importantly, so was our first pope, Peter."

"Face the facts, Julien. Bernard would be a difficult man to have as a friend, much less as an enemy. He's still unmatched when it comes to influencing a crowd, though. At this point we still don't know whose candidacy he's planning to champion. If there is anyone who might seriously offer competition to Pierleoni, they're not making it known. I want you to go to St. Peter's as soon as you've had your breakfast and talk to as many priests, bishops, or anyone else, as you can. Even if Roger is convinced he can work better with Pierleoni than any of the others, we need to know who his chief rivals are."

"I'll do my best."

"Good. Be sure to be back in plenty of time to go to Tullia's. I suspect that will be an entertaining engagement."

Further sleep was now entirely out of the question. Julien arose, a shade fretfully, and after a hasty wash went downstairs to see if anyone was about yet. He found a servant stumbling sleepily towards the kitchen and left word with him that he was off to an early Mass. Dawn had just broken fully by the time he reached St. Peter's, and he marvelled at the number of people milling about. Inside the basilica each of the many small chapels that bristled along the walls was presided over by a priest or monk haranguing his listeners in the course of saying a Mass. Julien realized this was the scene of active politicking to garner support for the various papal candidates.

He moved casually from one chapel to another, listening for indications of the public mood and the names of possible contenders for the tiara. At the first three chapels he visited, they were definitely for Pierleoni. At the third a young monk was demanding the excommunication of the vandals who tried to destroy two stone lions that were a gift of Cleopatra to Caesar. Clearly, he insisted, this was the work of Pierleoni's opposition. At the fourth chapel a middle-aged monk was denouncing imperialists and aristocrats, and insisting the choice of a new pope must be dictated by Cluny only. There were audiences for each of these speakers, but in none of the chapels did they seem greatly impressed by what they heard.

There was a disturbance at a chapel further towards the main altar, and the crowd began to shift curiously towards the source of the commotion. Vatican guards had pulled a young monk down from his pulpit and were attempting to drag him away. Julien edged into the crowd to get a better idea of what this was all about. He was about to ask a couple of students on his left who this wild-eyed young monk was when he heard a familiar voice.

"Julien. Stay where you are. I'll be right back for you."

Julien felt his head jerk in disbelief and his throat constricted. That was Brother Ralf! It could be no one else. He searched the crowd and thought he glimpsed him moving away with the guards and arguing with them. Julien started to move towards him but then remembered his admonition and stayed there. He strained for another glimpse, then thought he saw him again.

The public had now joined Brother Ralf and the young monk in shouting down the guards, and a lieutenant moved in to restore order. There could have been no clear-cut instructions for dealing with such occurrences during election time, and he eventually waved the guards away.

Ralf elbowed his way to Julien as soon as he was free, and embraced him earnestly. "I couldn't believe it was really you, dear boy. What in the world brought you to Rome? Ah, I can guess. Is it so?"

"Yes, more or less. And you're here as his emissary?"

"I am. I don't have to whisper his name. Abelard sent the two of us." He turned to the young monk who was with him. "Julien, this is Arnold of Brescia. As you can see, my time is fully occupied trying to keep him out of prison."

Arnold reached out and gripped Julien's forearm firmly. "Ralf speaks of you often, Julien. We both wish we could visit you in Sicily."

Julien studied his face intently. It was an honest, open face, with rather large features and the luminous eyes of a fanatic. He was raggedly dressed and not particularly clean, but those obsessive eyes did not permit you to dwell on any other feature of his person. "Arnold of Brescia," Julien mused. "Aren't you the commune-ist?"

"They call me so, yes. I'm back with Abelard now, but I welcomed the chance to return here for a visit. You can see that my popularity with certain factions in Rome doesn't appear to have increased much since I was last here."

Julien recalled Roger smiling but shaking his head when he spoke to him of Arnold. "What were you saying to the crowds that brought the guards down on you?"

"I told you I wasn't popular. I merely demanded that the new pope, whoever he might be, and I really don't care who he is, be forced to take an oath of poverty."

Julien thought of the luxury of Cardinal Conti's palace and winced. "But surely you don't seriously expect him to?"

"It's not a matter of what I expect. I'm no one. It's the only way he can serve God. And it isn't simply the question of poverty. Why doesn't the pope concern himself with man's spiritual guidance and leave the wars and politicking to the scum better suited for it."

"I gather you don't think much of princes either."

"I'm for self rule. The northern communes are working towards it, but if an ultra-conservative pope or a pro-imperialist one is elected, the first thing he's sure to do is move against them. But, enough of this. It's Ralf you want to talk to, not me. We'll meet again later and you'll probably be sick of my ranting, so why don't you two go off now and have a glass of wine?" His eyes had already fastened on a group of men some yards away who looked as if their discussion would soon lead to more direct expression and he began to move towards them.

Ralf put his arm through Julien's as they left the basilica. "Did you get my message?"

"Yes. Did you get mine?"

"No. I've been in Rome since before Christmas. It's been an exciting campaign, even if we've no idea who the final adversaries will be. All Rome appears to be behind Pierleoni."

"And Abelard too?"

"Yes, but with reservations. Pierleoni appears to be the best man, but Abelard is uncomfortable about the ease with which his fat purse brought him advancement. Still, Pierleoni has one edge beyond his popularity. Honorius recently appointed eight cardinals for the preliminary selection of the next pope, and Pierleoni is one of them."

"Good! But tell me about yourself, Ralf. You look happy, but thinner." He was alarmed by Ralf's extreme gauntness but felt he should modify his concern.

"And you're beginning to look like a man instead of a boy. It's not an easy time we have of it in Britanny, Julien. Abelard is being crushed by his enemies. Bernard of Clairvaux may easily be the most saintly man alive today, but he isn't content to simply challenge Abelard's beliefs. He's relentless in his persecution of them."

"I heard many would like to see Bernard made pope."

"He could have it if he wanted it, but he prefers to be the power behind the pope. Don't underestimate the extent of that power, Julien. I believe Bernard is already the most influential individual in the world. Let's walk awhile, shall we? I don't much feel like sitting.

"I've thought of Roger's role in this and as I see it, any of the other candidates will be determined to bring Roger quickly to heel. I assume you're aware of this and are preparing to negotiate with Pierleoni as the only candidate likely to give Roger what he wants in return for his support."

"Exactly. I didn't think it would be much of a secret."

They were just a short distance from St. Peter's when they heard a new commotion just ahead. The excited cries of the crowd and then screams drew them closer. Two monks were beating a naked man with leather straps while he screeched his public confession. "What is he accused of?" Ralf asked a neighbor.

"He's a priest's servant," the man answered. "He fought with another servant and drew blood. Nothing interesting." Most of the other witnesses found the spectacle at least moderately diverting, however, and were encouraging the monks to lay on more heavily.

"That seems rather strict," Ralf said. "The only times I saw that in England were towards monks convicted of heresy or sodomy, and it was always delivered at the church door right after Sunday Mass. But come; let's not add to this unfortunate man's distress. Tell me, are you working as Robert of Selby's assistant? We know he's Roger's subchancellor."

"On this mission I am. The rest of the time I'm a glorified secretary to Roger, although I've done next to nothing so far. I am learning Arabic, though."

"And how to win the hearts of Sicilian girls, no doubt."

"Ralf. You have no idea what Sicilian women are like. You never even get a chance to see most of them with all the veils they wear. The only ones who let you speak to them are the old, married women. The rest are kept away in the harem. It's depressing."

"All right, Julien, come on. Who is she?"

Julien looked at his tutor solemnly a moment, then broke into a relieved laugh and rapidly told him of his experiences with Ula and Claire.

"And Roger has flatly refused to entertain your suit?"

"Well, before I left he relented a little and said I could see her to say goodbye on condition that her mother be present. That morning I sent three messengers to their apartment asking if I might have an interview with her mother; the last one brought back word that the baroness had a headache. I'd lost my last chance of seeing Claire."

"But you did see her."

"Yes, I was surprised. A Sicilian girl doesn't contradict her elders' wishes so lightly. She came to the studio alone, just as I was packing some last minute things. Aziz, the Muslim friend I spoke of, was there and made some excuse to leave us alone. Can you believe it? He could've been just as severely punished as we if someone had found us out."

"Julien dear, I've never been in Sicily, but whatever the customs or history of a people, it doesn't much change human nature. I usually make that observation regretfully, but in your case I'm pleased. She obviously returns your affectionate interest."

Julien shook his head slowly. "She came only to refuse me. And yet she brought me this." He reached into his shirt and brought out a coral rose which he wore on a silver chain. "It's to protect me."

"Nonsense. Girls don't give sentimental gifts unless they're interested."

"You don't know Claire. She wanted to do something generous because she feels sorry for me and knows she's hurting me. When she started to leave, I couldn't bear the idea of not seeing her again, and I'm afraid I got carried away and tried to kiss her. That isn't done either."

A wry smile crept across Ralf's face. "Was she angry?"

"For a minute I thought she was kissing me back, but then she pulled away and got very angry. She told me to save my kisses for my concubine. That hurt me. She knows perfectly well Ula means nothing to me. I told her then that if I couldn't have her I would never marry."

"Did you mean it?" Ralf found Julien's tale more amusing than he dared let Julien see.

"Of course I did. At least, I did then. Ralf, when I'm around her it's as if no one else in the world exists. She was cruel enough to laugh at me when I told her that. But then she said we would remain good friends, because she has no intention of marrying either."

Ralf chucked his friend's chin. "But Julien, you idiot. That's as good as an acceptance."

"What do you mean? She couldn't have been more explicit. She said flatly she'd not marry me or anyone else."

"Poor Julien. It's absurd that you should have to listen to advice from an old celibate like me in these matters. Have you spoken to no one else about this? Selby?"

"Oh yes. I'm afraid our first week together I could talk of little else. Unfortunately, he gets impatient with me. He thinks I should be delighted at my good fortune . . . having Ula delivered to my bed every night like a bowl of fruit to be eaten before retiring. It's his belief all young girls are idiots and anyone who takes them seriously is doubly so."

"You can be sure he knows better. But have you ever thought of the risk Claire took in remaining alone with you in the studio, even for that fleeting goodbye?"

"I know. She might have been compromised."

"Exactly. And if the two of you were discovered, how could her honor be saved, however stained?"

"You mean by my marrying her?" Julien drew back warily.

"I do. Don't misunderstand me. From your description of her, colored though it may be, I see Claire as uniquely independent, a little headstrong perhaps, and assuredly spoiled, but not stupid. She must have considered the possible consequences of your rendezvous. While I'm sure she's not a girl who would come to you expecting or hoping to be discovered, don't you agree she would never have done so if the possibility of being forced into a marriage with you was as repugnant as she would have you believe?"

"I never thought of that. But what a terrible way to get married! And if her father were alive and felt himself sufficiently disgraced by her conduct, he could have her put to death, no matter how much I wanted to marry her. And I'd surely be disgraced for all time in Roger's eyes."

"Possibly. But only possibly. It might also get Roger off the hook. I'm sure he already has some idea of what to expect from Claire if he were to arrange a marriage she thoroughly disapproved of with some ally or kins-man."

"Then, you really think there's hope for me?"

"Far from it. I think you're a hopeless fool, and if you marry her, you'll get exactly what you deserve. Oh come now, I'm teasing you. I don't know the girl, but I'd say your chances are excellent. One bit of advice, though. I'd get rid of Ula somehow."

Julien sighed exasperatedly. "Easy enough to say, but how do I manage that? She was a gift from my Lord. And anyway, I don't think I have the right to return her or to pass her on to someone else. I'm not at all certain how those things work. I also think she may be stuck on me."

"Don't be so sure. You might be the answer to a maiden's prayer on a free marriage market, but Ula might well consider herself better off in the harem of a rich and powerful man instead of the plaything of a young puppy. I hope I'm not being too hard on your famous pride."

Julien stared at his tutor wonderingly, then smiled, "I'll do it. I'll speak to Roger as tactfully as I can and tell him I've been instructed by my spiritual adviser to subdue my flesh for a while. Someone will explain it to her, and she'll have to understand. Come on, aren't you ready for a glass of wine now? I've got to be going back soon. I'm to meet Pierleoni today at a dinner being given by his nephew's friend." They went into an inn for pilgrims and spent the rest of the morning speculating on the politics of the coming election.

When Julien returned to the palace, Cardinal Conti was already in the great hall, wearing his long ermine cloak with a train twenty feet long that was carried by four attendants who were skipping nimbly to avoid colliding with each other as he paced and turned impatiently.

"I'm afraid the reception will not be as heavily attended as we had planned. The English envoys sent their regrets a few minutes ago."

"I'm sorry," said Julien. "I looked forward to meeting my countrymen. They must have had pressing business."

"Nothing more than a simple meal," the cardinal went on, "and with some of the most fascinating women in Rome. It's not as if we were asking them to sign a contract. Well, never mind."

"What about the ladies I met last night?" Julien asked. "Will they be there? I found them charming. I don't believe I've ever met any ladies quite like them."

"Yes, charming, quite. They'll be there. Two of the oldest families in Rome, not as rich as the Pierleoni but much older. Impeccable credentials. You're simply no one in Rome without them. Today you'll be sitting on the left of another singularly gracious lady, Matilda of Canossa."

"I look forward to meeting her. Has there been any word yet from the emperor? Whom he supports?"

"I wish you wouldn't call him that. I know everyone does, but technically Lothair is still just a German king in command of the Empire. He'll be entitled to be called emperor only if and when the pope makes him one."

"And do you think your uncle would make him emperor if he were pope?"

"Lothair's support would entail some recompense, yes. Well, I believe it's time we were off. Selby is waiting in his chamber. Will you tell him we're ready?" Julien recognized that Conti was giving him the chance to have a few moments with Selby and was grateful for the man's tact. Robert sat up the moment Julien entered, wincing from the movement of his wounded arm. "The English cancelled," he whispered quickly. "What can it mean?"

"Obviously they're in no position to commit themselves. Were you able to discover who Pierleoni's chief rival might be?"

"Bernard of Clairvaux and Peter of Cluny will do all they can to defeat him, but neither man is a willing candidate. All Rome appears to be solidly behind Pierleoni, however."

"Yes, but Rome is hardly Christendom. Very well, on to meet Peter, Cardinal Pierleoni; with God's help, our next pope."

Tullia's villa was conveniently close by. It was smaller than Cardinal Conti's but reflected the same cultivated extravagance. The avenue to the entrance was flanked by dozens of welcoming white peacocks that had been surgically muted. They were greeted first by an aged eunuch and then by twin Chinese dwarfs armed with spears and a half dozen knives tucked into their girdles. When they were ushered inside, two young women with re- markably ugly features took their cloaks and led them into the reception room where Tullia was reclining on a silk covered dais. Her long blond hair had been artfully draped across her bare shoulders and then parted to reveal a bosom that was most ample, but no more so than the rest of her. She was undeniably a great beauty, but half again as large as Julien would have guessed a legendary courtesan would be. She raised her hand languidly for their greeting and signalled them towards the faldstools fanned out before the dais. Conti approached her and brushed her fingers lightly with his lips.

"Massima and Octavia are amusing themselves in the garden," Tullia said. "And your uncle's messenger was here a few minutes ago to announce that he and Matilda will be arriving any moment."

Her voice was distinctly sweet, and Julien thought a trifle childish. They were brought glasses of warmed wine and fruit juices flavored with cinnamon, and when everyone was served, the two ugly serving girls took their places at Tullia's side, craning their necks awkwardly to place their faces as close to hers as they could while they faced the guests and grimaced. The woman at Tullia's left was covered with hairy moles, while the other had beady pink eyes and a mouthful of black teeth imbedded in prominent pink gums.

Tullia fluttered her eyelids at Robert. "If you gentlemen are planning to stay in Rome awhile, you must allow me to show you some of our more interesting sights."

"There could be few to compare with what we see here," Robert stated as gallantly as he could.

Tullia smiled and arched her back, thrusting her bosom forward, while the attending women strained to keep their faces close to hers. "Perhaps you'd like me to show you the rest of the villa. It might even be a good idea to join the ladies in the garden." She raised her arms for the maids to help her rise and managed a standing position with more grace than Julien would have believed possible.

She led them down a long gallery lined with busts of Roman emperors in amber-colored onyx on porphyry pedestals into a sunny room lined with fern, palm, and hundreds of hanging geramiums. "This is my music room," she announced.

"I've never seen so much glass," said Robert, "and it's so clear."

Tullia laughed airily. "I believe the ladies are on the portico." She opened twin doors and they entered an eight-columned portico, where Massima and Octavia were seated on a double swing, kicking their legs in a manner that struck Julien as not very ladylike. They clambered off the swing and gave Conti a quick peck on each cheek before bowing to the others.

"The first apricot blossoms appeared only this morning," Tullia said. "Our shrubs are well protected by the garden walls. Shall we walk around? It's never too cold out here."

The garden was an intricate maze of hedge with ornamental flower beds in decorative shapes and dwarf fruit trees pruned and espaliered into fantastic patterns. In the center of the garden was a grinning, life-size Priapus whose enormous member had been recently decked with a bright garland.

"Oh you naughty girls!" Tullia wagged her finger at them. "Do you hope to improve on art or on nature?"

One of Tullia's dwarfs scurried up to her to announce the arrival of Peter, Cardinal Pierleoni and Lady Matilda of Canossa, but before he had finished, Pierleoni was already walking briskly towards them with Matilda following demurely behind.

The ladies kissed him quickly, and he held out his hand for a kiss of greeting and reverence from Robert and Julien. The ring he proffered was a cabochon emerald larger by far than any stone either of the Englishmen had ever seen, and Julien's eyes bulged as he bent over it. "Your Eminence does us honor," he muttered.

"I trust Duke Roger was well when you left him?" Pierleoni said. "Be sure to tell him that he is remembered daily in my prayers and that the Church will always be grateful to the Hautevilles for the recovery of Sicily to Christendom." His eyes had a sprightly twinkle that denied the formality of his greeting. The vigor of his step and the solid muscularity of his body were markedly different from the softness Julien had come to associate with the prelates of Rome. Peter and Robert eyed each other appraisingly, and seemed pleased by what they saw. Although Pierleoni was more than a dozen years older than Robert, they recognized each other as men who enjoyed making decisions, who prided themselves on their efficiency in dispatching problems.

"I know my duke would enjoy the privilege of meeting Your Eminence no less than I do, and God willing, will hasten to do so."

"Let there be no doubt, then, of the warmth of my welcome to him. The Church has need of such champions."

"I propose adding sustenance to your conversation," Tullia interrupted, "although I have never known your argument to lack strength. The dining table is prepared."

Julien was pleased when Matilda self-assuredly took his arm to be escorted in. Her smile was certainly encouraging, but she kept her eyes lowered. After a few steps he found himself thrilling unexpectedly to the warmth of her hand and to the perfume of her body. She must be well into her thirties, he guessed, but her figure is that of a girl. He studied her face as they walked, not certain how to begin a conversation. Her nose was quite long and very straight, and the light bounced sharply off the well-defined planes of her cheeks. He felt it was the most aristocratic face he'd ever seen, yet with all the pride and breeding reflected in her deportment and features, there was still a vulnerability he found attractive.

"You're rather young, aren't you," she said at length, "to be on such a responsible mission?"

Julien was stung by the reference to his youth. "I'm older than I look," he said defensively, then modified his voice politely. "I suppose I'm being educated."

"Ah, that's good," she answered, her smile now quite sweet. "And how is your education coming?"

He wondered if he was mistaken about the insistent pressure of her hand on his arm. It seemed, at any rate, that she didn't think of him as *too* young. The casualness of their introduction and the ease with which she was accompanying him to the dining room was something he'd never experienced. Are there many women in Rome like this? he wondered, and then, If Claire were Roman, would it all have been so much simpler? "I feel I have a great deal to learn," he answered her, "but I look forward to each new lesson."

"Something tells me your education has not been lacking in the essentials." She looked directly into his face now, and her smile, a trifle crooked, was very engaging.

Julien pressed her hand with his arm. "A student can only hope to be as good as his teacher."

"I'm not so sure. I can think of cases where a teacher might profit more from her students."

Julien tingled at Matilda's distinct use of the female pronoun. "Are you a teacher, then?"

"You flatter me. No, at the moment I'm trying only to be a student, like yourself."

He grew determinedly bolder. "Perhaps we could learn together, then."

"Do you think so? Well, let us continue this discussion at a more appropriate time."

Pierleoni led them in a prayer of thanks in a firm voice, pronouncing the words meaningfully instead of in the singsong, routine fashion Julien had become accustomed to at the monastery. Plates of fish and meat were passed around, and Julien found himself intrigued by a dish of chickpeas and fried squash blossoms. For a few minutes they fed themselves busily before Tullia opened conversation.

"Forgive me if I ask a presumptuous question, Peter, but I beg you to indulge my curiosity. Would you tell us what name you will choose as pope?"

"Your question is not as presumptuous as your assumptions, dear Tullia. Honorius still lives. But then, why not? I believe most cardinals must entertain the vain fancy of choosing their name as pope. I would be Anacletus. Anacletus, the second. I like the name and we haven't had an Anacletus for a long time. Saint Anacletus was our third pope. Saint Peter was still alive then."

Robert rose with his glass in hand. "May I propose a toast?"

"Indeed you may not." Pierleoni's voice was more matter of fact than reprimanding. "It would be disrespectful to Pope Honorius and probably very unlucky to me."

Robert took his seat again, mildly abashed.

There was a stir in the entrance hall. The door burst open and two cardinals in a state of extreme agitation rushed in, only slightly hampered by Tullia's dwarf servants, who had attached themselves firmly to their cloaks. Pierleoni paled and rose, clutching the table. "Honorius."

"Treason." The taller of the two cardinals was struggling for his breath more successfully than his heavy, wheezing companion. "Treason in the Church. Honorius died during the early morning hours. Chancellor Almeric and Cardinal Girard were with him. They kept it secret until they could convene the cardinals of their party. They secretly elected Cardinal Gregory of San Angelo as pope and are moving even now to present him to the people."

"Outrage!" shouted Pierleoni. "That is not a canonical election." He turned to Robert. "My enemies, the heads of the Holy Curia. This is completely illegal. There can be no election without me. Honorius himself designated me as one of eight cardinals to guide the selection. Robert, I want you and my nephew to come with me. I am going to convene a majority of the cardinals, and we'll have another election at once. Come, there's no time to be lost."

"I'll see you this evening," Robert whispered to Julien. "Send a messenger to Roger at once with the news. I'll have more details for him tomorrow."

The four cardinals and Robert left hurriedly, and Julien found himself alone with the women and a mountain of food.

"I heard Selby say you needed a messenger," Tullia said. "If you will accept my help . . . It's never too easy to find a reliable person in Rome."

"Thank you. Could I have pen and parchment please? If you can get a rider to Gaeta, we have a relay system of riders from there to Sicily that we set up on the way here." Writing materials were brought to the table and he started at once to compose his message. He made no attempt to conceal his writing from the others, and Tullia stood directly at his shoulder and peered frankly at the message.

"Nanno knows where to take this," Tullia said. "I can assure you, your man in Gaeta will have the message by tomorrow, delivered by a trusted member of our party. I beg your pardon, but I've never seen a stranger code."

"It's Arabic," Julien said. "Roger will be able to read it, but not many people in Rome will."

"You're very clever," Matilda said, reminding him again that her leg had been pressing his since they were seated.

He returned the pressure. Why not? he thought, almost aloud. While the other ladies were engaged in their leavetakings, she whispered to him to meet her at the house across the road from the old church of St. Theodore.

It was a simple matter to find the church. It stood halfway between Tullia's residence and the Circus Maximus in one direction and halfway between the Pierleoni villa and the Palatine hill in the other. Julien was so captivated by the charm of its ninth century octagonal construction, and by its enchanting paved courtyard, that he forgot the eagerness with which he had hurried to this rendezvous.

Her villa was modest in size but impeccable in proportion and style. She had been waiting for him, a little longer than she liked to, it appeared, and he wondered if she had seen him lingering at the church, but once the door was opened, she ushered him in and sent away the single servant who took his cloak.

Alone with Matilda in her chamber, Julien felt unaccountably awkward and uncertain how much aggressiveness might be permitted. He attempted to embrace her at once, but she adroitly sidestepped his advance with an invitation to make himself comfortable while she found wine for them. It was certain she was encouraging intimacy, and yet her unruffled demeanor belied the warmth of her invitation.

"Do you find me attractive?" she asked, somewhat noncommittally, as she poured his wine.

"Of course I do."

She looked at him levelly. "I didn't ask you if you found women attractive. Your answer was too quick and too compact."

Julien was flustered by her comment. "I don't understand. You asked me here, and I came."

"I asked you because I find you attractive. But that doesn't mean I'm going to allow you to push me on the bed just because you need a woman."

"I'm not that sort of person. Actually, I haven't been with a woman since I left Sicily."

"What a perfectly dreadful answer. How old did you say you were?"

"Twenty-one," he lied.

"Nineteen would be easier to believe. Certainly quite old enough to have developed a degree more grace with the ladies than you show. Tell me, what are women in Sicily like? We hear such odd stories."

Julien shrugged. "I can't say I know all that many. I know they're very different from the women here."

"But you don't know all that many women here."

"You don't have to know them to see what they are."

"I see. You believe all Roman women are whores."

"I didn't say that, but there doesn't seem to be much keeping them from it."

"You're ruder than I believed. It's not too late to have you thrown out."

"I wasn't calling *you* a whore. But I never saw so many, down by the banks of the Tiber. I was told there are only thirty-five thousand people living within the walls of Rome, and yet I'm sure you have more whores than London or Palermo."

"Well, about the Tiber whores, I admit you do have a point. It's the pilgrims, you understand. You've heard the Italian proverb, *Dove ci sono campane ci sono puttane?*"

" 'Where there are church bells there are whores.' I'm sure that was coined for Rome."

"It was. But make no mistake about the rest of us."

"I'm sorry, but what about Tullia? And La Assoluta? Aren't they high-class whores?"

"Tullia can pick and choose the men she entertains. A courtesan's value and reputation are not measured by how well she performs in her bed chamber, but by how she conducts herself in her role as a surrogate wife or hostess. It's too refined a concept for an Englishman. You wouldn't understand."

Julien began to feel he was being unfairly badgered. "Look, I'm sorry if I don't behave the way the men you're used to do, but well, if you'll forgive my frankness, didn't you invite me here to make love?"

"You're improving. But let me say rather that I invited you here for *my* pleasure. That is not to say that I don't expect you will enjoy it any less, but my motives are entirely selfish. There's no point in allowing you to make love to me until you understand what's expected of you."

"Well if you expect me to make love, let's go."

"You don't understand. You are expected to give *me* pleasure, instead of merely assuming that my enjoyment will be derived from knowing I satisfied you."

"Frankly, I haven't the faintest idea what you're talking about, but it doesn't sound normal."

"That's what I was afraid of. If you still wish to be a student, then listen to me. You're just barely over being a boy. Now I think boys are pretty enough, but rarely worth the trouble it takes to bed them. I sometimes think Greek men have the right idea about them. You do show some promise, I admit, but if you want to find out what it takes to be a satisfactory lover, you'll have to submit yourself completely to my teaching."

A moment earlier Julien had been aware of his blood coursing more rapidly and warming him. Now a chill gripped his gut and blocked desire. This woman's boldness, her candor, even her frank hunger for sex confused him. She seemed to be taunting him for his lack of experience while making it clear she found this innocence attractive.

The weeks with Ula had given him a rich initiation into sex, but when he reflected on it, he realized that the variety provided by Ula had not slackened his desire for something more involving. Was it because Ula was there exclusively for his pleasure? Matilda's words stung him with their truth. There had to be something more fulfilling, an ultimate thrill which would prolong satisfaction and leave him content. He thought of the promising look in Claire's eyes when they parted and decided that Matilda's course of instruction was likely to bring him no nearer to his fantasy.

"You honor me greatly," he said after a moment, "and I'm truly grateful for your interest, but I'm afraid that as a student I'd be a greater disappointment to you than you feel I'd be as a lover."

Matilda frowned and drew back. "Are you lacking vital parts?"

"No, of course not, or I shouldn't have come here. I find you a beautiful and thoroughly engaging woman, but I don't think I'm up to the challenge you offer. Perhaps I am too young, after all."

"Or perhaps I'm too old?"

"Not at all. Your years give you grace."

"Well, I certainly have no intention of begging you."

"Can't we be friends?"

"We might have, if you'd been clever enough to say something else just then. No, I'm afraid the thought of friendship with a boy under these circumstances—and I see you are still a boy—makes me shudder. May I see you to the door?"

"I wish we could talk."

"Please, no. I have the dreadful feeling you'd end up telling me all about some whining little virgin who fills your nights with dreams of ecstasy. No, I beg you to spare me that."

Julien choked on his voice. "Whatever you say."

"Where will you go now?"

"Back to Cardinal Conti's, I suppose, to wait for word from Robert."

She appeared thoughtful. "Perhaps I'll join you. We probably won't know anything more about the election for hours, but I'd rather not spend the rest of the day here alone." She extended her hand in a conciliatory gesture. "Let's forget about what I just said, shall we?"

Julien kissed her hand gratefully. "I deserve your anger. What a good person you are."

"Of course I'm not angry. I still rather like you. You really don't know a thing yet about women, Julien, but apart from your years, I suppose you can't have had much contact with them. First the monastery and then Sicily. My word! Is it true that Sicilian women are kept locked up?"

"Not exactly." He offered her his arm, and they left the villa chatting amiably, if not affectionately.

When they arrived at Cardinal Conti's, they discovered that news was not as long in coming as Matilda had expected. The story that Rome had two popes was already blanketing the city. A majority of the full college of cardinals had quickly swept Pierleoni in as Anacletus II, whereas a majority of the initial electors appointed by Honorius, which was to have included Pierleoni, had voted for Cardinal Gregory of San Angelo, himself also a Roman, as Innocent II. Plans were being made for both consecrations on the same day in the following month. While Anacletus' election was more canonically correct than Innocent's, they were both disputable, since the Church had not yet established hard, fast rules for electing a pope. Meantime, Anacletus was entrenched in St. Peter's with the support of most Romans, while Innocent took refuge in the area of Trastevere across the river from Pierleoni's villa.

When the news of the potentially disastrous rift in the Church had circulated through the city, the people took to the streets proclaiming the name of their favorite candidate and confrontations resulted in injuries and even some deaths. Meanwhile bands of priests and a few laymen stopped at Cardinal Conti's residence to offer congratulations and promise their loyalty to Anacletus' party. Matilda was pressed into duty as an unofficial hostess to greet the callers and thank them for their support. Julien mingled with the throngs of people that now filled the hall, and he could see any further conversation with Matilda grow increasingly unlikely. Conti and Selby did not return until well after dark, but they had no further news that was not already public knowledge.

Just as Julien was beginning to wonder if he would ever see his bed that night, he spotted Brother Ralf and Arnold of Brescia entering the hall, their faces almost completely muffled in their cloaks. Julien dragged Robert away from a group of Irish priests and hurried him across the room to meet his friends.

"I've looked forward to this meeting," Robert said to them. "You no doubt agree that Anacletus' victory is a victory for Abelard too?"

"If it really is a victory," Arnold answered. "Anacletus' enemies are too clever to dispute the canonicity of the elections, since there seems to be at least some question of validity on both sides, but Bernard has already started a campaign against Anacletus which is no more than character assassination and vituperation of the most vulgar sort. He addressed some of King Lothair's prelates this evening and we went to hear him."

"Tell me, please," Robert said. "I'd like to know what their campaign strategy is to be."

"I've already written down most of what we heard tonight so I can send it to Abelard. Here's my favorite quote from our holy Bernard. *"It is to the injury of Christ that the offspring of a Jew should have seized for himself the throne of St. Peter."*

Robert grimaced. "I'm not surprised. Bernard would have to admit privately that Anacletus would make at least as good a pope as Innocent, so where there is no argument in reason, you can safely rely on Jew-baiting as a course of action."

Ralf nodded. "Bernard rages at Abelard for daring to suggest that Jews are not culpable for the death of Christ."

Robert was taken aback. "Does Abelard go so far?"

"It is a principal tenet of his. Crime is not in the act but in the intention," Ralf answered. "Those who crucified the Lord, whether pagan, Jew, or whatever, without knowing that He was truly the Savior, did not sin."

"I'll have to think about that," said Robert. "Meanwhile, did Bernard say anything else that we can build an argument against?"

"That's it. The dispute will be settled only when the kings of Europe declare themselves. I can assure you Bernard will be very busy working on them."

"Anacletus will not lack friends. I'm sure you know my duke's support is wholehearted."

"With no offense intended to you or to the illustrious Roger, I'd like to point out that his hold on the dukedom is tenuous at best, since it's already contested by Lothair. No, the decision will come from Germany, France, and England. Without Lothair, Louis, and Henry, Anacletus will be driven from the throne in less than a year."

"We'll just have to do what we can, then. But don't underestimate the power of my duke. Julien, I'm truly pleased to have met your friends. You've told me a good deal about Ralf, and I find he's precisely what I expected, but I admit that you, Arnold, are something of a surprise to me."

Arnold smiled wryly. "Did you expect I'd be horned and tailed and carry a pitchfork?"

"Oh no. I've heard your enemies describe you as an anarchist rabble-rouser, but I've listened to your friends too, who describe you as ascetic and even holy. I'm pleased to see that you're a man, and maybe even a fighting man."

"I've a great deal to fight for." Arnold gripped Robert's forearm. "Perhaps we'll meet again one day, but now it's time for us to leave. We must go back to Brittany to work out a program with Abelard. These times demand faster action than most."

"We all have programs to work out, but I agree, time has rarely been so critical. God be with you."

They saw the two monks out the door, and Robert pulled Julien aside into one of the promenades. "Walk with me a moment before we go back in."

"With pleasure. That mob was beginning to depress me. I assume you worked out the details of our alliance with Anacletus earlier today."

"Of course. Roger will support Anacletus officially, and in return Anacletus will make him king of Sicily, Calabria, and Apulia, with more or less definite rights over Capua, Naples, and Benevento. So you see, our mission is virtually all accomplished."

"But what if Innocent should retain the papacy? All the other princes are holding off until they can see which way the wind blows."

"Don't you think I've checked to see what the possibilities of a conciliation with Innocent are? I wouldn't be worthy of Roger's trust if I didn't at least test the water with a toe. No, Innocent loathes Roger. He evidently thinks of him as a glorified robber baron to be stamped out like vermin. And Lothair's representatives here expect that Innocent will dangle Sicily as a bribe to the Germans for their support."

"If that's how it is, we can go back to Sicily right away."

"Don't be so impatient, Julien. Do you really miss those pretty dark eyes so much? No, the mission we came on is complete, but I'm afraid we won't be home for a few months yet. Anacletus wants to meet with Roger as soon as he consolidates his position here. It's his first order of business. We will escort him to Avellino, where, God willing, he'll formally invest Roger with his new title. With a little luck we should be able to arrange it for some time in March. I've already sent word to Roger, and I've no doubt he'll spring at the chance. Do you think you can wait that long?"

"No, but I will. Shall we go back in and grip some more arms? I expect we should be making new friends for Roger as much as for Anacletus now."

"Agreed. I see you seem to have a talent for making new friends fast. I couldn't help but notice. By the way, how was Matilda?"

"Oh, I'd say about average."

Chapter XII
KING BY THE GRACE OF GOD

Despite Robert's anticipation of an early meeting of duke and pope, it was not until the 27th of September, over seven months later, that Anacletus issued a bull declaring Roger king of the *regno*. The territories were granted to him exactly as had been previously agreed upon with Robert in Rome, with an additional clause giving Anacletus an annual payment of six hundred gold *schifati* from the new kingdom.

It was further decided that Cardinal Conti would officiate at the coronation in Palermo on his uncle's behalf. On Martinmas, November 11th, Julien set out from Avellino as the leader of Cardinal Conti's escort to Sicily. Robert of Selby had resumed his duties in the mainland capital, and Roger hurried back to Salerno as rapidly as Anacletus hurried back to Rome once their meeting was concluded.

When Julien and Conti reached Salerno, they found themselves beset on all sides with rumors and reports of new alliances favoring Innocent. Conti appeared lighthearted despite these stories and did his best to cheer Julien, who was brooding over the unfavorable turn of events. Their first day in Salerno they had a meeting with Robert after their evening meal. They were to sail for Sicily the next morning, and it was likely to be Julien's last meeting with Robert for a long time. Julien felt a pall hanging over them. He couldn't persuade himself that Roger's chances for a permanent hold on his crown were more than ephemeral.

As soon as they were seated informally around the familiar council table in the old castle with a cask of sweet Neapolitan red wine, Julien addressed his friends. "I think you're both whistling in the dark. Here it is months after Anacletus was elected pope, and Roger's still the only sovereign to support him. Not only that, but do you know of any king who's stepped forward yet to congratulate Roger on his new throne?"

"Don't get yourself into such a state," Robert said. "I admit it would have been more becoming for Anacletus to wait for his own universal recognition as pope before bestowing titles on others, but you surely can't expect Roger's brother rulers to welcome him with open arms in any case, now could you? That's not the way of the world."

"I don't expect them to send him flowers," Julien said, "but I did think one or two could have said something mildly encouraging. What of our own

King Henry? He's half Norman on his father's side, exactly like Roger and the two of us are. You'd think he'd be a little more friendly."

Conti smiled wisely. "Remember, Julien, there are those English who might feel that Roger owes England tribute because Henry is king of the Normans. If Roger were to give them that, I guarantee he'd receive recognition in return. He clearly doesn't want it."

"And need I remind you why the French aren't quick to recognize Sicily?" Robert said."We all know there's not a monarch in the West who hates non-Christians as openly as Louis the Fat does. And he remembers that the Sicilians alone never contributed to the Crusade that cost him so much in wealth and manpower."

"Well then, what of Hungary?" Julien proposed feebly. "King Coloman is related to Roger and they love each other. Why hasn't he stepped forward to say something?"

"Actually he has," Robert said, "but he can only do so informally. Take a look at the map, Julien. The kingdom of Hungary is surrounded by the Holy Roman Empire. King Lothair could crush Coloman in an instant if he had a mind to. It's Lothair, and Lothair alone, who's determined to beat Roger to his knees."

Although Robert appeared to be countering all Julien's arguments, Conti could see from the expression with which he addressed the younger man that he was distinctly proud of Julien's performance in the last months. Although Julien had told Conti when they first met that he was Robert's aide because he felt it might be imprudent to identify himself as Roger's representative, Conti had long since seen the independent maneuvering which established Julien's value to the crown. "You are both mistaken," Conti interrupted, "to believe it's the will of monarchs that steers the courses of their kingdom. It's the national churches and the great monastic orders that will choose. They alone will guide the rulers in deciding the destiny of the papacy. Bernard, Peter of Cluny, Norbert of Magdeburg, Wibald of Stablo . . . these are the men with whom the fate of the Church lies."

"Then, we really are without hope," Julien moaned. "If all the powerful churchmen except Abelard are against our cause, what can lie ahead but ruin?"

"I'm surprised at you, Julien," Conti admonished him softly. "Those aren't Christian sentiments. We must make the certitude of our faith equal to theirs and leave all else to the judgment of God."

"The certitude of faith!" Julien winced. "I'm sorry, but that's Bernard speaking. I prefer Abelard's wedding of faith with reason, but I'm afraid it doesn't hold out any more hope."

"Don't misunderstand me, dear boy," Conti said quickly. "When I suggest we rely on God's judgment, that doesn't mean I believe we shouldn't try to influence that judgment as much as possible."

"Buck up, lad," Robert said to him, jovially. "You're on your way to Sicily. Doesn't that lighten your heart? I should think that after all the past postponements this return voyage has had, you'd be jubilant."

Julien tried to perk up. "You're right, Robert. I can hardly wait."

Conti poured some more wine for them. "And can you imagine with what feelings I look forward to a couple of months away from the intrigues of Vatican politics? Drink up, men. Not one more heavy word from any of us. I feel the need to celebrate."

Their ship was a small, neat vessel of Arabian design that sat in the water well and hugged the wind in her full-bellied, truncated sails. The crew was Salernitan, Neapolitan, and Amalfitan, but there were also two Pisans, and one Venetian. Neither Conti nor Julien paid much attention to the crew, but they both disliked the Venetian as soon as they saw him. The Venetians were independent, but owed a great deal to the protection of the Holy Roman Empire that surrounded them. Conti thought of objecting to the man's presence, but it seemed inadvisable to invite further delay. Julien and the cardinal shared a large, comfortable cabin, and with winds as favorable as they now appeared, they seemed assured of a pleasant voyage.

On only the second night out Julien sensed the presence of a stranger in the cabin. It was a warm evening, and he was glad he hadn't covered himself. He lay quietly until his eyes grew sufficiently accustomed to the darkness to make out the alien form only a yard or so away. He waited until he saw the man's arm upraised before springing from his bed and leaping on him. Surprise is a convincing ally, and in an instant Julien had disarmed him of the wicked, curved knife aimed for Conti's throat. Conti, aroused, congratulated Julien on acting before he could use the equally effective blade under his own pillow.

Julien asked Conti if he very much minded excusing him from being there when they tried to extract information from the Venetian. He was embarrassed to reveal his squeamishness, but he doubted his capacity for being effective in these matters.

"Dear me," the cardinal answered. "I'd rather hoped you'd go in my stead. Oh well, I suppose it's really my duty."

Julien lay uncomfortably on his bunk to wait while Conti questioned the man. He had no doubt as to the outcome of the interrogations, since he remembered the alacrity with which the cardinal dispatched the thieves who had attacked Robert on their way to Rome. Still, who would act differently in these circumstances? Half an hour later he heard a splash outside his porthole that told him they had finished their business with the Venetian, and Cardinal Conti reentered the cabin a moment later.

"Thank Heaven it wasn't one of those difficult trials," he said. "The unfortunate man confessed before anyone had the need to draw blood. As soon as we reach land, we must send word to Salerno to have a certain Father Corsi arrested and executed at once before he tries anything else. This poor Venetian was simply misguided by him. I believe he was a good man, and I gave him complete absolution before he died. May his soul find Heavenly peace. Would you be so good as to pour me out some aquavit? I think we could both use a drink. It isn't easy for me to sleep on the water."

The rest of the voyage was swift and uneventful. As soon as they reached Palermo they were met by an impressive committee, but Conti asked if he might be allowed to spend the evening alone to recover from the trip and he was escorted immediately to his apartment. Julien found himself alone, and the palace didn't look as warm and inviting in the darkness as he recalled it. He made his way to the studio first to find Aziz.

It was empty, although it was still an hour before vespers. He inquired in one of the adjoining offices and was told that Admiral George had called a council and asked Aziz to sit in with him. There was no way Julien could disturb a meeting of the admiral's. He had wanted to see Aziz before anyone else, not simply because he was a close friend but also the man most likely to give him news of Claire.

Perhaps it was just as well. Julien decided to try to contact Claire directly to see if she would dare to come to him again. He called a eunuch and gave him instructions for reaching Claire's apartment, and admonishing him to be certain the message was delivered to no one's ears but Claire's. The message was simply "Come to the studio."

Julien bit his nails for the next half hour, wondering if the messenger had been able to deliver his words in private, or if he had made another serious error in trying to contact her so brazenly. When Claire finally appeared, she was dressed somberly and she had Aziz's child Ahmad with her. She entered the room quietly and stood on the threshold with her eyes lowered even after he rushed to her and impulsively grabbed her arms, not daring yet to embrace her. She disengaged herself with a slow, deliberate movement, still avoiding his eyes.

"Your message sounded urgent. What is it you need of me?" Her voice was intentionally icy.

"I had to see you, Claire. All these months I've thought of no one but you. Claire, why are you so pale? Are you all right?"

"I'm perfectly well, thank you. Is that all you wished to say to me?"

Tears welled into his eyes, and he did nothing to check them. "Claire, does it mean nothing to you that I'm back? Don't you know how much I love you?"

She raised her eyes then and looked at him squarely. Her lips weren't quite as firm as she would have preferred, but she managed to maintain the coolness in her voice. "You have no right to speak to me that way."

"I do. My feelings give me that right. Claire, I couldn't wait. I came straight to find Aziz for news of you. I was afraid that if I tried to reach you directly, your mother might hear of it. Darling, I knew I loved you when I left, but only when I was away from you did I begin to understand how much."

"I haven't behaved properly in coming here. My mother is far from well. If she were to find out I'm gone, she'd be furious with me, and rightly so. Now, if you have nothing else to say to me I'll go."

"Claire, how can you treat me this way! Have you no word of welcome for me? Not even a look to say you're glad to see me again?"

"Glad to see you? I've cursed you, Julien."

The tears that had welled into his eyes started flowing. "But why? When I have nothing but love in my heart for you."

"You talk like a boy. Do you ever think of your responsibilities instead of your passion?"

"Do you mean, then, that I have a responsibility towards you?"

"No, you bastard. Towards Ula. I can see you haven't asked about *her* yet."

Julien drew back as if she'd slapped him. "Ula! But I told you she means nothing to me. She was a gift, that's all. I'll never see her again if you wish. I'd already intended to leave her, I swear it."

"That's exactly what I mean. If you were a man, or if you had any depth of feeling, you couldn't talk that way. Is she nothing more to you than that? A gift?"

"Yes, I swear it."

"And now you'd like Roger to make you another gift. A somewhat more impressive prize?"

"I don't understand."

"I mean, you wouldn't hesitate to accept me as a gift, would you?" Her face was fairly blazing now.

"It's not the same thing. Claire, don't look at me with such hate in your eyes. What have I ever done in word or thought to injure you?"

"Injure me? What makes you think you have the power to injure me? I'm speaking of Ula, you pig. Did you ever give her a thought? No, of course not. Even now you haven't troubled to ask me what's become of her."

"Is she ill? I mean, what was to become of her? She's comfortably taken care of."

"You left her with child, you rotten whoremaster."

Julien grabbed the edge of his desk for support. "I never dreamed. I thought they—"

"You thought!" she sneered. "You never thought at all. That was your trouble. You never once felt the slightest responsibility towards her."

"I'll make it up, I swear. My child. Is it a boy or a girl?"

Claire's lips curled spitefully. "Is that your only concern?"

"For Heaven's sake, Claire, stop this. I know I've behaved badly, but I don't think about those things the way you do. So help me, it never occurred to me once, in all the time I was away, that I might have become a father."

"You still haven't become one. Ula bribed one of the eunuchs to abort the child two months after you left."

He wept openly into his hands. "Dear God, is this a sin I share?"

"I believe so. She could have applied through the proper channels for an abortion. It would almost surely have been permitted since you never thought to make any arrangements for a child if one were to come, but she, I'm sorry to say, is as stupid and thoughtless as you are. Doing it the way she did, and mind you, I know women do it frequently here, she took a great chance of being discovered and punished."

"How is she now?"

"Not well, and it's hard for anyone to get news of her. The idiot who performed the operation had only the vaguest idea of what he was doing. She was very ill for months. My sex forbids my giving you any more details. Then, because she had asked for an illegal operation, she had to be punished. As soon as she was strong enough to withstand the pain, the eunuchs beat her so badly she had to spend another couple of months in bed. I understand she's better now, but I can tell you she's not as strong or as beautiful as when you left her."

Julien had taken a seat on one of the faldstools and was holding his head dazedly while he listened. "I must see her right away."

"I'm afraid you'll find that's not possible. Forgive me for telling you all this as harshly as I did. I didn't expect you to take it so deeply. The truth is, she's no longer your property now, Julien. She's a prisoner of the state and no one is permitted to see her, but with a little luck she'll be married off in a year or two to one of the servants."

"That's not fair. She was given to me."

Claire bridled. "There you go again. Well, if you're still in Roger's favor, he'll probably make you a gift of another slave. Or you can always use the whores at your disposal in the town's stews."

"Stop it. That's not what I meant at all. Claire, I had no idea you hated me so much. I'm going to ask Roger's permission to make a retreat. Even if you never forgive me, I pray my God may have a softer heart."

Claire realized her last outburst was ill considered. "I don't hate you, Julien. You still need to become a man, that's all."

"I hate myself."

Her voice softened at the sight of Julien's genuine misery. "That would be very wrong."

"And why did you, of all people, have to know of this and be the one to tell me," he moaned. "I'm so ashamed."

"I made it my business to know. Perhaps I was wrong in doing so."

His eyes widened. "You made it your business to know? Then that means you thought of me while I was gone or you wouldn't have cared."

Her voice was hesitant. "I never said I didn't think about you. But I still don't approve of you."

"Couldn't you ever think about me kindly?"

"I often do." Her words issued slowly.

"I don't deserve to hear that. Claire, my dearest, do you know those words give me hope, the most hope you've ever offered me?"

"It's pointless, Julien. I was never intended for you. Look, I know you aren't the ogre I just painted you. Your history with Ula is unfortunate, but I'm old enough to realize that it is man's justice and not God's that rules women. Forget my criticism; I had no right to make it. Forget me. You'll meet a girl very soon whom Roger will approve of, and I believe you'll make her an excellent husband."

"Forget you? I could sooner forget speech. Claire, I'd dedicate my whole life to making you happy. I know I was stupid and impulsive, but I was green. I've been away for almost a year now. I've changed. I've met people—"

"Women too, no doubt?"

"Let me finish. Yes, women too, from whom I've learned a great deal. I met one woman in particular in Rome—I'm not ashamed of it—who made me see women very differently. Don't look at me that way. I didn't sleep with her, if that's what you're thinking, although I admit I wanted to at first. The point is, she said something about taking pleasure with a partner that made me think about how selfish I'd been. I believe you're right, Claire. I will make a good husband, an excellent one if I can, but it's *your* husband I plan to be, and that's all there is to it."

Claire laughed. "And that's all there is to it, is there? For a man who learned the lessons you claim you did, you didn't leave much ground for agreement or disagreement. What do I do now? Faint in your arms because you've decided I'm the wife for you? No thank you, young man, you've still a long way to go."

"I know I still speak impetuously, darling. All I want you to say—even a look will do—is that you'll give me the chance to make you love me."

"You mean the chance to *earn* my love, don't you?"

"That's it. That's what I meant to say. Please say you will."

She raised an eyebrow enigmatically and turned from him. "I must get back to my mother now. And I have to return Ahmad to his family. What do you think of all this, little Ahmad?"

Ahmad had been sitting in the corner, his eyes widened during the most heated moments of their conversation, never sure whether to cry at the sound of their voices or to run away and risk Claire's displeasure. He jumped to his feet when Claire spoke his name and started to drag her towards the door.

"Ahmad, stay. Don't you remember me?" Julien called to him.

The boy shook his head and continued to pull Claire away.

"I must take him now. Will you be in your studio tomorrow?"

"Yes, of course. Claire! Does that mean you'll come to see me?" She hurried away without answering, then turned and gave him a quick, but grave, smile when she neared the end of the corridor.

Julien opened one of the chests and poured himself a long drink. How could he reach Ula, he wondered. It would be embarrassing to face her. He couldn't. No, they would never allow him to see her again in any case. It was she who had behaved most foolishly, but he had wronged her nevertheless, if only by his attitude towards her. He had almost a year's pay coming to him. He would see to it that she received that, at least.

To think that I was almost a father. The thought thrilled him and actually warmed his loins. He never doubted his fertility, but even with the sadness of the circumstances, the news of her pregnancy elated him. It was as heavy a sin as he had ever weighted his soul with, but once he made a mental note to see his confessor in the morning, his thoughts returned to the prospects of making Claire pregnant. More than ever he was convinced she was the only woman for him. He saw her big with his seed and hugged his arms in pure pleasure.

Aziz entered some minutes later, and they fell into each other's arms. "This is the welcome I've been waiting for. How much I've missed you, dear teacher, dear friend."

"You never left our hearts. Julien, I'm afraid there's some very unpleasant news."

"Ula? Yes, Claire told me."

"Oh? You saw Claire? I'm sorry you had to hear it from her. She has been exaggeratedly upset about the whole affair. I've been sorry to see her so concerned."

"She really was that concerned, then?" Julien mused. "It must be because she knows how much I love her that she allowed herself to become so involved."

"Perhaps. I know she also dwells too much on the lot of the slaves, and particularly the women. I hope you're not still deluding yourself with hopes of marrying her?"

"I know of no other way I can be happy."

"Or unhappy."

"I mean it. I'm a one-woman man. Now that I've found her, it's she or no one."

"That's not easy, even at my age."

"I didn't say it was easy."

"Poor Julien. I can't bring myself to think of you as a celibate. It seems such a waste. You'd father such pretty children."

"I don't plan to be a celibate. I plan to teach her to— I mean, I plan to earn her love, and then—"

"Julien, I beg you not to make a mess of things. I don't doubt Claire has strong feelings for you. You may call it love, but that's not quite enough."

"Why not? You mean, you really think she might love me?"

"One question at a time, please. Remember, there is her mother, and then there is Roger. Neither will find you as convincing as she does. And yes, I believe the poor girl never passed an hour without thinking of you, whether in anger or sympathy. I suppose I'd have to call that frightful condition love in someone her age."

Julien embraced him. "Right now Roger can have no criticism of my behavior. As a matter of fact, I believe he's very pleased with me. When I see him tomorrow I shall ask him for permission to court Claire. He can't deny me that much, can he?"

"On the contrary, he could do so very easily if he has someone else in mind for her. You presume too much."

Julien's eyes had a faraway look that told Aziz he wasn't really listening to him. "Now that I dare to hope she feels something for me, I'll stop at nothing to make her my wife, and I swear she'll be the happiest woman in Sicily."

"Julien, every time I start to think of you as a man, you say something to remind me you still have a schoolboy's humors fevering your flesh. I insist we change the subject. During almost a year's absence I can't believe there was absolutely nothing to occupy your interest except Claire."

"Forgive me, Aziz. I take advantage of our friendship. I haven't even asked you how things were with you."

"That's all right, Julien. I wish I could tell you they were better. Another child was born to me, a boy, and it died within six hours. I'm afraid my seed is growing weak."

"Not you, my friend. Perhaps it is your wife who needs a rest."

"What, Fatima? No, she's not yet forty and strong as a mare. She drinks teas of herbs and rare grasses all day to strengthen the egg so that she may conceive again soon. I was told that the child Ula carried would have been a boy, but it's not always easy to tell that early. It's a good sign, Julien, and I want you to know how sorry I am that she deceived you."

"Deceived me? How?"

"Yes, she knew she was pregnant when you left, or certainly must have suspected it. It is a serious crime for her not to have told you. They must have added to the lashes given for her punishment after the abortion because of that."

"God, how she must hate me."

"It's possible. But if you must review your conscience, please wait, and do so when you're alone. Did you have many adventures in Rome?"

"It was exciting, but I wouldn't want to live there. I noticed only three occupations in the city. You can be a Vatican politician, a whore or pander, which I take to be the same thing, or make your living by fleecing the pilgrims. The honest people who tend the grain and bake the bread live outside the walls." He shook his head. "I'll bore you with my adventures later, but tell me, what's going on in Palermo?"

"Everyone's thoughts and efforts are aimed at the coming coronation. You can't believe the preparations! You'd have to go back to the most glorious days of the Byzantine Empire to find a ceremony to compare. Roger has brought in the finest Byzantine artists to supervise the decorations. He settled on Christmas Day for the coronation, even though he knew Cardinal

Conti would be here sooner. It will be the most lavish celebration the world has seen in modern times, and there's no chance his holiday will be overshadowed by Christ's, or at any rate that's what we irreverent Muslims believe."

"I hoped to speak with Roger tomorrow, even though I don't have an appointment. I wonder if I dare to if he has so much on his mind."

"Of course you can. He'll be pleased to see you. Why don't you accompany Cardinal Conti when Roger receives him? That's a perfectly natural thing to do."

"It's not exactly the circumstance I had in mind, but I suppose I might be able to petition him then for a more private interview."

"If you're so determined, I won't say another word. Enough! Will you dine with us this evening?"

"You are my family."

As soon as Julien found himself alone, he began to muse on his last words to Aziz. My family. It was true. England seemed so far away. He thought often of his family, but always sentimentally, and he wondered if he would ever be granted the chance to see his father again. Nigel was well over fifty now, and that was many more years than God gave most men to live. Perhaps one day, when Roger's lands were settled, he could petition for a year's leave to visit England. If he could only take his bride with him! He knew the sight of Claire at his side would lighten the old crusader's heart. But Roger's campaign was a long way from being won. His work was here. What if I'd stayed in England? He smiled at the idea of a career as a village priest or as a teacher in a monastery such as Durham. No, his home was in Palermo. He felt Sicilian.

Julien went to Cardinal Conti's apartment the next morning to pay his respects and to ask if he might accompany him to his audience with Roger, which was scheduled for late morning and would presumably lead into the midday meal. Conti had just finished a large breakfast of fruit and pastry and was in high spirits. "Remarkable fruit, dear fellow. I don't suppose I could get any of these to grow in my garden in Rome?"

"You might, if you shielded them from the winds. We grow melons like the one you ate in Sicily, but at this time of the year I'm almost certain the one you had came from Tunisia. We're expanding our relations with the North African coast, and it appears we'll be receiving tribute from all of their kingdoms before long."

"I seem to recall that your Sicilian navy suffered its worst defeat there."

"Yes, Mahdia. That was seven years ago. A great deal has changed since then, including the size of our navy. More importantly Prince Hassan realizes Sicilian corn means a great deal to him. He acknowledges Roger as his suzerain."

"I begin to understand the basis for some of the criticisms of Roger one hears in the north. Truthfully, don't you think he goes a bit far in indulging all these Muslims, and yes, these Jews?"

"But, I thought— Aren't you Jewish?"

Conti pouted. "Julien, you mustn't make the same mistake our enemies do. My forefathers were Jewish. I am not. Unlike the north countries, many of us Christians in Italy and Spain can claim Jewish ancestry. The Jews of Rome are quite ancient. Ostia had a community of at least ten thousand Jews at the time of Julius Caesar, and Romans descended from them have every right to be proud because they were among the foremost citizens. But to *encourage* Jewry is something quite different. And as for the Muslims, which of our Christian families in the north has not suffered a loss in the Crusades?"

"Very well, then, I'll answer your question so that there can be no misunderstanding between us. No, I don't think he goes too far in indulging Muslims and Jews. My closest friend here is an Arab. How do you think I learned Arabic?"

"Julien! Intellectual curiosity is all very well, but I must warn you to be careful. Aren't you ever troubled that these foreign influences might endanger the well-being of your soul?"

"Come now, you told me a Roman might well be proud of his Jewish ancestry. What makes an Arab so different?"

"Everything. Christ was a Jew."

"I'm delighted to see that's occasionally remembered in Rome."

"I still fail to see how you can equate Jews with Muslims. The Saracens are still the sworn enemies of Christ. You don't see Jews raising armies to fight Christians."

"No, nor even to defend themselves from them. Promise me you'll try to speak to some Muslims while you're here. You may find them stimulating. I'd particularly like you to meet my friend Aziz."

"I suspect he won't be the only infidel I'm thrown in with, from what I hear of Roger's court. I confess I was taken aback just moving through the palace to get to my rooms. It looks like he's flung open his doors to every race in the world."

"Except Germans. Roger believes, as most Sicilians do, that German customs are too different from ours to ever be assimilated here. There aren't many Germans who try to become Sicilians, but it's our fear that if they should ever decide to migrate, they'll do so with spears in their hands and their emperor at their head."

"We share that nightmare in Rome. I begin to think you Sicilians aren't as different from us as I had believed. I have another question for you, if you'll indulge me further. Roman Jews have always been curious about the Jews of Sicily since they both represent the older, more established Jewish colonies of Europe. Can you tell me how many of our cousins are here now?"

"Yes, I can. Aziz, the friend I spoke of, is an expert on the subject. Jews constitute at least ten percent of the population of all the larger cities, with a lower percentage in the smaller towns."

"I'd heard a larger figure."

"Well, a few minutes ago you chided me for asking if you weren't Jewish. If you wish to include those families that were once Jewish but no longer are, yes, the figures would be significantly higher. I'm ashamed to say it, but when the first Normans arrived, they found that after over two hundred years of Muslim rule there was such a general lapse of religious worship that the Christians could hardly be considered members of the Church, and that was true of the Jews as well.

"Following the Norman soldiers, there arrived a new army of monks who were very busy baptizing all those who had fallen by the wayside. It became a wholesale practice to baptize everyone on the island who wasn't a Muslim, so nearly every Jew here was at least temporarily a Christian. I'm not daring to venture a guess as to how many of our good Christians can claim Jewish ancestry. More than in Spain, I should think, and that would be considerable."

"My dear friend, it would give me pleasure to continue this conversation with you, perhaps with your friend Aziz included. But now to your future king."

Roger rose to greet them when they entered his chamber. He was alone except for two eunuch guards at the door and one of his cheetahs. He nodded perfunctorily to Julien, then bowed low to kiss Cardinal Conti's ring.

"Your Eminence does us great honor."

"The honor is mine, King Roger. No less than the privilege of consecrating you King of Sicily through his Holiness' grace."

Roger was silent a moment. "Am I not king, then, by the grace of God?"

"Of course you are. Through the offices of His representative on earth."

"But first by the grace of God."

"Do you speak of divine right, as did the Byzantine emperors? That is an eastern affectation which has never been digested in the Holy City. Your brother kings have not pretended to such rights for a long time."

"No, that doesn't surprise me. Such rights are best understood in these climates. I won't embarrass you by making an issue of it, but please remember that a majority of my subjects in Sicily are either Muslims or Byzantine, and the concept's natural to them. Regardless of the formalities you can choose to employ in the ceremony, my subjects will acknowledge that the kingship is mine through divine authority."

"I can't really be concerned what the Muslims think when it's clear we're not speaking of the same god."

"They might not agree."

"Be careful what you say." Conti's distress was evident, but Roger remained coolly polite. "Roger, will you swear to me that you will accept the sacrament I offer you in full Christian faith?"

"Do you question whether I accept the sacrament in faith or do you question my faith? Never mind. I will, and I am secure in my faith in Christ."

"There! That's a relief. Not that I doubted you for a moment, you understand, but rumors about you are so persistent. It would be unfortunate if someone tried to embarrass us after your coronation. Why don't we sit now and relax. Julien has been itching to speak with you."

"I'm truly happy to see you again," Julien said earnestly.

"And I you. You've served me well, and I shan't forget it. Robert told me how well you performed. He'll be here for the coronation, of course.

"Incidentally, I received another letter of commendation from Rome in addition to the praise from his Excellency Conti and His Holiness."

"Yes?" said Julien. "I can't imagine whom it would be from."

"A woman. I was ready to discount her impressions, but she expressed herself in the manner of a great and learned lady. It was Matilda of Canossa."

"Matilda!" Cardinal Conti broke in. "Well, that is praise, then. I noticed you were making a good impression on her, Julien, but I had no idea she'd take it upon herself to write a letter in your behalf."

"I suspect," said Roger, "the impression this rascal made was about six inches deep."

"Be that as it may," Conti intervened, "there are few people of either sex as close to St. Peter's throne, and for entirely disinterested motives. Her aunt was Matilda of Tuscany, and no woman is more noted for her piety and devotion to the Church.

"The niece Matilda's estimation of Julien's character may be considered on its own merits, regardless of any friendship between them."

Roger began to show impatience at all this praise of Julien in his presence. "All right, Julien. Is there anything else you urgently need to see me about?"

"Yes sir, but I'll wait for another time. I know you and His Emimence have much to talk about."

"Oh, we have plenty of time for our talks," Conti said generously. "It's a month till the coronation, and if you would extend me your hospitality, Roger, I should very much like to spend most of the winter here before returning to Rome. I find your climate most agreeable, and your kitchen surpasses anything imaginable."

Roger bowed his head lightly. "I promise to do everything I can to make your stay as pleasant as possible. Julien, don't beat about the bush. If you have some business for my curia, we'll take it up tomorrow, but if you want to speak about something personal, let's have it now. The cardinal is clearly your friend." He noted Julien's reticence and set his jaw firmly. "Is it about Ula? That's out of your hands now. I'll not say anything more about it, and you'd be wise to follow my example."

"No, it's not Ula. My penance there will be a private one. I really would rather wait until I can see you alone."

"If you wish," said Cardinal Conti, moving as if to rise, but going no further.

Julien appeared shocked. "Oh, no, Your Eminence, I wouldn't dream of inconveniencing you. I'm embarrassed you would think I could. No, this is a private matter I have no right taking up valuable time with."

Roger's impatience was increasing. "What makes you think I'm likely to be less busy tomorrow? Or next month? Don't be so bloody irritating, Julien. If you've a favor to ask, then out with it now, damn it, while I'm still in a good mood."

Julien hesitated only briefly. "I think I should marry."

"I think you're an idiot."

Cardinal Conti raised his hands conciliatorily. "Roger, please. I must remind you that marriage is a sacrament that cannot be denied him if he is of age. Discourage him if you must, but not in my presence."

"Very well, then." Roger started to rub his hands briskly. "I suppose you want me to choose a bride for you. One with enough money, I should think. No problem there, just give me a day or two to decide."

"No, my king. I know whom I must marry."

"Must? What is this must? Have you compromised some innocent girl? She'd better not be of good family, or I'll have your bottom caned for it."

"No, it's nothing like that. There's a woman I love absolutely, and I can't be happy without her."

"Heaven help us. Do I know this angel of delight?" Roger winked broadly at Conti.

"She is your ward, Claire."

"Claire!" he thundered, leaping from his seat. "I told you she wasn't for you. No, absolutely not! How dare you mention her to me again after I told you I had other plans for her."

"It's stronger than I am."

"Oh God, that phrase again. Every damn Sicilian who makes an ass of himself excuses it with 'It's stronger than I.' Well, you're still an Englishman, and wet behind the ears at that, even if you're my subject. Start making sense, boy."

"You haven't promised her to anyone else, have you?"

"It's none of your damned business what I've done. Besides, there's her mother to consider."

"But a word from you."

"Not now. Her mother is very ill, or didn't Claire tell you?"

"I heard she wasn't well."

"No, she's *very* ill. My doctors have been attending her for the last two months, and they don't hold out much hope. Julien, if you insist on being a fool, I'll choose a bride for you. I'll even give you your choice of two or three. What do you say?"

"At least give me some hope. All I ask is that you don't absolutely forbid the marriage."

"I hope you haven't been stupid enough to tell her what's on your mind. Oh, but of course you have. I forget what you're like. Julien, how can you possibly put your judgment in these matters above mine? When you came here, how many young women had you known?"

Julien blushed and didn't answer.

"I think I know. While you were at school you had half a dozen chances on holiday to pat the ass of some half-witted country girl. Perhaps there were a few more chances at a bit of tit on your voyage here. But answer me this. How many young women of Claire's class have you ever spoken to in your life?"

Julien felt thoroughly humiliated by now and continued his silence.

"Just as I thought. Claire's the first good-looking young girl of breeding you've ever spoken more than half a dozen words to, and so you're sure it's love. Damn! If any more of my court start acting as ridiculously as you have, I'll take every mewling troubadour and trouvère who licked his way into my kingdom and ship them to the first male whorehouse on the African coast that'll have them."

He was enjoying his dramatic speech too much to be entirely convincing, but Cardinal Conti was now blushing as fiercely as Julien. Roger dropped his voice and laid a hand on Julien's shoulder. "Seriously, my boy, you're making a dangerous mistake. I should punish you, but you know I won't. All right, leave us now. I have more important business to discuss with His Eminence, and there's no point having you hanging about like a sick lamb."

Julien hung his head. "Very well."

"See me in the morning. Early. And do me a favor. Go out and get yourself laid this afternoon. You'd be surprised how it clears the head."

Cardinal Conti had begun whistling off key. Julien hastily brushed his hand with his lips, then knelt and kissed Roger's hand firmly. "My lord."

"Get out, get out. I should've known better than to let myself get involved with a horny, gat-toothed redhead."

"I'm sorry if I've displeased you." Julien walked shamefacedly towards the door. This was not the reception he'd expected after he'd been away so long in his master's service. And in front of his friend, Cardinal Conti! He felt his humiliation turn to anger and paused at the threshold. "If you're so dissatisfied with me, perhaps you'd like to release me from my contract and let me return to England."

"What? How dare you? Is this the thanks I get from you? After all the honors I've just heaped on you? Why, there's not a Norman in my court who wouldn't give his left ball for a title like yours—and some of the best land in Sicily. You ungrateful little snot-nosed whelp!"

Julien wheeled and stared at him. "Honors?" He stumbled and almost trod on the paw of the cheetah who had seen him to the door.

"Yes, where have you been? Didn't you deliver your report to my curia when you returned as you were instructed?"

"I delivered it, but I was anxious to see someone, so I didn't stay to speak with them. Aziz didn't mention anything, and I've seen only him. And Claire."

"Dunce! If you did your work properly, you'd know that when you make a report to the curia you submit yourself to them for further questioning or other instructions. You were too busy sniffing after forbidden skirts. Forgive all this, Conti. The lad has no sense of protocol." He shook his head exasperatedly. "I wondered why the Devil you didn't mention it. I've made you a baron, you idiotic scapegrace, although if I were to tell you what I think of barons, you might not consider it such a compliment. You'll take your oath of allegiance on my coronation day. Not that the title means a damn thing, but it comes with a rather choice parcel of land."

Julien rushed to Roger and tried to kiss his hand again but he pulled back. "See me tomorrow, you bloody ass. I've had enough of your silliness today."

"I wanted no title, Roger. You do me honor I don't deserve."

"Well, I didn't want a title for you either, but it came with the land. Now get out, Baron di Furci."

"Furci?"

"It's a short way north of Taormina. You may even get to see it one day, if you're lucky. Now stop trying my patience. Get the hell out of here."

Julien felt he must look like a madman to the passersby as he dashed to his studio to tell Aziz the news of his windfall. A baron, before he was yet twenty! And his lands held in what must surely be the most beautiful part of the island. Aziz would of course be sure to tell Claire, and maybe even her mother. Now he had something to offer her. The Baroness di Furci! How well it suited her.

But first he had to have her, and Roger seemed no more inclined than before to give his consent. Not even to Baron Julien di Furci. What a pleasant ring it had. Of course, it meant that he would now be bound closer to Roger with ties of fealty. No matter. He had already pledged himself completely in his heart. He wondered if there would be time to visit Furci before the coronation. He still had not explored the eastern part of the island, but he knew that it was softer, warmer, and altogether more seductive than the northern coast.

Taormina was long a favorite site for the wealthy citizens around Etna to build their summer retreats. The Greeks from the ancient city of Naxos just below it used it as a resort and built a splendid theater there whose high arched walls were open to one of the most glorious scenes their poets had ever described, encompassing the cone of Etna, the dense gardens of the villas, and the scimitar curve of the sea-green coast. Julien felt thoroughly intoxicated. There would be some income from the estate too. He hoped it would be enough to impress Claire's mother.

Aziz was delighted to hear the news, but returned quickly to his customary sobriety. "I know you'd like me to tell Claire of your good fortune at once, but I must tell you she is more concerned with other matters just now. Her mother took a turn for the worse during the night. It is as if something were eating her from within, and the doctors can do no more."

"Poor Claire. What does that mean for her future, if her mother were to die now?"

"Roger would most certainly hurry her marriage. It would be impossible for her to live alone in the palace."

"Aziz, you must help me."

"What do you expect me to do? Dictate to my king?"

"Tell me how I can reach him. There must be something I can say to him which would make him change his mind."

"Julien, your king has just done you a great honor. It would be unseemly to make other demands on him. I advise you to hold your tongue, unless you want him to think you ungrateful."

"Perhaps if I were to tell him how much better I could serve him if I were given my wish. With Claire by my side, there's no limit to how far I could go."

"Give us all some peace, Julien. Look, why don't you dine with my family this evening? I was recently given some extraordinary wine from the slopes of Etna. We'll celebrate your new title."

"For a man whose religion forbids wine—"

"I never drink in public."

Celebrate they did. When Julien went to Roger's chamber to keep his morning appointment his head was still throbbing.

Roger was in a grim mood. "You embarrassed me, Julien. Don't ever ask me—in front of strangers—for anything you know I can't give you. It makes me appear ungenerous."

"I apologize, Roger. You must think me an ingrate. But I truly didn't know you'd already honored me so greatly."

"That should have made no difference, but I'm ready to forget it. Now, I'll say one more word to you about Claire; then I forbid you to mention her name to me again. Forbid you, do you hear?"

"Yes, my lord."

"Her mother knows she cannot live long, and it's Theodora's wish that Claire be married to her cousin, Alexis of Copertino. He's a fine man, a few years older than you, although probably not much richer. Did you know you're rich now, Julien? Furci is a handsome settlement, and you deserve it. Don't make me regret my choice by acting stupidly. Conti and Anacletus both sing your praises, and Selby says you acquitted yourself every bit as well as he could have hoped to himself. I think of you as my chief secretary now, and it's right for you to have an income that suits your position."

"I promise to do everything in my power to make you feel I'm worthy of the trust you've placed in me." Julien answered humbly.

"And you will respect my wishes about Claire?"

"I respect your every wish, but how can I obey? I still love her more than life itself."

"Those are the words of a child. You certainly don't expect me to countermand what may well be a friend's deathbed wish. Claire turned sixteen last June. I can't delay her marriage any longer. The first banns will be read before my coronation, and since we must assume that her mother won't live much longer, Claire must be married when a decent interval after the funeral has passed. Now, as for you, it would be well for you to marry as soon as possible. I gave it a good deal of thought last night, and I've come up with three prospects for you to choose from."

"Roger, please. I have no heart for such thoughts."

"In that case, I will choose for you." He rose and began to pace the room. "The first candidate I thought of was Cunegunda of Salerno. She's a distant relative of the royal house, and although she doesn't have much money, you can't find a better name. She's fourteen and they're anxious to marry her off quickly. I hear she's a great beauty. The women of that family are noted for their splendid breasts and thighs. She'll bear you many a fine son."

"Roger, please. I don't—"

"Be still. Then there's Constance, the widow of John of Mortain, a distant relative of my father's second wife. She's two years your senior but utterly charming and quite, quite rich. That would be a most advantageous match. She was married to her former husband for only a year before he died, but I know he adored her. She bore him one child, but it died at birth strangled on its cord, so there's no fault to her there.

"That's one Lombard and one Norman. I also think you might fancy Anne of Lecce. They're rather snobbish Greeks but well educated and fairly rich, although I seem to recall there's a great number of children to share the inheritance. Maybe not. You'd have to wait a year or two anyway. I believe Anne's thirteen, but George of Antioch, who knows them better than I, says she can't be more than twelve. No, that wouldn't do, you're too hot to wait that long. I think it shall be Cunegunda. What do you say? Would you like to meet her? Or Constance? They'll both be here for the coronation. You can have either one, but if you take too long deciding, I warn you—I'll make up your mind for you. No, it will be Cunegunda. I've decided. You'll find her irresistible."

"I'm sure she's as lovely as you say, Roger, and I promise to go along with your wishes, but not now."

"When, then? When your juices are dried?"

"Only after Claire is married to another and I know that she is completely lost to me. Then I shall marry anyone you wish me to as quickly as I can, and I'll do my best to make her a good husband. But I can't promise to love anyone except Claire."

Roger glowered darkly, "Julien, I warned you against repeating these idiotic troubadour fantasies. Damn those French milksops! They do nothing but encourage excessive masturbation in my finest young men. Am I doomed to see a whole generation given to sighs and fluttering hearts?"

Julien bit his lip. "It's well known how much you love Queen Elvira, Roger. Am I wrong to aspire to that same love?"

Roger stopped his pacing abruptly and stared at Julien as if he were a stranger. "You can't have any idea what that love is." His voice was softer, almost melancholy. "Yes, of course I love her. Absolutely. But I hadn't seen her before I married her. I prayed that I would love her, and because she is as good as she is lovely, I find I do. But real love comes after the marriage." He lifted his voice and resumed his pacing. "Now, from all I hear, this Cunegunda is worthy of any man's love. She sounds like a prize piece of flesh, ripe and juicy. You'll start pawing the ground at the first whiff of her, boy. Love will follow, never fear."

Julien was silent. There must be more to it than that, he thought.

"And now you'll be kept very busy for the next month. Busy enough, I hope, to cool that hot blood of yours. You've already missed out on all the initial preparations for the coronation, but there are still a great number of details to be attended to. I want this to be the most spectacular event in anyone's memory." He clapped his young friend's shoulder heartily. "This isn't just my coronation, Julien. We're celebrating the birth of a nation. On Christmas Day the kingdom of Sicily will take its place beside the great nations of the world. We are about to have our day in the sun."

"I pray the day may be a long one." Julien crossed himself.

"Please. You don't have to remind me of my enemies. I'll deal with them when I have to. Don't think I underestimate them for a minute, but at least for now, the Holy City and St. Peter's throne belong to Anacletus, while Innocent remains in exile. Without Bernard at his side, Innocent would be nothing. Nothing."

Julien nodded. "Conti and I had reason to believe Lothair has opted for Innocent. Has there been any confirmation of this?"

"He hasn't. At least not yet. Just when it looked like Lothair would declare for Innocent, Anacletus excommunicated Conrad of Hohenstaufen, Lothair's chief enemy and the only other claimant for the imperial crown. That should sit well with Lothair. All right. I'll want you with me when I meet with my curia this afternoon, but in the meantime you can familiarize yourself with all that's been—"

Roger was interrupted by a loud knock at the door. Before his eunuchs could answer, a handsome, weather-beaten man with a blond beard and a powerful, muscular body entered excitedly. Julien recognized him as George of Antioch, Roger's emir of emirs whom he had seen only on a few occasions when George addressed the curia.

"May I speak freely in front of him?" the man asked with a nod towards Julien.

"Absolutely. You've met Julien. He's now Baron di Furci, my secretary."

George acknowledged Julien curtly and proceeded with his news. "There was an important message brought to my office from France. The Fat called a church council at Étampes to help him decide which pope he should support, and as you can guess, the whole council was totally dominated by Bernard. There was no contest. It hardly took any time at all."

"Who was at the council to speak for Anacletus?" Roger demanded.

"Abelard's men, but they didn't have a chance against Bernard."

"That's hard to believe," Julien said. "They're as skilled in argument as any, and the canonicity of Anacletus' election is sound."

"Bernard was too clever to go into it. I have a quote here which will give you an idea of Bernard's argument. Listen. *'The adherents of Anacletus have made a covenant with death and a compact with hell . . .'* And later, *'The abomination of desolation is standing in the Holy Place, to gain possession of which he has set fire to the sanctuary of God. He persecutes Innocent and with him all who are Innocent.'* If you read on, you'll see that he didn't allow any reasonable inquiry into either's right to the throne."

"So the French have gone over to Innocent." Roger's face was ashen. "I hadn't expected this so soon. Julien, please leave us now, and take these papers with you. I've some things to go over with George."

Julien bowed to both of them and returned to his studio.

It was less than forty-eight hours since he'd returned to Sicily and he felt like he'd been catapulted into a whirlwind. It was too much for him to digest in such a short time. And this Cunegunda! He conjured an image of a florid Lombard aristocrat with too much jewelry and too much flesh. There was no sense antagonizing Roger further just yet, but he was sure he'd have no Cunegunda sharing his bed. He was so depressed when he entered his studio he was almost piqued to find Aziz in high spirits.

"Julien, it's not seemly of you to be so long in the mouth when Allah has been so generous with you."

"Has he? I don't recall ever praying for a title, or money."

"Sit down and cheer up, lad. I have an idea. It's a bit farfetched, but in your present dismal circumstances, it might be worth a try. Have you ever seen the Baroness Theodora?"

"Claire's mother? No, I was never presented, although I did see her once with Claire, but at some distance. I remember, I thought she looked very proud, and still quite lovely. But she refused to see me when Roger tried to arrange a meeting just before I left. She'll have no part of me, it seems. She's most unfair."

"Do you think she'd recognize you if she saw you again?"

"I doubt it. I don't think Claire told her who I was the day I saw her."

"Excellent. Listen to this. Theodora is receiving guests this evening. I expect the doctors may have hinted that she can't hope to live much longer, and she has decided to see her friends. It will be quite informal, and I know she wouldn't mind our taking along another guest. Why don't you come with us? She may even take a liking to you."

"No, no. Not if she absolutely refused to see me before."

"Correction. She refused to see Julien Fitz Nigel, an upstart only recently arrived from the primitive wilds of England, who had the bad manners to thrust himself upon her daughter with no respect for protocol. I plan to introduce her this evening to Baron de Furci, a cultivated gentleman who is a polished addition to Roger's court."

"Aziz, you're wonderful! But what if she does see me, what good will that do? She's already expressed her final wish to Roger that Claire be married to her cousin Alexis."

"What of it? Before you left for Rome, Roger was all for marrying her to one of Bohemund's relatives. Nothing's been arranged yet; he has too many other things to think about. Don't be so fainthearted. If nothing comes of this, you'll at least know you tried everything."

"And I'll see Claire again. Good, I'll go. Thank you, Aziz."

"I've already warned Claire that I'd ask you to come with me, and she promised to behave exactly as if she's meeting you for the first time."

"She did?" Julien's earlier mood was suddenly reversed, and he gave Aziz an impulsive hug.

For the next two hours Julien tried to summon all his powers of concentration on the papers Roger had given him to study, but at last he had to admit that it was hopeless. He left the palace and walked awhile, then went to a nearby bathhouse frequented by aristocrats and wealthy Lombard merchants, and spent a long time having himself shaved, massaged, and rubbed with scented oils until his skin was radiant. He returned to his apartment and selected a robe that he had bought in Rome and not yet worn. It was woven of a fine, tan wool which he knew was a shade that flattered him. He was satisfied when he looked at it again that he'd make a good impression. There was a matching cloak with a fine embroidered border, but he decided the night was too warm to wear it and he reluctantly put it aside. As a last thought, he took out a fine linen wimple in a blue-violet that he thought would suit Claire when he saw it in Rome. Theodora had Claire's coloring, he recalled, and it might please her. He felt fully equipped for his campaign now and set out for Aziz's apartment with a light spring to his step and a jaunty tilt to his head.

Baroness Theodora was reclining on a pile of cushions in the center of her chamber. She was far younger than Julien expected, probably still in her thirties, he thought, and it was obvious that Claire or one of the maids had skillfully painted her face to re-create the bloom that had dissipated with her illness.

A dozen guests were seated solemnly around her in a semicircle. Introductions were made very gravely, and the baroness flickered her fingers lightly towards Julien. He accepted her invitation by carrying them lightly to his lips as he knelt before her. He handed her the wimple without speaking, and she stared at him puzzledly before she nodded her head in thanks.

Claire was seated far to the side with her head bowed. When Julien moved to pay his respects to her, she held her hand out timidly and he was tempted to seize it, to press it to his mouth, and devour it with kisses if he could do so unseen by the other guests, but he thought better of it and allowed his lips to hover over it fleetingly.

"The doctors have warned my mother not to exert herself," Claire said. "If she doesn't join in the conversation it's not because she is less than delighted by it."

Aziz took the initiative and cheerfully directed the conversation into the most optimistic appraisals of recent affairs. Plans for the coronation were foremost in everyone's thoughts, and it appeared that the parties and other entertainments for it were to last for well over the next two months. The women of the Tiraz were working from dawn until dark, and every seamstress and silk worker in the city was turning down requests for more and more elaborate robes for the festivities, while the price being asked by the merchants for jewelry and precious stones had doubled in the last month.

Theodora kept the violet wimple Julien had given her next to her and glanced at it periodically, returning her gaze to Julien often. He was able to catch her eye each time, and after a while she would hold her gaze longer and longer until he realized she was openly staring at him. Aziz, meanwhile, skillfully wove hints of Julien's many virtues and of the honors and estate he had just been given into the conversation, and Julien saw Theodora's interest in his talk enliven.

After only an hour Claire rose and announced that the reception was ended since she had promised the doctors she wouldn't allow her mother to tire. The guests rose to their feet and queued in front of the baroness to make their farewells. When it was Julien's turn and he bent to kiss her hand, he heard her whisper, "Stay."

He started abruptly and looked at her questioningly. Her lips formed the word again unspoken. Julien drew to the side and whispered to Aziz that he would like to join him at his apartment later if his family would still put up with him, and Aziz squeezed his arm in answer.

The maids had already begun to lead Theodora to her bedchamber, where she was put to bed and propped up comfortably on more pillows. Julien heard her call to her daughter. "Send me the young baron and wait outside." Claire did not dare to look at Julien when she motioned him into the room, but she thought she heard his heart echo the tattoo of her own.

"Baroness."

"Come closer. My voice is very weak." He looked for a stool to pull over to her bedside, but she impatiently gestured for him to sit on the bed close to her and he did so, faintly uncomfortable at the unexpected intimacy.

"You're clever, young man."

"I? But why? I've barely said two words to you."

"Do you think I don't know who you are? Or do you perhaps think I don't know my daughter?"

"I beg your pardon, madam. I assure you I meant no offense in coming."

"Nonsense. I know exactly why you're here. Let me tell you why I wouldn't see you when you first asked for an interview through Roger."

"That's quite all right, madam. You don't—"

"Quiet. Do you think I haven't seen more than my share of Norman adventurers coming down to win or steal anything they can? Let me tell you, I married one. Yes, he was no better than any of you. Or did you think we Greeks loved our Norman conquerors? Well, I admit I finally did come to love my husband, but I swore I'd have no part of any more rough, Norman scum that leave home to rape their livings. Certainly not for my Claire."

"I'm sorry. Perhaps I should leave. You're straining yourself."

"Let me finish. I'm not so deeply prejudiced that I don't love Roger.

But Norman though he is, he was born here and is one of us. He knows exactly how I feel. I made him swear he would never marry my daughter to a Norman. Forget about that nonsense of her marrying Bohemund's relative. He had to improvise something for your benefit."

"I had no idea you felt so strongly about it, madam. The sight of me must displease you. I apologize for it and will bid you good night now."

"Stay where you are." She reached forward with unexpected energy and pressed his shoulder down. "I had three sisters, and they were all raped by Normans. So were two of my aunts. The only reason I didn't meet the same fate was that my husband Serlo knew he could advance his career faster with an advantageous match. Do you understand?"

"I'm sorry we caused you such pain. But I'm only half Norman. My mother's lands and the women of those lands were raped by the Normans too."

"Yes, and Claire is half Norman as you are, but you are a man, and there is a great difference there."

Julien was silent, not knowing how to continue. Her hand reached out and lay on his for just a moment. "Claire spoke to me this morning."

"Yes."

"The silly girl threatens to take the veil if she is forced to marry my cousin Alexis. Did you know she thinks she's in love with you?"

"I didn't dare hope so." Julien thought he was going to faint, and wondered how she could bear this airless room.

"All right. I admit I was wrong about you. I don't know what you were like before, but I see Roger has done his best to make you respectable, and you speak Greek better than any Norman I've ever heard. Very well, if you really love Claire I see no obstacle to the match. I'll tell Roger tomorrow that I release him from his vow."

Julien stared at her, not certain he could believe what he had just heard and wondering why she would try to make such a bad joke. There was a buzzing in his ears and a flush rising to them so that he had to grip the corner of the mattress to be sure he wouldn't fall over on her.

"Are you all right? We can work out the details of her dowry and the morgengab tomorrow. I'm growing tired now."

Julien pressed his eyes shut to drive back the dizziness.

"Did you hear what I said?"

"I can't be sure."

"Claire brings a handsome dowry with her. She's my only heir."

"That's not— I mean, I don't care. It's only Claire I want."

"And I want her happiness. Do you know what a morgengab is?"

Julien confessed he didn't, although he'd heard it spoken of as part of a marriage contract.

"It was originally a Lombard institution, but it's practiced all over Roger's lands. It's a husband's gift to the bride to ensure her independence in case of some unforeseen problem. Not that I believe either of you would give the other grounds for divorce; it simply makes good sense, and the only people who don't do it are the ones who can't afford to."

"She can have everything I own."

"You know that's not possible. Everything she has will be yours, except for what you expressly state as a gift from your own estate."

"Then, she shall have Furci."

"That's more than is necessary or usual. But please leave now. My daughter and I can work out the rest of the details together."

"I'm sorry if I tired you. But did she really say she loves me?"

"She'll have no one else. Go. And Julien—"

"Yes, madam."

"God bless you both."

He leaned forward and kissed her on both cheeks. "You are a great lady."

When he left her chamber, he looked cautiously to see if Claire might still be around, but the only person in the room was an old serving woman who was anxious to show him to the door as promptly as she could. He hesitated there a moment. "Can you tell me if I might see Lady Claire?"

The woman appeared outraged by his request. "At this hour? In her own apartment? The very idea!"

"But we're engaged."

"All the more reason if that be true. Would you like me to call a eunuch to escort you back to your own quarters?"

Julien raced through the labyrinth of corridors to Aziz's apartment and found his friend waiting for him with a glass of wine in his hand and a delighted grin on his face. There were a dozen or so of his children present and his wife, Fatima. The children immediately surrounded Julien and began tugging at his robe playfully. "A wedding, a wedding!"

Julien looked at Aziz in amazement. "How did you know?"

"Dear Julien, did you really think it was my idea to have you see Theodora? I suspect you may be marrying a cleverer woman than you deserve."

"It was Claire?"

"Of course. She knows her mother's chief concern now that she's so ill is that she be provided for and happily married. You've seen how strong willed the girl is. Once she decided she really wanted to have you, she had to find a way to get her mother to accept her decision. Roger was no problem, because he would have to respect the dying woman's wish. I admit it helped your case greatly that you now have a position and title to offer Claire. What we didn't expect was that the baroness would guess your identity so quickly, but the minute you entered the room she was on to us."

"Did you speak to Claire?"

"Briefly, after you followed her mother into the bedchamber. She had a fairly good idea of the interview that would take place. Did Theodora ask you many questions?"

"No, I had very little to say. She guided the entire interview."

"I'm not surprised. Women have a way of working out men's destinies between them. Drink up, Julien. My word, I think you're still in shock. You don't look at all like a happy bridegroom should."

"I must see Claire."

"Not likely. You'll be informed soon of the date they've set for the wedding. It would be presumptuous of you to expect to see her alone until then. I expect Theodora will invite you to her apartments again very soon, and if you're lucky she may allow Claire to be present, but I wouldn't depend on it."

"Oh no! How can I not tell her what I feel? This is the most important thing that's ever happened to me. I can't keep it to myself."

"You may tell me all about it if you wish, Julien. I promise to be a sympathetic listener, but I beg you not to overdo it lest you inflame my passions as well." The children all laughed at this and Julien felt foolish, but then he joined them in laughter, and in another minute he was seated at the table, roaring until he hurt.

"You'd best spend the night by our fire, Julien. It won't do to have a madman roaming the palace halls."

"How soon?" He struggled to regain control of himself. "How soon do you think they'll want the wedding?"

"Because of the baroness' grave health, I'm certain you'll be married as soon as possible. You Christians take three weeks for the reading of the banns, so that should bring us very close to Christmas. I shouldn't wonder if they decide to have you marry on the morning of Roger's coronation, your Christmas Day. What a holiday that would be! You would have your great religious celebration, a joyous marriage, and Roger's introduction of the kingdom of Sicily to the world. You'd surely have no trouble ever remembering your anniversary."

Aziz's prediction was an accurate one. Julien was allowed to see Claire just twice between the announcement of their betrothal and their wedding, and never alone. The next month was the most frantic of Julien's life, because his responsibilities for Roger's coronation were in no way diminished by the preparations for his wedding. At midnight Mass, Christmas Day, 1130, he married Claire in the modest chapel of St. Mary Magdalene, next to the Cathedral of Palermo. He had wanted Cardinal Conti to officiate, but the pressures of the coronation were too devastating to him, so the couple were wedded by Bishop Le Clerq, the French bishop of Troina, who had baptized Claire.

Pride constricted Julien's throat as he saw Claire at his side dressed in a flowing robe of cream-colored silk embroidered with hundreds of pearls the size of small peas. Her waist was loosely cinched in bands of pale gold alternating with silver, and her silk slippers were entirely encrusted with baroque pearls. Her hair had been plaited freely with jasmine blossoms and their fragrance reached the acrid veil of incense that permeated the chapel.

Julien wore a robe of fine white silk, with a girdle studded with rough nuggets of turquoise, and over it a cloak of natural-colored raw silk caught at the throat with an emerald clasp. Never had he felt so elegant. The cloak had cost him more by far than all the clothes he had ever owned in his life, but Aziz insisted on the purchase, and he was pleased when he saw Theodora's approving glance and the color that rushed to Claire's cheeks when he took his place next to her.

Roger had found it impossible to attend, but he sent his two eldest sons, Roger and Alfonso, now thirteen and eleven, as his viceroys. They were handsome boys, young Roger in many ways already a man, and although Julien had seen them only half a dozen times, they always treated him with courtesy and respect. The ceremony was a brief one, and when it ended young Roger gave Claire his father's wedding present, a pair of small but exquisite cabochon rubies set into earrings.

Theodora was carried back to her apartment, shaken by the strain of the day's events, but otherwise in fine shape, and Julien led his bride through the mobs of people outside the cathedral, where his well-wishers had assembled together with the crowds that had come for the coronation.

Their bedroom was bright with the lights from the thousands of lanterns that festooned the entire facade of the palace. Although the night was cool, there was a warming African breeze that carried with it a tropical languor. Claire's mouth tasted like ripe figs. He swore to her there could never be another woman for him, and she yielded herself to him gracefully and without embarrassment, to his repeated declarations of unimaginable joy.

They slept only after dawn had tinged the sky, then rose just before noon to prepare for what to every other Sicilian was to be the day's major event. That morning the streets of the city had all been carpeted with good red wool, and for days carts from all over the kingdom had been delivering tons of blossoms to turn the city into a flowery park. Every balcony and terrace was hung with silk banners in gay colors, and it was as if the city itself was being crowned.

From every corner of his kingdom, Roger's vassals had assembled to do him honor and to rival each other in the splendor of their clothing and equipage. Wealthy shippers and merchants from Genoa, Pisa, and Venice were there by the thousands, anxious to determine what the possibilities for increased commerce and expanding wealth in the new kingdom might be. Peasants and poorer townsmen too had walked or ridden their carts to see the events that were likely never to be paralleled in their lifetime.

It was almost impossible to get through the streets. Carts and benches had been set up wherever they could be squeezed in, and from these the merchants hawked food and drink as well as every conceivable souvenir of the event. Julien found it intoxicating. In what was already the most exotic and colorful city in Europe the infusion of foreigners out to celebrate in their own ways made the atmosphere fabulous. Native Italians, Normans, Greeks, Saracens, Lombards, as well as visitors from every corner of the world were speaking excitedly in their own tongues and adding to the clamor of the streets.

A parade had been proceeding through the major streets of the city since early morning. Dancers, musicians, and acrobats from as far off as the Atlas mountains took their turns entertaining the crowd, but their popularity was shadowed by the tremendous reception given to the procession of animals. Prince Hassan of Tunisia had gathered beasts from the African interior seldom if ever seen in Europe for his coronation gift to Roger.

Many of Roger's people were familiar with lions, leopards, camels, and even elephants. Indeed, their appearance on mosaics dated back to the days when Sicilian animal dealers supplied the arenas in ancient Rome. It was the giraffes that created the greatest commotion. The crowds found their appearance totally unbelievable and cheered them spiritedly.

At last Roger appeared at the end of the arcade that led from his palace directly to the cathedral. He was mounted on his white horse, all but hiding it beneath the magnificent sweep of the purple and red robes which trailed a dozen yards behind him. The path from the palace to the cathedral had been carpeted in heavy purple silk, then buried beneath thousands of red carnations. His entourage reflected not the heraldic pomp of the northern kingdoms but the richness and splendor of eastern courts, in the midst of which Roger maintained an aloofness so elegant, the aura about him was less earthly than divine.

At the cathedral, Cardinal Conti was waiting to anoint him with chrism, the sacramental oil, and then Robert of Capua, as first vassal of the new kingdom, placed the crown upon his head. This was followed by the nobles swearing fealty to their sovereign, among whom Julien proudly took his place.

In the palace, servitors dressed in sumptuous silk garments created just for the occasion served an endless succession of dishes in vessels of pure gold and silver. And over Roger's regal chair, a motto had been freshly painted in gold leaf: *"A Deo Coronatus"* . . . "Crowned by God"!

Cardinal Conti studied the new ruler's impassive face as it scanned the chief vassals and magnates of the church lined on either side of him. A smile that seemed lightly tinged with arrogance formed itself on Roger's lips, and Conti felt he understood the extent of Roger's message. He acknowledged no obligation, either to the pope or to the barons and people of his realm. Here was a supreme monarch who was consciously styling himself in the fashion of the Byzantine emperors. The cardinal rapidly made a mental note to include that observation in his next letter to Anacletus.

BOOK TWO

EDEN'S GATE

Chapter I
IN THE GARDEN

Julien smoothed his palm across his belly a few times and prodded the flesh with his fingertips speculatively. I'm going to get fat if I don't exercise more, he reproached himself.

The hammock he was cradled in was perfectly still, and if he closed his eyes he could feel himself poised weightlessly between heaven and earth, so extraordinarily calm was this peaceful midday. The children must still be having their naps, he thought, or it would never be this quiet. Even his falcon was asleep on its perch in the shade. He shifted his weight and looked out across the courtyard of the still new villa. The only movement was from a gecko sunning itself on the tiles around the fountain that twitched toward a passing insect. Furci was every bit as romantic and beautiful as he could have hoped. And Claire was so happy here. That was most important.

Two hundred yards from their gates the sea was dense with tuna, swordfish, and every conceivable type of shellfish, while the gardens, both in the atrium and surrounding the outside walls, rivalled Eden in their profusion of fruit and flowers. It was no wonder Claire told him so often how much she preferred this simple, pastoral existence to the noisy public life of Palermo. Julien snobbishly enjoyed the knowledge that the word idyll was coined by Theocritus to describe the pleasant country life of Sicily to the sophisticates of Alexandria.

But now for the last few weeks, he was fed up with puttering about the garden pruning and weeding. He needed something more to do. Every day he would ride for an hour or two. He'd take the dogs with him, those beautiful Vizslas that were a gift from King Coloman, but they too missed the excitement and the activity he could no longer give them. Hunting was quite out of the question since that broadsword caught him in the shoulder. Even polo had become too difficult, and he'd taken up that eastern game with so much enthusiasm. Doctor Giacobo was quite firm on the subject. As if he needed to be! Julien knew he couldn't swing a mallet or hoist a lance into position without grimacing.

Still, it was better than it used to be. Swimming every morning helped, even if he could no longer use the strokes he was more accustomed to. And the other wound in his side was fully healed now, although occasionally an unexpected twinge would remind him that the flesh just below his waist on the right side had been brutally savaged.

Julien hadn't expected to fight. Roger had been clear about his status as a noncombatant. But who can predict the tides of battle! When all seems lost and you have to fight for your life, then fight you must. And even if his first battle had been a total disaster, at least he and the few survivors were acquitted as brave men.

It surprised Julien to learn that his actions had been described as heroic. In reflection it seemed to him that a better soldier or a stronger man would have undoubtedly been killed pursuing the battle further, while his only instinct had been for survival. Roger was genuinely delighted to find him still at his side after the rout, and he even chided himself for not insisting Julien go back to Salerno before the battle. He needed his skills at court far more than he needed another sword on the battlefield. Apart from his sincere affection for Julien, Roger knew he could be trusted absolutely.

Julien was proud that Roger relied on him more and more. At council meetings he rarely made any inspired judgments, and infinitely more experienced councillors were available. But Julien knew he had a knack for relating comfortably to the various factions at court better than most. The Greeks trusted him as much as the Arabs did, and the Normans and Lombards had to admit their respect.

When Claire first saw his scars, even though they had healed and lost their angry color, she became ill, and for weeks she wept every time she saw his body until his caresses urged her from her morbid fears.

Julien raised himself on an elbow and stared at the fountain which was trickling water into its basin so gently that he couldn't hear a sound. Why would anyone complain about having to spend so much time here? he asked himself for the third time that day. With three wonderful children and a beautiful wife, isn't that enough? The weight of his body on his elbow pained him, so he allowed himself to slump back into the hammock.

No, he felt no regret. His father's strong admonishments against bloodshed had left their mark. Julien had learned to appreciate Roger's techniques for avoiding battle, which included everything from diplomacy to outright bribery. He knew he should have stayed behind that fateful day at Nocera. Even when the battle turned against them, he still had time to leave. Then he found himself suddenly in the thick of it. The infantry had all been cut down or taken prisoner, and the bravest knights around Roger had all been slaughtered. Acting instinctively, Julien seized a horse and lance to help the handful of others clear a path for their escape to Salerno. There were only four knights left with Roger and Julien when the gates of Salerno were slammed in the face of the pursuing Rainulf.

If it hadn't been for his wounds, he'd have accompanied Roger on his last campaign, the only time since his taking service that Roger had gone to the mainland without him. It was just as well. Roger was still smarting from the defeat at Nocera, and this time he was accompanied by his Muslim troops instead of his Christian army. Julien had already heard some of the backlash from the Italian clergy, who complained, predictably, of Roger's using "the enemies of Christ" to shed Christian blood.

Those damned rebels. As if there weren't enough threats to the kingdom from Lothair and Innocent without those bastards. During the last five years, he'd joined Roger in one campaign after another to quash the rebels. Of the troublesome nobles, Robert of Capua and Rainulf of Alife were certainly the most disobedient. Robert of Capua, the same chief vassal who placed the crown on Roger's head and renewed his vows to him before all the others, had broken away from his lord less than a year after the coronation. And Rainulf of Alife was Roger's brother-in-law! True, Rainulf and his wife never got along, and when she turned to her brother for help as she often did, Rainulf was quick to use the excuse to rise against his king. Julien was perhaps more bitter about Rainulf's repeated defections than he was about Robert of Capua's, but the memory of the flight from Nocera did not encourage magnanimity.

Julien swung out of the hammock and paced irritably about the garden for a while, then sat in a corner where he could watch the wisps of smoke from Etna thread across the startlingly vivid Mediterranean sky.

He remembered how Etna used to frighten Claire in their first year at Furci. When they arrived to spend a week or two at the newly completed villa, she seemed perfectly enchanted with everything about the place. Then early one morning, when they were lying in bed not yet fully awake, Etna rumbled ominously and he felt her jerk upright in bed and tremble until pulled back down and comforted with his caresses. Now she told him she found the rumble soothing.

On several occasions he listened to her tell the children that it was King Arthur sleeping beneath the mountain, and then she would have to repeat one of the many Sicilian legends of the great warrior and his court. Near Claire's mother's home in the tip of Italy's heel, the castle of Otranto had a magnificent mosaic floor illustrating the life and deeds of Arthur, and she had been taken to see it as a child. She told Julien the first morning they lay in bed together that she had promised herself that time in Otranto that one day she would marry a handsome knight from faraway romantic England.

How the children loved stories! Adelaide, the firstborn, named for Roger's mother, was barely four, but she could repeat many of her favorites. Peter, named of course for Abelard, would simply listen wide-eyed and not say a word, but then a day or two later he would ask a totally unexpected question about a detail of the story. Still a baby, Nigel would shut his eyes and blow little bubbles through his pouted lips until the story ended.

Julien loved best to tell them the tale of Persephone, although Claire had cautioned him not to at first, because she feared it might frighten Adelaide. Not at all. It quickly became Adelaide's favorite.

Adelaide would gaze at the summit of Etna when clouds formed grotesque shapes around it to see if she could spot Pluto sitting and spying on Persephone as she went about the garden gathering flowers. Persephone's abduction to the underworld carried no terror for her. Adelaide's eyes would fill with tears only when Julien described Demeter, the gracious corn goddess, mourning her daughter's loss so grievously that she allowed all that grew in field and garden to wither and die. Then when Persephone was permitted to return to earth, Adelaide would clap her hands in joy, already resigned to the gloomier months of the year when her heroine would sit by her husband in dark Hades with her three-headed dog at her feet.

During their first year of marriage Julien would protest that the journey to the villa was too long. Even though he took with him as much work as he could, he was never completely easy spending more than a week or two away from court. Roger fully appreciated Julien's ability to phrase a controversial document as flatteringly as possible in each of the three court languages, so that the reader would be subtly convinced that the document favored his case more than it actually did. Yet Julien knew that the staff could change mercurially, and he was sensible enough to be aware that his position was most secure only when he was directly in charge. He'd advanced well for a man still in his mid-twenties, but many careers more illustrious than his had ended sooner.

Then, earlier in the year Queen Elvira died and Roger's grief was towering. Affairs of state were rejected, pleasures put aside, and even his harem was forced to observe a period of fasting and abstinence. He refused all consolation, not even allowing his children to see him except rarely. From the seclusion of his chamber he refused all messages from his curia, but the administration of his state continued smoothly, thanks to the tight organization he had already set up. And while his ministers continued to dispense the king's law with unwavering efficiency, Roger simply withdrew completely.

Julien was forced to admit that he had absolutely nothing to do in the palace except continue his studies, and by now he was able to read Arabic texts as scholarly as any Aziz could produce for him. Claire was able to persuade him to withdraw with his family to Furci until such time as he should hear that Roger had left his mourning and needed him, but the short letters he received from Aziz were generally uninformative and encouraged him only to stay on. Since Claire was pregnant again with her fourth child, he was grateful for the chance to be with her during her confinement, but he knew the situation in Palermo could not continue much longer as it was.

Roger's unmitigated grief was beginning to create a sort of scandal, and some of the priests voiced their criticism more boldly, charging him with the sin of uxorism. To prolong the state of mourning for such an unreasonably long time was unseemly in any man and absolutely dangerous in a monarch. Roger's subjects began to wonder what unnatural hold this woman had on him, and stories of Elvira's witchcraft and the ancient Iberian rites she practiced began to be whispered, even abroad.

Elvira had never shown any interest in affairs of state, and preferred to remain detached from the business of the realm. Intelligent, she dedicated herself entirely to Roger's personal needs and to the upbringing of the seven children she had borne him during their fourteen years of marriage.

She had been brought up in one of the courts of Spain, the daughter of Alfonso VI of Castile, and was little more than a girl when she married. Roger was then twenty-six, and a stirring figure; the matrimonial catch of the season. He had already been maintaining a harem for years, but Elvira's background and the proximity of the Muslim states to the Castilian court made her more tolerant of these aspects of Roger's life than another princess from the north might have been. She never criticized his fondness for his concubines, accepting them as naturally as she did the falcons in his mews, the horses in his stable, or the cheetahs that he handfed chicken livers to twice a day.

Roger gave her no reason to doubt his love. The women of the harem were his toys and in no way competed with his queen for his affection. Most usually after he had dallied with his favorite of the evening, he would dismiss her and retire to Elvira's chamber, where he would talk to her for hours and sleep at last folding her in his arms, then wake to make love to her more often than not, because Roger was a man of lusty appetite.

Roger's grief was aggravated by the fact that Elvira's fatal illness had been transmitted to her by him. When he returned from the battle of Montepeloso, he had a high fever and the doctors were greatly concerned. Elvira insisted on personally nursing him day and night, and after he recovered, the most skillful administrations of his doctors, who were certainly the finest in

Europe, could do nothing to save her. She had allowed herself to grow weak and tired from the long vigils by his bedside, and the infection finally brought her down.

The doctors were worried about a recurrence of Roger's illness when his grief took on such exaggerated proportions. He could neither eat nor sleep, and on those infrequent occasions when he allowed himself to be seen, he was gaunt and haggard, looking much more than his forty years. His seclusion was so rigidly imposed that the rumor of his death began to circulate throughout Europe. There had been no public appearances in over three months, and Julien was concerned over how widespread the stories of his death had become. Once, when he went to Messina to shop for gifts for Claire and the children, he passed the Genoese community of shippers and traders that had a settlement there, and he heard a Genoese priest swear he'd attended Roger's secret funeral.

A commotion from the kennels just outside the Furci house shattered the peace of the siesta hour. The three servants entered the courtyard from the far wing. First to appear was Abbas, the powerful Tunisian eunuch who not only looked after the family's needs but could be relied upon in an emergency calling for a show of strength. He made a rapid obeisance to Julien and strode towards the villa entrance to see who might be disturbing their tranquillity. One of the two maids ran off to quiet the dogs and another proceeded to the children's room to see if all was well there.

Julien waited in the courtyard, unwilling to show himself in case it was a caller he wasn't anxious to see. They had friends in the neighboring villages, but it was unlikely they would call at this hour.

Claire quietly joined him. She moved slowly, her delicately boned body already swollen with child. "I told Rima to keep the children in bed for another half hour or so," she said. "I think Nigel's the only one of the three that ever sleeps."

Julien embraced her and led her to a bench in the side garden. He looked at his wife's body with pleasure, loving the way it shaped itself to the miracle growing within. As he sat next to her, he whispered, "How lovely you are."

"That voice is familiar," Claire said, turning away. "It must be someone to see you. Yes, it's Thomas. I'm sure of it."

"It must be word from Roger." Julien rose as Abbas ushered Thomas into the garden.

Thomas was pale and looked distraught, but Julien assumed he was tired from his journey. Thomas embraced them both; then Claire made an excuse to leave them alone.

"How are Griselda and the baby?" Julien asked as soon as they were seated, and caught his breath the moment the question was out when he saw the pained look on Thomas's face. Thomas had married the daughter of Roger's building commissioner shortly after she turned fourteen, and they had a child two years later.

"They're dead, Julien, both of them. There was nothing we could do to save them."

"Dead! But they were so healthy when I last saw them."

"I'd been working so hard. I had to spend most of my time in Cefalu, and I left her alone for weeks at a time. Perhaps this wouldn't have happened if I could've been with her. The doctors think she picked up an infection from shellfish and transmitted it through her milk to the baby. They fell ill at the same time and were already gone when I reached them a day later."

Julien put his arm around his friend's shoulder. "I feel for you. I suppose Claire will have to know, but I hate her to hear these things when she's carrying a baby."

"There's more bad news, Julien. Your friend Aziz. He started to write you and then asked me to tell you instead. His wife Fatima lost their child and is still very weak herself. Now there's no reason to let Claire know that yet."

Julien nodded numbly. "You must stay here with us for a while and recover from your grief."

"I thought I might, but it's really not such a good idea. The voyage has already helped me. I needed to be alone with my thoughts for a while and I already feel much better about it. I should be ready to return in a day or two. Julien, I actually came here to ask you to go back with me."

"Back? Why? Has Roger recovered his senses? Did he send for me?"

"No, he still grieves. That's the problem. There's a real threat to the kingdom now. These rumors of Roger's death have circulated everywhere, and they encourage his enemies. It's not just rebels like Robert of Capua and Rainulf of Alife now. Even the Byzantine emperor has offered Emperor Lothair money and troops to fight Roger. And the Venetians are out for Sicilian blood too."

"I suppose it was only a matter of time once Lothair was crowned emperor."

"But it isn't Lothair," Thomas said. "Can't you guess who's really behind this whole campaign?"

"Bernard."

"Of course. Read this. It's a copy of Bernard's letter to Lothair." He took a folded page from his purse and handed it to Julien.

"It ill becomes me to exhort men to battle; yet I say to you in all conscience that it is the duty of the champion of the Church to protect Her against the madness of schismatics. It is for Caesar to uphold his rightful crown against the machinations of the Sicilian tyrant. For just as it is to the injury of Christ that the offspring of a Jew should have seized for himself the throne of St. Peter, so does any man who sets himself up as king in Sicily offend against the emperor."

Julien refolded the letter and returned it to Thomas. "It doesn't surprise me."

"I didn't think it would. You know, I remember how much I used to distrust your arguments in behalf of Abelard when I first met you, Julien. I've changed many of my ideas since then. Oh, I was forgetting. There's another letter for you—from your old tutor, I believe."

Julien reached for it eagerly. "Ralf. I wanted him to come to Sicily for Nigel's baptism. He's been invited to stand for each of my children, and he's never been able."

"Perhaps for your next one. Would you like me to leave you so you can read it? It looks like a long letter."

"No, no." Julien stayed his friend with an upraised hand. "I'll just glance at what he says." His eyes swept over the page. "No, he won't be able to come." He paused a moment. "Our friend Arnold of Brescia has returned to the communes of northern Italy. Good. I really believe that's where his vocation lies." He put the letter down a moment. "I hope it didn't sound as if you were a less desirable choice for Nigel's godfather, Thomas. I owe so much to Ralf."

"Please don't mention it. I consider it an honor and I couldn't love Nigel more if he were my own son. May I see him?"

"Of course. Claire's probably getting them all ready to see you now." Julien turned back to his letter. "Let's see. Ralf sends congratulations to Robert on his confirmation as governor of the mainland. And, oh yes, this will interest you. Arnold went to Rome to see Lothair crowned and sent a first-hand report on that event."

Thomas's interest immediately quickened. "Tell me."

"It seems Lothair and his queen met Innocent at Viterbo, and they marched on Rome together. When they got there, they found the city still solidly in Anacletus' hands—and much too strong for the pitiful army they'd brought with them. They were hustled to the Lateran by their supporters, and Innocent quickly crowned Lothair and his queen. But it must have been dreary when they knew that meanwhile Anacletus was holding court with his cardinals at St. Peter's and probably laughing at them. Need I mention that Robert of Capua and Rainulf of Alife were present at this second-rate ceremony?"

"The swine! After all Roger's done for them." Thomas seemed genuinely indignant.

"Well, what happened next should amuse you. No sooner was the ceremony over, when Lothair mustered his empress and his few troops and lit out for Germany as fast as he could. Now that he had what he had come for, he couldn't wait to get back. Innocent, Bernard, Robert of Capua, and Rainulf all found themselves stranded in an unfriendly city with no military support. The latest word is, Innocent is already back to a new exile in Pisa. Well, what do you make of that?"

"That letter was written months ago. Lothair is already mounting his campaign against us, and now that he's emperor, he'll have no trouble raising an army to be reckoned with. You'll not fight again though, will you, Julien? Quite apart from Claire's upset, you have no idea how much your wounds worried all your friends."

"Not likely. Roger didn't hesitate to leave me behind on his last campaign, and I was just as glad. I had no appetite for seeing him revenged for the defeat at Nocera."

"No one likes it, least of all Roger." Thomas had set his jaw firmly. "You'll be going out with him again, though. We can both be certain of that. I just hope there's never an occasion for you to fight." They both remained silent a moment.

"You must be tired after your journey. Shall I call one of the servants to prepare a bed for you? You can see the children after you've rested."

"No, please. This is fine. I'm happy to be with you, Julien. We haven't had nearly as much time together as I would have wished. Those long trips, and now Furci is so far."

"I miss you too, Thomas. I wish you'd come to Furci sooner. You'd be comfortable here, maybe even happy."

Thomas looked about the garden as if he were trying to absorb all its details, to fix it in future memory. "Tell me, Julien, did you ever dream of a life like this years ago? No, not at Durham, but even when you first came to Sicily."

Julien found the question odd. "No, I don't suppose I did. Why do you ask?"

"Perhaps because it's not the life I foresaw for you either. Although it's everything I would have dreamed of for myself."

Julien cocked his head quizzically. "I don't understand. Every man does well to have a fine home in the country for his family, doesn't he?"

"You're not every man, Julien. When I first met you, you know how much I mistrusted you. Then, as I came to know you, I saw you as a dreamer, an idealist. No, don't look that way. I mean that in the best sense. I often think you would make the best priest I'd ever know."

"A priest? I?" Julien laughed, but he was instantly aware of how hollow his laughter sounded.

"Why not? When you wanted to spend your life at Abelard's side?"

Julien's eyes fastened hard on Thomas. "I'm a man now, Thomas. I suppose I've changed, but I like to think I still have the same reverence for my old master."

"I'm happy to hear that. It doesn't surprise me, but can you truly say you have no regrets for the turn fate gave your earliest hopes?"

Julien spoke slowly, as if he were choosing his words cautiously. "I believe I've been very lucky, Thomas. What I have always loved most in Abelard is an attitude towards men, humanism if you will, and it's my good fortune that the country I came to reflects those attitudes more closely than any land I know of. I suppose I was meant to serve. I'd have served Abelard gladly. I still would if I could, but I serve his spirit as best I can in the services I give Roger. Does that make any sense to you?"

"A great deal. Forgive these questions. The loss of my family makes me lonely and nostalgic. On the boat here I was reminded often of our trip from England to Sicily, and I confess I was . . . not exactly homesick . . . just wondering what my life would be if I had remained there. Don't you sometimes regret having left England? For not joining Abelard?"

"Regret? No. I think of both my native country and my teacher with as much love as ever, but I don't feel deprived of them. My love for both is immediate enough to keep them close."

"Then I do envy you, Julien."

Acutely aware of his friend's loneliness, Julien lowered his eyes without answering.

They were interrupted by Claire and the children. "Adelaide wouldn't be held back any longer. She had to say hello to you. How are you, dear Thomas?" Adelaide ran to their visitor and unself-consciously twined her arms around his neck.

"My word. I'd forgotten what a lovely young lady you are! And that hair, what an extraordinary shade of red."

"With a little luck it may darken in time," Julien said wryly. He motioned Claire aside and whispered to her of Thomas's loss. Thomas caught the look on her face at the news and signalled her with a smile that it was quite all right now.

Adelaide was followed on Thomas's lap by Peter who had been standing by, tottering and uttering shrill squeals while Adelaide embraced him, and then one of the maids carried Nigel over for his godfather's kiss.

Thomas's eyes were brimming. "You are the most blessed of all men, Julien."

Julien's face became troubled, but he kept silent.

"You mustn't be made uneasy by my loss," Thomas continued. "I'm still a religious man, and it helps me over the rough spots. And before Queen Elvira died, Roger gave me enough new projects to keep me occupied night and day for a lifetime. Did you know he wants a chapel built in the palace? And I'm not even through with Cefalu."

"Yes, the Palatine Chapel. I worked on the budget. He wants it to be not large but overwhelming in its beauty. A jewel. I'm sure you're the one man who can get it done, and Roger would never have assigned it to you if he wasn't delighted by what you've accomplished at Cefalu. That immense mosaic of Christ the Almighty is surely more beautiful than any mural in Byzantium, and I love the dignity of the two towers."

"Thank you, my good friend."

Claire took Nigel from Thomas's lap. "You must stay here with us as long as you possibly can, Thomas. We're very easy to live with, and there's plenty to do if you want it, but I promise we won't try to plan your days for you."

"I'm afraid I can't stay long, much as I would love to."

Claire looked from Thomas to Julien in alarm. "You came to take him back with you, didn't you?"

"We'll talk about it tonight," Julien said softly. "There's nothing to be concerned about."

"Can we take a walk by the seashore?" Thomas asked. "All of us. And I'd like to carry Nigel, if I may. It would make feel like I'm really part of your beautiful family."

"A wonderful idea," Julien said. He glanced at Claire, who was still pale, although she said nothing. He searched for a neutral subject of conversation. "By the way, did you hear anything else about the fire reported in London?"

"I did. I'm sorry to say it was infinitely more devastating than the first word we received. King Henry wisely kept it quiet because he didn't want his enemies to hear how utterly destructive it was, but the losses were the greatest in our history. I'm afraid my conversation isn't nearly as lighthearted as our reunion calls for. Do you think the water's warm enough for swimming?" It wasn't, but they cavorted in the sand and collected shells until Abbas came to announce their meal was ready.

At the close of the day, Julien was relieved when Thomas announced he wanted to retire early. Julien and Claire were uncommonly solemn as they undressed for bed. Julien slipped under the light cotton coverlet first and watched, fascinated as ever, while Claire loosened her hair and brushed it before slipping in beside him. She pressed her back against his chest and cradled there so that they were nested like a pair of spoons. His arms moved around her, one hand cupping a breast while the other lay lightly on her belly, marvelling still at the tightness of the skin surrounding the wonder within.

"Let's talk about it," he said after a while.

"That you must go back to Palermo? I expected it. I hope you don't mind if I don't go with you."

"You amaze me."

"Why? It's only natural, isn't it? You have your duties and I have mine." She sighed softly. "It's been a blessing to have you all to myself for such a long time, but I knew it couldn't last. I have to confess I even thanked God one night for allowing your wounds to keep you with me all these months. I just hope you understand my reluctance to go with you."

"Of course. I'd rather you were with me, but by all means stay here with the children if you've a mind to. It's just that I keep wishing your mother were still alive to be with you during these difficult weeks."

Claire pressed his arms with hers. How warm and strong he felt. Her body shuddered lightly with pleasure. "I miss her a great deal, but I know how grateful she was to have lived long enough to see me married and even to see her first two grandchildren. She never expected to last that long, and I think somehow she would have fought harder to stay with me if she didn't believe I was going to be all right."

"I know. She told me too that she felt she had finished what she was put on earth for. But I want you to promise me that if you're feeling even slightly unwell you'll send to Taormina for Dr. Giacobo. And you must get word to me at once."

"I promise. Tell me, has Roger sent for you or was it something Thomas said to you that made you decide to return?"

"There's still no direct word from Roger, but he mustn't keep himself closeted any longer. There's a new crisis forming in the north, and it calls for a major effort from all of us."

Claire's body went rigid. "War?"

"We're certainly threatened." His hands stroked her body delicately until he felt the tenseness leave her.

"Do you think you'll have to go with him again?" Claire had trained herself not to allow the anxiety she felt to color her voice, but her right hand moved to his side and fingered the welts that laced his skin there.

"I told you Roger never asked me to fight, dearest. At Nocera it was entirely my choice, and that was under circumstances I'm not likely to face again."

"But will you have to accompany him?"

"I don't know anything yet. And even if I have to go, it may not be for months yet. First I'll have to discover what Roger's program is. I might even be able to come back to you before the baby is born, or soon after."

She stretched languorously in his embrace. "Do what you must. If I find I'm nervous about having the baby here, I promise to return to Palermo, but I have full confidence in Dr. Giacobo, and he's found an excellent woman to help me after it comes. It really is a lot easier for me here, darling."

"I'll be happy knowing you're well taken care of here, and I'm sure it's better for the children." He lay quietly a moment. His flesh had awakened to the pressure of her body, and he gripped her more closely. In a moment he felt her wetness answering his need for her. He groaned and fastened his mouth on the nape of her neck, and Claire, with only the slightest movement of her body, accommodated him and they rocked, sobbing, until they were released.

Chapter II

MADNESS

The boat Julien sailed in was trim and swift, and he arrived in Palermo the last week of May to find the entire city still in mourning, not simply for Queen Elvira, but as a reflection of Roger's unremitting grief.

The palace, though, was stirring with news of other events. Word had reached the curia that the mainland rebels were already massing in Naples. Robert of Capua had staged an attack on his duchy, and the city of Aversa, one of the first Norman strongholds, had fallen to them.

Ushered into Roger's chamber, Julien saw his king, still wild-eyed with the madness of his sorrow, struggling to understand the excited reports of two Arab members of his curia.

"Julien, can it really be as bad as they say?"

"My lord, there's no question that Lothair is on his way, however long it may take him. And this time he'll have a proper army to reckon with, instead of the few thousand he led to Rome. Byzantines, Venetians, even the Milanese have swung to him. If we move at once, though, I'm certain we can still count on mainland support."

"Well, I haven't been entirely asleep. I was afraid something like this would happen. There's a fleet under Admiral John and an army under Chancellor Guerin waiting for my word to attack. Julien, we must leave at once for Salerno. I need to speak to Robert of Selby, and then we'll stamp out this vermin once and for all. Are you free to leave? Claire and the children all right? There's no time to waste. Queen Elvira would never permit me to risk our sons' patrimony so recklessly." There were still dark pouches beneath his eyes, but Julien saw the old fire that had been missing these last months return and set the orbs crackling with vitality. Whatever misgivings he'd felt about Roger's sanity were firmly dispelled.

On the 4th of June they arrived in Salerno and immediately joined Robert of Selby, who assured them of the continued loyalty of the Salernitans. Roger was aware of how skillful Robert's administration had been and congratulated him. In truth the natives of the city had always despised the penny-pinching ways of the Lombards who had ruled them before, and they'd grown very fond of Robert for his openhanded bonhomie.

After Roger's long period of inactivity, he was in no mood to waste more time. A few days of conferences with Robert convinced him of the best course of action. Aversa was still in the hands of the rebels, but they abandoned it at once on the news of Roger's approach. It was put to the sack, and the ruins were strewn over the ground in keeping with Roger's policy: the first cities to fall suffer the most as a lesson to the others. As predicted, the cities around Aversa immediately sent messengers assuring Roger of their good faith.

Julien watched these campaigns with mixed feelings. He knew the rebels must be suppressed and Roger's punishment was no more severe than might be expected from any other ruler, but he could no longer stomach these bloody skirmishes.

By midsummer they broke camp to return to Salerno and wait for the next move. Julien was awakened in his tent one morning, when they were still two days' march from the city, by the sounds of a great commotion in camp. He rose and saw that the priests who had accompanied the troops had packed their belongings on mules and were preparing to leave. Some of the clergy were Salernitans, but a great number had joined the army while they were well engaged in their campaigns. A few of these were committed to Innocent, although the great majority professed a sincere support of Anacletus' cause. Julien approached an Italian monk a few years younger than he and asked him what was going on.

The monk turned to him with unexpected bitterness. "Ask your baptized sultan. It seems he prefers to be a leader of infidel hordes."

Julien didn't question him further but went to Roger's tent. Roger wasn't there but his personal attendant, the eunuch Hadim, was boiling water for his master's tea. "Do you think there's any chance of my seeing King Roger this morning?" Julien asked him.

"I doubt it," Hadim replied. "He's very upset. Didn't you see the priests leaving?"

"That's why I want to see him. We can't afford to let them leave. It's very bad for the morale of our troops."

"It's because of troop morale that Roger sent them packing," Hadim answered, and Julien was reminded that Hadim was not a Christian.

"These aren't matters that concern you," Julien told him. "Where is your master?"

"Here I am." Roger stood in the entrance, glowering and in no mood for Julien's questions.

"Isn't there something you can say to the priests to keep them from leaving?"

"Why in the world would I want to do that? I threw them out! They're supposed to be here for the comfort of my Christians, to shrive them and keep up their morale. Instead, I found the filthy traitors trying to convert my Muslims behind my back."

"I'm sorry. I didn't realize—"

"You know my rules. If I'd caught a Muslim imam trying to convert my Christians, no one would suggest I was acting improperly if I had him drawn and quartered, and I would too! I know it's bad for the morale of my Christian soldiers, but think how much worse it is for my Muslims to have those black-robed sneaks trying to make them abandon the faith of their fathers. And you also know I need to have troops I can count on in case of a confrontation with the papal army."

"Roger!" Julien appeared genuinely shocked to hear Roger voice something he knew quite well but didn't expect to hear from his lips.

"Oh, grow up, Julien. You should know by this time whom you can trust or what to expect from your spiritual leaders." He pronounced the word "spiritual" scornfully. "No, no, no!" he continued. His face was almost choleric in its anger, and he stopped only when he had realized that Julien and Hadim were standing motionless with downcast eyes. "All right, Julien, all right. Will you have a cup of tea with me now?"

"I wasn't really questioning your judgment, Roger," he said softly. "I was only concerned for our men."

"I've little patience left, Julien. Don't you add to my problems now. I've had very upsetting news. Our siege of Naples was doing well, but the Pisans have just relieved them."

Hadim poured their tea, and Roger seemed soothed the moment he held the warm cup in his hand. Although Julien was still alarmed by what he felt was Roger's lack of prudence with the priests he recognized that Roger needed the sympathy of his friends. "Worse things could happen than losing our priests," Julien told him. "We'll be back in Salerno within days. Our Christians aren't likely to have their souls tried too sorely before then."

Roger clasped Julien's wrist. "Do you think I behaved badly? It's supposed to be very unlucky to dismiss a priest."

"If we were facing a battle, I'd think it was a very bad sign," Julien said. "Let's just hope our campaigns are all behind us now. We'll find some way of dealing with the Pisans."

When they arrived at Salerno, Robert greeted them with the news that the Pisans had swept down from Naples to Amalfi, and there with great relish sacked the city that had so recently been one of Pisa's most powerful competitors in Mediterranean shipping. Now the Pisans were busily ravaging all the neighboring towns.

"I don't like surprise attacks," Roger said, "But I think we can repay them with their own coin. As soon as our troops are rested, I'll cook something up for those Pisans they won't be likely to forget."

Roger decided to leave his Christian soldiers to the defense of Salerno while he took his Muslim troops with him, as inconspicuously as possible, to the wild mountainous area behind the Amalfi coast. He didn't have to wait long. The very next day the Pisans attacked Ravello, and Roger's men descended on them from the sheer heights that back the city. The battle was short but bloody. Seven thousand of Roger's Saracens killed or took prisoner fifteen thousand Pisans and drove the rest back to Naples.

"It couldn't be a more complete triumph," Julien announced to his king on Roger's return to Salerno. "The Pisans have had their teeth pulled. What do you want to do next?"

"Follow them," Roger answered. "We can reinforce the siege of Naples with my Muslim troops, and I've a mind to teach the Neapolitans a lesson. We'll burn their vineyards right up to the city walls."

"But Roger! If Naples returns to us, and I'm sure they eventually will, they'll be suffering for years and years to come."

"Let them," he replied. "And which of their neighbors will dare to speak of my harshness when they see how these towns have suffered at the hands of the Pisans? I know what I must do to ensure that a lesson is well learned."

Just days later Naples found itself securely hemmed in by Roger's troops, and it appeared the siege would be a success, but Roger had no patience with this most boring form of warfare. Julien was sure Roger would soon speak of returning to Sicily for the winter.

No word of Claire had arrived with any of the ships that brought provisions from Sicily to Salerno, and now Julien had begun to worry. He estimated his fourth child had been born about the time the Pisans were being routed from Ravello. It was unlike Aziz not to have sent a note advising him of Claire's well-being and announcing the birth.

Everyone in Roger's retinue was kept busy the next few days making plans for a great ceremony. It was chiefly to allow Roger to introduce to the world his eldest son and heir, who had already distinguished himself on the battlefield since the age of fifteen. The people of Salerno clearly adored the handsome young Roger, and when he was presented to them in front of the cathedral built by his great-uncle, the Guiscard, the crowds demonstrated their enthusiasm unreservedly. Roger was invested by Cardinal Peter as duke of Apulia and heir to the throne of the kingdom of Sicily. Although just barely eighteen, the people acknowledged him not only as his father's heir, but as heir to the mantle of the Guiscard.

To punish Robert of Capua for his repeated defections, Roger then installed his second son, Alfonso, as the new Prince of Capua. Tancred, his third son, who was still not quite fifteen, became Prince of Bari, while a son-in-law, Adam, and Simon, a cousin, were given the defense of the Terra di Lavoro, to be served in succession or jointly. The only one of Roger's surviving sons not granted a title or honor was William, who was a scant year younger than Tancred, and it was the first sign that Roger was not overly fond of the brooding, heavyset, thick-browed boy. The youngest of the lot was Henry, who was sickly from the start and not expected to live to manhood.

By distributing the mainland kingdom among sons and kinsmen, Roger installed Hautevilles in all the scattered conquests of the earlier Normans. It was a major step in the disclaiming of the creaky structure that had existed, and Roger was able to turn his eyes back to Sicily with a good deal of satisfaction.

Julien had never seen Roger look more weary, but he knew that it was the fatigue that falls after a major accomplishment. On their last evening in Salerno, he went to Roger's rooms for a farewell entertainment. Roger's three sons were there, as were Robert and a few of Roger's favorite Lombard councillors. It was a sentimental celebration. Roger was never particularly fond of music or poetry, but he knew his eldest son was, and for the young duke he had asked Iqbal, an Arab poet from his court, to entertain them with his songs. The concluding selection of the evening was an elegy in the popular Arab style, a lament for the loss of Sicily to the Normans, and Julien saw in the eyes of Roger and his family a love that echoed the poet's.

Weep as you will your tears of blood,
O grave of Arabian civilization.
Once this place was alive with the people of the desert
And the ocean was a playground for their boats.
O Sicily you are the glory of the ocean . . .
You were the cradle of this nation's culture,
Whose fire like beauty burnt the world.
Sadi the nightingale of Shiraz wept for the destruction of Baghdad;
Dag shed tears of blood for the ruination of Delhi;
When the heavens destroyed Granada
It was the sorrowing heart of Ibn Badrun who lamented it;
Unhappy Iqbal is fated to write your elegy . . .
Tell me your pains, I too am immersed in pain.
I am the dust of that caravan of which you were the destination.
Fill the colors in the pictures of the past and show them to me;
Make me sad by telling the tales of past days.

After the poetry reading they were joined by more officers from Roger's military staff, and the celebration grew more determined. Wines were consumed in vast quantities as toast followed toast and the merrymaking took on a more ribald tone. By the time it was apparent that all memories of the battlefield were resolutely erased, a dozen pretty women entered and were hailed with another round of toasts. Robert whispered to Julien that they were the most beautiful *bolognesi* to be found in the south.

A sloe-eyed girl with dark lashes and a torrent of bleached hair tumbling about her shoulders gave Julien a look that demanded his attention. He approached her and found she spoke only Greek and the local Salernitan dialect. She told him her name was Annunziata, and she begged him to return to her before the evening ended. He turned to another of the women nearby and found that she had the same limited linguistic range. Confused, Julien went to Robert. "I thought you said these lovely women are from Bologna. It isn't so. They're all southerners. I haven't heard one yet speak Italian with a northern accent."

Robert looked at him oddly and broke into a laugh. Julien felt rebuffed, and turned to young Duke Roger. "Didn't you hear him say they were the most beautiful *bolognesi* around?"

"Yes, I did," Roger answered. He pulled Julien aside. "Lower your voice. Sometimes they get offended and then they're not much fun."

Weaving in place, Julien had to shake his head to focus on Roger's words. He blinked uncomprehendingly.

The young Duke smiled. "They aren't from Bologna at all. Don't you know what a *bolognese* is?"

Julien shook his head vigorously.

"It's to your credit that you don't have smutty friends, Julien. The women of Bologna are reputed to be extremely passionate, and they are also much freer than our southern women. In order to preserve their maidenheads for the man they marry, they have learned to perform oral sex so well they are celebrated throughout Italy for that skill. If a woman does a *bolognese*, that means—"

"I understand," Julien said uncertainly. "What do you take me for? They're all friends of Robert's, aren't they? That's good enough for me."

"Yes, that's right." Roger smiled. "Actually it's a very considerate touch. Just what you'd expect from Robert. Since most of the men will be returning to their wives soon it greatly lessens the chance of their taking the pox back to their families. My father could not have found a more considerate governor for this province."

Julien stared at the duke and blinked a few times, then shrugged. "There was too much salt in the food tonight, don't you agree? I don't know when I've had such a thirst. How about another cup of wine?"

Julien's conversation with Duke Roger was the last thing he remembered before he awakened. His senses were still so dulled, he recognized only with difficulty that he was in the same room he'd used whenever he was in Salerno; the bed was the same, but still something seemed changed. He winced when he realized he wasn't alone in bed. Not only was he not alone, but it was Annuziata with him, and she was growing increasingly aggressive in her ministrations. His head was throbbing from the evening's debauch and he was parched with thirst. He rose halfway in bed and pushed her shoulders with his hands, but it was an ineffective gesture. She grasped his hands and drew them down to her breasts while she continued working on him. He sank back on the bed and shut his eyes until it was over, repeating to himself, Forgive me, Claire, forgive me. I'll never let anything like this happen again. Never, never, never! He accompanied his release with a racking sob and was quiet again. Annunziata rose and rested against his shoulder for a few moments before either of them spoke.

"Please go," he said. "I think my purse should be on the chest near the door. Take what you want and leave me."

"There's no need. Governor Robert has taken care of everything. Why are you sending me away so soon? It's scarcely dawn. Didn't I please you?"

He hesitated briefly, then nodded.

"You drank too much to be any good last night, but I knew you'd be up to it in the morning. Wouldn't you like me to bathe you before I go?"

"No. Thank you, no. I think you're very attractive, but I'd rather you left me now." He sounded miserable.

"All right." She rose and stretched her body, catlike, and Julien couldn't resist peeking between his half-shut eyes.

She's incredible, and then, remorsefully, What a beast I am. No better than an animal. A pig. A monster. I don't deserve you, Claire, but I'll make it up to you somehow. He remained in bed, brooding for several more minutes. Is it your pride? Did you think you were better than other men? Well, you know better now. He staggered to the water pitcher at length and drank a good deal but the bad taste wouldn't leave his mouth.

Chapter III
AFTER THE FALL

The palace in Palermo rang with cries of victory when the fleet carrying Roger and Julien approached, although it had been far from a decisive victory. Naples was still under siege, and Robert of Capua had managed to escape and make his way north to the Emperor Lothair, where even now, with tears in his eyes, he was begging the monarch to hasten his trip south to crush Roger. No matter. The siege was under control, the emperor was a long march away, and the equivocal state of affairs could last for many more months before a crisis appeared. Returning heroes were to be hailed with festivities. The public demanded it, certainly expected it more than the heroes did.

Julien had to fight his way through the crowds of joyful citizens choking the halls of the palace as he made his way to his studio to look for Aziz. The studio was empty and looked as if it had not been used for weeks. He rushed to the neighboring offices to get information about Aziz's whereabouts, and found a message waiting for him. Aziz had gone to Furci with his wife and son at the request of the Baroness Claire.

Julien's fingers felt thick and unresponsive as he tried to pen a message to Roger explaining that he had to leave at once for the east coast. He checked further with a few friends to see if there was any other news of her, but no one had heard a word, and they could only say that Aziz had left very suddenly.

There were no ships leaving for Taormina that day, but he was too impatient to wait. The captain of one of the galleys that had accompanied them from Salerno knew Julien and respected him. Julien had no difficulty convincing him of the urgency of the trip, and a few pieces of gold ensured a prompt departure. From Palermo to Furci was just one hundred and sixty miles by sea, but the uncertainty of sailing schedules and the capricious weather along the Sicilian shore could easily add days, even weeks, to the journey.

For the entire trip the sky was padded with dark clouds along the coast, and a raw autumn wind fueled Julien's foreboding of something dreadful. At the straits of Messina, the whirlpool Charybdis was in a rage, and the captain was able to steer the ship to the mainland side of the straits only with great difficulty. They anchored below Scylla and waited for more hospitable currents before going further. Julien was chafing with impatience. If the captain had managed to moor the ship on the Sicilian side, he could have disembarked and taken a horse the short distance to Furci. The sea road was a good one, and well travelled. Now they were stranded in an eerie, twilight sort of haze that the sun couldn't pierce even at midday. The mists of the Fata Morgana shrouded the coast and tricked their senses. Julien was certain now that some evil was dogging him, and he reviewed his recent sins to see if they merited such terrible retribution. His prayers brought him no comfort, and he bribed the captain with another three pieces of gold to risk his ship and crew by daring the crossing without further delay.

Current and wind fought each other for four hours before the ship completed its hesitant crossing to the Messinese coast. The fishing ships that usually speckled the water for as far as the eye could see were all moored, waiting for the ghostly haze and the demons of wind and current to be exorcized. Julien found himself praying as fervently as he had during the shipwreck at Cefalu.

The night was moonless and thick as a sponge when the ship approached a cove just north of Furci, and Julien was let down in a boat with two seamen to row him to shore. His lantern could intrude in the darkness for no more than a yard, and when he felt the beach beneath his feet and had tipped the sailors, he felt wrapped in a void deeper and inkier than any he could imagine. With even the lightest scattering of stars, there was scarcely a man who couldn't find his way, but deprived of these guiding lights he was entirely at the mercy of unknown forces. The wet sand forced him to plod laboriously, and the blackness made it harder to keep track of time. He continued his search, nonetheless, hoping that the void would uncover some landmark, even a familiar rock, that would guide him to his villa, but the night would yield nothing. His damp skin was covered now with the pink grit of the sirocco that had swept over the coast.

He stumbled and fell, and felt himself trapped, then gratefully realized that he was tangled in the mesh of some nets that fishermen had spread on the sand. He knew they couldn't be far and started shouting to rouse them. A glow flickered hesitantly in the near distance, then grew stronger, and when the first fisherman reached him, Julien was screaming wildly, with tears tracking unchecked through the sandy coating on his face.

The sleepless nights and the terror of wandering in the blackness of the sirocco-swept beach had drained his energy and the fishermen carried him the half mile to his house. They refused money for their services and stayed just long enough to be sure someone in the villa had heard them.

The dogs answered first. Julien called to them by name and their howling increased.

The eunuch Abbas, who slept in a small room off the entrance, ran out to him within minutes after the dogs alerted him and led Julien back into the main hall. Abbas refused to answer any of Julien's barely coherent questions, knowing that Aziz was already on his way to them. When his old friend arrived, he rushed to Julien and cradled him a moment before either of them spoke.

"She's going to live, Julien. She's all right, but your son was stillborn. We thought we were going to lose her, but she's a strong woman with an even stronger will. She'll be fine now that you're here. Don't worry."

Julien's bloodshot eyes were roving strangely. "I want to go to her."

"Not now. She's heavily drugged. She wasn't able to sleep or eat for weeks. By the way, you look perfectly awful yourself. Why don't you get some sleep and you can be with her in the morning?"

"No, I must at least see her first. I won't disturb her." Julien brushed Aziz's arm away and stumbled towards the door to his bedroom.

The lantern's yellow light picked out a face so wan and wasted that Julien sucked in his breath and began to sob. The pinched nostrils seemed to be fighting for breath, and her lips were so bloodless they barely outlined her mouth. He leaned over and kissed her, then stroked her shoulder gently, but she made no response.

"It's better to let her be," Aziz insisted. "Her drug is a strong one, but it was necessary. She blames herself for the death of your baby, and she still suffers a great deal. Her fever lasted for weeks, and for a while she used to cry out to be allowed to join her baby in death."

Julien recoiled. "What a horrible sin! And what of the other children? Did she have no thoughts of them? Or of me?"

"Try to understand. She was desperately ill, Julien. I'm sure it will be all right now that you've returned. Women sometimes become morbid when they go through their pregnancies alone, and hers was a difficult delivery. It may have been a mistake to leave her here with just the servants. She should have had the company of someone close to her."

"It was her choice, and I thought the children would be enough. When did you arrive?"

"Dr. Giacobo sent for us almost a week before the delivery. He suspected then that something was wrong with the baby. We arrived the day after she was delivered, and have stayed at her side ever since. You know how devoted Fatima is to her."

"Yes, and I'm grateful to you both."

"Come, Julien. I insist you get rest. It's best we don't disturb her further."

Julien dropped off to sleep without undressing and slept like a rock until awakened shortly after dawn. Aziz was squatting by the side of his mattress boiling water over a spirit lamp. "Don't get up. Your tea will be ready in just a few minutes."

While Aziz was brewing the tea, Julien dropped off again, an uneasy doze that was almost a waking dream. He stood at Claire's bedside for their reunion, and she was lovelier than ever as she lay asleep with her dark hair fanned out over her shoulders in loose curls. Her eyelids fluttered prettily and then opened. A low murmur of pleasure escaped from her lips, the sound he always heard at the onset of his lovemaking. He leaned forward eagerly to clasp her to him and she whispered his name huskily, then nestled contentedly in his embrace. He awakened and felt a chill from the still damp air.

Aziz had his arm around Julien and was easing him to a seated position while he urged the hot tea to his lips. It was scalding, but he drank it greedily, then sank back on the bed. "Take your time. Claire is awake now, but I feel I must prepare you. She's been through a great deal, and you mustn't expect too much. She's still exhausted."

It took more effort than Julien expected to lift himself from bed. He splashed water on his face and changed into a fresh shirt quickly while Aziz continued to reassure him the worst was over and there was nothing Julien could have done for her if he'd been there.

When he reached her bedside, Claire was lying perfectly still, her eyes wide open. The sockets were so hollow her stare seemed sightless. She made no sign of recognition until he called her name, and then stirred only slightly, blinking hard to focus on him. Julien bent forward and kissed her on the mouth. The foulness of her breath was startlingly pungent, but he kept his lips on hers until she pushed him away and started to pant for breath. He saw that she was frowning, and she studied him as if he were an intruder.

"Claire. Oh darling, what's happened to you? If you only knew how much I've needed you."

"Why did you come back?" Her voice was fretful.

He started at this, but Aziz steadied him with a reassuring squeeze of his arm. "I'm going to take care of you. You'll soon be well now that I'm here. I'm going to see the children now, but I'll look in on you again in a little while, after you've had more rest."

Her thin lips turned inwards on her mouth, and she closed her eyes.

"Come, Julien," Aziz said. "The children are in the courtyard. The storm blew over during the night, and there's even a bit of sunshine today." Julien allowed himself to be led away.

"She acted as if I were nothing to her."

"Don't take it so. For the last month she's been locked in a struggle with death . . . the same death that stole her child from her. When she's stronger she'll be her old self again. It's up to you to help her by not demanding too much. Even her children can give her no pleasure right now."

The courtyard was drenched in feeble sunlight. One of the serving women was rocking Nigel, the youngest, in his wooden cradle, while Peter was ambitiously digging a hole nearby with a spoon as long as his arm. A swing had been set up between the trees, and Aziz's son Ahmad, who was now a reedy boy of nine, was sending Adelaide higher and higher into the branches while she screamed delightedly. He caught one of the ropes when he saw Julien and lifted her down gracefully so that she could greet her father.

Julien was shaken by his daughter's loveliness. She was wearing a turquoise silk robe in the Arab fashion, and her red hair tumbled about her shoulders in a dazzling cascade. She wet his face with kisses and clung to him so earnestly, he thought his heart would push its way out of his chest.

Peter was howling to be picked up, so Julien carried his daughter to him and they all settled around Nigel's cradle. "What a lucky man I am! Does she see the children?" he asked Aziz.

"Just for a few minutes in the morning and afternoon, and then they're brought in for prayers just before they go to bed. We're very careful not to tire her, and the children seem to be understanding."

"I should think they'd be better for her than all the medicines in the world. Aren't they the most beautiful children you've ever seen, Aziz?"

He stood Peter next to Adelaide and studied them both. It seemed to him they had grown beyond all expectation since he'd last seen them. Peter was almost as tall as Adelaide, with sturdy legs and a firm, childish paunch, while Adelaide was as lissome and trim as her mother. He found her girlish features so provocatively pretty that he stretched to plant another kiss on her cheek. In his haste he had brought no gifts for them, and he made up his mind that as soon as he could leave Claire for a day or two he would ride to Messina to find some pretty things for all of them, especially for Claire.

He noticed that Aziz's eyes were misty. "Dear Aziz, how lucky I am to have you as a friend. It means everything to me to know that you and Fatima were with her during this terrible time. Heaven bless you. Now I think I'll go back to her for a few minutes. There are so many things I long to say to her."

"Not yet, Julien. It's too soon. She's aware that you're back at least, and that's sure to give her a boost, but you mustn't tire her. Chances are she wouldn't understand much of what you said to her anyway."

"But I've been away for months. I'm sure she needs me."

"Your children need you too. Stay with them awhile, then go in to see Claire around noon."

"Very well," he answered sulkily. The surge of warmth he felt towards Aziz a moment ago was replaced by resentment. What could Aziz understand of what he felt! He'd probably even be amused to know that he kept his promise of fidelity up until his last night in Salerno. Not another man that he knew of on the campaign had been as virtuous. Even Roger, for all his recent mad grief over Elvira's death, had brought three of his women with him.

Adelaide left his side to return to Ahmad, who smoothed her hair, which had been disarranged in Julien's embraces. Julien looked at the tender way the boy groomed her. Ahmad stood more than a head taller than Adelaide. He was almost too thin for his age, with long, narrow muscles, and a sensitive, even feminine face marked by great, round brown eyes that could soften or chill with his changing moods.

"Ahmad is almost a man now," Julien said to Aziz.

"He is a man now," Aziz announced proudly. "He was circumcised while you were away. He may no longer spend his days in the harem. He's earned the company of men."

"Congratulations," Julien said, knowing that the rites of introduction to manhood were a source of much pride to an Arab father. "You'll have to start making plans for him."

"Plans? Oh, you mean his education. There's plenty of time for that. He writes poetry. I think that's sufficient occupation for a boy his age. Julien, the children will be perfectly happy if we just stay here with them while they play. Tell me about the campaign. We hear it was a smashing success."

Julien chided himself for his momentary resentment of Aziz and proceeded to describe the events of the last months. Aziz chuckled approvingly and applauded when he heard of Roger's surprise attack on the marauding Pisans. When it was almost time for their noonday meal, Fatima came out to them.

After a few brief moments with Julien and her husband at breakfast, Fatima returned to Claire's bedside, where she had nursed her every day since her arrival, insisting on supervising every detail of her patient's convalescence.

"I think this would be a good time for you to see her, Julien. She was able to swallow some tea and a little fruit juice. That's better than she's done so far, but don't stay too long."

Claire seemed more alert. She turned her face when he tried to kiss her, but didn't withdraw her hand when he took it in his. He stayed with her for only ten minutes, whispering endearments and words of encouragement, and when he left it seemed to him that she had tried to smile. That evening she drank a full cup of broth for the first time, and Fatima was optimistic about an accelerated recovery. "You're good for her, Julien, but don't expect too much too soon."

In a week Claire was able to sit up in bed, but answered questions only in a faint monotone or with a gesture. She continued to resist any display of affection Julien attempted towards her, but did appear to welcome his presence more, and even seemed amused by his fussing around her.

Weeks later Fatima and the maids arranged a couch for Claire in the main hall, where she could feel more a part of the household affairs, and she responded well. She took a more direct interest in her children, and even ordered Adelaide to go wash her face and hands one day after Ahmad had been teaching her to play jackstones. That night Julien took heart and decided to sleep in her bed. He had no intention of making any sexual demands on her, but he was desperate for the warmth of her body next to his. She watched wide-eyed as he undressed, then slipped softly in next to her. He reached out for her gently, almost tentatively, and was dismayed to find her shrink from his touch and begin to tremble.

"Darling, it's all right. I won't try to make love to you. I just have to be near you. I know you're still far from well, but I need to show you how much I care for you. Please don't turn from me."

It disturbed Julien to notice how fetid her breath still was, but he braced himself and tried to kiss her. She dodged him, and he was able only to plant a peck on her ear. He took her face in his hands and felt that it was wet with tears.

"Dearest, what's wrong? I'm not going to hurt you. Don't you understand how much you mean to me?"

"Please. Sleep somewhere else."

"But this is my place, next to you. You belong here in my arms. It's my right, Claire."

She started to sob. "Please. No."

He left the bed without another word and went into the anteroom. Sleep seemed a long ways off. He masturbated angrily, almost punishing himself with sharp, stabbing strokes, but there was little relief, and he fell asleep only when the first cold light brushed the sky. It embarrassed him that it was clear to everyone he still spent his nights on the mattress in the anteroom.

"I don't know what to do," he said at last to Aziz. "She doesn't want me near her. I tried again last night. She seems so much better, and yet, she'll have nothing to do with me. Nothing. It's maddening."

"You mustn't try to hurry her," his friend replied. "Why don't you go to Taormina or Messina and get yourself a woman? It's not good for you to go so long."

"I don't want another woman. I want her."

"Come now. There are times when you sound like the boy you were when we first met. You still have her as your wife. She loves you, even if she wants no part of lovemaking yet. Be patient. In the meantime it's bad for your health to go so long without a woman. After all, you're not a monk with atrophied balls."

"I'll wait for her no matter how long it takes."

"My friend, while you were on the mainland . . . you didn't have a woman in all that time, did you?" Aziz turned his face away politely as he asked the question.

Julien felt a wave of heat rise towards his eyes. He decided he shouldn't mention his passive encounter with Annunziata. "No, I have self-control. I'm proud that I decided to wait for her."

"Yes, but do you remember how hysterically you behaved when you arrived here . . . sobbing like a woman, and raving? I suspected then that you were suffering from a lack of sex. Those humors thicken if they're not released, and then they clog the passage of ether to the brain."

"I know I was half mad, but that was only from my fear for her. I knew something terrible had happened."

"But don't you see? Your grief would have been more controlled if you had been exercising your manhood. That madness was womanish. Once a man knows the pleasures of regular lovemaking, it's dangerous to revert to celibacy."

"Well, what of Roger? He was mad too after Elvira's death, worse than I, even though his women visited him during all those months of mourning."

"Yes, but think what he'd have been like if they hadn't. No, I suggest you ask Dr. Giacobo if he doesn't agree. I'm speaking for your own good, Julien. Find yourself another woman. Or do it for Claire's sake. You'll be a better husband and lover when she receives you again."

"I said I'll wait. I can find relief by myself."

"Dear friend, you still know so little of women and the fancies they take. I'm not saying this to hurt you, but has it ever occurred to you Claire may never wish to have you again? It's possible."

Julien's eyes blazed. "How dare you! Now you really do presume too much, Aziz. If you weren't my most respected friend, I'd strike you for that."

"Another few months without sex, and I'm sure you could. Be a good fellow, Julien. Go have a talk with Dr. Giacobo."

"First I'd better have a talk with Claire. It's time we spoke openly." He fought to calm himself as he made his way into the hall where Claire's bed had been moved to the window to catch the thin streams of autumn sunlight that warmed the room. Fatima saw the look in Julien's eye and withdrew politely.

"Are you feeling stronger today?"

She looked up and smiled. "Much stronger. You're all pampering me by making me lie down so much. I'm really quite recovered."

Julien beamed at the sight of her. Her flesh had begun to fill out again, and except for some of the darkness that still clung below her eyes, she was indeed close to her old self again. He sat on the couch and took her hand.

"I'm so happy to see you well again, my dearest. And so beautiful." Color rose to her cheeks and made her still lovelier. He pressed her hand briefly to his mouth.

"All these weeks. I've been . . ."

She placed a finger over his lips. "Julien, please don't."

"But you're my wife. Is it wrong for me to want you? I know you're not strong enough yet, but at least I want you to know how much . . ."

"Julien, I can't."

"What do you mean, can't? Was there an injury during the birth?"

"No, at least I don't think so, but it doesn't feel the same. I don't want to cause you any more pain, Julien, but when you touch me, it's more than I can stand. That first night when you came to my bed and put your arms around me, it gave me pain, down there. I can't help it."

"But that will pass in time. Oh darling, I promise not to make love to you if you don't want me to, but I must feel you close."

She shrank from him, almost in terror. "No, don't." She pressed her face into her hands and wept quietly.

Julien stiffened and rose. "Then . . . even my touch—"

"I'm sorry, I know it's unnatural. You don't deserve this, Julien."

"No, I don't believe I do."

That afternoon Julien went to see Dr. Giacobo, but the good man admitted he could do little more than offer advice. He was more than pleased with the progress Claire had made, but the medical aspects of her problem provided no ready answer to Claire's rejection of her husband's advances. He was able to reassure Julien only that there appeared to be no physical abnormality or injury. "Before this unfortunate occurrence," Dr. Giacobo asked him, "was your wife a passionate woman?"

"Yes, very."

"All the more difficult. Women who don't enjoy lovemaking may sometimes use an unfortunate experience such as your wife had as an excuse to relieve themselves of their duties towards their husbands. In your wife's case, this appears not to be so. I can only suggest that you be patient and trust in God's will. But please let me caution you against forcing her. I know husbands do try it all the time, and I've heard some doctors recommend it, but it's never been my experience that it was successful in the long run. No, certainly not with a sensitive woman like Claire."

Julien drew himself up indignantly. "Of course I wouldn't force her. I'm an Englishman. But still, it *is* my right, isn't it? She should recognize my need for her. I mean, even if she didn't enjoy it, don't you think she should try, at least for my sake? After all, it's not like she has to get it up, is it?"

"I do believe she loves you, Julien, and that should be enough for you right now. You have other women, don't you? Give this one a rest."

Julien's eyes moved towards the door. "Thank you, doctor. I appreciate all you've done for her."

He brooded after this visit, unable to find pleasure even in the charms of his children, and conversation with Aziz had begun to bore him. He was surprised one morning when Fatima came to him with a warm grin on her face and announced that Claire had asked if he would see her.

Claire had put on a new gown of wine red silk and was pacing the floor when he entered. It almost irritated him for a moment to find her so apparently vivacious, so attractive, and yet know he must still maintain his distance from her. He approached her rather formally and saluted her with a quick kiss on the cheek. He did notice that she seemed to receive it more cordially than usual.

"Julien, believe me, I know how hard this has been on you. Look, I'm feeling quite well now. Well enough even to travel."

"To travel? What are you getting at?"

"Yes, I'm ashamed of myself for keeping you and Aziz away from court for so long. And it's unfair for Fatima to be so long without seeing the rest of her children. I've decided I don't want to spend the winter in Furci. Why don't we all return to Palermo together?"

Julien grabbed her shoulders excitedly. "Do you mean it?" The weeks of inactivity and his conflict with Claire had seemed to him to be dulling his brain, and he had already decided to return to Palermo, alone or with Aziz, at the end of the month. From the little news that reached him, the affairs of the kingdom didn't seem to be exceptionally pressing, and Roger hadn't even bothered to answer his last letters, but he increasingly found the prospect of an idle season away from court unbearable. If Claire and the children were with him, he'd throw himself into his work, and then perhaps the wait for her feelings about him to change might be less frustrating.

"Claire, this is too good to be true. I didn't dare hope you'd leave. You know I need my work, almost as much as I need you, don't you?"

"It's not good for a man to be idle. It's all my fault."

"Don't say that. I'd stay here forever if I thought it would help you."

"Thank you, but I really want to go too. After all, we originally thought of this villa for our summers and holidays, didn't we? I think it might be depressing for us to spend the whole winter here. No, I've no right to keep any of us from Palermo any longer. It will be good for the children too."

"You're really sure? And you're strong enough?"

"My dear, I simply don't have enough to do here. I'll be busier in Palermo, and then you'll see how strong I become. No, it's all settled. Let's tell Aziz and Fatima right away. They're as anxious as you are to go, I know. Do you think we'll have to wait long for a ship?"

"For a party of eight? If I can't hire a boat, I'll buy one. This is so wonderful! For the first time in ages, you're the Claire I knew." His hand rested a moment on her shoulder, but she put it down gently.

"Don't think I don't know how hard it's been for you. Thank you, Julien."

A week later they were in Palermo and moved into the new apartment in the palace which Julien had bid for months ago in anticipation of his larger family. Claire pronounced it delightful as she moved from room to room, making mental notes for the incidental changes she planned, to Julien's amusement.

Claire had given up her duties in the rug warehouse when they married, and he had heard her fretting more than once about the lack of organization there now. Although she had never proposed it, he wondered if she might not enjoy working there again a few hours a day. It might help ease the pain of her tragedy, he thought. It might even help heal our relationship.

While Claire was running her finger critically across the finish of a linen chest, he suggested it quite abruptly. She spun around, her eyes vibrating with excitement. "Julien! You wouldn't mind? It's not done, you know. A baroness, and married."

"Not if it's just for a few hours a day. The children are well cared for, and I can't imagine anyone whose opinion we value criticizing us."

She impulsively kissed him quickly on the mouth, then drew back, embarrassed by her spontaneous display of affection.

"Don't pull away. I liked that very much. As a matter of fact, maybe you should work all day."

"I'm sorry. That wasn't fair. I know I'm cheating you, Julien."

"It won't matter after you come back to me."

"Please don't say that. I can't make any promises."

"But wouldn't you like to be my wife again? You used to enjoy it."

"I wish I knew. I'd do it, gladly, for your sake, but I don't think I could bear it."

"All right, Claire. I'll speak to Abdullah right away about your assuming some of your old duties in the warehouse."

"No, I'll do it. He knows me better than he does you."

"Yes, but how would it look? I'm your husband."

"Julien, you agreed not to treat me like a slave."

"I didn't mean it that way. I was only trying to help." She didn't answer, but she stopped to squeeze his hand when she walked past him.

There was a knock on the door, but before Julien could answer it, Thomas Browne rushed into the room, his eyes unnaturally bright, but his face ashen. He gripped Julien's arms and fought to catch his breath.

"Julien, thank God you're back. King Henry is dead. Roger has declared three days of mourning in the kingdom."

Chapter IV

THE CHANCELLOR AND THE EMISSARY

June was Julien's favorite month, and he congratulated himself today for living to see his twenty-sixth June. He tried to remember as many of them as he could, recalling first the feeling of the warm soil trickling through his fingers when he was a small child playing in the fields on his father's estate; then the June mornings at Durham, when it seemed the world had finally awakened again after a long, drugged sleep. After these there were the voluptuous Junes of the south, when the labors of spring were rewarded by a crushing extravagance of fruit and flowers.

He looked about him, and it seemed to him that in clarity and beauty this morning surpassed any day in June the world had ever seen. The steady breezes that had carried his ship so reliably from Palermo to the shore of the mainland mingled the scent of blossoms with the clean salt of the sea, and it exhilarated him. He hugged his arms in sheer pleasure.

He could see the Amalfitan coast stretched out to the north, its whitewashed villages dazzling in their brilliance, and he wished his journey had not ended so soon. Part of his pleasure derived from the prospect of seeing his old companion, Robert of Selby, but he was glorying too in the freedom of being at sea. He hadn't guessed until he had left Palermo behind how very much he needed to get away. The last few days on shipboard had been so relaxed, so cradled, he was tempted to tell the captain he wanted to postpone his arrival so that he might sail further up what he believed was the most magnificent coast in the world.

It was out of the question of course. Time was pressing upon him, and besides, Naples was under siege, and the other coastal cities were too unsettled to be hospitable. Imperial spies, spies from the maritime cities, and spies from the two papal courts were swelling all the coastal cities of the south, breeding plots and counterplots, foiling their adversaries' plots, creating intrigues, spreading dissension, and ultimately cancelling and contradicting each other so that nothing was resolved.

The last year and a half in Palermo had been exceptionally trying. Roger had grown more demanding, and also testier as he became more worried about the threat to his kingdom. When Julien worked alone with him, their relationship was informal though businesslike, but at court Roger insisted more and more on what seemed to Julien were excessive formalities and observances of protocol. There was now a good deal of grumbling heard that when Roger gave an audience his visitors were expected to execute reverences which had hitherto been reserved only for the most austere and powerful of the Byzantine emperors.

Julien felt embarrassed the first time he saw Roger's feudatories prostrate themselves and touch their foreheads to the ground in the king's presence, but Roger's demands on certain nobles were inflexible. When Julien hinted to Roger of the growing criticism of court ceremony, he laughed and said he was glad to hear it. Julien was taken aback, but when he thought more about it he recognized the source of Roger's amusement. It was always towards the most pretentious aristocrats of his court that his demands for pomp and formality were most strictly enforced, and it was his enemies and critics that were most impressed, even if adversely, by this outward display of power. When Roger was entertaining the intellectuals of his court, which he much preferred to do, it was Roger who rose first when a respected geographer, physicist, or sometimes even poet, entered the hall, whether they were old friends or merely respected visitors. This too was general knowledge and a certain source of annoyance to the nobles he despised.

Julien had worked hard after the return from Furci. He sat in on all council meetings, and Roger personally briefed him daily on the course of the emperor's campaign and their counterstrategy. There was no doubt Roger was preparing him for a crucial mission, more critical even than his trip to Rome, and Julien exercised his intelligence as keenly as possible to be equal to the exceptional demands he knew would shortly be made upon him.

If he hadn't thrust himself so energetically into preparations for the emergencies that faced the kingdom, he would have found it far more difficult to get through the last year. He watched Claire grow stronger and bloom with the loveliness of regained health, and it increased his bitterness. He admitted that in no way could he reproach her for inattentiveness or for lack of loving attention, so long as it was outside the bedchamber. She was softer towards him than ever, more anxious to be understanding and generous. No matter at what hour he returned to their apartment, she was waiting for him to attend to his comfort. But it wasn't enough. A touch, a caress, a chaste kiss and no more, could sadden and sometimes even anger him. He worked every night until he was exhausted enough to sleep without the troubling thoughts of the arms and kisses he longed for so achingly.

There were months of this, and then almost a year ago he went to the room of one of the Tiraz workers who had flirted openly with him every time he visited the workrooms. She was warm and soft, and she yielded at once to the rush of passion he unleashed at her. The next morning he sent her an expensive flask of perfume and thereafter avoided the Tiraz as much as possible.

A few months later his passion was gnawing at him so insistently that he was certain it was interfering with his work. He opted for as impersonal an encounter as he could think of and visited a discreetly elegant whorehouse in one of the residential sections of Palermo. The Greek manager saw the glitter of the coins Julien poured onto his table and promptly matched their gleam by flashing his gold teeth in an appreciative grin. He gave effusive thanks to God that he had a woman staying there worthy of such a distinguished guest. Her name was Mirgin and she was a Turkish dancer, newly arrived in Palermo, and personally schooled in all the arts of the bedchamber by the chief eunuch of the Sultan of Baghdad himself.

Mirgin turned out to be about Julien's age; a shade older, he felt, than the woman one might expect for the large sum he'd laid down, but he had to admit she was extraordinarily good looking, with a fierce mane of black hair that bristled out from her head in all directions, and a full complement of white teeth.

She led him to a low-ceilinged room thick with stale incense and motioned him toward a pile of cushions while she prepared to do a dance for him. Julien was thoroughly bored with the dances of the Near East. They were an invariable part of the entertainments he was expected to attend, and he was anxious to resolve the purpose of his visit, but he resigned himself to watching her perform.

Mirgin was definitely a dancer of no small talent. She remained amply

clothed during her dance, which surprised him, but then he grew unmistak-
ably aware that the undulations of her body, seen under multiple layers of
thin silk, were exciting him. He moved to grab her whenever she slithered
near, but she eluded his grasp and continued her dance, only at the end
shedding her clothes as she extinguished all but two of the candles and
approached him, almost as if she were stalking prey.

Julien had considered Ula an expert lover, but Mirgin's aggressions
were beyond anything he had experienced with a woman before. She made
him understand that she expected him to assume as much passivity as he was
capable of while she explored his body with an enthusiasm matched only by
her extraordinary skill. Julien stayed with her all night, and in the morning
he left her a sum of money equal to what he had paid the landlord for her
services. It was clear she considered him extravagant, and she begged him to
return to her as soon as he could. Julien nodded absentmindedly.

He felt more numb than tired at work that day, but the melancholy was
as strong as ever. He even found he was disappointed because Claire didn't
reproach him with so much as a glance for spending the night away from
home.

He didn't visit the whorehouse again until a month later, a short time
before he was to sail to Salerno. He paid the Greek pimp who was un-
disguisedly delighted to see him again, and decided that perhaps this time he
would do well to be more explicit about the sort of woman he hoped to find.
He admitted that Mirgin was unsurpassed in her knowledge of the arts of
love, and perhaps even a genius at invention, but he felt he would be happier
with a woman who was not quite as zealous. The Greek looked at him
craftily, waiting for another hint of his client's taste.

Julien kept thinking: It's Claire I want, but he was offended at the idea
of describing her in hopes of finding a substitute in such a place. "The truth
is, I like to feel the aggressor," he went on. "With Mirgin, everything was
her idea, and I'm not saying I didn't enjoy it, but I'd prefer someone more
naive, someone who wasn't such a practiced whore."

"I think I understand. Younger, of course?"

"Well yes, but the most important thing is, I don't want an aggressive
woman. I believe it's a man's place to lead."

"You came to the right place, my lord. We have many clients of your
refined taste, and it just so happens that today I have the perfect partner for
you. I absolutely guarantee your satisfaction. She is, of course, a bit, shall we
say, rarer?" He paused until Julien allowed a few more coins to trickle to the
table.

The pimp led him to a room that was larger and more sumptuously furnished than the first he'd visited, but the air was every bit as nauseatingly thick with incense. When the door closed behind him, he made out a figure lying on a bed screened off from the rest of the room with embroidered silk hangings. He undressed quickly in a corner, then pulled aside the drapery and sucked in his breath sharply at what he saw. A thin wren of a girl, no more than a child, stared up at him wide-eyed. Her breasts were unformed and her ribs were poking through her fleshless torso. One of her ankles was tightly confined in a heavy iron manacle attached by a long chain to a metal ring in the ground.

"How old are you?" he gasped.

The girl's lips trembled as she answered. "Thirteen."

"Well, I guess that's old enough." His eyes moved towards her naked groin, and he wondered if she were still hairless or if they shaved her to increase her youthfulness. He realized at the same moment that he had not only lost all his desire but was even uncomfortable, actually repelled at being there. "What's your name and where are you from?"

She moved over to make more room for him on the bed, and he sat down awkwardly, wishing he hadn't undressed before seeing her.

"My name is Adele. I think I'm from Syria."

"Very well, Adele. Have you worked here long?"

"Only a month, but I was in Egypt for a year before they bought me."

He recognized her fear of him and it disturbed him. He reached his hand out to touch her shoulder, hoping to comfort her, but she shuddered and shrank from his touch.

"Don't be frightened, Adele. I'm not going to hurt you." She shook her head dumbly, and then her eyes widened with increased fright when she saw Julien start to rise from her bed.

"What's wrong? I said I wouldn't touch you." He looked around the room for where he'd left his clothes.

"Please don't go. They'll beat me if they find out you didn't want me."

"Beat you? Don't be silly. I've paid for you. What I do with you now is my business."

"No, no, don't go." She reached out and tried to pull him closer, then jabbed her arm out and tried clumsily to clutch his limp prick.

Julien grabbed her wrist, then sat down on the bed again at a more discreet distance. "You're really frightened, aren't you?"

"Believe me, if they find out you did nothing, it will be terrible for me."

"No it won't. I can take care of that. If they're abusing you, I can have this house closed. King Roger has laws for this."

"You don't understand. He owns me. If you did something to punish him, it would only be worse for me later."

"Slaves are protected under Sicilian law whether they're whores or not. King Roger had a man fined last year and his farm taken from him for beating his slave to death."

"I beg you not to say anything. Even if they didn't kill me, there are worse things." She suddenly grabbed Julien's hand and thrust it between her thighs. He drew it back quickly and recoiled from her, shaken. Her flesh had felt dry and cool.

"Don't do that. Will you believe me if I promise you I won't let them hurt you? I have some influence in this city."

"No, please stay. If you won't take me, then at least pretend you did."

"I have no stomach for this. Do they send you many men?"

"Not many. They charge a lot of money for me, I hear. Sometimes the men are angry with me because they had to pay so much, and then it's bad."

"You aren't ready for any of this yet. You lied to me about your age, didn't you?"

She was silent, but Julien recognized the troubled look of a child who doesn't sufficiently understand what's happening.

"I thought so. And the men they send you . . . they often enjoy forcing themselves on you, don't they?" He realized that this question must sound foolish, or even incomprehensible to her, but his memory recalled men he knew who dreamed of child rape. His first experience in the sack of a town had taught him much he wanted to forget. The girl was looking more frankly frightened now.

"Do you think they would sell you to me?"

She stared at him in disbelief. "But why would you want to buy me? We haven't even done anything."

He slipped his clothes on quickly. "Get dressed and wait for me."

"I don't have any clothes, and I can't go anywhere with this." She gestured towards her manacled ankle.

He gritted his teeth and went out to confront the Greek. In his purse he always carried a meaningless document that bore Roger's seal, which was useful for impressing illiterates. The pimp was startled to see him so soon but did not mistake his mood and retreated, placing the table between himself and Julien.

"I suppose you know that the girl you sent me to is only ten."

"That's not possible. I bought her from a reputable dealer. Besides, she had lots of experience before I got her."

"Show me the documents for her purchase."

"I don't have any. Come now, we're both men of the world. It's never been necessary before. What is this, and who are you anyway?"

"I'll tell you in good time. How much did you pay for her?"

"A hundred gold bezants."

"You're a craven liar. More likely two or three. Here are ten. See that she's decently clothed and sent to the palace, to Baroness di Furci. If she's not there in one hour, and in good condition, I will see to it that this sink is closed and you'll be wearing those teeth as a necklace."

"Why didn't you say you wanted to buy her, my lord? I understand perfectly. Excellent judgment, excellent. I must compliment your taste. But ten gold bezants! You saw for yourself she's worth far more than that. She'll be as tight as a bride for years yet. You wouldn't want to cheat me, would you?"

"No, I don't want to cheat you. I really want to break your neck. Now move quickly or you'll have all of Roger's personal guard as your guests for the next month."

"This is an outrage. I'll bring it to the courts."

"Good! You have one hour to get the girl to the palace. Move."

When Julien told Claire he had engaged a new nurse for the children, she looked at him curiously but didn't question him further. She knew Julien was aware that the staff they already had was more than adequate for their needs, but the firmness with which he announced his decision was something she hadn't noted in him before.

Adele arrived only a few minutes after Julien, and Claire was startled to see how young she was. Adele admitted at once that she was not quite twelve. Claire was about to express doubt as to the girl's ability to handle three children, the oldest of whom was only five years younger than she, but a glance at Julien's brooding expression cautioned her to be still.

The children were already in their beds, so Adele was shown directly to the room she would share with the two other women they employed. She looked at Julien and then at Claire unbelievingly. Her mouth began to twitch and Julien thought she was about to cry, but instead her shoulders hunched up and her body tensed as if she'd been seized by a sharp cramp. Her head jerked to the side with a spasm that shook her frame and then she relaxed. Julien looked at her wonderingly. She had apparently lost her faculty for tears.

Claire looked askance at the ragged robe Adele was wearing and found her a loose fitting shift of her own that swept the floor. It made her look even more like a little girl. Julien smiled happily when he saw his wife embrace her before leading her off to bed. He waited for Claire to return, trying to compose a story on how he came upon the child that she might find reasonable, but when she joined him again she still had no questions. He read quietly until she decided she would retire; then she kissed his cheek a shade more lingeringly than usual.

Next morning Claire introduced Adele to her children with genuine enthusiasm. Adele showed a creditable talent for dressing Adelaide's hair, and Julien heard Claire tell the servants they must be very gentle with her. For the rest of the day Adelaide taught Adele how to play her favorite games, and it was clear the newcomer would fill an unique position with the children, far more a companion than a servant.

As Julien stood at the ship's rail, he felt again his familiar ache for Claire, only now it wasn't the simple yearning for her that he'd lived with so unhappily these last months. He was aware of their separateness, and it had little to do with being denied her bed. *I love her more now, though differently.* Perhaps it's because I no longer sleep with her that I can appreciate her fine qualities better, he thought, and he congratulated himself on having chosen such an exceptional woman. Abelard could be no more exultant in the gifts of his Heloise, he decided. Claire was to be treasured, no matter what.

The formalities at customs were brushed aside at the first glimpse of Roger's seal. Julien was either remembered or expected, and a slave was brought up at once to conduct him to Robert of Selby's offices, now housed in a palace in the heart of the city, directly across from the Norman cathedral.

Salerno had not changed much, except that it looked more prosperous than he remembered. In this part of the city there was not the medley of race that he had become accustomed to in Palermo, or even the flow of foreigners around the university area. Here Italians and Lombards seemed fused in the Salernitans he saw; they were taller and moved more energetically than most Apulians or Calabrians. He was pleased to see the pace of the city's business, and his ear delighted once more to the soft Greek tone of the Italian he heard.

Robert was alone in his inner office and appeared surprised to see him. "Julien. Welcome. I've not made any preparations for you, though. I didn't think you'd be here until sometime in July."

"There was no time to lose. Too much has been happening, and Roger has worked out a strategy with his curia that I'm to acquaint you with. Will you arrange a meeting with your council as soon as possible, please? Tomorrow would be best. Are they all to be trusted? What I have to say is vital."

"I think we've weeded out all the malcontents. How's your family?"

"Healthy, handsome, and graced by God, thank you. And now I have an announcement that will please you greatly."

"It's true, then?"

"Oh, you've already heard about Guerin? Yes, it's true. He died a good death, at peace with God and secure in his faith. May Heavenly peace remain his. I hope you don't mind that it is only I who am to invest you as the new chancellor in Roger's name. He prefers it to be a simple and quick ceremony. It's absolutely impossible for him to leave Palermo right now, but he promises when next you meet, the archbishop and he will reinvest you with all the ceremonies due you. I feel greatly honored to declare you our new chancellor, Robert. Accept my congratulations with my love." He embraced Robert and kissed him on both cheeks.

Robert was moved but oddly controlled. "I confess I couldn't be more pleased. I've worked for this."

"You've earned it. Guerin was a fine man, but you know Roger had always hoped to see you his new chancellor after the old man went on."

"Yes, he's been generous enough to say so to me often. That's why it's no great surprise. I heard an unconfirmed report of Guerin's death this morning, but I had no idea Roger would act so fast. Frankly, I wish he'd move as fast in areas more critical to our welfare."

"I understand perfectly what you mean. Will you allow me to wait till our meeting tomorrow before discussing this with you further?"

"Must I wait until then?"

"It was Roger's suggestion."

"And where Roger suggests, we follow."

"So long as we have one king and one God."

"Then, let's have the council meeting right away. We don't have to wait till tomorrow. Why don't you take a nap, and I'll have my men assembled for you in two hours?"

Julien had always marvelled at Robert's swift course of action. It was no wonder Salerno's government functioned as smoothly as it did. Roger could have chosen no one more capable of reflecting his own goals in the kingdom. But although the two seemed perfectly in tune, Julien wondered how Robert would react to the information he was about to present to the council. He felt certain the course of action Roger had decided on was not what Robert would have initiated independently.

The meeting convened in a council room furnished exactly like a dining room with a long trestle table and benches at one end. Robert pulled Julien aside to whisper to him. "Tell them about my appointment as chancellor later. I want to get on with the more important business."

Julien made himself comfortable and proceeded to address the council in an informal fashion. "Your concern for the affairs of the last months is no greater than what we feel in Sicily, but to explain our program I want first to give you the facts as we see them and what lies behind them.

"On the surface it appears that Emperor Lothair has succeeded in mustering all available forces to create an enormous body of men with one single purpose. It's simply not true. We also thought he'd created a triumvirate in the old Roman tradition, but it seems now that if Lothair tolerates the other members, it's because he has no choice. His son-in-law Henry the Proud is ruthless, ambitious, and would love to see old Lothair dead. Conrad of Hohenstaufen is Lothair's traditional enemy, tolerated only for the sake of peace at home."

"Granted," Robert said, "but what of all the other men they've picked up in Italy with Innocent and Bernard?"

"I'm coming to that. Those who joined Henry because they were Innocent's followers aren't necessarily friends of the Empire."

"Yes, I can see that," Robert admitted. "We were surprised that Henry didn't put Innocent in St. Peter's when he had the chance."

"It was no surprise to Roger. Henry and Innocent had their first major falling out over the spoils of war when they took Viterbo, and it's been getting steamier between them ever since."

A young Norman in the council interrupted Julien. "There had to be more reason for Henry's not installing Innocent on the papal throne."

"There was," Julien said. "Henry was committed to meet Lothair with the rest of the imperial army in Bari no later than Whitsuntide. He didn't have the time to take Rome from Anacletus. And by the time they got to Bari, Innocent and Henry were at each other's throats."

"So you believe that the emperor's priority for installing Innocent in Rome is pretty low, eh?" Robert said. "I'm not sure that isn't wishful thinking. Seems to me the quickest way to make Innocent's place in Rome secure is by crushing Roger first. We're the only real support Anacletus has. I'll wager that's their strategy, and it's good."

"Maybe so," Julien said, "but they still have to crush us. Now do you think Lothair's made any new friends in the south? One of his first stops was at the shrine of St. Michael in Monte Gargano. A most commendable Christian act, wouldn't you say? But before he left, he stripped the shrine of all its treasure: gold, silver, gems—even the precious vestments were looted.

"Then, Roger's rebels in Apulia got a taste of imperial justice as he moved through their towns. In addition to castration of the defeated enemy, Lothair has another favorite punishment. He left behind village after village filled with slit noses. Once Lothair leaves the area, the rebels will welcome Roger back with open arms."

"Fine, but he's on *our* doorstep now, with the greatest army since the Great Crusade." Robert was beginning to show his irritation. "Why aren't we better equipped to meet them? What's Roger waiting for? Unless he moves fast to muster all the troops he can and finds us new allies, his cause is lost."

"And he'll continue to wait. That's precisely what I'm here to tell you. No matter how large the imperial army is, they are not united. Innocent and Bernard are at Lothair's throat, and Henry and Conrad are seeking only their own ends."

"I disagree, Julien. They may not all think as one, but they *are* united—against *us!* Roger has no allies I know of."

"But he *does,* Robert. He has several. I know many of you expect Roger to carry on this war in the tradition of his fighting ancestors. That's not his style. Our king represents a new generation of Normans. No, Roger will not direct a clash that will leave the fields of Apulia soaked with his subjects' blood."

The council members raised their voices protestingly and Julien allowed them to grumble among themselves and speak out before he quieted them with a gesture. "I told you we had allies. The first of these is time. Look, we're already well into June. If they can't conclude the war by early fall, they'll never make it north in time to get through the Alps before the passes are all closed by snow.

"The thing we feared most was that Lothair would mass a huge navy with the help of the northern maritime cities. If he were to attack Palermo by sea with a strong force within the next month, the war would undoubtedly be his. Fortunately for us, the Germans are never comfortable at sea, and he doesn't really trust any Italians, not even the Venetians. Lothair is committed to doing battle on land, where his troops can be relied on, and that decision will undo him.

"We have another powerful ally that he's just beginning to find out about, and that, dear friends, is the Apulian summer. If we can just stall him long enough, those northern root farmers will never make it through August. They have no defense against the marsh fevers that plague that area, much less the heat. Already the grumbling among his troops is growing. His feudal contracts for service are almost overdue, and even the emperor can't force a soldier to fight much longer than he's contracted for. The crops at home will soon need harvesting, and that's of more concern to his men than which Italian is pope, or whether some Norman reigns in the south. They've been gone ten months already, thanks to the length of time it took Lothair to mass them, and they still haven't seen an army to fight."

Robert kept shaking his head. "Does Roger really think he can fight this war by not fighting?"

"That's exactly what he proposes to do. Frankly, we wouldn't stand a chance in open battle with them. Our plan is to stall them as much as possible. Our agents aren't idle. Everywhere in his camp you can see the distrust growing between army and Church."

Neither Robert nor the council members appeared convinced. "It's just not enough to go on," Robert said.

"I agree," Julien said. "But we have a few more tricks up our sleeves. As soon as I conclude my business with you gentlemen, I'm going to Bari as Roger's emissary."

"You? To negotiate terms? But where will that leave us?"

"Let's say I go not so much to negotiate as to play at negotiations. The terms I will offer Lothair will be totally unacceptable to Innocent and Bernard, and I suspect they eventually won't interest Lothair very much either. But I've got to convince them they're worth considering. I hope not only to widen the rift between the two forces, but to keep them involved in discussion for as long as possible."

Julien nodded to a venerable Lombard named Gandolf whom he respected for his judgment. The old man's voice was even, but still charged with emotion.

"I believe I speak for all of us at this council when I say we're confused, to put it politely, by the official analysis of this emergency. It's perhaps more oriental in its reasoning than we Italians are accustomed to. If Roger can really avoid bloodshed by these wily tactics, then of course we're all for him, but allow me to state *our* case. Roger is in Palermo, and I agree that Lothair's army isn't likely to make it to Sicily, and even if they were to get as far as the Straits of Messina, the advantage would be ours. And you may be right, granted, in saying that all efforts must be made, short of shedding blood needlessly, to avoid even that battle.

"But we're here on the mainland, not in Sicily. What if Lothair decides it would be wisest to take Rome, install Innocent at St. Peter's, and then continue home, ignoring a Sicilian campaign? If he were to do so isn't it likely that he'd come west first to take Salerno so that he'd at least be able to say he subjugated Roger's mainland capital and taught his enemy a lesson?

We too have often felt that Lothair can't take Sicily and put Innocent on the throne as well because of the time involved. Is Roger banking on Lothair changing his goals and so sacrificing us?" The council applauded him loudly.

"Thank you, Lord Gandolf, for your insight. What you say is true. I've already given Robert sealed instructions to be opened only in case the city is directly threatened by the imperialists. I'm not at liberty to divulge its exact contents but only to swear to you that Roger has no intention of sacrificing the loyal people of Salerno to his interests or to the overall good of the kingdom. For this I ask you to accept my word and your king's."

"We don't question Roger's good faith," Gandolf replied, "but think of Lothair's reputation. Look at what those troops did to Bari, to say nothing of the other towns."

"Capua was spared."

"Only because Robert of Capua was there with a handy bribe of three thousand pounds of silver to keep the troops in line."

"We have silver too. And Benevento was spared because they acted diplomatically. If Innocent and Bernard were to permit Salerno to be sacked in spite of generous terms offered, they would be injuring their reputations."

"We'll have to discuss this further among ourselves. I'm afraid it's a risky course Roger is embarked on."

"Discuss this among yourselves by all means, but you'll see there's no course open to you which offers greater insurance. There's no more I can say. Robert, can you arrange to have horses and a dozen men ready to accompany me to Bari? The imperialists have already been informed of my coming and are honor bound to grant me safe conduct through the city. I have two of my own men from Sicily with me, but I need an entourage befitting my mission. I'd like to leave tomorrow morning if you have no further business with me."

"By St. Aidan's bell, I'll go with you myself if you like."

"I'd love it, but it's out of the question. Roger was quite firm on that point. Need I remind you who you are now? Will you inform these gentlemen of your new honors after I go, or would you like me to tell them now?"

Gandolf nodded his head. "There's no need to say it. If Roger wasn't intelligent enough to make Robert his chancellor, he wouldn't merit our loyalty. We assumed he would follow Guerin. Congratulations, Robert!"

Julien bowed. "I leave you to your congratulations, then. If you'll excuse me now, I need to prepare some papers for my journey. Good day, my lords."

Julien was satisfied that he'd been reasonably convincing, but as he left he felt his knees shaking unaccountably. Was it the strain of my argument?

he wondered, and then he recalled the nausea that had gripped him when he described Lothair's mutilation of the Apulians. *What am I walking into?* He knew when he accepted the mission that it would be dangerous, that he would be confronting an awesomely powerful man whose considerable anger must now be whetted by the frustrations of his campaign. Julien walked faster, then broke into a run and got back to his room just in time to be sick in his water basin.

Julien joined Robert for dinner with his staff but resisted his invitation to spend the rest of the evening in their company, despite the fact that Robert was celebrating his appointment with a feast featuring a superb selection of foods and wines that looked as if it would last for hours. He spent the rest of the night in prayer, and at dawn he wrote out his last will and sealed it, to be opened by Robert in the event of his death.

Morning seemed to have arrived so soon. Then he remembered this was the shortest night of the year, perhaps a good omen. He kissed the wooden crucifix Claire had given him before he left and placed it back around his neck. He would need long days to do the work ahead.

He washed, then decided to walk about the city for a breath of air before seeing Robert. The men Robert had selected to accompany him to Bari were already waiting in the square outside the cathedral. Robert had chosen wisely. All twelve men were a full head or more taller than Julien, the blondest giants that could be found in the city. Julien smiled to himself. The two men he had brought with him from Sicily were tall and blond as well. It wasn't a bad idea to allow the Germans to believe they would be engaging northern supermen in battle.

All of his escort were dressed in heavy iron armor, and Julien pitied them and their poor horses. At best it would not be a comfortable journey, and he was glad not to have to wear armor himself. Roger had pointed out it would be more fitting for an ambassador to present himself as a man of peace. In Sicily Julien had taken to wearing Arab dress whenever he rode. The cotton trousers were suited to riding, and the loose robe worn over them was comfortable in warm weather. On sunny days he even chose to wear a turban when on horseback. It was not considered an affectation in Sicily, since it offered sensible protection from the sun and absorbed sweat. Out of deference to the aims of his mission, however, Julien had chosen conservative western clothing for the trip.

He introduced himself to the men and inspected them briefly. He knew he would be with them for quite a while, perhaps even be dependent upon them for his safety, but there was no time now for more than the most cursory appraisal. Most looked too young to be seasoned warriors, but they were nonetheless impressive. All were remarkably handsome, and although they were big, they moved with the responsiveness of finely trained athletes. He judged the oldest of them to be two or three years younger than himself, and for a moment he felt the hand of time upon him.

It wouldn't do to keep them waiting. He reentered the governor's palace to say goodbye to Robert, and found the new chancellor surrounded by his staff and already involved in the business of the day. "I won't detain you, Robert. I believe I have all I need for the journey. Those look like fine men to have at my side. My thanks. I promise to bring them all back to you safely. Wish me Godspeed, my friend." They embraced, and Julien read the concern in his friend's face.

He led the men out of the city at a fast pace, anxious to ride as far as possible before the heat of midday set in. Although the distance was not great, the terrain was mostly hilly and he knew progress would be slow. Since the Salernitans knew the territory better than he, they took charge of the itinerary and found the most advantageous paths. They were able to change horses once at Potenza, and by urging themselves and their beasts to the limit, they found themselves at the outskirts of Bari in just five days.

Once in view of the city, they were surrounded by imperial scouts who started an attack at the sight of men in armor, but Julien dismounted at once and waved a parchment roll in the air, demanding to be taken to Lothair. He was correct in assuming none of them would dare disobey anyone waving a document, but the scouts continued to flank his men with their swords drawn and were on their guard every step of the way.

As they drew closer to the city, they found the stench appalling, and once inside the walls, a grisly sight was spread before them. Gibbets had been erected all along the main road to the center of the city, and the three hundred Saracens who had defended the citadel were hanging from them, naked and castrated, their bodies and faces savagely mutilated. Julien clasped his crucifix and muttered a prayer for them as they passed.

The leader of the scouts who had been riding well in advance of the party dropped behing to speak with Julien. "They've been up there for two days now. Had to teach those dogs a lesson, but they'll all be thrown into the sea tomorrow."

"It's ghastly," said Julien. Even his experience in battle had not prepared him for anything so awful.

"Never mind, they're all heathens. Wasn't a Christian soul to be saved in the whole lot." Julien didn't answer him, but clenched his jaw and rode as erectly and proudly as he could despite his fatigue.

The castle where Lothair and his staff were quartered was within the city walls and on the sea, built to withstand attack from land and water and large enough to shelter a large percentage of Bari's population if need be. When Julien and his company were admitted to the castle gate, they were told their hosts were at dinner and they were kept waiting at the entrance while one of the scouts went to inform Lothair's party of their arrival. This was the first time Julien found himself on enemy ground, but his desire to set a proper example for his retinue gave him courage.

A few minutes later one of Lothair's staff appeared to say that Julien was expected at the emperor's table and that his men were invited to join the junior officers at a lower end of the hall. Julien was surprised at the readiness with which he was being admitted to the emperor's presence, but he followed without betraying any sign of emotion.

Julien was led to a table raised on a crude wooden dais, where Lothair was seated with forty or so others. The emperor was gnawing an ankle of mutton, and it took a while before his attention could be directed to the arrival of the stranger. Julien made an obeisance as soon as he caught Lothair's eye, and waited for a place at table to be indicated to him. Lothair blinked at him a few times, then signalled his staff to make room for him at one end. Some bowls were pushed aside, hips were grudgingly shuffled, and Julien squeezed himself onto the bench. The emperor returned to his mutton, and the conversation at table, such as it was, resumed.

From his place Julien was able to study Lothair and the people around him. Lothair's costume was not distinguished by any sign of his high office, and there was no standard or other insignia to indicate his rank. He appeared at table as a leader of fighting men without pretension of majesty. Julien knew the emperor was elderly, but he wasn't prepared to see him looking so weak and tired. The men at his side had to incline their heads to hear him when he spoke, and between mouthfuls he paused and sighed, almost gasping for air. This is not just a tired, aging man, Julien thought. He is ill.

The man on Lothair's right Julien judged to be the emperor's son-in-law, Henry the Proud of Bavaria. He looked every whit a warrior. His dark moustache bristled fiercely, and his voice was profound and loud. He was the largest man at table, not simply the tallest but also the broadest, with a fist the size of a cantaloupe. His face and coloring aren't really too different from Roger's, Julien observed, with his thick black hair and that oddly Semitic cast to his features. Henry's eyes fastened on Julien's only once or twice, but they were not appraising. Julien felt their coldness go through and past him.

On Lothair's left sat Conrad of Hohenstaufen, a middle-aged man whose mien was as threatening as Henry's, but suggestive of a more heightened intelligence. His face was roughly chiselled and his large, blond head gave him a firmly leonine air; but his manners were refined, and the composure of his face reflected none of Henry's arrogance.

Julien was so captured by this trio it took him a while to realize that opposite Lothair and his party only clergy were seated. He had to strain to see if Innocent might be there. He half rose in his seat before ascertaining that both Innocent and Bernard were indeed present, side by side, and seated directly opposite Lothair.

Innocent was in his late sixties, calm and ascetic, and he didn't carry his years well. The bitterness of his exile and his shabby treatment at the hands of his imperial allies had pinched his face and given it a martyr's cast. There was very little food on his trencher, and he seemed entirely absorbed in the conversation of Bernard on his right.

Bernard was twenty years younger. There was an air of fatigue and resignation about him until one saw his eyes, which alone animated his face, reflecting his determination. The years of self-discipline had left his tallish frame gaunt, and his flesh was lusterless, but those magnificent eyes were eloquent testimony to his gifts. His reddish blond hair was thinning and lank, but he wore it much longer than Julien expected, and his beard exhibited a total lack of interest in grooming. The contrast was striking. Innocent, whose role in the Church was political and extroverted, sat reflectively, while Bernard, the chief monk of an order dedicated to contemplation, was vigorous and demonstrative, an almost palpable energy emanating from the prematurely withered frame.

Julien was ignored, if not actually snubbed, by his neighbors at table. After a while a surly servant approached him with his trencher of bread. It was rough brown bread such as only the poorest peasants ate, and Julien judged the flour had not been very clean, but he was hungry and fell to his food with good will. There appeared to be every kind of meat and fish imaginable, but he found them poorly prepared.

When he had eaten less than half of what he had expected to, he put the rest aside and gave all his attention to a continued scrutiny of his dinner partners. It appeared to him these soldiers had no taste for vegetables or salads. He longed for the more discriminating diet of Sicily, or even the pleasant, simple food that he and his men had been able to find in the small villages on their way here.

These are the enemy, he thought, and it chilled him. The fact that they were breaking bread together seemed ironic. How great is my danger? he wondered. It wasn't so long ago that Pope Gregory VII had castrated Henry IV's emissaries to abash the emperor. Could he expect much more from these savage-looking warriors seated opposite him? It seemed the best he could do was to remain unruffled, observe protocol as strictly as possible, and to honey over the more abrasive demands of his proposal.

He disliked Henry the Proud instinctively, and chided himself. Roger had repeatedly warned him never to allow instinctive aversions to personality to influence his dealings. "Take note of your feelings," he'd been told, "because they'll be right more often than not, but enter all discussion as if you truly believe the man you're talking to is hiding the fact that he wants to give you everything you ask for." Julien admitted to himself that Henry was certainly a man to command respect, even fear.

Conrad was more interesting, more appealing even, yet when he glanced at Julien his face was scornful, haughty. He had been within a hair of claiming the imperial crown for himself and had doubtless never abandoned that ambition. These were certainly strong men to reckon with.

The more he watched Lothair the more Julien found himself feeling sorry for him. He decided the leader's greatest fault was probably that he had no patience and little understanding of anything foreign to him. He didn't understand the south, and what he didn't understand, he hated. However famous he was for his piety, it didn't abate his impatience with the Church's quarrels. If I were a German, Julien thought, I'd probably admire him a great deal; however, it is my great good fortune that I am not. Certainly Lothair appeared to be the most reasonable of the three. Julien broke off these musings, reminding himself that, Not until we face each other at the bargaining table will I be sure what sort of man I'm dealing with.

Instead of a more formal presentation to the emperor, a servant came to him as the meal drew to an end to escort him to his quarters. None of the objects of his scrutiny even glanced at him as he rose to leave, but he made a low bow anyway, then followed his guide out of the hall as proudly as possible. These were strange manners indeed, even for a court in camp. When Roger was on campaign, no one would have dreamed of leaving his table without some express sign of dismissal. He tried to reassure himself that the laughter he heard behind his back was in no way meant for him.

He expected to be quartered somewhere in the castle, but instead he was led to another building a half mile away which might formerly have been a sentry house. His cortege was already waiting, trying to settle their possessions in the meager space. Inside the house there was a row of narrow cots along both walls with a chest at the foot of each; hardly deluxe accommodations. Outside their door were four armed guards, and all weapons except their daggers had been taken from his companions.

"You can't blame them for not trusting us," Julien told his men.

"I don't think they trust each other any more than us," observed a young man named William of whom Julien had taken note on the trip. "It smells of assassination in the inner circle and mutiny in the ranks." William was half Norman and half Italian, the finest athlete, and also the one best liked—an obvious leader. He stripped off the rest of his armor, stuffed it under his cot and stretched out, flexing his muscles impatiently. He, more than any other, seemed to be enjoying the adventure, even when circumstances were unfavorable.

Julien watched the contractions of the young giant's powerful body and suddenly felt envy mixed with his admiration. "William," he chided, "you shouldn't lie there naked like that without hanging your netting first. You'll be bitten raw by morning. The mosquitoes here are the size of humming birds."

William sprang from his cot and quickly set up the frame for his netting. "Our dining hall was ringed with armed men," he went on, "and they weren't stationed there against outside intruders. It seemed to me these men were from three different commands, and they kept eyeing each other uncertainly."

"I thought we were going to get our first good meal after that long journey," said another man named Mauger. "What rot it was." Mauger was William's closest friend, all Norman, and the grandson of one of the Guiscard's lieutenants. The sun had leathered his skin and left his hair almost white in its blondness. He was acknowledged to be the best swordsman in the company, his powerful arms wielding the heavy double-bladed weapon like a straw. He arranged his netting and stretched out on a cot next to William's.

"If this is the way their officers eat, then Heaven help the foot soldiers," Julien said. "It's no wonder the men are grumbling. I think the Baresi must be bringing them all the spoiled fish they can find for their kitchens, and that meat had a definite greenish tinge to it. By the way, there was no conversation worth reporting at my table. Did any of you hear anything valuable to us?"

"No," answered William, "but I recognized one of the priests at your table. He's a deputy judge from Salerno."

"Excellent," Julien answered. "Make no attempt to contact him or indicate in any way that you recognize him, though. I've no doubt there are many others of us about, but I certainly didn't expect one at my table."

Next morning Julien washed and dressed carefully. There was no word yet from the castle, but he knew he would see Lothair, and he expected some exchange. At noon their guards escorted them to the dining hall. Julien saluted Lothair with scrupulous formality, and the emperor responded with a single, curt nod. Julien tried, then, to pay his respects to the other notables at the table, but they pointedly ignored him, so he took his place quietly.

Back at their quarters, William came to Julien, disturbed. "I think they're insulting us. You should have had a private interview by this time, or at least have been given a date for one. And the men at our table treat us as if we weren't there. We continue to be courteous, as you instructed, but if we try to speak with them, they ignore us and go on speaking German, even though I've heard a number of them use Latin."

"Continue to be correct in your manner with them. If they're insulting us, then it's the kind of insult we should enjoy," Julien answered. "Let them take as long as they wish before they see me. My mission will be half won if they continue to snub us long enough."

"I did overhear something today that will interest you," William said. "There's sickness in their camp. They're making jokes about it at this point, but it could be serious. It appears the men are all coming down with diarrhea, and one of the guards was laughing a merry storm because someone from his platoon fainted and fell into the slit trench."

"Very funny," Julien sneered. "Tell our men I want them to be sure to wash their hands before every meal, and before and after they use the privy. This is to be strictly obeyed by all of us."

"It already is," William answered. "We were all trained in Salerno, remember? And our doctors in training camp were all from the university."

"Good. I think we've found yet another ally. Roger will be pleased to know that their arms may be fighting us but their asses are working for us."

It was another four days before Julien was informed that the emperor would see him after the noonday meal. The imperial troops had now been in Bari a full month, and there were confirmed reports the army was infected with marsh fever. Half the citizens living on the Apulian plain were infected with this enervating and greatly feared disease, which the doctors believed rose from the bad air of the marshes and called *mal aria*. Julien knew that an adult from another part of the world had less resistance to the bad air, and the initial attacks would be ill sustained.

When he and his men were escorted to the castle that day, they could tell from the smell that hospital tents had been set up behind a densely screened area. Even on this ten minute walk, two of the guards had to leave to relieve themselves, which they did by the side of the road, and William grinned broadly at them when they returned.

Julien was aware of an indefinable change in the atmosphere of the dining hall. Lothair returned his greeting in his usual matter of fact way, but Henry first condescended to give him a slightly more pronounced nod, and it seemed for a moment that Conrad had actually attempted a smile.

When the meal was over the guards did not appear, so Julien kept his seat at table. At length Bernard rose and addressed the emperor. "Your Imperial Majesty, we believe there is some business at hand that might be of interest to us." He nodded towards Julien. "Are we mistaken?"

"I don't know what this young man has to say, if anything, so I can hardly guess if it would be of interest to anyone." The emperor's voice, barely louder than a hoarse whisper, was flattened to let them know how boring he found the whole matter.

"Is he not Roger's ambassador?"

"Roger, as you know, has many ambassadors among us. It's possible this one merely wants a look at us. If you think he may have something significant to say, then by all means join us. I, for one, intend to take a nap first." He turned to Henry, then Conrad. "I assume you gentlemen wish to stay here to finish your wine? Very well, I shall expect you in my reception room in one hour." He waved to an attendant, who brought an hour glass to the table, inverted it, and set it in front of the emperor's place. Bernard winced and paled, but Innocent put a hand on his arm and patted it comfortingly. When the emperor had gone, Henry and Conrad stretched and yawned pointedly a few times, then announced they would meet the others in good time and left the hall.

Julien continued to sit politely at his now vacant end of the table, waiting either for the guards to conduct him to the emperor or for Innocent and Bernard to address him. They seemed to be whispering to each other again, with their heads lowered secretively, until he realized they were both at their prayers. He bowed his head and joined them. When he looked up, Bernard smiled at him and nodded. Julien wasn't sure what he meant by the gesture until Innocent signalled him to come closer. The sands in the hour glass had only a short time left to run.

Julien knelt as devoutly as he had ever learned to, and kissed Innocent's hand, then Bernard's.

"You don't look Norman," said Bernard. His voice was unexpectedly friendly, and his eyes were soft. "Are you a Lombard?"

"I'm English," he answered, "Norman English on my father's side."

"Ah yes," Bernard said, amused. "One of those. Answering the call of fortune in Sicily, are you?"

"I pray that whatever call I hear is sent by God and not his enemy," Julien answered gravely.

"Please continue to do so," Bernard said tartly. "I'm sure you know that the land you've chosen to serve is filled with God's enemies."

"I was taught that those were everywhere."

"Your Latin is too good. Where did you study?"

"At Durham Abbey, Excellency."

"Durham, eh. If only the good Benedictines there were as zealous in training the spirit as they are the tongue . . . but never mind. You're a member of Roger's court?"

"I am the Baron di Furci, yes."

"And the message you bear is from Roger's own lips? You're not part of some cabal of his noblemen?"

"I know of no cabals, or of any noble men against their king." Julien carefully drew out "noble" and "men."

"Their king, is it? I see." Bernard's manner had become increasingly brusque, and now his tone was reproachful. "And the message from this ruler of Muslim hordes . . . I assume it is for the emperor. Was there no other message for his pope?"

Julien turned to Innocent, who had remained thoughtfully aloof during Bernard's questions. "He wishes Your Eminence good health, sir, and hopes that you may one day include him again in your prayers."

Innocent colored at Julien's form of address which was proper for addressing no one more exalted than a cardinal. "Your suzerain knows there is only one way to have his excommunication lifted."

"I'm a simple emissary and no judge of such matters," Julien answered, lowering his eyes. Innocent had a serene, spiritual quality which affected him. It was a relief after the stinging charge of Bernard's words.

The presence of these two august and powerful men made the skin at his nape prickle, and the informality of their conversation didn't stop him from feeling overwhelmed by the ponderousness of his mission. He had to remind himself that all his study and training had led to today's work, and this was not the time for him to falter.

Bernard rose. "The sands are almost all down. I don't believe we would be disturbing the emperor if we were to go to him now." Bernard led them through the hall, guiding his pope by the elbow, and brushing aside the guards who tried to escort them.

The emperor was waiting in an almost bare room, seated on a crude throne, really no more than a high-backed chair with arm rests that differentiated it from the low-backed stools lined up before him. He had slipped his shirt over his shoulders, and a servant was mopping his chest and back with a wet cloth. He struggled to slip back into his clothir ᴛ when they entered. Julien kissed his hand and waited to be told he might sit.

"Find Henry and Conrad," Lothair said testily to one of his staff.

"It's possible we arrived early," Bernard conciliated.

"Sit down, sit down. I suppose you've had a chance to satisfy your curiosity about this tadpole from Roger's muddy pond."

Rather than being offended by the Emperor's peevishness, Julien smiled.

"What's funny? Are you an idiot, too? Don't you know I'm your enemy?"

"I'm aware of you as my host, Your Imperial Majesty, and I've not yet been granted the opportunity to thank you for your hospitality."

"You sound French to me. Are you sure you're Sicilian?" Julien bowed his head in assent.

Conrad and Henry entered, carrying their wine goblets, and slouched on stools, barely acknowledging the others. Julien was reminded that it was Anacletus who had excommunicated Conrad and wondered how much less courteous Conrad might have been towards him.

"All right, let's begin." Lothair suddenly appeared stronger and thoroughly redoubtable as he addressed himself to the affairs at hand. "The only terms acceptable are complete surrender, of course. The tyrant knows that. Are you here to see if there's some way he can save his hide?"

Julien raised his head and smiled affably. "I'm here in the interests of averting bloodshed, that of your troops as well as our own."

"Our troops! Is this Roger's impudence or your own, puppy?"

Henry the Proud waved his hand impatiently. "I see no point in going on with this. If Roger were serious about discussing terms of surrender, he'd have sent a soldier to plead his case. This fellow doesn't look like he could swing a broadsword without falling off his horse."

Julien neither flinched nor reddened. "King Roger honors his soldiers, of course, but our sovereign does honor as well to many who could in no way distinguish themselves in battle."

"Yes," Henry sneered. "We're well aware how he fills his court with popinjays, pagans, and parasitic poets who were not tolerated in their own lands, while he sends heathen armies to spill the blood of Christians."

"Your Imperial Majesty," Julien began, deciding to address himself more profitably to Lothair alone, "King Roger sends me in good will to salute you and to see if you may not recognize goals of mutual benefit."

Julien's dismissal fired Henry's anger. "It's only *our* goals that are exclusively to the benefit of Christendom. I think the pretender Roger loves Muslims and Jews too well to ever serve our course."

Lothair glared at his son-in-law. "I remind you of your responsibilities."

Henry jumped up from his stool and headed for the door. "I leave those to you. I'll not sit here and suffer the mewling of a milksop in the service of a baptized sultan."

"So be it," Lothair said grimly, but in a weakened voice. He was not indulgent towards his heir's temper.

Conrad rose slowly. "I am of the same mind as Henry for once. There can be no benefit from this." He drew himself to his full height and looked down at Julien contemptuously as he fingered his dagger. "I'd send Roger's minion back to him with a reminder of how we punish apostasy."

Julian flinched for the first time since the interview began, but Lothair seemed unperturbed, and waited silently until Conrad had left. "Am I to understand," he began slowly, "that Roger is prepared to relinquish the imperial lands he has usurped and to disavow the anti-Pope Anacletus?"

Julien breathed deeply before answering. "Regarding King Roger's claim to these lands, I beg Your Imperial Majesty to recall that King Roger's claim is to lands that are all part of the Norman conquest of the last hundred years, either inherited by him directly or ceded to him peacefully and with due legal process by other Norman families without direct heirs. There are no competing claims honored by an earlier pope."

Bernard raised his voice for the first time. "You forget, do you not, the papal claim to these lands?"

"We recognize the pope as the rightful suzerain of every monarch."

Lothair started to say, "I fail to see how—", but Bernard raised his hand. Julien felt transfixed by the intensity of Bernard's stare.

"Would Roger, then, be prepared to acknowledge Pope Innocent II as the rightful pope, as have all the other crowned heads of Europe?"

"I can say without hesitation that as soon as any evidence is presented which discloses that Pope Anacletus is not the rightful pontiff, an emissary would be sent at once to discuss it further. Has any new evidence been uncovered?"

Lothair sighed. "Is Roger so foolish as to think he can send you here to say he will acknowledge me as his lawful suzerain and that I'll then just turn on my heels and let the matter rest there? Come now."

"I assure you, King Roger doesn't take your campaign here so lightly. Because he has always acknowledged that you have traditional rights in Apulia, he is prepared to make an offer I am convinced you will find interesting."

Lothair glanced at Innocent, who was clenching his jaw, before he answered. "Does Roger forget why I'm here?"

"I suggest that the sparing of Christian blood is in the interests of the Church as well as of the Empire and Sicily."

"Sacrilege!" Bernard snapped. "Don't you see, foolish boy, the very fabric of the Church is threatened by Roger's obstinate allegiance to that spawn of the Devil?"

"That may be, and the threat to the Church is of pressing concern to Roger, but it is not my mission to defend his conscience there. That would take a much abler mind. I ask only that you judge whether the proposal I offer may not have sufficient merit for your consideration in light of the vast slaughter that threatens both our peoples."

"Go on," said Lothair, wearily.

"King Roger is willing to divide his kingdom. He proposes that the mainland be established as a separate duchy with his son Roger as the lawful duke, invested by you, and with you as his suzerain."

"And Sicily?"

"King Roger would keep that as his kingdom. Your Imperial Majesty admits he has no claim there."

"The man must think I'm in my dotage," Lothair replied after a moment. "Under terms like these, he'd be free to continue exercising his hold the instant my back is turned. Does he think I'm unaware he's just waiting for me to leave? I know what sort of loyalty to expect from Italians. No, Roger must be crushed. There's no other way I can believe the scourge of this accursed south land will be ended."

"Your Imperial Majesty does King Roger an injustice. Of course he recognized you might entertain some doubts towards his intent, and he offers you his son Tancred as a hostage, to return with you to Germany and to be held by you there as a token of his good will and fealty."

"I want none of his sons." But Lothair's eyes had gone thoughtful.

"You would be able to return to Germany with your army intact. Your Imperial Majesty, it is believed by many that your troops are in no condition and of little inclination to pursue this war to the shores of Sicily."

"What? My men? How dare you! Do you know how seriously outnumbered you are? There isn't an army in the world that could stand up to my fighting force."

"I agree. But there isn't an army in the world that could stand up to another two months of marsh fever, diarrhea, and insufferable heat, when there is no well-defined advantage to them in the victory."

"The advantages to *me* are clear cut."

"Very well, then. Let us assume all your fighting men have precisely the same objectives you do. Does it really matter so much whether Roger sits on the throne or his son does, so long as his son does you the full homage you expect from Roger? Consider the alternative. If you persist in your campaign, you would allow the dukes and barons who have wrecked the land for so long to take power again. Then how long do you think it would be before they were at each other's throats, fighting for power and sacrificing their subjects to get it? There can be no lasting peace in that solution."

Lothair pursed his lips. "My claims are nonexistent with a man like Roger in power. He takes too much on himself. No, the tyrant will be crushed."

Bernard was smiling with his eyes downcast, while Innocent looked fretful. Julien swallowed hard and resumed his argument. "I cannot believe, Your Imperial Majesty, that my proposal is so utterly without merit that it doesn't deserve longer consideration. Won't you weigh what Roger offers and think of your troops as well as the citizens of this land before you give me a final answer? I beg you to receive me again in a week, when you have pondered further."

"A week? You must be mad. Stay if you will, but only for another three days, and then you must be gone or I'll not answer for your heads."

"May I see Your Imperial Majesty in three days, then?"

"I still think you'd be wiser to leave now. My generals have no love for you." He nodded for Julien to leave.

Julien knelt and kissed the hands of all three before he went to the door to wait for the guards' escort back to his quarters. The refusal was outright, but even if Lothair wouldn't change his mind the old warrior had something to think about. Surely there must be some temptation there. He was clearly worried about the possibility of outright mutiny, and even tensions within his inner circle must be exasperating.

Julien felt lighthearted as he marched back, more from relief than accomplishment. He quickly reviewed the interview to see if he could recall any serious errors in judgment, when a new thought crossed his mind and his knees turned to water.

"St. Blaise's throat! I was alone in a room with the three most powerful men in the world."

The guard came closer and studied Julien curiously to see if he too might be taken with marsh fever like many of his comrades.

Chapter V

SIEGE

Julien rose earlier than usual the third morning after he had offered Roger's proposal to Lothair, wanting to be as fresh and alert as possible even though he knew the emperor wasn't likely to change his mind. By the water tubs behind the sentry house he was immediately aware that something unusual was stirring in camp. There were only two guards on duty, and they greeted him nervously. They had lost some of their reserve over the last few days, and even seemed friendly in the few words they exchanged with their charge.

"You'd better take your men and go at once," one of them said. "Your horses are tethered to the trees right around the bend. We've received no new instructions for you, but no one said to detain you, either. Just go."

"But I'm to see Emperor Lothair today."

"Not likely. We're breaking camp."

"What? On the march again? Where?"

"Just take my word for it and get out of here, if you don't want to answer for the lives of your men."

Julien hurried back inside and found William was already awake. "Listen. We've got to wake the others and pack our things at once. The Germans are breaking camp and we've been warned to get back while we still can."

"But what of your talk with Lothair? We can't go back to Salerno without a definite answer."

"Keep your voice down; the guards are right outside. Of course we're not going back to Salerno. First we've got to find out which way they're headed. There's been more grumbling than ever among the men and it's finally forcing Lothair's hand. Today is to be the hottest day yet, and they'd be mad to cross the plain into Calabria in this."

William and Julien wakened the rest of the men and informed them briefly of what was going on. By now the sounds of the imperial army making ready to march were unmistakable. "Just a few miles west of here there's a hilly forest," William said. "I suggest we keep under cover there while we try to determine their movements. We'll have to stay close to them for a few days at least to be sure of what they're up to. It means being very cagey. They're bound to keep their scouts in the area."

"We could move a lot faster and more quietly if we didn't have to wear this bloody armor," Mauger moaned, kicking at the formidable arrangement of mail and plate stacked neatly under his cot.

"I know it's uncomfortable," Julien said, "but you can't risk not wearing it. The danger of running into soldiers is too great and you must be protected."

"But what about you?" William asked. "You're totally vulnerable."

"I'll have to take my chances."

"Then, stay close to William and me," said Mauger. "We'll be your fighting arms, and I vow they'll have my life before they get near yours."

Julien gripped his arm. "I'll never doubt it."

They reached the hillside and waited impatiently, but not until sunset did the sentry in the topmost branches of an oak tree throw down an acorn to signal that the imperialists had started to move. Julien peered into the branches and the shadowy silhouette raised its arm and pointed.

"North," Julien whispered excitedly. "They must be faking."

"It sounds too good to be true, I admit," William said, "and yet, there'd be certain mutiny if he remained in Bari much longer. Even though the townspeople are still terrified, it would only be a matter of time before a band plotted mischief."

"I wonder if it's only that," Julien mused. "They seem almost desperate to get out of town if they're leaving at this hour. They certainly can't go far tonight."

"I agree it sounds daft. No army starts to move at dusk unless it's part of battle strategy. Maybe he just wants to keep his men busy to get their minds off their complaints."

"Perhaps so," Julien answered. "They can't be returning to Germany. He'd have been better off accepting Roger's terms. No, I think it's likely they're headed nearby . . . for the Apennines perhaps. I expect he'll look for a cooler spot to spend the night and give his men a breather from this heat. We'll have to follow as closely as we can with safety, and wait for his next move."

Julien's surmisal proved correct. The army spent that night on a plateau just north of the city, and two days later set up camp still further north. Julien and his men were able to find shelter in nearby Megara, a village of two hundred inhabitants before Henry the Proud and his men marched through it on their way to Bari. It now held sixty.

The townspeople welcomed Julien and his men cordially, then turned sheepish on learning Julien's identity. They admitted they had rebelled against Roger twice in the last decade despite the fact that he had treated them generously. But, they explained, this was because they were of Greek heritage and had traditionally supported the Byzantines. If the choice were now between Roger and the emperor, as it seemed to be, it was a clear-cut one.

Julien felt he could hardly chide them for their defections when he viewed the appalling destruction around him. What was left of the wooden frames to buildings was scorched, and even the stones smelled of smoke. He could hardly bear to look at the children. They were so drawn, and they had the haunted eyes of old, beaten men. He thought of the three healthy children he left behind and shuddered at the horror that could be visited on his own family if Lothair's troops ever got to Sicily.

Although the harvest this year was meager because the imperialists had set fire to their fields and vineyards, the villagers gladly shared the little they had. They ate bread made of chestnut flour with fresh radishes and beets, and later the town elders elected to send two of their women to the imperial army camp to sell the last two baskets of radishes and see if they could learn anything of the army's movements.

A week later Julien and his men suspected the imperialists were making ready to move again, and they watched expectantly. Mauger bet William his carved silver belt buckle that the Germans would continue north. When they started westward, William accepted the prize with little cheer. Yet their route seemed still uncertain. If they were headed for Salerno, they were certainly not taking a direct road.

The sound of battle reached their ears two mornings later, and they knew the imperial army was attacking Melfi. The battle was over by midafternoon; there was never any question of a contest. The soldiers stayed in the city overnight, the next day, and then another.

"Why Melfi?" Julien asked. He couldn't calculate what strategic advantage occupation of the city might give.

On the morning of the fourth day, Julien listened grimly as Mauger reported the scouts had seen Lothair's troops heading south.

"I think we'd best go to Melfi first," William said. "We can travel faster than they and we should see if we can help the Melfitani." Julien was quick to agree. Melfi had a reputation for loyalty, and it had always been spoken of to him as a pleasant place.

When they approached the city, the smell of burning that greeted them told the story. No one came forward to greet them when they entered the battered walls. Hundreds of the townspeople were lying in the street, dreadfully dismembered. It had been a swift and merciless massacre. Julien estimated it would take a week to bury all the dead, and led his men to the church instead. If there was no time to take care of the bodies, they could at least try to consign their souls to peace.

The church, predictably, had been stripped of all its treasure, including the altar cloths and vestments. They knelt on the stone floor and prayed silently, with the stench of the slaughter still in their nostrils. While still at prayer they heard a stirring, and then what seemed like a muted groan coming from behind the altar.

Julien rose stealthily, signalled to William, and bade the others to continue their prayers but to stay alert. Behind the altar they found two figures, both still alive. The young woman looked at them with such unreserved terror that Julien's stomach lurched at the sight of her. She was covered with blood but seemed otherwise unharmed. The man stretched out on her knees was a priest, and a quick inspection showed that he had been castrated and his tongue cut out. His jaws were moving up and down mechanically, and his eyes had bulged nearly out of his head. He had lost most of his blood, and it was obvious to Julien the man couldn't live. He signalled to William to finish him off mercifully, and William withdrew his dagger. As soon as the woman saw the blade, she screamed and fainted.

"It's just as well," Julien said. He carried her to the altar and went to the font to see if there might be some holy water to revive her with. He bathed her temples for several minutes before she began to regain consciousness, and by now the others were all hovering about. Julien tried to reassure her with soothing words, but the young woman saw only a group of armed men and the terror that had accumulated over the last days wouldn't be so easily dispelled. She posed an unexpected problem.

"She can't stay here," William said. "No one could be allowed to remain in this charnel house."

"Let me take her," Julien said. "My horse has less weight to carry than the others. Do you know if there's another town nearby where we can leave her? The rest of the Melfitani must've gone somewhere."

"That depends on which way we're headed. Don't you want to follow the Germans south?"

"We have no choice." Julien shrugged.

"Then, there's not another town I know of on today's march. Tomorrow, perhaps, we can leave her somewhere."

"Until we know what the army is up to, we're powerless to make plans. And there's no point trying to ask her anything. She carries on like I'm the Devil himself every time I go near her."

"First she needs a bit of cleaning up." Julien again admired William's practical approach. "We should be able to find some other clothes in one of these houses. Mauger, will you look for a gown for her?"

Mauger returned a short while later with two simple cotton shifts. "These are from what looked like the richest house in town. I daresay the mistress' finer things were taken, but these should do well enough."

The young woman seemed more in control of herself when they motioned her to go behind a screen to change. When she came out, Julien realized she was much better looking than his first impression of her. She appeared to be of Lombard stock; blonde, but not as fair as most Norman blondes, with hazel eyes that glinted yellow. She was as tall as he, with large bones firmly padded at the hips and bosom. A bit of thickness at the wrist and sturdy columns of thigh suggested she was a peasant, but her skin was as clear and soft as that of the most pampered aristocrat, and her teeth were unmarked and even.

Pleased to see her more composed, he asked, "Where are the rest of the townspeople?"

"They ran away. I don't know where." She had a slight lisp which made her sound girlish and more defenseless.

"What of your family? Did they get away? Why did they leave you?"

"My husband was killed. I have no one else. The priest you saw was my husband's brother, his only kinsman." She started to cry. "When I saw your dagger, I was sure you'd kill me too." She paused a moment until she regained control of herself. "I beg you to do me no harm. I'm a poor defenseless woman and whatever you do to me the Blessed Virgin will be watching."

"Madame," William answered gallantly, "it would damn our souls forever to take advantage of your distress. Any man who dares insult you will have to answer to me."

"We're royalists," Julien added. "Consider yourself under King Roger's protection."

"Sicilians!" she gasped. Her eyes filled with terror again.

"Trust me, madam," Julien said coolly, "whatever your previous experiences may have taught you. What's your name?"

"Gaitelgrima."

Julien winced. "These Lombard names are difficult for me. Perhaps you wouldn't mind if I called you Gay?"

"My husband did. I thank you, sir."

"I am Julien. Is there a village nearby where the Melfitani might have gone for refuge?"

"There's nothing very close, and I can't guess where they would go. I have no one to turn to in any case."

"Come now, you must have had friends, neighbors."

"Not many. I've only been here since I married two months ago. And you see what happened to my husband and brother-in-law."

"Have you any idea what made the imperialists behave so cruelly? Such a massacre! Were they provoked by something?"

"Not by our men. This has always been a peaceful city, as you must know. No, it must've had something to do with the plot on the pope's life."

Julien was instantly all attention. "What? A plot? Tell me, quickly."

"It happened the first night. We yielded the city at once. They seemed content to let us be, but they had Sicilian agents in their camp, and it was they who created all the mischief. They bribed some of the soldiers with gold and got them to agree to kill Pope Innocent and Bernard, and all the cardinals with them. It didn't surprise us much when we learned of it. There was already such bad blood between the papists and the soldiers that the papal tents were set up at quite a distance from the imperial camp. When Emperor Lothair heard what was going on, he rode to them with all his guards just in time to foil the assassins. The pope's personal guard had already been killed, and it would've been a matter of only minutes before the rest of them were all done in too."

Gay seemed to enjoy being the center of attention and continued her story, scarcely pausing for breath. "When word of the treachery reached the rest of the troops, they rioted among themselves. The townspeople were frightened when they heard about it, and abandoned the city as quickly as they could. Then a number of the soldiers entered the town and went mad with anger when they saw the people trying to leave. They killed everyone they could get their hands on. Although my brother-in-law was a priest, he had never declared for either Anacletus or Innocent; that issue isn't important to simple people, but he stayed behind to help those in need of a priest. I ran to him after I saw my husband killed, and he tried to hide me in a cupboard behind the altar. No one was safe anywhere. The soldiers came to the church to see what they could steal, and when they were about to uncover our hiding place, my brother-in-law stepped out and gave himself up in order to save me. Oh, how I curse this damned war and all the devils who fight it."

Julien looked at her reproachfully. "You should be thanking Heaven for having escaped worse harm."

Her eyes narrowed. "At the time it wouldn't have mattered."

"What a way to talk. You know what those soldiers would have done to you."

"They'd have done it to a corpse."

Julien stepped forward and embraced her gently. "Forgive me. I didn't mean to speak to you so sharply after all you've just been through. Come with us now."

"With you?" Her eyes took on alarm again. "How can I?"

"You must, dear girl. There's no telling how long it may be before the Melfitani return, and you certainly can't stay in this ghastly place. Perhaps we can leave you at some convent. The nuns, I'm sure, will care for you."

Gay sufficiently recovered to manage a faint smile when she allowed Julien to lift her onto his horse. She was unaccustomed to riding, but she hugged his waist tightly. Several hours later, when they stopped to rest, she seemed resigned to whatever was decided for her.

As Julien and Gay sat in the shade and munched bread and cheese, she offered more information about herself. Her parents were killed in a Norman attack when she was still a child, and she had been brought up by a grandfather on a farm just a few miles west of Trani, near where Lothair's troops had rested before advancing westward to Melfi. She was betrothed while still a child to a kinsman named Falco, but the marriage was postponed several times because of her grandfather's failing health. There was no one else on the farm, so from the time she was fourteen, she had to seed, plough, and harvest the crops in addition to her domestic and nursing duties. Only when her grandfather died was she at last able to make the trip to Melfi for her wedding. She had no claim to her grandfather's small farm, which was entailed to his liege lord, and her husband was much too poor to settle a morgengab on her. Her brother-in-law had some modest holdings, but these would now fall to the Church.

Julien found her direct way of speaking becoming, and he felt she sustained her misfortunes with more fortitude than he expected from a girl of her class. Gay did not surprise him when she announced her determination not to return to Melfi, no matter what. She even seemed pleased to have her future decided by someone she'd known only a few hours.

They rode for two uneventful days until they saw the imperial army settle down again by the cool shores of Lagopesole, another unaccountable maneuver. The lake and its village were charming, but their military advantage was doubtful.

On the second day there they saw a long train of clergymen arriving from the north. Mauger returned from town that evening and reported that the army was likely to remain there for quite a while because an important council was being held in the papal tents. The clergymen were representatives from Monte Cassino, anxious to confirm the monastery's status and to avoid any future reprisals from either the imperial army or Innocent's forces.

The council went on for days, but thanks to Mauger's spying, news of its outcome reached Julien within hours. Innocent had grown increasingly irritated by the imperialists' lack of consideration, and had been reproaching Lothair even more insistently for the indignities suffered by him when he was travelling with Henry the Proud. Nothing less than the unqualified capitulation of Monte Cassino would satisfy him. Innocent held Abbot Rainald at Lagopesole until he submitted a formal renunciation of Anacletus and his clergy, and a condemnation of Roger and his kingdom as well.

Julien found the council's conclusion regrettable—but not irrevocable. With these negotiations out of the way, a decisive step was likely. Lagopesole was in the center of the peninsula, midway between Bari and Salerno. If the army headed north, it could mean they were pushing towards Rome in an attempt to install Innocent there, or even that they were headed back towards Germany, with or without Innocent's installation. A move to the south or southeast could mean they were bringing the campaign to Sicily. If they were to turn west, however, their target would undoubtedly be Salerno. To Julien's surprise, he saw that the bulk of the army intended to remain in camp at Lagopesole, while a thousand or so horsemen left and headed west.

Julien and his men spurred their horses to make every minute count. It looked like the attack the Salernitans had feared for so long was on its way. Gay's future was forgotten temporarily, as all efforts were directed towards alerting Robert of Selby to the dreaded event that threatened the city. As they approached Salerno from the eastern hills, they saw another army camped a day's march northeast of the city. Mauger reported the army was Robert of Capua's, and that they were busily building siege machines.

They circled southward and arrived at Salerno after sundown to find the gates firmly barred. Only with difficulty were Julien and his men able to convince the sentries of their identity. Julien left Gay and his men at the apartment Robert had given him and headed straight for the chancellor's palace. He found Robert still in his office, working by candlelight with an aide whom he promptly dismissed.

There was no time to waste on formalities. "Robert, there's a large army of Germans on their way here. We couldn't see the banners too clearly, but they looked like Henry the Proud's colors. We estimate their number to be at least one thousand horses. They're certainly being sent to help Robert of Capua, whose army is massed northeast of here."

"Yes, I expected something like that," Robert answered. "The Germans wouldn't want to miss out on their share of the loot. But I'm afraid you don't know the worst, Julien. There are almost five thousand ships out there blocking Salerno from the sea. Wibald of Stablo was finally able to get the Pisans to come through with the help they've promised for so long, and they're out for our blood. We had to lift our siege of Naples to free every man we could to defend Salerno."

Robert's objectivity had a steadying effect on Julien. He could still hear his heart pound, but his voice was calm and surprisingly firm.

"How many fighting men do you have here?"

"All told, only about four hundred. And forty galleys. We're vastly outnumbered."

"What of Roger's instructions? Have you read them yet?"

"I did as soon as I learned the attack was coming by land as well as sea. And you? Were you able to make any headway with Lothair?"

"No, but the war isn't lost yet."

Robert found Roger's message, unrolled it and reread it thoughtfully.

"He anticipated exactly this," he said at length. "And as you told us, his wish is to save the city at all costs. He wants us to surrender to Lothair's army as soon as they appear at the gates. I'm authorized to offer him a ransom up to the entire contents of our treasury in return for our lives and the sparing of the city. Do you think Lothair will accept such an offer?"

"I hope so," Julien answered, "but it will be Henry the Proud we have to deal with. He's a good deal more inflexible than the emperor, and far more cruel." He gave Robert a detailed report of the mutinous feelings among the soldiers, the continuing hostility between Henry and Innocent, and the sorry physical condition of the troops.

"Do you have enough food and water to submit to a long siege if it should come to that?" Julien asked of Robert finally.

"More than enough. We've tried to provide for any eventuality. Will you stay here with me, or do you plan to return to Sicily? I can still slip you through. The Capuans won't be encircling us for a day or two yet."

"I'll stay with you, my friend. But let me send a messenger to Roger while we still can. I'd best write it at once." He found a pen and started to write as he continued. "Meantime, I believe the men you gave me would like to see their families. Oh, and I have a woman with me. She was widowed at Melfi. I thought I'd leave her with the nuns of the Holy Cross here. She has no one."

"By all means, let the men see their families, but tell them to be back at the palace before morning. I know you found them good companions. They were handpicked from my personal guard; they're the finest men to be found anywhere."

"I agree, emphatically. And you should make William your captain. He's as brave as he is intelligent, and I'd trust him with my life. The rest of the men have already accepted him as a leader." Julien finished penning his message to Roger and sealed it. "Here you are. Let's get it off at once."

"Good. Consider it done. Now, about this girl you have with you . . ." Robert's eyes lost their severity for an instant and almost winked. "Is she pretty?"

"Very, but not at all my type. She's one of those big-breasted blondes."

"Is she, now? Are you sure you want to turn her over to the sisters? I might be able to find another husband for her. Why don't you bring her by and let me have a look at her?"

"I might do that. Wait for me, I won't be long."

When Julien returned to his apartment, he found the men already knew pretty much what was expected of them and left at once to pay their respects at home. Gay was stunned by the rapid turn of events, and she seemed almost numbed at the prospect of witnessing another assault. "But you musn't worry, Gay. You'll be perfectly safe with the sisters. Whatever happens to the city, they wouldn't dare risk the scandal of doing harm to a Salernitan convent."

"Whatever you say," she said bitterly.

"No, it's not just what I say. It's time for you to make a choice now. I told Chancellor Robert about you, and he's shown an interest in your welfare. He even believes he might be able to find you another husband here."

"So, is that to be my choice, then?"

"Yes, and it's a rather good one, I should think."

"Is it?" Her eyes searched his.

"Well yes, don't you think so?"

She turned away. "No. First you tell me you want me to make a choice, and then the choice you offer me is— I'm sorry. I don't want to seem ungrateful . . ."

"What is it, then?"

She kept her back turned. "One of your men has already asked me to marry him."

"I'm delighted to hear it. Who was it?"

"William."

"Oh, but that's wonderful. Congratulations, Gay. There's not a better man to be found, nor a handsomer one if it comes to that. I fancy he's already turned the head of many a pretty girl in these parts. I couldn't want anyone finer for you. You're very lucky."

She turned and faced him squarely. "Julien, do I have to marry him?"

He looked at her oddly. "What are you saying? You should be thrilled."

Gay remained silent and cast her eyes downward, pouting.

"I swear I'll never understand women. What's wrong with you?"

Tears came and she made no attempt to wipe them but stood in front of him with her head lowered and allowed them to course freely.

"Is it too soon after losing your husband? Is that it? Of course, how thoughtless of me! You probably loved him a great deal, didn't you? And after only a few months . . ." She started to sob at this, and Julien moved forward to comfort her. He placed an arm around her shoulder and brought her head gently to rest on him, then circled her waist with his other arm and started to rock her gently. She felt very good. Gay's arm rose from her sides trembling, and found Julien's body, embracing him timidly at first, and then she hugged him closely to her with a gasp. She tilted her head and searched for his lips, found them and fastened her mouth there in a long, hungry kiss.

It happened unexpectedly, but Julien's response was spontaneous, and he covered her throat and shoulders with kisses. Gay moaned and struggled to plant her kisses on his eyes, his brow, his nose, anywhere her mouth could find. They continued frantically tasting each other's desire until she fell back, breathless.

"Remember Gay, I already told you I was married."

"It doesn't matter. It's you I want, any way I can have you. Take me with you, Julien. I never loved my husband. Never. I did my duty towards him, but he never allowed me to feel anything like what you've awakened in me. Take me, Julien, and let me live as a woman instead of a dumb brute."

"You're foolish, Gay. William would make you an excellent husband. He can offer you so much more than I."

"I've been married. I don't need it again. And as for your wife, I don't mind sharing you. I understand from the things you told me how much you love her."

"There wouldn't be much sharing." He bit his tongue. "Your place with me would carry no station, you know. I couldn't live with you openly."

"But you'd come to me whenever you could, wouldn't you? I'd wait forever for that."

Julien tried again to swallow the lump that was blocking his throat and ventured one last attempt to resist the voluptuous frame that filled his arms so abundantly.

"This couldn't be happening to us at a worse time. We face a siege by land and sea, and the forces against us are staggering."

"Then, why don't we leave now? We could still get away and return to Sicily. You've done your job."

"No, I couldn't do that. Besides, I've already announced my decision to stay. But are you sure you know what you're doing?"

"I do, I do." She started to kiss him again. "Julien, answer me truthfully. Do you think you could ever learn to love me just a little? I know you love your wife, but if you tell me you can give me even a small part of your heart, then I'll have no doubt as to my choice."

"Yes, I can promise you that, Gay. I hadn't realized how much I'd come to care for you, but I need you very, very much. I'll find a little house for you in Palermo, and you'll never want for anything. You'll see. I promise to do all in my power to keep you from ever regretting your choice."

"Then, take me now, Julien. Do it."

He pressed her again in his arms and then half released her. "Not now. Robert is waiting. Tonight."

She suddenly thrust her hips forward, and he felt her heat almost sear him. He became aware again of the great mass of her breasts. He'd never felt so much pliant flesh trapped between himself and a woman. Whenever he squeezed, her breasts flattened and oozed almost to his shoulders. They ground their bodies together, and he stammered guiltily. "But I—I have a report to write out." Even as he spoke, though, his hand had started to hike her skirt up, and he felt her fingers searching to free him from under his shirt. "It's important," he gasped as he felt her hot hand close around him.

They sank to the ground and rolled on each other deliriously, and then her hips rose to greet him, and they locked. It lasted only one or two frenzied minutes; then they rocked in each other's arms, sobbing their relief.

Julien rose after a while and adjusted his robe. "That cleared my blood, but tonight my dear, tonight I will lead you into a garden of delights." Gay did not seem entirely displeased with the quick eruption of his passion, but Julien knew she was still unschooled in lovemaking, and he looked forward to evoking new and longer responses from this apt pupil. His desire for her was greater than he had expected, and he wished he could continue to lie with her now, to fondle her and discover her further. It isn't right, he reflected, for a man to be without a woman to tame his passions. Claire was the mother of his children, and he grew more sure with time of his deep love for her. But Gay made him feel like a man again, and the tenderness he felt towards her warmed his whole body.

Gay told him she was going to the cathedral to light a candle to the Virgin in thanks for her prayer being answered, and Julien hurried back to Robert's office mentally composing his report on the outcome of his negotiations with the emperor.

Robert was frowning when he entered the office. "What were you up to? I thought you said you were coming right back."

Julien colored. "I had some personal business to attend to."

"I'll say you did," he roared. "I sent a servant around to see if you needed anything, and he reported such a thumping going on, he believed you were engaging the whole imperial army in hand-to-hand combat. Was it the girl you spoke of?"

Julien laughed. "Yes, it was. Trust you to know of everything that's going on almost before it happens."

"No matter. I can still find her a husband. The city's full of men who'd be happy to have any wife I choose for them. I'm afraid, though, that in her slightly used condition, I wouldn't feel honest demanding a morgengab for her."

"That won't be necessary. I'm taking her back with me."

"Ah, so it's that serious, is it? I thought you had forsworn all others for the love of the beautiful Claire." His voice was faintly mocking.

Julien shrugged. "We're men, aren't we?"

"And subject, therefore, to all the weaknesses of such. I just believed you were different. I'm pleased, actually. It often seemed to me that you were a little too doting. It doesn't do to let a wife unman you, you know, as I hope you've found out."

"Yes, I found out. And what about you, Robert? Aren't you anxious to have a legitimate heir to all you've carved out for yourself here? I know you probably have more women than any man could wish for, but isn't it time to have a proper family, instead of breeding bastards as fast as you can?"

"My dear Julien, when I first met you I addressed you as if you were my son. Then, shortly after that, I welcomed you as my companion and peer. Do you now propose to assume the role of my father?"

"You're incorrigible, you old whoremaster. No, my beloved friend, I'd not change you for all the gold in Sicily. I just want you to have as much as life can hold."

"Oh, but I do. And do you realize that if I deplete the treasury as Roger expects me to, there'll be a danger of cheating thirty or so bastards out of their patrimony? Our king is a hard man. Come, we need a drink. I've a cask of the finest wine in Italy that I've been saving for some extraordinary celebration. Will you help me see to it that it doesn't fall into German hands? They'd probably boil it or mix it with equal parts of honey, and we must save these glorious vintages from such an ignoble fate."

When Julien returned to his apartment he was reeling from the quantity of wine he'd consumed. He grinned foolishly at Gay, who was already in bed waiting for him, and staggered towards her, fumbling clumsily with his clothing. She looked at him with frank dismay, but rose and helped him undress for bed, trying to avoid his heavy breath. Once in bed, Julien pawed at her breasts, mumbled incoherently, then sank onto her shoulder, a thin stream of saliva escaping his mouth.

Gay freed herself and sat upright in bed, then struggled to push him on his side away from her. "Is this the garden of delights I was told to prepare myself for?" she said aloud, but Julien had already begun to snore. Her mouth curled in contempt. "Never mind," she said. "It's better by far to be a rich man's whore than a poor man's wife." She stared at him thoughtfully a moment, then added, "Or any man's wife."

Chapter VI

HEALING

Two days later, on the 17th of July, Salerno was under full siege. The hard-pressed Amalfitans, in return for a promise of imperial protection against the Pisans, had joined the other enemy ships in the harbor. Robert of Capua's forces wheeled their giant machines in a semicircle around the city, and the Salernitans knew it was only a matter of time before his army would be joined by the imperialists. Julien and Robert of Selby could do no more than keep to the city, and wait patiently for further developments.

On July 24th Henry the Proud arrived with his thousand troops and the battle began in earnest. Stones half as tall as a man were catapulted from the high wooden towers overlooking the walls of the city, and although the walls were thick and strong, the constant battering began to exact its toll. There were still no casualties to speak of, but Julien knew Robert's defenses could not hold up much longer.

The city waited. Robert sent a messenger to Henry's camp, asking if they might discuss terms, and the messenger was sent back with a rude answer. Julien's heart sank. Roger had seemed certain the imperial troops would not be able to resist so handsome a bribe. Another emissary was sent out with a promise of an even greater sum, but he returned with his nose slit by way of answer.

Two weeks later, Lothair arrived with the rest of the army as well as Innocent, Bernard, and the full papal retinue. The Salernitans panicked at the news, but Julien saw it as promising. He insisted Robert send another emissary directly to the emperor this time, and even offered to go himself. Robert was skeptical, but couldn't afford to leave any chance untried. He refused to let Julien go, however.

The emissary was received with great courtesy, and the promptness with which the emperor placed Salerno under imperial protection indicated his great relief at Robert's offer. For a sum of gold which was only half of what Robert had been prepared to bargain for, Robert and his men were to be allowed free exit and the city of Salerno was to be spared.

Henry the Proud was furious as soon as word of the truce reached him. He stormed to Lothair's tent, where the old emperor had virtually closeted himself. There was only a servant with him, bathing his temples with tepid water.

"So! I see you no longer feel you have need of guards," Henry fumed.

"It's one of the fruits of peace I most enjoy," Lothair answered softly.

"Your appetite for fruit is too easily appeased. We had a fabulous king-dom in the palm of our hand, just waiting to be squeezed dry of its riches. What were you thinking of? Certainly not of me. I'll not respect the terms of this cowardly peace, and I'd be surprised if Conrad did."

"You will, because you dare not do otherwise, nor do you have the power to," Lothair said calmly.

Henry bristled. "What was the use of creating a triumvirate if you weren't planning to consult your partners?"

"Lower your voice. You were my partners in the administration of an army. Kindly remember I am your uncle as well as your emperor. You will offer your advice only when I ask you to."

"Does it mean nothing that I am to be an emperor in my turn?"

"In your turn? Yes, well, just remember it isn't your turn yet. You were ill-advised to come to me like this. I've no patience with your bad temper today."

Henry drew himself up, and his sheer bulk seemed to threaten the frail monarch. "You'll need more than patience to explain your actions to my troops. I promised to fill their helmets with Sicilian gold before the summer was out."

"That was foolish. I don't care a fig for explanations—or for your promises. I made my promises to my troops a long time ago, and I intend to keep them."

"You made promises to me too."

"So I did. As long as you remind me of so many promises, I'll recall the one I made to my God—to see my men safely home to their farms and wives."

"But you've given the war away!" Henry shouted. "Salerno was ours."

"It was, and I've given it back to its citizens for a handsome ransom, which you'll share as well as all our men. We don't return entirely empty handed."

"Empty handed! You made them a gift of the city. They would have paid ten times as much."

Lothair waved a hand impatiently. "That's talk. What I received was half of King Stephen's yearly income from all of England."

"Precisely. And I'm told that Roger has more yearly income from Palermo alone than Stephen gets from all of England."

The emperor smashed his fist down on the table next to him in his first display of temper towards Henry. "Will you be still? I'm an old man, and it's God I think of making my peace with. I'd be happy for no more than the assurance that I could see my fatherland once again before I die. You forget that you had all the healthy, active troops with you, while I travelled with the unfit. Do you know what it meant to me to hear the groans of the sick and dying when I was trying to fight my own pain long enough to get a few hours of sleep? Don't you have a nose, man? Didn't you smell the air when you came into this camp? Do I have to tell you the nature of that smell? Get out of here and leave me the peace of my last days."

Henry scowled at the old man, then turned to leave but looked over his shoulder at the entrance. "It looks as though I'll be emperor sooner than I expected," he said cuttingly.

Lothair stared at him levelly and whispered hoarsely. "Don't count on it."

Julien and Robert were wild with joy at the news of the emperor's generosity. But instead of accepting the terms of free exit, Robert opted to retire with his four hundred men to the castle stronghold above the city, the same citadel where he and Julien had been housed on their first visit to Salerno. It was an ideal place to wait out further developments. Lothair and a picked company of his men moved quietly into the city and occupied the castle in the city's center, while Henry and Conrad sulked with their troops in the camps outside.

The Salernitans started a three-day holiday to celebrate the peace by rolling casks of the finest wines to the town squares and setting them up to give free drink to all. Toasts to Roger's health rang through the city, and torches kept the streets bright for the revellers till dawn. The troops who accompanied Lothair were quickly as pleasantly oiled as the Salernitans, and the feeling of peace was genuine.

On the second morning of the celebration, word reached the Pisans of the emperor's terms. They came to the city and confronted Lothair with nothing short of savagery. They felt they had been sold out, cheated of both their booty and their revenge. Disgusted by Lothair's coolness in the face of their rage, the Pisans stormed out, deciding instead to speak to Robert, and climbed to the citadel to discuss terms of peace with him.

Robert was as amused as he was delighted by this unexpected *volte face,* and he entertained the Pisans with the most sophisticated food and wine at his disposal. The admiral of the Pisan fleet was a rough, outspoken man named Giacomo, himself direct in his dealings and instantly attracted to Robert's straightforward, easy manner. By the end of the evening, he and Robert were swearing eternal friendship.

Robert was able to convince Giacomo that the Pisans' best interests now lay in going to Palermo at once and telling Roger of the new turn of events. Giacomo agreed to this enthusiastically. Sicily was a competitor in trade, but he had no direct complaint against the kingdom, or Roger. Robert's assurances that he would be welcomed in Palermo, and even rewarded for his defection from Lothair, sent him back to the harbor in high spirits to make preparations to move the entire fleet to Palermo to make peace.

Julien and Robert had every reason to be jubilant. Lothair was technically the victor, but Salerno was spared, and Roger was far from crushed.

Apulia belonged now to the Empire, but the question of its disposition still remained. Before Lothair could make another move, he was obliged to set up a government which could be relied upon and whose loyalty to him was unquestioned. Julien went down to the city every day to follow the course of events there. Rainulf of Alife, Roger's rebellious brother-in-law, was chosen as Apulia's new leader, and instantly approved by both Lothair and Innocent. Yet despite the fact that papacy and Empire agreed on the choice, it opened yet another rift between them. Each party claimed the sole right to invest Rainulf in his new territory.

Julien watched the bitterness grow, and it seemed for a while that Rainulf would never be invested. At last an announcement was made. A solution had been found, and Robert joined Julien in the square outside the cathedral to watch the ceremony.

"They're making bets all over town on who will bestow the gonfalon on Rainulf," Robert said.

"I know, and the odds are exactly even everywhere," Julien replied.

The gonfalon, a pennoned lance, was used to confer the rank of office, and giving it was as symbolic as placing a crown on a monarch. There were a few short speeches before the main ceremony and the townspeople crowding the square were obviously bored.

"Rainulf looks embarrassed standing there," Julien observed.

"I can see why," Robert answered. "Look. They're *both* going to hand it to him."

Innocent and Lothair moved towards where the gonfalon lay on a cushioned table, bowed formally to each other, and then Innocent grasped the point of the lance while Lothair took the shaft, and together they moved clumsily towards Rainulf. They took turns delivering portions of the speech of investiture, and then, after signalling each other with a glance, held out the lance to him.

The townspeople snickered behind their hands at the undignified ceremony which the Church's highest officer and the most potent crowned head had staged.

"Think of how amused Roger would be if he were witnessing this ridiculous farce," Robert said.

"I plan to write him a full description," Julien chuckled.

The new duke of Apulia was then given eight hundred knights to secure his territory, but as Robert guessed, they were chosen from the unfortunates who had accompanied Lothair to Salerno, not from the fitter knights of Henry's contingent.

The ceremony over, Lothair and Innocent made ready to go with the imperial army to settle the lesser questions of Benevento, Capua, and Monte Cassino.

Julien returned to Gay feeling lighthearted, and recounted all the details of the ceremony, which appeared not to interest her at all. He gave up trying to make further conversation with her after a while and undressed for bed, although he didn't feel much like making love that afternoon. It simply appeared to be the only thing to do.

At the end of the next week, word reached Robert's office of Lothair and Innocent's victory for the creaky brand of rule the Church conservatives preferred, at the expense of the citizens of Benevento. Meanwhile, the citizens of Salerno had already gone back to doing pretty much what they had been doing before the siege, and Chancellor Robert's knights came and went freely from the citadel.

Julien and Robert waited, anxious to see what the next imperial move might be.

It was now the second week of September, and the army was further from the shores of Sicily than it had been in months. A new campaign seemed less likely than ever. Instead, Lothair's forces were doing what they could to shore up defenses against any move of Roger's on the mainland.

Word reached Salerno that Lothair and Innocent were approaching Rome, but cheers went up in Salerno when, a day later, they got word the emperor's army had bypassed the city and continued northward. Anacletus' hold on the city was still too strong for them to take it without a major conflict. Lothair, no less now than his men, was determined to reach the Alps before the snow set in and separated them from their lands, and Innocent had begun to irritate him more than ever. The emperor was now well out of the arena, and whatever troops he left behind as a reminder of the imperial power were insignificant.

Roger lost no time in setting out from Sicily to reap the greatest advantage possible from the new turn of events. A day of feasting and celebration was immediately declared in Salerno to welcome their ruler back to his mainland capital. On October 2nd Roger landed as though the victory were entirely his. All the battles had been Lothair's, but it was clear to all that once he left, the war was won by Roger.

Although Roger was exultant he entered the city with as little pomp as possible, almost stealthily, and hurried Julien and Robert to a conference in the first hour of daylight. "I want no celebration," he instructed. "There'll be plenty of time for that later. My first need is to conscript men for my army, and I'd like them to be sober."

"I thought your troops were following you from Sicily," Robert said, frowning. He knew the Salernitans would not welcome the idea of assisting in a new campaign, especially since there had been no significant military aid from Sicily during the siege of their city.

"Yes, they should be here in a day or two, but they're just my Christian troops, and I doubt they'll be enough. If I use my Muslims again to teach the rebels a lesson, I'll have the Church falling on my neck. Do what you can to discourage heavy drinking. I never have to worry about that with my Muslims, but these Italians will be unmanageable at the first sacking if they're not curbed now."

Julien's expression reflected his distaste. He didn't relish the idea of accompanying Roger on yet another punitive expedition, but he remained silent. Roger caught his mood nonetheless. "I don't think I'll want you with me on this leg of the campaign, Julien. Perhaps it's just as well for you to stay here and wait. I understand you're not likely to consider it a hardship to remain in Salerno." He winked broadly at Robert.

"How did you know about her?" Julien wheeled and confronted Robert accusingly.

Roger and Robert laughed good-naturedly. "No, it wasn't your friend here," Roger said. "You should remember it's my business to know everything about you. Come now, don't give it another thought. It goes no further." He turned to Robert. "Now, back to business. I intend to get rid of Robert of Capua first. I doubt it'll take long."

Robert snorted. "I expect he'll take to his heels again as soon as he hears you're on your way."

"I hope so. He's not worth more than a week's time. Then I should stop at Naples. I don't expect much of a problem there either. Prince Sergius is tired of all this revolt, and at his age I believe he'd welcome the chance to renew his vows to me. And I'm really quite fond of him."

"I hope there won't be any surprises," Robert said, "but at this point it sounds like a fairly cut-and-dried operation."

"Let's hope so," Roger said. "I'd like to leave as soon as my Sicilians get here. I hope to be back with you in no more than a few weeks. Why don't we rest now. I'll meet with you again towards noon."

*   *   *   *   *

Julien walked back to his quarters uncommonly slowly. He was relieved not to accompany Roger on this operation, but he was also tired of Salerno. What's more, he was becoming positively bored with Gay. He delighted in her voluptuousness and she easily excited him, but he couldn't remain in a room with her when they weren't making love without a sense of growing irritation. Reading was out of the question if she was anywhere nearby. He tried once to teach her chess and came closer than he ever had in his life to striking a woman at the end of the first evening. Occasionally he could bribe her to go to the markets, but she didn't even seem very interested in shopping for herself.

Gay flung herself around him as soon as he walked in, and he kissed her firmly but perfunctorily. "I have some letters I must write," he said. "Why don't you go buy yourself some earrings or something?"

"But what about Roger?" she pleaded. "You haven't told me yet when you'll be leaving or how long you'll be gone. You never tell me anything anymore."

"I'll be here for a while. Please. I've been postponing this letter."

"Who must you write to?" she asked, her voice a bit distracted.

"My wife."

"Your wife! What's she going to do with a letter?"

"Get out of here, Gay. I'm very busy."

When she left, Julien addressed himself to composing a letter, but his thoughts seemed either trivial or insincere. He put it aside and tried to begin a letter to his friend Aziz, but was forced to give that up too after a while. He put his writing tools away regretfully. I'll wait until I can tell them for certain when I'm returning, he thought. He folded his arms across the table and laid his head down on them. I should be very happy. He made up his mind to insist that Robert give him some work to do in his offices for the next week. He needed it badly.

Chapter VII
BATTLE

As he predicted, Roger subdued most of the western mainland within weeks, and with minimal casualty to his troops. He returned to Salerno ahead of schedule to rest and make ready to challenge his archenemy, Rainulf of Alife, who ruled uneasily as duke of Apulia. While Roger was away, Robert of Selby had put Julien in charge of conscripting every available soldier that could be mustered from the countryside for the approaching Apulian contest.

Roger's rest was a short one. He announced barely a few days after his return that he felt the army was strong enough to take on Apulia. Julien grew suddenly sentimental when it was time to take leave of Gay. She had become more tolerable in the last fortnight, particularly since his new occupation kept him away, if not actually out of town. He held her in his arms a long time the morning of his farewell, and he believed he felt the start of something close to love for her.

Once on the march, Julien found he really didn't think about Gay very often; certainly nowhere as often as he thought of Claire. And there were so many things to think about now. This could be a crucial battle. If there was doubt as to its outcome, it wasn't apparent in his companions. The mood was more that of a triumphal march. Recent victories, most of them uncontested, had made Roger's soldiers heady.

Only a short distance out from Salerno, a scout from the north reported that Bernard had left the frustrated Innocent to fend for himself and had joined Rainulf at Rignano, just north of St. Michael's shrine at Monte Gargano. Word of this winged swiftly through Roger's ranks, and the men were seen to cross themselves and spend more time in prayer; and an increasing number of amulets and relics began to appear on their persons. There was no Christian who had not heard that Bernard was already a saint able to perform miracles that rivalled the most magical phenomena ever witnessed. Roger cursed himself for not bringing more of his Muslim troops. Still, his numbers were superior to Rainulf's. Even the aging Prince Sergius was by his side with a party of Neapolitan troops, and his ranks were still being swelled by former rebels.

The two armies massed a short distance from Rignano. Roger held a last council in his tent with his chiefs of staff and advisers to confirm plans for the next morning's attack, and, satisfied that his strategy was a good one, dismissed everyone except his son Roger, Julien, and Robert.

Roger's tent was larger than any of the others by half and raised off the ground with planking that was covered with thick carpets against the dampness and chill of October. This tent was surrounded by a ring of smaller tents which housed his personal dining room, his kitchen, his household eunuchs, the women he brought with him, and certain privileged noncombatants—in this case Julien and Robert, two astrologers, two historians, a geog-

rapher, three poets, and seven musicians. In his own tent Roger kept the few
pets that he never failed to travel with. On this campaign it was his white
gibbon and two cockatoos.

The air in the tent was already thick with the incense the eunuchs liked
to burn—frankincense liberally spiced with herbs, charms, and ground up
semiprecious stones to ensure their master's health and the success of the
expedition.

Julien, Robert, and young Duke Roger made themselves comfortable on
cushions while Roger stretched out on a table to be massaged and oiled by
Hadim. He had barely disrobed when a guard appeared excitedly and announced in a tone reflecting his own disbelief: "Bernard of Clairvaux is
outside with two monks as his escort and asks that King Roger grant him an
audience."

Roger quickly signalled Hadim to bring his robe and asked that Bernard
be escorted in.

Bernard stood in the doorway with his hands raised in a gesture of
peace. Roger went to him immediately, knelt, and was offered a hand for a
kiss. Bernard appeared to be in no mood for formalities. He was dressed in a
ragged monk's robe, and his reddish hair was longer than usual and more
dishevelled. He seemed thinner and more racked by pain than the last time
Julien had seen him, and his eyes had the intensity of a man with a raging
fever. Julien was reminded that the details of Bernard's newest diet were
circulating widely and the knowledgeable ascetics now judged barley water
and boiled beech leaves indispensable to the purification of the spirit.

"Beloved son," he addressed Roger, "I came here to ask you to tell your
men to lay down their arms."

The Sicilians all stared at him in amazement before Roger spoke. "I
cannot. My cause is a just one."

"You must think of the price that's already been paid for your stubborn-
ness. How much more blood must be shed?"

"Very well, then. I will accept a surrender from Rainulf and will spare
the city and his life."

"Don't you understand? Rainulf has been invested by the pope. *Your*
pope, if you wouldn't persist in your hopeless support of the anti-Christ.
Doesn't it trouble you that the wisest, most dedicated men of the world
acknowledge only Innocent?"

"The pope I acknowledge is in possession of the throne of St. Peter and
has done nothing to indicate to these wise and dedicated men that he is
unworthy of that exalted chair."

Bernard's irritation revealed itself in the rasp of his voice. "Be reason-

able. If you honor Innocent's investiture of Rainulf, I will personally intercede for you with His Holiness, and I am certain peace can be made with no
reprisal."

"That's not possible. And furthermore, I feel no need of forgiveness for
my actions."

Bernard observed an intent silence before speaking again. "Roger, so
you truly accept Christ as your savior?"

"I do, and always have."

"Then you must accept the judgment of his authority on earth. There
are already too many disturbing stories circulating of your lack of support for
the Mother Church in Sicily."

Roger drew himself up haughtily. "How can you speak to me of stories?
My record stands for itself."

"And yet your history shows an unduly great number of Greek religious houses established under your direct patronage."

Roger became defensive. "There's a reason for it. When I first began to
rule, I had more Greeks living in Sicily than westerners. As more westerners
moved in, I've issued more grants for western churches and monasteries."

"I see. And what of this mosque you're building?"

Roger stared at him, astonished. "That's simply not true. No new
mosques have been built since my father's day. My Muslim population is
actually diminishing."

"And yet I have reliable reports from my priests that at a short distance
from your palace even now a new mosque is rising."

Roger threw his back and laughed. "Your priests are not very percep-
tive then. What they saw is the groundwork for the construction of St. John
of the Hermits, which I'm building for the Benedictines. There was an old
mosque on the site, and I'm incorporating part of it into the new structure.
The finished church will indeed resemble a mosque, because it will have five
domes in the Arab style. I find that the architecture is harmonious to my
city. I'm sure you have friends among the Benedictines. You should have
questioned them before you came to challenge me with stories. There's
nothing new to these ridiculous rumors. My father before me and I have had
to counter absurd charges of conversion to Islam or to the Greek Church for
all our lives." He suddenly stepped forward and seized the heavy wooden
cross which hung around Bernard's neck, raised it dramatically to his lips,
and kissed it fervently. "There, now. I wasn't struck by lightning, was I?"

Bernard had changed color and shrank from Roger's touch. He glared at
him now as if stung, and narrowed his eyes. "Do you deny, then, that you're
sponsoring a book by the heretic Nilus Doxopatrius?"

"What? Nilus a heretic? Nonsense, he's a Byzantine, and one of the most brilliant thinkers in their Church."

"Are you or are you not sponsoring his book?"

"Yes, of course I am. I sponsor many books."

"And do you know that one of the infernal claims he makes in this book is that when the imperial capital was transferred from Rome to Constantinople in the 4th century, the Holy Father lost his ecclesiastical primacy?"

"I find it an argument that's well supported and therefore worth writing down. If I had to personally agree with all the arguments that find an audience in my kingdom, I'd have a fraction of as many books written, and not nearly as many interesting people to chat with. As a matter of fact, I've just published some new editions of Ptolemy and Orosco that I personally find contradictory and confusing, but it would hardly be to my credit to deny their value because of my personal prejudice, now would it?"

Bernard looked horrified. "We have no concern with trivia. I warn you, Roger. This battle will be lost to you. Hear me now." He paused dramatically, then shouted, "Christ will fight on the side of your adversary."

"Do you believe that?" Roger lost his poise only briefly.

"I know it."

"Then, I can only suggest that you have been seriously misled by yet another of your many sources of information." His voice had regained its evenness.

Bernard's eyes blazed now in a totally unnatural way. "Come back to your Church, Roger."

Roger soberly bowed his head, then knelt before Bernard. "Before you leave us, Holy Father, will you give me your blessing?"

Bernard drew back a moment. "You know I cannot. You are under a strict ban of excommunication."

"But are you certain of its validity, Father? It was never delivered from Rome, you know."

Bernard stepped back, bowed, and left, the two silent monks who had escorted him scurrying to keep up.

When Bernard was gone, Roger spun sharply towards the others in the tent. "Did any of you think to see if any of the guards were standing within earshot?"

Julien and Robert were both embarrassed. "No," Julien answered. "How could we leave without being dismissed?"

Roger waved his hand. "I know, I know. But at times like these, you should've taken the chance. You're not southern enough yet. Do you know what could happen if word of this gets around camp? I'm talking about the business of Christ fighting on Rainulf's side. I'm absolutely sure Bernard intended it to be overheard by the guards. These damned superstitious Italians! If I had my Muslims— Never mind." He shook his head passionately. "Damn those holy hypocrites. Why don't they make up their minds whether theirs is the kingdom of Heaven or of earth? Oh, how I despise political priests. Give me the sainted hermit any time who is so revolted by humanity that he vomits at the approach of human scent."

Next morning young Duke Roger led the attack. He proved himself a gallant soldier, worthy of the Hauteville name, by meeting the enemy head on and driving them south along the road to Siponto on the Adriatic.

Roger led the second attack. He charged bravely, but without equal skill, and his assault met with unexpected resistance. As soon as the Sicilians saw the tide of battle turning, they grew confused and undisciplined. Word spread among the men of a vision of Christ seen on a cloud over the rebel army, and there was a general rout. By the end of the day, over three thousand of Roger's men lay dead on the battlefield. Among them was Duke Sergius, the thirty-ninth duke of a noble Neapolitan house, fallen in the service of a man whose name was unknown a hundred years earlier.

Rainulf returned to the little village nearby, where he had lodged Bernard, and, weeping as he knelt, communicated the news of his victory to the triumphant abbot who smiled securely and renewed his blessing on Rainulf.

The atmosphere in Roger's tent as they prepared to march back to Salerno was as lugubrious as it had been triumphant when they set out. Julien felt the demoralization of Roger's defeat as keenly as any of the combatants. In fact he regretted not participating in this rout far more than he would have if they had been victorious. He had been at Robert's side all morning as they checked on the condition of Robert's personal guard. Of the fourteen knights that had accompanied Julien on his mission to the emperor in Bari four months earlier, both of the Sicilians and three of the Salernitans were killed. Mauger escaped with the loss of an ear, but William and two others had wounds serious enough to take them out of action. William had accompanied Julien and Robert back to the royal tent at Roger's request and was waiting now to see his king.

Roger turned from his wash basin and allowed Hadim to dry him as he scanned the dozen or so people waiting to see him. He looked like he hadn't slept in a week.

As soon as Roger spotted William, he went to him first and, embracing him gently out of consideration to his wounds, kissed him firmly on the mouth. "I owe you a great deal. Have my doctors seen to your wounds?"

"I've had attention far more than I'm worthy of," he said, but he had difficulty hiding that he couldn't move his right arm. He'd taken the brunt of a lance in his shoulder while covering Roger's retreat, and the doctors had told him the arm would probably regain only part of its function.

"You're certainly a splendid-looking fellow. I hate to think of your military service ended. Robert, can't you use him as a noncombatant on your military staff?"

"Of course I can. With your permission I'd like to make him a captain."

"And I'd like to make him a gift. Robert, do you remember when you were showing me those remarkable estates about five miles above you on the Amalfitan coast? Wouldn't one of those suit him nicely?"

"It would suit anyone. I'll see to it."

William fell to Roger's feet and tried to kiss them.

"Come, come. That's no way for a hero to behave. No matter what the outcome of the battle, I want you to have full honors when we're back in Salerno, for I swear I've never seen a braver man in battle. Another dozen men like you, and it wouldn't matter how many visions Bernard could conjure."

Julien stepped forward to embrace and congratulate William, and the others followed. But as soon as William left the tent, a pall descended once again, and although there was no further business for his staff, Roger seemed reluctant to dismiss them. No one was anxious to be alone. A poet was sent for, and only after he had recited for nearly two hours did Roger allow the others to leave him.

Once back in Salerno, Roger continued to brood in the palace there. It was November and ordinarily he would be making plans to return to Palermo for the winter, but he was still uncertain whether to contest Rainulf's hold on Apulia again. Morale continued low among his men, but the territories held by the rebels were too critical to his kingdom to be dismissed lightly.

Julien was no less moody. Since their return, he had virtually nothing to do, and he spent far many more hours in Gay's company than he had expected to. He longed to return to Palermo, not only to see his family again, but so that he could make arrangements to have Gay quartered where she would be accessible to him when he wished it and quite out of sight when he didn't. Although he continued to make love to her regularly, he had to admit that there was now more release than pleasure in it. Her attempts to amuse him made him long for the straightforward, easy relationship he enjoyed with Claire, and he winced at the vulgar things that seemed to convulse her. If I could combine the gifts of the two women in one person, he said to himself, there would be no man in the world happier than I. Meantime, if Gay suspected his restlessness, she gave no sign of it. Under her new regimen, she added another pound or two to her frame each week, and while they still suited her, she made no effort to take on any new activity which might check them.

A temporary respite from boredom was provided when emissaries from Benevento arrived to sue for peace. Roger decided to take Robert and Julien to Benevento at once as an antidote to his restlessness.

At Benevento they were greeted by a cheering populace. Roger rewarded the citizens with a royal charter which relieved them of many of the exactions which he, his Norman predecessors, pope, and imperialists had all imposed on them. Although Benevento was technically a papal city, Roger's attitude was that it belonged to him as much as any other city within the boundaries of his kingdom. The Beneventans were at last given the charter they had so long sought granting them communal rights, and the hoary exactions demanded by Innocent on his last visit could now be comfortably ignored.

On their way back to Salerno, the abbey of Monte Cassino was restored to Roger's camp, and Wibald of Stablo was forced to return to Germany after little more than a month as abbot. He fled hurling anathema after him and vowing never to rest until he was revenged on the tyrant Roger. The news seemed to cheer Roger enormously.

Once returned to Salerno, they found the city in an uproar. Bernard had sent messengers, not to ask for an audience with Roger, but to announce that he was on his way there to see him.

Julien was excited but wary. "He simply refuses to give up," he told Roger. "It must gall him that you're the only king who has been able to listen to him without eventually yielding. When I saw him fix his eyes on you that way at Rignano, I had a dreadful feeling if he kept it up long enough, you'd do or say whatever he asked you to."

"I was aware of it," Roger said. "There have been other mystics with a gift for imposing their wills on weaker minds, but we shall see if my mind is the weaker. If it is, then he deserves anything he can get from me. Now I know what sort of man I'm fighting, and I swear he'll never have another victory over me like the one at Rignano."

"He has another argument on his side this time," Julien continued. "Anacletus' most devoted clergymen have grown bitter about the length of this contest. If the schism doesn't end soon, there's real threat to the structure of the Church. Never has a papacy been contested this long."

"I'm a reasonable man," Roger answered, "and I'm willing to review the case. Very well, let's send Bernard an answer right away. Give him the usual form of address, without any flattery, and tell him we shall be pleased to open the question of the papacy for further consideration. But I'll be damned if I'll allow him to stand me in a corner and chastise me like a truant schoolboy. Ask him if he would be kind enough to bring three cardinals with him to plead Innocent's case, and we'll request Anacletus to send three cardinals to present his side. I don't know why someone hasn't done this before. This crisis needs a good, clean debate on the issues. It will be a relief to us all."

When Bernard arrived, he was accompanied by no less a personage than Cardinal Almeric, the papal chancellor whose hastily organized machinations had placed Innocent on the throne the fateful morning of the previous pope's death. With them were the highly respected Guido of Castello and Girard of Bologna. Bernard wore his usual simple gown of rough cloth. His face more than ever reflected the privations of his ascetic life and the strain of the struggle of the last years. Roger welcomed them with accommodations equal in splendor to his own.

The three cardinals from Rome arrived the next morning. Anacletus sent his papal chancellor, Peter of Pisa, a man noted for his piety and blameless life. With him were Cardinals Matthew and Gregory. The debate was promptly scheduled for next morning.

Julien did not sleep that night. He was awed by the holy aura of Bernard's presence, but he trusted him less than ever. The man's savage attacks on all who contradicted him and his insistence on absolute adherence to his own interpretations were repellent. He thought of how mercilessly Bernard had hounded Abelard. Julien also sensed that the saintly Bernard was not above envy. However much he could hold the support of the Church primates in his condemnation of Abelard, Bernard still knew Abelard was studied by the most intellectual of the clergy, especially the younger scholars, and that only fear kept many of them from openly embracing many of his ideas.

The debate was to be held in the main hall of the citadel that overlooked the city. The cardinals from the opposing teams faced each other from opposite sides of the hall, while Roger and a party of ten councillors, including Robert and Julien, were seated on a dais at the far end of the hall. It was Roger's intention to invite Bernard to be seated with him, while the cardinals took turns reviewing their arguments for each of the papal contestants.

Bernard made his appearance only long after the others were all seated and waiting to begin. He bowed low to Roger when he entered, and then ignoring his invitation to join him on the dais, Bernard stood in the center of the hall opposite him and flung his arms wide for silence. *"All Christendom favors Innocent. Only you and your kingdom resist him,"* he pronounced.

Roger sighed. "Will you not accept my invitation to join me here while we hear these illustrious churchmen review their cases? They're anxious to begin."

Bernard did not answer, but proceeded instead to pace one side of the hall and then the other, fixing each cardinal one at a time with his intense, probing stare. He chose a position at length from which he could direct his address to all three sides of the room and then began his oration. His eyes were flashing now as they roved from one face to another, fastening finally on Roger's. Julien caught his breath, fascinated by the virtuoso performance. Bernard's voice rang out deeper and stronger than Julien had ever heard it. He scribbled rapidly, pausing only when Bernard did, to steal another glance at the presence that now seemed enraptured by his own words.

> *The robe of Christ, which at the time of the Passion neither heathen nor Jew dared to tear, Pierleoni now rends asunder. There is but one Faith, one Lord, one Baptism. At the time of the Flood there was but one ark. In this eight souls were saved, the rest perished. The Church is a kind of ark . . . . Lately another ark has been built, and as there are two, one must of necessity be false and will surely sink beneath the sea. The ark which Pierleoni steers, if it is of God, it shall be saved; and the ark which Innocent steers, if it is not of God, it must needs be that it sink: then shall the whole Eastern Church perish and all the West: France, Germany, Ireland, England, and the barbarian kingdoms, all will be lost in the depths of the ocean. The monks of Camaldoli, the Carthusians, the Cluniacs, those of Grandmont and Cîteaux and Prémontré and innumerable others, monks and nuns, all must be drowned in one great whirlpool, down into the deep. The hungry ocean will consume bishops, abbots, and other Princes of the Church, with millstones tied about their necks.*
>
> *Of the Princes of the world only Roger has entered the ark of Pierleoni with all the others perished, shall he only be saved? Can it be that the religion of the whole world should perish, and the ambition of Pierleoni, whose life is so plain to us, should gain for him the Kingdom of Heaven?*

Not until afternoon did Bernard begin to show any signs of tiring. The tribunal recessed, and Roger confessed he was exhausted by the man.

"But when will they discuss the canonicity of the elections?" Julien asked. "I'm anxious to hear the others."

Robert shrugged. "Perhaps now that Bernard's had his say, we can get the cardinals to present their cases tomorrow morning."

Next day Bernard arrived again after all the others, and stood in the center of the hall as before. When it appeared he intended to speak again, Roger rose in his chair to protest, but Bernard silenced him with an imperiously upraised hand and recommenced his astonishing flow of rhetoric. He repeated this feat on the third day, and again on the fourth. Midway through the fourth day's oration he paused, and Peter of Pisa, Anacletus' chancellor, rose to his feet.

"At last," Julien whispered to Roger. "I wondered when one of them would dare interrupt him to say a word of his own." There was a light stir among the cardinals, and then a hush as Peter of Pisa advanced from his place and proceeded gravely towards Bernard. When he stood no more than three feet from him, he flung himself abruptly to his knees and began to confess his sins in a faltering voice. Trembling, he implored Bernard's forgiveness and begged him to take him back into the bosom of the Church.

Bernard raised himself and stretched his arms upward, looking triumphantly from one cardinal to the next. They were all shocked speechless. Bernard raised Peter from his knees and embraced him. Matthew and Gregory, the two cardinals who had accompanied Peter from Rome, shielded their eyes in embarrassment.

Bernard next took a few steps towards Roger, and holding his gaze firmly on him, invited him to come forward and declare as well for his champion. Roger rose and spoke very slowly, but with his vigorous voice lending emphasis to his words. "You have the gratitude of all of us here for allowing us to witness such an extraordinary testimonial. However, I find your arguments too complex for a layman. Will you not allow me a few days to mull the import of your argument? I do not find this so shallow a decision it can be made on the spur of the moment."

Bernard's face was crossed by a flicker of annoyance, but he had no choice except to bow and withdraw.

Roger called a meeting the next day with Julien and his chancellor. "You're not going over to him, are you?" Julien asked. He was concerned by the rapt attention Roger had paid Bernard during the last days of his oration. It seemed impossible he wouldn't be at least influenced by the man's words.

"Julien, my boy, he had no argument for me. He's taken four days to tell me only that I'm wrong because it's impossible that everyone else is, and I'm afraid that's the wrong approach to use on anyone as stubborn as I. I'm as concerned as anyone about the threat to the Church, but if I were to renounce Anacletus without a better reason than the one he offers, I'd never forgive myself."

"I'm convinced Bernard would welcome the chance to get Innocent to confirm you in your kingdom," Robert said. "At this point all you need do is ask."

"I'm sure that's why he's here," Roger replied, "but if I were to allow myself to be convinced by him, I'd also insist my son be confirmed as duke of Apulia and that the treacherous Rainulf be banished once and for all, and I suspect that might stick in Innocent's throat. I don't deny it may one day come to that, but right now I'm content to stall for more time. Time has always been my ally, Robert. I trust it more and more."

"What a terrible blow it will be to Anacletus to learn his trusted chancellor went over to Bernard after all these years of loyalty," Julien said. "I feel sorry for him."

"Anacletus must have seen the handwriting on the wall. It actually pained me to ask him to send his cardinals here to review his claim. No, I'll not betray him. I honestly don't believe he can hold the throne much longer, but I'll not be the man to give him the final dagger thrust."

On the fifth day after the tribunal ended, Bernard sent a short note to Roger demanding an answer. Roger sent for the abbot at once, and had him led directly to his audience room. Here Roger was careful to seat himself well above Bernard and, dispensing with formalities, insisted that Bernard remain seated for their talk. "The questions raised by this tribunal frankly confuse me," he said. "But I want you to know how grateful I am for your coming here. You do me a great honor."

"What appear to be the greatest problems often have the simplest solutions," Bernard answered in a surprisingly soft voice. "Why not accept the inevitable, Roger? Pierleoni will still be an anti-pope, even if he were to sit on St. Peter's throne for seven times the seven years he's held it."

"I wish I found it as simple as you make it sound. No, I'm afraid I need more time."

"More time?" Bernard's voice rose with his irritation. "The tribunal started nine days ago, and I'm sure you've thought of little else. What more could you hope to know?"

"It isn't just that," Roger said. "I shouldn't make a decision as grave as this one without the counsel of my curia. I must go back to Palermo and

convene them at once. Will you do me the honor of joining me? I'd like to
invite the cardinals who were kind enough to come here to present their
arguments to join me as well."

Bernard was clearly disappointed. "I'm afraid that's impossible. If my
arguments haven't already prevailed upon you to see reason, I doubt I could
do more in Palermo. I will recommend, however, that at least one cardinal
from each side accompany you for consultation. Cardinal Guido will go with
you to represent Innocent's interests." He rose, and Roger nodded his permission to leave.

Julien and Robert joined Roger a few minutes later, and he told them of
his conversation with Bernard.

"It's clear to me he's written you off," Robert said to Roger. "If he felt
there was still the faintest chance of winning you over, he'd not have hesitated to go to the ends of the earth with you."

"I must go back, Robert. I know how much there still is to do here, but
I can't stay away from Palermo any longer."

"I miss it more than I thought I could ever miss any place," Julien said.
"And it's six months since I've seen my family."

"It appears to me you haven't had quite that much occasion to miss
them," Roger teased. "Will you take Gay back with you?"

"I plan to."

"Won't you find that a bit sticky? You told me your arrangement with
Claire would never permit any outside alliances."

"That seems such a long time ago."

"You'll tell her, then?"

"No, of course not. I'm buying a house for Gay."

"Your conventions amuse me," Roger said. "How much simpler it is to
just use the harem. It's cheaper and infinitely more convenient."

"One day, perhaps. My marriage hasn't come to that yet, thank God."

Roger and Robert smiled at each other, and Julien caught the implica-
tion that they believed the day would come quite soon. "I still prefer that a
woman be all things to her husband," he protested, "but if this can't be, then
accommodations must be made."

"Make them, Julien, make them." Roger patted his shoulder. "You've
served me well these last months. Let me make you a gift of the house for
Gay. Or, perhaps I should say, I think you should have a pleasant study away
from the palace, where you can follow your intellectual pursuits."

Julien didn't enjoy the ironic ring to these words, but he knew Roger
was honoring him as well as sporting with him. "Thank you, my lord. And

now, if you don't need me further, I'll find Gay and tell her we're leaving soon for Palermo. She'll be pleased."

"Good, leave us now. I have tiresome details to discuss with Robert."

Gay was in his room arranging flowers when Julien came in. "Julien, I had to throw out all the flowers in this room and pick new ones. They had brought you chrysanthemums. Imagine!"

"Yes, I asked for them. I thought they'd be beautiful in this room."

"Julien! What's wrong with you. Chrysanthemums are only for the dead. Don't you know anything?"

He shrugged his shoulders. "It doesn't matter. Listen Gay, I have good news. We're going back to Palermo, this week!"

She dropped the vase she was holding and it shattered on the tiles, splashing water on their ankles. She had turned waxen.

"Gay, what's wrong? I told you I'd be taking you back with me. It's just a little sooner than I expected. Roger is homesick."

She sat on the divan and started crying softly, but she kept her face turned and made no answer.

"I don't understand. You seemed so pleased." Her sobbing grew louder and he sat next to her to comfort her, but she shrank from his touch.

"I can't go."

He pushed her away from him angrily and rose to his feet. "What the devil are you talking about?"

"First you must promise not to kill me. I know you'll beat me, but promise me you won't kill me or maim me or knock out any teeth."

Julien was growing more irritated and shook her roughly by the shoulders until he heard her teeth chattering. "I told you from the first that I'd never beat you. I despise men who beat their women. Now tell me what this is all about."

"I want your promise first."

"Damn it, I promise." He pushed her away angrily and strode to the window. "All right, out with it!"

"I don't deserve to be your mistress."

"Stop that and get to the point."

She started crying again and he was tempted to slap her until she stopped, but he stayed by the window taking deep breaths of the cool air. "You would be right to kill me. I've been unfaithful."

He wheeled and faced her. "Unfaithful? What, you a whore? I don't believe it!"

"It's true. It happened before I knew what I was doing."

"Who was it, bitch? Tell me before I cut your lying trull's tongue out of your harlot's head."

"Please, you promised. When you went away to Benevento, I was all alone and I felt so sorry for him. You mustn't do anything to him, I beg you. It was all my fault."

"Out with it, you common cotquean. Who was it?"

She remained silent, sobbing softly until Julien grabbed her shoulders again and shook her. "Tell me, you damned Jezebel."

"It was William," she faltered, chattering the word.

"William! I don't believe it, you lying trollop." He pushed her away with such force, her neck jerked as if broken.

"You promised not to hurt me. Please, Julien. He was so kind to me, even when I told him I wouldn't marry him because of you. Then, when he came back wounded, it broke my heart to see him that way and I knew he meant a great deal more to me than I'd dreamed."

Julien strode over to her and twisted his fingers in her hair. "I ought to break your neck, you draggle-tailed strumpet."

"You promised, you promised," she screamed.

"I can have him exiled for this. Or even unmanned!"

"You mustn't. William loves you more than he's ever loved any man. He told me so himself, many times. He's avoided you since your return because he's sick with guilt."

"So that's it. I wondered why he stayed away. Oh, how could you! Both of you! I loved him, too. I told Roger there was no braver man in Salerno, and I asked Robert to make him his captain." He released her and sat down on the couch next to her. "Is this what one is to expect from women, then? Roger does well to keep his in the harem. Foul, foul, foul. This could never have happened in Palermo."

"Forgive me, I beg you."

"Forgive you? How can I? Do you know what would happen to you if I were a more impetuous man? No, you've injured me too greatly." His memory summoned a vision of William's massive frame stretched out on the cot in their barracks near Bari, and he remembered how struck he had been by his good looks. He raised his hand again to strike her, then put it down.

"Julien," she pleaded, less anxiously now, "I must have your forgiveness. My life has been so miserable since it happened."

"How many times did you do it with him?"

She looked at him strangely. "Just once."

This seemed to calm Julien a bit. "I don't know, perhaps I will be able to forgive you in time. Roger always says time is his ally. Perhaps it's mine too. After we've been back in Palermo awhile, I may find the pain of your treachery faint enough to forgive you, but not now. Not yet."

"Oh, but Julien, I can't go to Palermo with you."

"Yes, yes, it's all right. I'll get over it. I must learn to be bigger than life's chicanery."

"But you don't understand. I can't go to Palermo."

"It will be all right, Gay," he said more impatiently. "We'll make a new start there."

"Julien, I'm trying to tell you I can't go to Palermo . . . because I'm staying here with William."

"What?" He jumped to his feet as if stung.

"William needs me."

Julien was sputtering in his rage. "Needs you? Has it come to that? Well, what about me, you foul-bellied fornicatrix?"

"Julien, the hurt I've done you is already done. It would be worse for all three of us if I went away with you. You wouldn't want to have me, knowing I still have feelings for William, would you?"

"What does a wretched jade like you know about feelings? I'd expect more sensitivity from a ha'penny upright."

"I don't blame you for being angry, but it's stronger than I am."

"Oh no, do I have to listen to that too, you dreary slut, you dross from the brothel slop pot."

"No man has ever made me feel the way William does."

"That's exactly what you said about me our first night," he sobbed. She silently turned her head away.

"You mean he's a better lover than I am?" Before Julien realized it, his voice had ended in a scream. She cowered as he raged, until he had exhausted both his body and his epithets.

"Go!" he said at last. "Take your things and get out of here. I have no further claim on you." He averted his head when she began kissing his hands. She finally quit, and he watched her pack her belongings without further comment. There was a cheerfulness beneath her nervous bustling that increased his depression. When she was all packed, she stood at the door a moment before speaking.

"You'll feel better about all this once you're home, Julien."

He turned to her and narrowed his eyes. "I'll never be able to trust a woman again."

"I never meant you harm, Julien, and it's not as if you were really in love with me."

"Don't speak to me of love, trollop. It was *you*, remember, who spoke of your great love for me. Is woman's emotion that shallow?"

Her voice grew unexpectedly tender. "Julien, I wanted to love you, and for a woman sometimes that's enough."

"You'd better go now."

"I left the jewelry you gave me on the chest, with the silks."

"Take them. I've no use for them."

"No, I have no right to them."

"They're yours, and I certainly don't want to look at them again." He went to the chest and rolled up the trinkets and clothing left there into one of the scarves. "These were given to you in good faith."

"I can't, Julien. William wouldn't wish me to."

"Why not? He's not planning to make you his wife, is he?"

"No, of course not. But I'll do all I can to be worthy of him."

"Then, it's no stain on his honor if you keep what you earned as one man's whore before you became his."

She snatched the bundle from his hands and hurled it into a corner, then ran out of the room and down the corridor, sobbing.

Julien called after her. "Gay! I didn't mean that. Hold up a minute. I really wanted you to have those things. Don't leave this way. I was angry. You can't blame me for that."

She paused at the end of the corridor and walked back to him slowly. "I'm not blaming you, Julien. I haven't forgotten that it's I who have injured you, and that you're still my benefactor, but I can't ignore my feelings. Or William's."

"Take them, please."

"I couldn't bear to look at them. They would remind me of my infidelity."

"I'll throw them out the window, then."

"Don't be childish," she said, then caught herself.

He gripped her arm roughly and raised a hand to strike her.

"Stop it, Julien. If you had wished to kill me, I could not have resisted, but you chose not to and now you must let me go."

"I trusted you."

She sighed. "I know you did, Julien, and I repaid that trust badly. But you still have Claire, and I know how much you love her. Look, you're returning to her now. Take that happiness and leave me mine." She leaned forward impulsively and kissed him on the mouth. "I'll always be fond of you."

Julien turned and walked back slowly. His cheeks were still blazing with hurt. I'll never trust a woman again, except for Claire. Never. I suppose it serves me right for making a fool of myself over such a lowclass slut. That trollop isn't fit to lick Claire's boots, and I made so much of her. To think I was even going to give her a house!

He remembered then that the house was to be a gift from Roger. Roger! How was he going to tell Roger and Robert of his humiliation? And what if he were to see William again? Men were killed for less.

No, William is still a good man. And really, Gay wasn't such a bad sort. Stupid, perhaps, but not really bad.

He decided the safest course was to say as little as possible about the whole affair. If anyone were to mock him for his role in this adventure, he would turn a deaf ear. He knew by the mores of the south he was an object of ridicule, but then William was even more so, and Gay not even worth considering. "And after all," he said to himself, "I *am* English."

Chapter VIII
THE SCHISM ENDS

It was natural that Palermo would celebrate their return with a holiday, but when the ship pulled in, Julien saw that the city's mood was far gayer, almost frantically so, than he had expected. The harbor was decked with garlands, and thousands of citizens had turned out to welcome the conquering heroes. They walked from the harbor to the palace on flower-strewn carpets, while overhead multicolored silk banners fluttered everywhere and jugglers, musicians, acrobats, and dancers thronged the streets in an almost wanton spirit of carnival.

What did it matter that western Apulia was still in rebel hands? The emperor had retreated and was even now trying to make the difficult passage across the Alps, despite the fact that the passes were already blocked with snow. The greatest threat Sicily had faced since the coming of the Normans was at an end, and its citizens joined in a fervent celebration of peace.

Julien rushed to his apartment to see Claire and the children, and found the rooms hollow in their emptiness. Rousing one of the servants, he learned that Claire had taken the children to Furci for a few weeks, but that word had already been sent to her of his expected arrival and she was probably even now on her way back. He was disappointed, but not bitterly so. After so many months without him, Claire must have longed for the intimacy and peace of Furci. He found an invitation from Aziz to spend his first evening with him, and Julien was consoled by the prospect. There was sure to be a great celebration in the main banquet hall tonight, and he suspected Roger would have to attend, but only because he was coerced by his rank. If Queen Elvira were still alive, no holiday imaginable could have stirred him from her chamber.

There were nine children with Aziz and his wife, and Julien was even more grateful for the invitation when he felt himself a secure part of their warm circle. After dinner the children were dismissed, and the three adults stayed on to chat over innumerable pots of tea.

The apartment they lived in was very much like his own. The room they entertained in held four divans and dozens of pillows, and the finer rugs were hung on the walls. Damascene trays on low wooden tables were organized geometrically between the divans, and Fatima insisted on serving the tea herself.

Julien was shocked to see Fatima so changed. The voluminous gowns she wore could not hide the fact that her figure had lost its roundness at the breasts and hips, but her belly was unnaturally swollen, as if she still carried a child.

Only when Aziz mentioned somewhat more sternly that she was tiring herself did she leave the men to have a few words alone.

Aziz's concern was apparent. "She continues to conceive," he said, "although she's well into her mid-forties. She pampers herself when she's pregnant and manages to carry the child for a few months, but she always loses it, and when it happens, oh Julien, how she suffers! She's had four miscarriages in the last two years."

"You know the answer to that," Julien said somberly. "You must stop sleeping with her."

"How? She insists. You know I don't need her for that. I have other women I see regularly, and I still go to the bathhouse once a week or so."

"The boy Ishkar?"

"Ishkar! You jest! He's a fine person, but he must be over thirty now and retired to his villa in Erice. No, no, I'm a pederast, not a pervert."

Julien knew his friend was teasing him, but also that he was trying to cover the gravity of his concern with a pleasantry. "You must remind Fatima of the threat to her health when she insists, and be firm."

"I *am* firm. But you've no idea how demanding she can be."

"It's rather the reverse of my situation, isn't it?" Julien said ruefully.

"It's occurred to me," Aziz said. "I hope you've learned to resign your-self more gracefully to God's will. Thank Him daily for your beautiful, healthy children, Julien. Allah has been good to you."

"I do, Aziz."

"And it seems the infant you lost has been replaced by the presence of Adele. I don't believe Claire could do without her. They all love each other so."

Julien felt a surge of warmth in his chest at these words. "Let me leave you on that note of love. I've kept you from your rest too long." He embraced his friend and returned reluctantly to his own apartment.

It had been a cozy and sentimental evening, and Julien felt comforted by the familiarity of his own bed when he retired to it. He found he enjoyed his home more and more as he grew older, and most of all when he returned from one of Roger's campaigns. He knew it would be only a matter of time before he was called upon to join Roger in yet another expedition, but there was always the hope that the next campaign would be the last. And tonight he was warmed by the prospects of his family's return. They would be able to enjoy Christmas together at any rate. He smiled at how unthinkable Christmas away from Palermo was to Roger.

Julien slept late the next morning and was awakened by the sound of workmen outside the palace. At the window he saw them stripping the festive silk banners from the walls and replacing them with swags of rough, black cloth. He dressed quickly and went to Roger's audience hall, where he found his king already in mourning. The holiday was over. "Our illustrious suzerain, Lothair, Emperor of the Holy Roman Empire, died on December 3rd," Roger announced. "I have asked for Masses to be said for his soul throughout the kingdom."

It was amazing that the mood of the palace should have changed so abruptly from festivity to mourning. And yet Julien never doubted the sincerity of Roger's respect for the emperor. Even as Roger demanded the utmost formality in the obeisances of his subjects towards himself, he was determined to accord all marks of respect to the dead emperor, however harshly they had regarded each other while he lived. "He died a bitter, disillusioned man, but he was a brave one," Roger continued. "His army was demoralized and mostly disbanded, but at least God granted him his last wish, which was to see his fatherland again. He died in a small village in the Tyrol, and it seems certain he knew his death was at hand. He was seventy-two, after all, an age not granted to many of us."

Julien bowed his head for a moment, then went to a table at the side of the hall where mourning bands had been laid out for the court, and slipped one on his arm. How curious it seemed. What would Lothair think to know he was being accorded all the rites of mourning at the court of the man he had usually referred to as "the half-heathen king," or "the ruler of Muslim hordes?" But then, what would he think of the fact that Roger had already undone most of the imperial work of the last years on the mainland? Roger, Julien reflected, could afford to be generous.

When they returned from Mass, they were intercepted by one of Roger's aides. "Your Majesty," the man said, "the cardinals who accompanied you to Sicily are anxious to know when they may be permitted to meet with your curia for further discussion of the papal contest."

"By the devil's third ball," Roger said irritably, "I was hoping to have peace from them for a while. Find them guides and take them, but separately, on a tour of the city and all its churches and monasteries. Then see if you can interest them in a short excursion to the monastery of the Holy Spirit outside Trapani. Entertain them royally, but without the royal presence, if you please." Julien smiled, and took his seat at the table. His monarch was back in form.

A week before Christmas Claire arrived in Palermo. Julien was alerted to her ship's approach and went to the docks to meet her. He saw Adele first, at the ship's rail, struggling to hold up little Nigel for his father's inspection, and at first scarcely recognized her. She was dressed in a pretty blue kirtle with a matching cloak, and looked like a rich merchant's daughter. He'd never seen her face so merry or so pretty. Adelaide came to the rail next, leading Peter by the hand and showing him how to wave to his father.

When Claire appeared, she was veiled, but the sparkle of her eyes gave evidence that the preceding months had swept away the last traces of her illness and left her as radiant as when he first met her. Her flesh had filled out a bit, and he thought it suited her. When he came ashore, he held her in a long embrace, and her eyes told him how greatly she had felt his absence. This look stirred his hopes and he pressed her to him more closely, but she held up a hand and withdrew gracefully.

"Why are you veiled?" he asked her. "You know I don't expect it of you."

She inclined her head and kept her voice very low when she answered. "I perform so few duties for you. I feel that the least I can do is see to it that my public appearance can give no man cause to question your honor, no matter how contemptible such a man may be to me."

"Claire," he said, "that's so unnecessary," but he felt secretly thrilled by her answer.

They dined alone in their apartment that evening. Claire insisted she wasn't tired and would do all the serving herself so the staff might be free to retire after the children were in bed.

Julien was overwhelmed by the considerations she showed him. He ate course after course of the special dishes she prepared while she chatted cheerfully, reporting on every note in their children's progress and dwelling on each of their virtues. He, no less eagerly, wove the details of his adventures into her stories. There was a pause, and he took her hand, which she let him hold for a while before she rose to bring him a favorite dessert prepared of whipped egg whites with sweet wine, vanilla, and almond milk. Afterwards she poured them each a glass of the heavy, sweet wine of western Sicily that she knew he enjoyed after dinner, and they sat quietly together, aware of each other's contentment. "I'm happy only when I'm around you," he said at length.

"If it weren't for the children, I don't know how I could bear your being away so much," she answered, and the glisten in her eye communicated a great deal more to him.

He decided to take courage. "Claire, my beloved, it's been such a long time. Won't you let me share your bed tonight?"

"Dear Julien, I was so afraid you would ask me that. I know I have no right to refuse you, but it wouldn't be fair of me, either, if I allowed you to without my wanting it too."

"But if I promise not to impose myself on you? Just let me hold you in my arms and sleep with you. I'll not ask for anything else."

"I would love that too, but I know you too well, Julien. Of course I want to be in your arms, to be your wife, and I hate myself for fearing it so."

"But you seem so well now. You never looked better. Perhaps it will be different this time. If I'm very, very gentle. I swear that the minute you say it hurts you, I'll—"

She sealed his lips with a finger. "Julien, Julien! My darling, I've lighted enough candles to the Virgin to make Palermo as bright as day. Believe me when I tell you, it's my greatest wish."

"Did you see Dr. Giacobo when you were at Furci?"

"Yes, he's an honest doctor. He admitted he doesn't know how to help me. He could only encourage me in my prayers. And I've been to see Roger's chief doctor, who cared for Elvira until her death. It was the same. Did Aziz tell you about Fatima?"

"Yes, poor woman. It pains him greatly."

"I wish I could be like her . . . giving myself to you even if it brings my death closer."

"Don't ever say that. That's the last thing I would want."

"Then you'd believe I love you."

"But I do believe it." He brought her hand to him and kissed it tenderly. Julien poured more wine, and after another hour of sentimental conversation, he was able to convince her to allow him into her bed, with a firm promise that he would not try to make love to her. He found he was shaking as he undressed and slipped in next to her.

Her warmth and the feeling of his arms around her were electrifying, and he felt drunk with the perfumes of her body. They lay quietly for minutes with his mouth fastened on the nape of her neck and her hair cascading over his shoulders, teasing him with every breath he took. His hands moved tentatively, gently, and then more boldly as he began to explore her breasts. He felt himself choking on his desire. He rolled a nipple between his fingertips and he felt her body go rigid, but she said nothing and lay still. He stopped for a moment, hoping she would relax again, and then allowed one hand to move to her waist and stroke her with the lightest brushes. He felt the rigor in her muscles increase again, and stopped his movement.

He was throbbing fiercely now and began caressing her again, urged on by the insistent straining of his loins. He inched slowly closer to her thighs, then swept his hand across her belly and let it rest just above the soft tuft of hair. It seemed her breathing had stopped, but then he decided it was the thunder of his coursing blood that drowned out everything else. He stretched his hand downward, and allowed his fingers to brush her nest, and as he touched her she broke into half-stifled tears.

He lay motionless, but her body continued to rock in sobs until he pulled away from her and apologized. She didn't answer him but continued sobbing, more quietly, almost mechanically. His desire was so fierce now, he felt a searing pain in his groin and belly. He rose, and left her to go to his couch in the anteroom. He could still hear her crying, and he muttered curses on himself. His desire was no longer fierce but the pain persisted. He masturbated perfunctorily, coming after a long while with a groan of relief. In minutes he was asleep.

It was growing closer to Christmas. Julien had never been particularly sentimental about the holiday, but this year he was exceptionally grateful to have his children around him. Their love did a good deal to make up for the loss of Claire's bed. He was aware that Claire tried to make up for the love she denied him at night with á hundred affectionate attentions during the day, but these small favors became ironic reminders of his loss, and without his children he would have recognized no home. Aziz alone was familiar with the true turn their marriage had taken. The servants knew that Julien spent his nights on another couch, but were committed to a loyal silence.

The cheeriest note in the household was now Adele, who genially busied herself with more duties than she was assigned. While Claire was at work, it was she who managed affairs. Still half child and half woman, she became an indispensable part of the family. Julien delighted in watching her as she moved about, fussing with the children, arranging flowers, organizing meals and social activities. She was growing prettier by the day, and he found himself looking for her quick smile.

Roger had turned moody again. The news from Rome was invariably gloomy. Innocent had been smuggled into the city, and although Anacletus still held St. Peter's, the Vatican, and Castel San Angelo, the presence of Innocent in the city had weakened his claims. The cardinals who accompanied Roger to Sicily were growing bored and became importunate in their demands for his decision. Both of them were eager to leave for Rome and insisted on an answer before Christmas Day.

Christmas morning Roger called Julien into a private meeting, and together they composed a letter which was written, signed, and sealed in triplicate, so that both cardinals would have a copy to return to Rome with. The letter was addressed not to either of the claimants, but to Bernard.

> *Most reverend and beloved abbot:*
>
> *We have consulted all the evidence presented to us as well as our conscience, and humbly submit our decision to you. The only clear charge you have laid is that His Holiness, Anacletus, was guilty of the sin of simony during his youth. It pains us to recall that virtually all members of the order of Cluny have similarly been charged with buying ecclesiastical preferment.*
>
> *Since we are not of the cloth, we view the sin of simony differently than our betters in the Church do. Pierleoni, as he was known at the time of this sin, had a great deal of money. Despite the biblical reminders of a rich man's difficulties in achieving entry to Heaven, we do not view the possession of wealth as a sin per se.*
>
> *We find it deplorable, even as you do, that the hierarchy Pierleoni entered should already be so notorious for offering preferment through the*

employment of gold, but given this state of affairs, we believe that if he didn't use existing means to hasten his advancement, he would have been a fool. We further believe that it is easier for a man to rise above the sins of his youth than it is for him to change being a fool.

Since Anacletus' assumption of the papal tiara, there has been no evidence of misconduct, licentious behavior, or flaw of character unbecoming a man of God. It appears, rather, that Anacletus is the very model of a Christian statesman.

As to the authenticity of his election, we have waited nearly eight years for any evidence which seriously disputes its canonicity, and have yet to see any.

Under the circumstances we feel it would be an affront to the dignity of his office to withdraw our support, and believe we have no choice but to reaffirm our loyalty to His Holiness, Anacletus II.

> *Yours in Christ,*
> *Roger II, Rex Siciliae*
> *pro gratia dei*

Cardinal Guido accepted his copy of the letter sadly, but gave Roger his blessing before leaving for Rome. Cardinal Gregory of Anacletus' camp was only slightly less solemn. He celebrated a Mass at the cathedral, and both men took separate ships back to the same city with their messages.

On Twelfth Night the holiday celebrations finally came to an end, and the city and the court took stock of their prospects as they faced the year ahead. Roger knew he would soon have to return to the mainland to finish the tiresome task of subduing the last pockets of rebellion. Rainulf of Alife was consolidating his hold on eastern Apulia, and there were new reports that Innocent was raising a papal army to strengthen his defenses there.

Roger called a meeting of his curia right after Twelfth Night, and for the next two weeks they argued over the best strategy. Roger had little heart for the coming campaign, and his lack of enthusiasm was reflected by all his ministers.

The conference came to an unexpected end when a messenger arrived with the news that Pope Anacletus II had died on January 7th. There was no doubt that the defection of his chancellor, Peter of Pisa, and the presence of Innocent in Rome had both contributed to the rapid decline of his health. Shortly before he died, he had received word of Roger's unwavering loyalty and had gone to his rest with a prayer for the kingdom of Sicily on his lips.

The messenger, a young Roman bishop, waited a moment and then continued. "Cardinal Gregory, who was recently a guest at your court, has been elected Pope Victor II by the cardinals of Anacletus' curia, and he awaits your approval and the assurance of your support."

Roger looked wearier than Julien had ever seen him since he had recovered from Queen Elvira's death. "My approval? Very well, bring it to him, then, but I give it with the certain knowledge that it is meaningless. The schism is ended and I thank God. Can I really be expected to exert myself now, on behalf of another aspirant to the tiara who has so little credibility? No, his days as pope are surely numbered, no matter what history decides for Anacletus. Go, give him my approval, then, for all it's worth. I'm sure he's wise enough to know that it's no more than my reluctance to declare for Innocent so soon." The messenger bowed and prepared to withdraw.

"Stay a moment. I have one last thing I would like to do for my friend Anacletus. There are some Byzantines working here who are undoubtedly the world's finest at their craft. I reserve for myself the right to donate a monument for Anacletus' tomb. I want him to have a porphyry sarcophagus like my father's."

The bishop remained silent and turned his head away.

"Well, why don't you say something? I can have my artists return with you to Rome and start at once."

"I'm afraid there can be no tomb, Your Majesty. The body of Anacletus has disappeared."

"Disappeared? Impossible!"

"No sir, it's true. It's a horrible thought, but it appears that Innocent's followers stole the corpse to ensure that no one could do it reverence. Innocent is trying to quiet the scandal, but the people of Rome were rioting when I left and crying for his relics."

"So this is how those saintly men conspire to secure their place in history! A wise, pious pope occupies the throne of St. Peter for eight years and his defamers plot before the corpse is cold to erase his name. Very well. Let the world proclaim the saintliness of Innocent and Bernard. I've learned much about power from them. As soon as I can organize my forces, I'll return to the mainland to put down my traitorous subjects in Apulia once and for all, and woe to the rebellious scum who stand in my way and dare to brandish the tiara and keys in my face."

The city of Palermo went into official mourning for three days, and Roger led all the others in his grief. Bitterness at court was heightened, when at the end of the mourning period, a copy of Bernard's letter to Abbot Peter of Cluny was circulated:

> *Thanks be to God who has given victory to the Church. Our sorrow is turned into joy and our mourning into the music of the lute. The useless branch, the rotting limb has been cut off. The wretch who led Israel into sin has been swallowed by death and thrown down into the belly of hell. May all those like him suffer the same fate.*

It was late in March before Roger was ready to return to the mainland.

He called a council of his curia at the news that Conrad of Hohenstaufen, rather than Henry the Proud, had been elected king of Germany, and they seemed relieved that the expedition would be postponed no longer. Afterwards, as he often did, Roger asked Julien to accompany him back to his quarters to get a more relaxed perspective of the recent events.

"My curia seemed just as pleased with Conrad," Roger complained, "but it's only because they hate Henry the Proud more. Now we have not only a disputed papal throne, but a disputed German crown as well. A clever pope never bestows a crown any more unless he has much to gain or he's forced to."

"What of your crown, Roger?" Julien asked. "Are you telling me you'll have to force the pope to recognize it?"

"Do you doubt I may one day have to? Cardinal Gregory—I still can't bring myself to call him Pope Victor—has no chance of securing his power. When he goes, I'll have no choice but to recognize Innocent. If I don't, they'll accuse me of prolonging the schism most unnecessarily, and they'll be right."

"Then, why not recognize Innocent now?"

"Not yet. There's no advantage in it. But let's finish these plans for the campaign another time—I'm tired of strategies. Now, tell me, Julien, when you joined me, did you have any idea you'd be spending so much time away from your family in the thick of intrigue and war?"

"I do so no less than you."

"That's not answering my question. I really want to hear what you think."

"Very well. First of all, when I came to you I had no family. I think what I feared most was that my life would be boring, that I'd be tied to a desk copying dull bits of legislation until my eyes got too bad. After all, I was no soldier, no priest—what else was there?" Julien paused before he continued. "But there *was* something else too. I was afraid of you."

Roger laughed. "Nonsense!"

"Yes. I was. Many people are. And I'm not talking about the boot-lickers who shade their eyes from your awesome radiance."

Roger laughed again more loudly. "You're very amusing tonight, Julien."

"I was so anxious to please you, I would've found your displeasure very hard to take. I suppose I was too sensitive for a young man."

"You're too sensitive for a mature one, too. I've often told you that."

"Perhaps so. But, do I like the life you've made for me? Yes, I do. Apart from the fact that it isn't boring, you've never really disappointed me; not in things that matter, and I set high standards for your conduct."

Roger suddenly turned thoughtful, and looked at him oddly. "I think you're telling me more than I should hear. Don't say things like that to me. I like myself too well when I see myself through your eyes. Perhaps that's why I want you around me so much, but I'm afraid I may be tempted to let it influence me one day, and that would be a mistake. I'm a king, Julien. Our choices are sometimes capricious, but they're the royal choice. I'm bound to disappoint you one day. It's inevitable, and I don't want you to hate me when the day comes. How did we get into this! I thought I was asking whether you resent the separation from your family."

"I miss them when I'm away, of course, but I feel no regret for any of the missions I've been on. Is that what you wanted to hear?"

"When you go home tonight, ask your wife to include me in her prayers. I know she already does, but I want her special prayers. Tell her I have no taste for shedding more of my kingdom's blood, and yet it must be done."

Chapter IX

ADELE

It was with relief as much as joy that Julien watched Palermo's shore draw close. His family was waiting at the docks as he hoped they would, but this time there was no great festivity in the return of the troops, only the satisfaction that things were somehow working out and would grow better.

The events of the campaign had been predictable. They led a pitiless expedition in the neighborhood of Benevento, Alife, and Ariano, in which Rainulf, his ranks newly swollen by the papal forces Innocent was able to muster, tried without success to lure Roger into direct battle with him. Roger preferred instead to continue to mop up the last strongholds not directly occupied by Rainulf, but it would be months before all resistance on the mainland could be overcome. At least there was less bloodshed than there had been on earlier expeditions. Many towns surrendered at the first news of their arrival, and where they did not Roger's retribution was swift if not merciful.

In May, Pope Victor saw no further excuse for prolonging the schism, and laid down his tiara and robes, but this was treated by Roger as a mattter of little concern. He declared his recognition of Innocent in the most matter-of-fact way, and sent messengers out with the word that Innocent II was now to be recognized as Father and Lord in all the lands of the kingdom. Innocent made no move to acknowledge his capitulation, and it seemed to affect the conduct of his campaign not at all.

With the coming of fall, Roger's thoughts turned as usual to Palermo, and he decided against any further skirmishing against Rainulf in favor of wintering at home. It had been a tiresome, largely uneventful expedition. Little was resolved, but Roger's position was more secure, and with the schism now behind him he felt free of the commitments that had troubled the first eight years of his reign.

Julien swore he would put all thoughts of the last months away from him and concentrate on his family. He marvelled at how rapidly his children seemed to grow every time he left them out of his sight, and no one could convince him that this wasn't a unique phenomenon. But the greatest surprise on this return was Adele's appearance. The first bloom of womanhood had come on her, and she was now a pretty young maiden who blushed when he embraced her. She was still quite small, however, and Adelaide had quite overtaken her in size. Claire had outfitted all of them in new robes for his return, and he was delighted by the charming picture they presented.

Despite her outward serenity, Claire seemed troubled. She looked as lovely as he remembered her, but the cheer of her greeting was clouded. Julien knew she worried more and more about him whenever he went to the mainland. She told him often how haunted she was by the fear that he might one day find himself again in the position he was in at the rout of Nocera and be forced to pick up a sword in his defense. Today Julien sensed that there was more to her gravity than this concern for him, and he questioned her as soon as they were alone.

"Claire, something's wrong. Have you been unwell again?"

"It's your father, Julien. I was trying to find the right moment to tell you."

Julien caught his breath and went rigid. "Dead?" An image of the old crusader as he had last seen him, heavy with the sorrow of their parting, swept across his memory and he felt his body rent by a single convulsive sob. He crossed himself. "How?" He moved closer to Claire and placed his arm around her as if it were she that needed comforting.

Claire yielded to his embrace and stroked his face lightly before she spoke. "He was aged, remember."

"But he was tough too." Julien's voice cracked.

She continued in a voice so solemn it reminded him how recently she had been gravely ill. "England's been wracked by war again."

"I heard. Why can't Stephen and Matilda keep their nasty squabbles to themselves instead of embroiling the whole country in civil war!" he muttered bitterly.

"It's worse than that. The Scots took advantage of the unhealthy situatiuon there to invade England, and there's been a bloody war in Northumberland and Yorkshire."

Julien's eyes widened. "Godwin! He went off to fight them, didn't he? Is he all right?"

"He's fine. The biggest battle was not far from your home. The Battle of the Standard. They wiped out the whole Scottish army. It was a massacre, and when it was over they threw all the bodies of the Scottish soldiers into great pits. It was dreadful. Dreadful! The English now call the area Scots Pits."

Julien shuddered. "How awful. I love the Scots, wild though they are. What a terrible mistake they made."

"Your brother distinguished himself, Julien. He's a fine soldier, brave and devoted to his fellow knights. But when word of the battle's fury and the wanton shedding of blood reached your father, he was taken with a violent attack that left him unable to move or speak, and he passed on only after he had witnessed your brother's safe return."

Julien crumpled to his knees and crossed himself again. "Oh, my poor father. I hope you've found the peace due you. These damned wars! I've been cheated of ever seeing that good man again. Roger promised me many times that as soon as the mainland was brought to heel, I'd be given a sabbatical so I might go back to visit him. We'd almost done it, Claire. It was so close. I'd already started making plans to take you and the children to England with me. It would have meant so much to him to see his grandchildren. If only he could have lived another year." He paused and wept unchecked. "Was there no other news of home? Godwin? My sister?"

"Godwin is strong and well, and hopes to stay at home to manage the estates which have fallen to him. He'll be looking for a bride next. Your sister Ediwa prays day and night for the security of your soul. Those are not my words, Julien, but hers. She is now abbess of St. Anne's in Yorkshire, a great honor for so young a woman."

"There's something else you're not telling me."

"Yes. It's your other brother, Geoffrey. I know you think of him often with tenderness, and I pray for him daily as I know you do. He died . . . shortly after your father did."

Julien's body contorted as if it were wracked with pain. Claire dropped to her knees to join him in prayer. "Before we pray, Julien, did you know that Roger too had a brother who was a leper, an older brother?"

"He has never mentioned him except once, but I felt it was an added link between us as well as another reminder of the vulnerability of kings. I believe he was consigned to a lazar house as poor Geoffrey was."

"Yes, and he too is dead now. I console myself with the knowledge that their God is more merciful than their fellow man."

When they finished their prayer, Julien was dry-eyed again, but he looked ashen. "This has been a bitter year. I'm sick to the death of the sight of blood, and now the hand of death has fallen heavily on my shoulder." He embraced Claire firmly. "I need you very much, dearest."

Claire stayed in his embrace and soothed him as best she could. He seemed fully in control of himself, but a darkness had entered his spirit that Claire had never seen there before. She never questioned him about the battles he had witnessed, and he much preferred to tell her the details of Roger's strategies and the clever way they outwitted the forces of their enemies. Today, death had a special meaning for them, and she felt the weight the bloodshed he'd witnessed in all these campaigns had laid on him. She knew she must help him erase memories of burning cities and mutilated bodies, and she felt that it was a challenge to her womanhood, even more than bearing his children and being his companion.

They had an early dinner, then Julien went to call on Aziz. Aziz seemed tired and much older, but he perked up at once at the sight of his friend. Fatima was obliged to send her apologies. She felt far too unwell to receive him. Aziz whispered to Julien that she had been confined to her bed for the last three weeks, and he believed she was far too weak now to ever regain her health. Fatima continued to lose weight everywhere but in her abdomen, yet she remained cheerful and grateful to Allah for each new day allowed her on earth.

Julien admired the stoic way his friends dealt with their trials and felt a twinge of shame for the exaggerated importance he attached to his estrangement from Claire. Aziz had heard of the death of Julien's father, but he made no attempt to offer consoling words. As Julien spoke to him now he realized his counsel over the years had made Aziz as much a surrogate father as a friend, and he felt even greater affection for him.

Aziz's voice softened when he spoke of Claire. "You should rejoice in your family, Julien. God has showered you with riches, and of all these a loving wife is first."

Julien gave an involuntary wince.

"Yes, I know, Julien, and I still say to you, be grateful."

"I *am* grateful, Aziz. But it still gnaws at me, to have her so close and so loving and still have her refuse me. It hurts."

"You must try harder to understand her. Claire isn't simply refusing you. What she is refusing is the prospect of another pregnancy. She went through hell the last time she tried to bear you a child. That is her pain. If it were possible for her to enjoy the fruits of love without carrying its seeds, I believe she would yield to you gladly."

"No, there must be more to it than that. I've offered to withdraw my seed before I spilled it, and we used to be versatile in our lovemaking. No, she'll have none of it."

"The act is the symbol of her pain, Julien. Any sex act. She can't separate them, and the thought of it is impossible to her."

"Perhaps so, but knowing that doesn't help."

"She thinks of your happiness all the time, Julien. Make it easier on her and find yourself another woman. I believe she would not only understand but would be happy for you. It certainly needn't threaten her position as your wife. She would still be loved above all others."

"I've tried whores, as you know," Julien said bitterly. "There's little satisfaction there."

"Perhaps you would allow me to make a suggestion."

"No thanks. I've never appreciated your refined eastern taste."

"Come now, don't be sarcastic. I believe you can do much better than that frightful whorehouse you told me about. There are other places in the city I'm sure you would enjoy more."

"A whore is a whore. Who cares if she lies on a fancier bed!"

"Still, I know of a place you might like. It's far more relaxing than the usual brothel. You'll meet a number of accomplished women and be in the company of the more respected men of the city. There's song, and dancing, and wine, and it's not nearly so cut and dried as the usual whorehouse experience."

"I'm not really interested, Aziz." He paused and bit his lower lip a moment.

"Look, let me take you out one evening this week. We may both enjoy it."

"Well, why not? It's been a long time since we were out on the town together. But you said they served wine there. Won't it be wrong for you to be seen in such a place?"

"Not at all. Many good Muslims go there. These are the new Sicilian whorehouses that started in Messina, as you might have imagined. They're already popular with anyone who can afford them." The two friends agreed to visit one of the houses the very next night.

Julien was pleasantly surprised by the sympathetic appearance of the place. It was located in a discreetly prosperous suburb south of the city's center and resembled any of a number of attractive villas owned by the wealthy tradesmen of the city. Inside he was able to recognize two sons of acquaintances at court, a member of the curia, and a noted astronomer, all of whom greeted him with a cordial smile. The scene was not dissimilar to the entertainments he often attended with Claire at the apartments of his associates. Servants passed among the guests with wines, sweet cakes, and nuts, while a dozen charming hostesses mingled with the guests and took turns dancing, singing, and reciting poetry. There were three young eunuchs, one of them skillfully painted and splendidly dressed in a woman's silk robe embroidered with a small fortune in jewels and skillfully painted. The merrymaking seemed polite and controlled, yet nonetheless genuine, and Julien congratulated Aziz on his selection.

A servant approached them with goblets of wine which Aziz refused in favor of mint tea, but Julien drained a glass and promptly took another. Aziz hid his concern, but he had never seen Julien drink so avidly. Less than two hours later Aziz cautioned him that he was drinking like an infantryman, but by now Julien had fastened his attention on a young Moroccan woman with a lithe, brown body and a dazzling smile, and his friend's words went by unheeded. When he started to stagger off with her to one of the bedchambers, Aziz told him he would wait but Julien now seemed entirely beyond caring.

It was past midnight when the Moroccan girl emerged from the room and told Aziz that his friend was still fast asleep. Aziz allowed him to sleep another half hour, then paid two servants to carry him back to the palace with him on a litter. Julien was asleep most of the way home, and Aziz roused him with difficulty when they arrived at his door.

"I had no idea your unhappiness went so deeply, dear friend. Can you make your way to your bed without waking the household?"

"What do you mean?" Julien mumbled. "I'm not unhappy at all. I had a wonderful time."

"I hope I didn't make a mistake," Aziz said. "I forget about these slumbering northern passions and what a fearful thing it can be to wake them. Good night, Julien."

Julien waved him away and made an uncertain path towards his bed.

Julien found it difficult to face Claire at breakfast, not because she showed any sign of reproach, but because he felt sicker than he remembered ever feeling in his life, and he was certain every detail of last night's carousal was etched legibly into his face.

Roger was no easier to speak with, and he went through the morning's business mechanically, waiting for the midday break so he could sleep an hour or two after his light meal. He felt somewhat better by afternoon, and by evening was chuckling over the night's experience. He paid another visit to Aziz, who looked at him apprehensively.

"Don't worry, old boy, I won't let that happen to me again. I guess I must have needed it though."

"I'm not going to scold you, Julien, but it seems a pity to get yourself into a condition that makes it doubtful if you can fully appreciate the charms of the woman you're with."

"Nonsense, I may have been a little lightheaded, but she didn't find me unappreciative. That was a most enjoyable place, and I thank you for introducing me to it. I plan to go back. Will you join me? Tomorrow perhaps?"

"No thank you. I don't like to leave Fatima too often, and happily, an occasional afternoon visit to the baths is enough to ensure the tranquillity of my evenings."

"As you wish. Do you remember that beautiful Spanish girl you said had skin like the flesh of a melon? She went off with one of the other guests before I could speak with her but I think I'd like to spend some time with her when I go back."

When Julien returned to the brothel the next evening he did try to be more careful about the amount of wine he took but he was still feeling somewhat fuddled by the time the Spanish girl led him to the bedchamber. The wine seemed to make the evening so much easier for him, and she was as fine a beauty as he remembered, with a great mane of untamed hair and a body as hard as rubber. He cautioned her to see to it that he left in time to be home well before midnight, and for a little while he believed he felt free from care. He was only slightly fuzzy when he awakened the next morning, and by the time he washed and drank some fruit juice, he felt he'd be able to perform convincingly at work.

By the end of the month he had slept with all of the girls at the house who attracted him, as well as a few who did not. He counted his glasses of wine now, allowing himself no more than three at the dinner table, well mixed with water, then another three during the course of the evening, and a last one after he had finished making love.

Claire never chided him for spending most of his evenings away from home, but she started to grow more silent, and in the mornings he was sometimes aware that she had been staring at him. As gentle as ever, she continued to show her customary attentiveness, but she wasn't as eager to discuss the details of the day's affairs. She was now working a full four to six hours a day in the carpet warehouse, but the children never lacked her attention, even though Adele was a capable nurse and companion to all of them and never tired of their company.

March arrived and the family had a pleasurable outing to Mount Pellegrino, picnicking among the almond blossoms. The mountain could be seen from every part of the city, but it took them two hours to ride there in a gaudily painted cart drawn by two horses. They feasted on cold meats and pickled vegetables, and there was plenty of wine and fruit juices. Claire seemed more vivacious out in the clean spring air than Julien had seen her for a long time, running with the children and playing their games as if she were one of them. She would hug them impulsively every so often or squeeze and pinch Adele to see if she could make her giggle.

"Julien, please try not to make any plans for this Friday evening," she told him. "It's Adele's birthday, and I want us to have a celebration at home. I know she'd be very disappointed if you didn't attend."

Julien looked over to where Adele was playing with the children. How odd it seemed to him. "Is she to be fourteen, then? It's hard to believe. But yes, I can see she's very much a young woman now, isn't she?"

Adele chose not to use any cosmetics, and never dressed her hair with the ornaments that were so popular, although Claire was always making her gifts of combs and inexpensive jewelry. She dressed no differently from Adelaide. Claire sometimes even bought them duplicate robes, but her body had definitely rounded into a woman's shape.

"She'll be wanting to marry and start a family of her own soon," Julien said. "Will you mind losing her?"

"Of course I'd mind. You can't imagine how much I depend on her. But she tells me she doesn't want to marry. At least not yet."

Adele looked towards them from where she was plaiting Adelaide's hair with almond blossoms, and smiled sweetly, as if to confirm Claire's words.

As the afternoon wore on and it grew time to leave, Claire stretched out on the grass next to Julien and appeared thoughtful. They looked at each other quietly for a long time. "I wish we could be like this forever," he said.

"I wish you could be as happy as you've made me, Julien." She let him take her hand and press it to his lips.

Adele's birthday party was as festive as any given for the children. Adelaide watched for everyone's birthday and insisted they all be celebrated with a party, and she loved Adele almost as much as she did her mother.

Aziz and Fatima arrived with their son Ahmad, and Thomas Browne appeared too, but he stayed only a short time because the Palatine Chapel was nearing completion and made heavy demands on him. They played games and sang songs before dinner, and then sat down to a meal of Adele's favorite dishes, including stuffed eggplant and fried squash. Afterwards they ate quantities of rich cakes trimmed with brightly tinted sugar creams, and everyone, including all the children except Nigel, was given cups of sweet muscat wine to toast Adele with. Then it was time to distribute presents.

Everyone had brought something for Adele, but Claire had bought gifts for everyone there as well, and by the time all the combs and scarves and ribbons had been passed around and admired, the evening had slipped away. Julien found he was greatly amused by his first social evening at home in a long while, and it made him realize how many evenings of late he'd spent carousing, but his twinge of remorse was light and only momentary.

He stayed up to read long after the others had gone to bed, and as he poured himself another glass of wine, he realized he'd drunk much less than usual. When he finally turned in to sleep, he felt once again the pang of loneliness that always reached him in his bed, and he debated whether or not to get up for another glass of wine to help him sleep.

As he lay there wakefully, he thought he heard a faint sound and then he was aware of another presence in the room. His eyes widened and in the darkness he could make out a figure moving towards the bed. He could feel his heart begin to thump against his chest, and the sound was distinct. His lips formed the word "Claire."

She slipped into the bed noiselessly and his arms quickly fastened around her as his lips searched for hers, and then he realized abruptly that it wasn't Claire, but Adele in his arms. She returned his kiss passionately, and they embraced hotly for several minutes before he could speak. "Adele, this is Claire's house too. You know this isn't right. You mustn't let me take advantage of you."

"You're not taking advantage of me. I love you with all my heart, and I'll have no other man but you."

"But think of Claire. You know we can't hope to keep this from her."

Adele remained silent but pressed herself a little more closely to him.

"Are you telling me she knows? Yes, of course she does. You wouldn't have dared come here unless—" His body rippled with a shudder of excitement.

"Do you like me well enough to make love to me?"

"Adele, you're beautiful, but it's still wrong."

"Because I was a whore?"

"You were never a whore, Adele. Don't ever let me hear you say that. You suffered a great deal, but you must forget all that now. You promised me you would."

"Then, make love to me, Julien. I owe my whole life to you." She gripped his hips with her hands and pulled him closer.

"She does know, doesn't she?"

"Know? She knows I love you. How could she not? I thought you must know it too."

"But how could she—"

"She loves you even more than I do, Julien, and she wants you to be happy. But this wasn't her idea. It was mine."

"It can't work. What if you become pregnant? The children. Adelaide is at an age when it would never do."

"If I had your child it would make me happy beyond my dreams. And don't worry about the children knowing. Children don't care about such things. Not if they're as happy as yours. If I had to, I'd live in the harem while I carried your child, but I don't think it would be necessary."

The insistent urging of her body had aroused him to a point where he knew he was beyond argument. He uttered a groan and began to cover her slim body with kisses, while she stuffed her fist into her mouth to stifle her screams of pleasure. Not since his first night in Claire's arms had he experienced such a night of sweet, abandoned lovemaking. And Adele, awakening to the first experience of sex that carried joy instead of fear released herself to him in a torrent.

A week later a messenger arrived at Julien's studio. After a moment Julien recognized him as one of the men who had carried him home from the whorehouse the night he went there with Aziz. The man was ill at ease, and mumbled a string of formalities until Julien insisted he get to the point.

"My master has missed your visits. He hopes that nothing has happened to offend you, and asks for the privilege of being your host again. We have six new girls, as beautiful as any in Palermo, and we look forward to your approval of them."

Julien smiled. The message was not unexpected. "Tell your master that as a host he is unequalled in Christendom, and I would not hesitate to recommend his establishment to any of my friends in need of his services. But as for myself, I'm afraid my evenings are occupied with pressing domestic business." He reached into his purse and withdrew some coins. "Here, this is for you. Give the rest to the girls and tell them to buy themselves something pretty." The man prostrated himself before Julien and withdrew singing hymns to his countless virtues.

Julien had already accomplished a good deal of work that morning, and went to his window to look out at the courtyard below. It was his habit when he worked to refresh himself periodically by gazing down at the palm trees and the play of water in the fountains between them. He felt very good about himself today. "How lucky I am to have such an extraordinary wife," he reminded himself again. He looked forward to every evening spent with Claire as much as he did the nights spent with Adele. What if the arrangement were unorthodox? It was still less bizarre than many of the domestic arrangements of Sicilians he knew of. The Greeks and Arabs had their eunuchs and pages, and more than a few Normans and Lombards seemed to have begun to find the eastern vice attractive. The harems were filled with concubines, and the whorehouse keepers were rich. It seemed to him the only people who might still observe the standards he respected in his youth were either people he wasn't likely to meet or people who couldn't afford any other arrangement. England was different, of course. He knew his father Nigel surely would have been shocked by his ménage, but that was another country.

When Julien had last seen his confessor, the old man appeared frankly bored by Julien's dramatic introduction to his recitation of this recent sin, and showed some interest in what Julien had to say only when he presented him with a series of questions intended to ascertain whether Julien were guilty of heresy. He appeared satisfied by the answers he received and gave Julien absolution, a blessing, and the kiss of peace with no reprimand or other reference to his domestic arrangements.

Julien admitted to himself that he never felt more content. He drank less now, and Roger seemed more pleased with him than ever. He had just given Julien a piece of choice land on the city's outskirts in lieu of the small house he had promised for Gay. Now Roger was hinting that he wanted to build Julien a small pleasure palace on it, similar to the string of elegant villas he kept for himself around the countryside. Julien's woolgathering was interrupted by Roger's entrance.

"Julien, how long will it take you to get ready to leave?"

It seemed like a cold fist had gripped his gut. "Whenever you say."

He knew that Roger would have to return to the mainland soon and that spring was a logical time to leave, but he now loathed the prospect of accompanying him on yet another campaign to punish the insurrectionists. Roger caught something of his mood.

"I wouldn't ask you with me if it weren't important. I'm not particularly keen on leaving Palermo myself just now, but it's essential that I be in Salerno before the month is out. Rainulf is ill with a mysterious fever, and if he dies I want to be ready to move in before the traitors find another leader for their rebellion."

"I wasn't thinking just of my own comfort," Julien answered. "We've never been so busy with internal affairs—the new assizes you were preparing, the plans for a standardized currency, the last details for your Palatine Chapel . . ."

"They'll all have to wait. But once this mess on the mainland is cleared up, I swear all my energies will be devoted to Sicilian interests."

"Is it true that Innocent is calling a new Lateran Council?"

"It's just a rumor so far, but it would be logical," Roger said. "I would assume he's anxious to consolidate his position now that his papacy is no longer questioned."

"It will be interesting to see if it has any more significance than the first Lateran Council," Julien said. "I can't think of anything that one accomplished except to embarrass a lot of priests who found their marriages annulled."

Roger laughed. "We'll see. I don't have to ask you if everything is well with your family. You wear their happiness on your face."

Julien colored as he smirked. "Yes, they've never been better. It hurts to leave them this time. But no matter. I'll clear up my affairs at once and be ready to leave when you are."

"I hope this will be my last trip to the mainland, and if there is to be a peace negotiated, I can't imagine doing it without you. I'm calling a meeting of my curia this afternoon. Try to attend."

He turned and left as unceremoniously as he had entered. Julien looked at the pile of papers and books on his desk and sighed. It would have been such an important season if only he'd had more time. The bureaucracy would keep things moving smoothly while they were gone, he had no doubt, but the results he and Roger and so many others had been working so hard for would have to wait for God alone knew how long.

Julien's leavetaking of his family was tender but abrupt. They too knew it was only a matter of time before he would have to go again, and they were resigned to it. On the eve of his departure Claire's good night kiss was a lingering one, warm enough to reignite his hopes. She sensed it, and as she drew away, she glanced towards his bedchamber and lowered her eyes. It was her way of indicating that Adele would soon be with him to offer her farewell. The girl was not long in coming to him. Julien made love to her with a passion that was punishing in its intensity. She stayed in his bed until dawn, waiting with him until they heard the first sounds coming from the servants' quarters before he would release her.

Robert was waiting at the Salerno dock when the swift dhow carrying Roger and Julien pulled in. Julien was pleased to find his old friend looking so optimistic after the gloom with which he had greeted him last year. Roger's greeting to Robert confirmed the pride that he felt in his chancellor. The entire western portion of the kingdom had repeatedly proven its satisfaction with Robert's sensitive administration.

Roger waved aside the litters waiting for his party, and started towards the chancellor's palace on foot, anxious to use this opportunity to chat informally with Robert and bring each other up to date on recent affairs. "What of the second Lateran Council?" Roger asked. "Has there been any word yet on it?"

"Yes there has," Robert answered cautiously. "I'm afraid you figure rather prominently in it. Innocent devoted one common excommunication to you and your sons, as well as all the bishops consecrated by Anacletus."

"Well, that's not very new, is it?" Roger's voice was light, but he was frowning. "Does he expect this new excommunication to be more powerful than the last? What else?"

"He excommunicated Arnold of Brescia too, and reserved some of his choicest anathema for him. It seems Arnold is now the chief enemy of the Church instead of just its chief critic."

"That doesn't surprise me either," Roger said. "Of course I don't share Arnold's political views, but I can guess it's his religious zeal more than anything else that Rome finds indigestible. Go on."

"They banned usury, and tournaments, and now monks are prohibited from studying law or medicine. That sounds like Bernard's doing. It was well attended though. He had five hundred bishops there."

"And against heresies. Did he come out with a strong statement?"

"No, he didn't. There again, it was just a confirmation of earlier statements."

"That's where he should have taken his firmest stand. I'm surprised Bernard didn't demand a declaration with some teeth in it. The new sects are gathering strength fast in the north countries. I had even hoped that he would set down some tight rules of procedure for the election of a pope. God knows it's needed, but he probably doesn't want his own election looked into more closely. So much for the Lateran Council. What of Rainulf? Does he still live?"

"Yes, but barely. He can't last much longer."

"Good."

Julien started and looked at Roger in astonishment. True, Rainulf was an enemy who had been forgiven by Roger and then turned against him again many times, but nonetheless he was greatly loved by his subjects and he had proved himself as brave a man in battle as Julien had ever seen. Roger, who was so genuinely touched at the death of Lothair, now seemed to discredit himself by exulting in the approaching death of this other enemy, who happened as well to be his brother-in-law and onetime close friend.

Roger caught Julien's reaction and snapped at him. "You find me hard, do you? What about my mercy to him time after time after he broke his sacred oath? Does it mean nothing to you that breaking such an oath makes him untrue to his God as well as to me? I've watched you, Julien, and I'm seen how often your stomach turns at the sight of bloodshed. I don't like it either, but blame *him* for it, then, damn him. I know his people love him, but the harm he has done them outrages me."

It was the first time Roger had turned on him in someone else's presence, and Julien felt dreadfully shamed. But Robert was tactfully silent.

The confirmation of Rainulf's death reached them a week later, and it was accompanied by reports of universal mourning and heartfelt grief throughout eastern Apulia. Julien watched Roger's jaw set stubbornly as he heard the report, and he thought he could read jealousy in his steely eyes. Was it, he wondered, because Rainulf was a warrior in the tradition of Roger's ancestors?

It seemed so contradictory, because Roger took his greatest pride in his skill at outmaneuvering his enemies.

The royal mainland army was now gathered in force at Salerno and Roger decided it was time to make a move. While he was still debating his first point of attack, word arrived that Innocent had massed an army of a thousand knights plus numerous foot soldiers, and was even now moving south to challenge Roger. With him were Robert of Capua and Rainulf's younger brother, Richard. Roger lost no time in sending scouts ahead to meet Innocent and ask for a parley.

On that same evening in May, Vesuvius erupted for the first time in one hundred years, and it was said to be the most awesome eruption since Pompeii had been buried eleven hundred years earlier. Benevento, Salerno, and Capua were darkened by a curtain of ash that terrified its citizens, but fortunately the only loss of life was in a few remote and sparsely populated villages near its slopes. The next day when the threat subsided, there wasn't a fortune teller or astrologer on the southern mainland who wasn't consulted for advice on the portent of this significant event. The prognostication offered Roger was invariably the same: "The throne of St. Peter is in danger." Roger listened to them all without comment, then sent messengers to the north to find out if Innocent's soothsayers were telling him the same thing.

Not unexpectedly, Innocent agreed to a parley, and it was decided that the papal party would be met at San Germano, first by royal emissaries and immediately after by Roger, accompanied by his son Duke Roger and Julien.

The trio of Sicilians lost no time getting to the elegant bishop's palace of San Germano, where Innocent was waiting with a retinue of nearly three dozen followers. Julien saw Roger blanch when he recognized the treacherous Robert of Capua at Innocent's elbow, but young Duke Roger touched his father's arm reassuringly, and it seemed to calm him.

After a round of formal addresses, they took seats. Robert of Capua made certain he was on Innocent's right and facing Roger, but he kept his eyes cast down as Innocent spoke. "Before we can proceed with other matters, we have first to settle the matter of our beloved son Prince Robert's duchy. We ask that all lands to which he has title be restored to him by Roger de Hauteville and that he be recognized once again as the rightful ruler of Capua."

Roger couldn't quite conceal his astonishment at the boldness of the request. He leaned forward until he was within inches of Robert of Capua's averted gaze, and answered coolly, "Never."

"Duke Roger, we ask that you do this as a testament of your good faith. Once you have satisfactorily established that faith in my eyes, you know I am only too anxious to discuss the question of your royal crown."

"No man can point to an instance in which I've shown bad faith to anyone I've promised my loyalty to. It is rather Robert of Capua's repeated and perverse faithlessness to me that makes it impossible he ever again be granted the trust of peer or suzerain."

"I demand this of you, Roger."

"You cannot command me to move against my Christian conscience. In the eyes of all Christendom, in this affair I have absolute right on my side. Solemn vows were broken." He emphasized the last four words separately.

"Are you aware that we have an army of a thousand knights and over four thousand footmen camped nearby?"

"Threats will not make an honest man of Robert of Capua."

"Your refusal of reconcilement tries my patience, Roger."

"*I* refuse to reconcile? For eight years I've given that vile traitor every chance imaginable to make and keep peace. Each time he rebelled, I forgave him and took him to my bosom again, and the snake never hesitated to turn against me the moment he saw the opportunity to do so. He is a patent danger to my kingdom, and I can brook no new dangers."

"You have no kingdom unless we say you do."

Roger's jaw clenched and he turned to his companions. "This is getting us nowhere. Your Holiness, if you will meet with me again tomorrow, perhaps we can review the business at hand more dispassionately."

"As you wish. Before you leave, I feel I need to remind you of my office. You cannot fight divine will. Truth is adamant, and will not be changed."

Roger smiled broadly as he bowed and withdrew.

Duke Roger seemed crestfallen by this initial exchange. "Was it wise, father, to leave before you even touched upon his confirmation of your crown?"

"It would be pointless. He's determined to structure the terms before any discussion can be held. My best chance is to keep at him every day on the chance that he'll meet me once without Robert at his side. You can hardly expect Innocent to change his terms with Robert pressing at his elbow."

The next day the two parties met again, and Julien was disappointed to see Robert of Capua take the same seat at Innocent's right. This discussion proved equally unproductive. They met for eight days. Robert of Capua was always present, and Innocent refused to budge from his demand that his ally be reinstated before he would discuss any confirmation of Roger's crown. It appeared to be a hopeless stalemate.

At the end of the eighth day's meeting, Roger turned at the door on his way out. "Your Holiness, I'd like a brief recess if it doesn't inconvenience you too greatly. Some small business has come up that needs my attention. A fortress to the north of here is up in arms. It appears they listened to the rantings of some young hotheads, and they're in a state of anarchy. I must take my soldiers there to restore order before the good citizens are made to suffer needlessly. I doubt the operation will take more than a week or two. May I propose that we meet again here in a fortnight? I promise in return for your considerateness that when we resume our discussion, I'll try harder to let myself be guided by your views."

Innocent was startled, but he could do nothing but accept.

"What's this all about?" Julien asked as soon as they were out of the palace. "I haven't heard anything about new uprisings in the north, have you, Roger?" he asked the duke.

Young Roger smiled and winked at his father. "We had an interesting chat after breakfast. I think we're all a bit tired of looking at Robert's smug face."

"I know the way that bastard thinks as well as he does himself," Roger said. "This time I'm going to give him enough rope to hang himself. I'm sure Innocent can't be budged unless the game changes."

Julien responded excitedly. The cunning look in Roger's eye was one he knew well. "Don't keep me in suspense. Tell me what you plan to do."

"It's not so much what we plan as what we allow Robert to plan. His fortunes have varied considerably over the years, but never has he found himself sitting as pretty as he does now. He has the double advantage of an angry pope on his side and a much larger army than he could possibly put together himself, and all within a day's march of his duchy."

"I see," Julien said. "You think that once we're away he'll try to get Innocent to put him back on his throne by force."

"He'd be a fool not to try," Roger answered. "For one thing, think of all the time Innocent has spent these last years in the shadow of Henry the Proud and Lothair, begging them to install him on his throne and becoming increasingly bitter at their attitude. I'd expect him to be somewhat favorably disposed to Robert's demands. Also, you know what happens with an army the size of theirs if it's not employed. The men get restless and unpredictable."

"Meantime, we're not going north at all. We follow them until the time is right to strike," Duke Roger said.

"Exactly," his father agreed. "Robert may know this territory as well as we do, but the papal army doesn't. We also have the advantage of surprise."

That same day Roger and his son led the Sicilian army towards the north, taking care to pass as closely as possible to the papal camp so that their departure would be unmistakable. As soon as they reached the mountain just outside San Germano, the troops were deployed through the forest to wait for a move from the papal army. It was a short wait. The next morning they saw the papists break camp and start to move towards Capua. The Sicilians reassembled their forces and followed close behind, keeping to the cover of forest.

Roger's army watched village after village fired as the papal army left an appalling trail of dismembered bodies behind them. The papists had been hastily recruited and were mostly unprofessionals from northern Europe who were attracted to Innocent's campaign by its promise of rich booty. Roger saw to it that his soldiers visited each village the papists passed through, not only to see if any of the surviving villagers could be helped, but also to whet his soldiers' appetites for vengeance upon the aliens who had been so ruthlessly despoiling their homeland. By the time the papal army had reached the town of Galluccio nestled in the foothills outside Capua, Roger's soldiers were seething with their passion for reprisal.

They saturated the mountains that ringed Galluccio, cutting off any chance of exit, and when they judged the northerners had finished soaking the village streets with blood, they struck.

The papal army watched with horror as young Duke Roger burst upon them from ambush with a thousand disciplined knights. They put up a brief struggle against the Sicilians and then turned heel in face of the first resistance they'd seen. Thousands were drowned in their pell mell flight across the Garigliano River, and the Sicilians still pursued them. Robert of Capua lost no time in taking to his horse as soon as he saw which way the battle was going and fled to the safety of the north, leaving the increasingly confused Innocent and his convoy of cardinals to the haphazard defenses of the few troops still left them. It would have been hard to imagine a more total disaster for the papists.

Innocent was taken prisoner together with his cardinals, and with exaggerated politeness they were escorted to a safe shelter in the nearby town of Mignano. Roger, now determined to squeeze as much personal satisfaction as possible out of the situation, sent the pope an obsequious petition, begging him for the favor of an audience.

Innocent's haughty refusal came back at once. Roger repeated his request on the second day, praying that the "Divine Will" be bent just slightly in his direction, but Innocent refused again. His champions had deserted him, his troops were slaughtered, he was a prisoner in hostile territory, and still he persisted in behaving as if his command over Roger was absolute.

On the third day he was still unable to conceive of how powerless he was, but he agreed to see Roger. Roger entered his quarters casually, asked politely after his comfort, and presented him with a formal petition. "No need to hurry," he told Innocent, "but I suggest you talk it over with your cardinals before you make a decision."

Roger suspected his cardinals had fewer illusions about his awe of papal power. He was correct. They prevailed upon Innocent to be reasonable, and the struggle between the two men was over. At once the pope sent for Roger, who had been waiting nearby with Julien and his son, confident that peace was at hand.

Innocent greeted them, shaking with suppressed rage. "I am your prisoner, then? You would dare?"

Roger knelt and kissed his hand. "What an unthinkable idea. You are my guest. A *king* can express only love and loyalty to his pope. The attitudes of lesser mortals are considerably less predictable, of course."

Innocent blanched. "You make light of your conduct. Very well, then. Let us discuss terms."

Roger raised his hand towards Julien, who produced a scroll he'd spent an entire morning preparing. "I thought I could save us discussion by offering a list of our terms. I'm sure you will see that there is absolutely nothing here that you can disagree with."

"Really!" Innocent said icily, taking the document. "That remains to be seen, doesn't it?" He started to read. "On the earliest possible date King Roger of Sicily is to receive absolution and his excommunications are to be lifted entirely. He will be invested in his kingdom, according to the rites of the Church." He turned to Roger. "I was ready to give you this long ago, if you'd only been reasonable."

"I thank you with all my heart. Please read on."

"King Roger's eldest son Roger is to be confirmed as duke of Apulia and his second son Alfonso as prince of Capua. What!"

"Yes, the dear boy's going to be so pleased. I've already sent for him. The citizens of Capua really love him, you know."

"That's impossible."

"Your Holiness, it's impossible that they not have a prince. Alfonso is still a lad, but he'd never run off in battle and leave you to fend for yourself. You'll find him a strong ally."

"I cannot."

"Of course you can. And I in my turn will swear homage to the Holy See and pay full reverence to my pope. There's no point disturbing your cardinals again, but I'm sure they're ready to congratulate you on receiving Palermo, the largest and wealthiest city in Christendom, back in your camp."

Innocent sighed and sat down wearily. "I would prefer that Palermo belong to a less powerful kingdom with a less obstinate ruler." He reached his arms out to Roger and embraced him, then embraced the duke and Julien in turn. "Peace."

Julien was feeling giddy as the three Sicilians walked back to the royal tent. At the entrance he leaped impulsively and clicked his heels. "We actually did it! I feel like getting drunk for a week."

"Calm down, my friend," Roger said. "Before you get carried away, let me remind you of eastern Apulia. Not till I take back that part of my kingdom held by Rainulf will I really feel that total victory is ours. I know it won't be long now, but I want you both to see to it that the men keep celebrations down to a minimum. I can't have them too relaxed, as long as there's more fighting to do."

"Yes, I agree," his son replied. "Then too, as long as Innocent's still with us, he's bound to be sensitive about his defeat. Instead of rubbing his nose in it, it's time we mended our fences."

"Spoken like a true prince," his father answered proudly.

Julien had sobered quickly at Roger's words. "I think you need an impressive public display of your peace with Innocent," he said. "Something to dramatize it for the people."

"An excellent idea," Roger replied. "I'll suggest to His Holiness at once that we visit Benevento together. Since it's technically a papal city even though it lies in our territory, our joint appearance there will give some meaning to the truce."

Innocent readily agreed, and when they arrived at Benevento the citizens could scarcely restrain their joy. It was the first promise of a lasting peace they had seen in a long time. Roger was feeling particularly magnanimous by now, so he made a point of visiting all the great churches of the city and distributing liberal endowments to all the monastic houses. Julien attended him on these pilgrimages, making his prayers for a speedy return to Palermo as fervent as any he could remember.

At Santa Sofia a murmur went up when Roger prostrated himself fully before the altar as the humblest penitent. Were it not a church, they would have cheered. Julien grew increasingly amused by the response to what he suspected were no more than Roger's most daring theatrics. He strolled about the ancient church, visiting the side chapels filled with artistic treasure that dated back as far as the days of Rome's empire.

His eye was caught by the sight of a slim form raised on a dais before the altar of one of the smaller chapels. It was the figure of a saint, probably her embalmed relics, dressed in nun's clothing and lying on her side. The position reminded him first of the relics and statue of St. Cecilia that he had seen at Rome and was impressed by, but then something else about the lightness and petite stature of the figure intrigued him. He stepped into the chapel for a closer look. The saint's form was raised almost to eye level. It seemed odd that she should have her back turned to the worshippers, but then he remembered that St. Cecilia did too.

He realized abruptly what had most intrigued him about her. The saint's diminutive body seemed exactly like Adele's. He looked at the tiny wax hand that lay on the skirt with a rosary twined through the fingers, and it seemed he was looking at an exact replica of Adele's hand. A surge of nostalgia suffused him, and his eyes misted. A young priest approached him with a friendly smile. "A local saint. These are the preserved relics of Saint Genovefa, a virgin and martyr of Benevento."

Julien acknowledged the priest's cordiality and was then embarrassed by the tears still in his eyes. "My eyes dazzle. She died young."

"She was just fourteen. Come closer if you wish." Julien accepted the invitation and stepped around the dais for a look at the saint's face. He recoiled at once in horror. Beneath the wimple, a naked skull stared back at him.

"She used to have a silver mask," the priest said, "but when the imperial armies passed through the city, it disappeared mysteriously."

Julien took his eyes away and shuddered. He realized his body was covered with a thin coating of chill sweat. "I'm sorry. I just didn't expect . . ."

The priest was looking at him strangely. "Would you care to lie down? I think you've taken some bad air."

"No, I'll be all right. I'm just tired. May I make a gift to your church for the replacement of her mask? I'll have the money sent to you at once."

"That's extraordinarily generous," the priest beamed. "Please tell me your name, and I'll see to it a Mass is said for you in this chapel every week and your name blessed in all our daily prayers." Julien told him his name and thanked him again for his courtesy. He rejoined Roger at the main altar, but his knees wouldn't stop trembling.

In early August, Naples renewed its vows of fealty to Roger. It was a city that had been woefully disheartened by the loss of its great Duke Sergius, and the people had suffered miserably during the long months of siege.

Innocent finally returned to Rome, allowing Roger the time to make plans for the last step of his campaign. He was determined now to snuff the last embers of revolt in the territories that had been held by Rainulf.

Roger led his army first towards Troia, which was Rainulf's last capital and where he had died. The town's capitulation was so rapid it was obvious they had just been waiting for the chance to welcome Roger back. Julien was delighted. It looked like his long months away from home were finally dragging to a close, and that he could even look forward to being in Palermo by the end of September if all continued to go as well. He almost reeled in shock when he heard Roger's answer to the envoys.

"Tell your people that I will never enter their city as long as the traitor Rainulf rests there."

The envoys exchanged desperate glances. What Roger demanded was appalling, but they were helpless. Julien turned his face from them, embarrassed.

"Your Majesty must instruct us what we must do to comply with his wishes. We cannot disobey you." But their voices were bitter.

"You mean you dare not," Roger persisted. "I want Rainulf's lieutenant, the man who was his partner in treason, to be the one to break open the tomb himself. Then I want Rainulf's body to be dragged through the streets by his officers so that all may see the reward of treason. After that, whatever is left of his body is to be sunk in a cesspool outside the city walls."

Julien's horror at these words was as great as the townspeoples'. The insult to the dead was too dreadful even for a man of Rainulf's repeated treachery. And apart from Julien's dismay at this breach in the accepted code for treating a fallen enemy, he remembered that Roger had never dared face Rainulf in battle while he was alive.

"Go on. Bring your people my message. You're getting off cheaply," Roger continued. "It would be just as easy for me to put the city to the torch and let your blood run through its streets. Now go. My army will remain here until my command is executed." The envoys left sorrowfully, but at dawn news reached camp that Roger's horrible request had been fulfilled.

"I still won't set foot in that city again," Roger said. "I never even want to hear its name mentioned to me."

Julien saw young Duke Roger lower his head in shame. He felt drawn close to the youth and wished he could tell him how unlike his father he felt this behavior was, but he feared too that this was a side of his king that he might see again.

Roger was still in a foul mood. "We have important affairs at hand," he roared. "Tell the engineers to get busy building siege towers. We march on Bari at once."

Julien's heart sank. He remembered how long the siege of Bari by the imperial forces had lasted, and theirs was a much larger army.

Julien's misgivings were not ill-founded. The siege of Bari lasted for fully two months. Thirty towers set up by Roger pounded at its walls incessantly until it was forced to surrender. Terms were quickly negotiated, and they appeared to be merciful, calling mostly for an exchange of prisoners, but Julien suspected Roger's still vengeful mood would not be satisfied. Then too, there was still the bitter memory of the hanging and dismemberment of the three hundred choice Saracens by the imperialists that Julien had witnessed when he entered Bari to meet Lothair.

They had scarcely taken over the city when one of Roger's knights who had been held prisoner there made a petition to his king. He claimed he had been blinded by Prince Jacquintus' direct orders during the siege of the city, in violation of all laws governing the rights of captives. Roger gloated triumphantly. Now he had the excuse he needed to make an example of the ringleaders. The deposed prince and ten of his councillors were given a public hanging, while still another ten were blinded.

Duke Roger saw how distressed Julien was by Roger's vindictiveness, and called on him later that evening. "There's nothing more we can do about Bari," the duke said, "but I took a solemn vow at Troia that I will prevail upon my father to grant Rainulf a Christian burial. He won't refuse me for very long, I promise you. He's made his point, and I think I can convince him now that he does his name no credit by behaving as he has towards Rainulf's corpse."

"He's changed so much," Julien answered. "I can understand cruelty on the field of battle, and I've learned to expect that sort of cruelty from his enemies, but I always believed my king was above such petty rancor."

"He'll be himself again when we return to Sicily," young Roger said. "He's been disappointed so often with the treachery of his mainland nobles that I believe it's maddened him. But once he's back home and involved with administrative affairs, he'll be the man we both knew again."

Julien recalled that Roger loved to say revenge was a dish best eaten cold, and he was doubtful, so he could only say he hoped the duke was right, but he was pleased by the gentleness of this redoubtable young warrior. My sons, he reflected, will grow up under Roger III, and there will be no finer king anywhere.

It had been an incredibly fortunate year for Roger. The former dynasts of Capua, Naples, and Bari were dead or exiled, and Roger's one dangerous native rival was exiled in the north with little chance of forming another alliance. The kingdom was completely his, and his rights to it had been legitimized by the pope. The last forces Lothair had left to maintain imperial power had been stationed at Troia, and they lost no time heading for the north as soon as they heard of Roger's approach. In Germany it would take a miracle for the king to mount another expedition against the south, especially since his own position as ruler was so precarious. But most warming to Roger was the recognition that his heir, the young duke Roger, was a favorite with his subjects. Even many of the rebels who strongly resented Norman domination were swept up by the popular enthusiasm for the handsome, soldierly duke.

The city of Salerno wanted to declare a week's holiday when the royal forces returned, but Roger insisted that celebration be kept to a minimum. He announced that he wanted to hold a domesday instead, dispossessing all his enemies of the land they held and holding them to the oath instituted by the first Normans that they be exiled "beyond the mountains."

Thomas Browne was waiting for them in Salerno when they got there. Roger had sent for him as the best man in the kingdom to conduct a domesday accounting. Roger, together with Julien, Robert, and a half dozen of the city's elders, sat down to an initial meeting with Thomas. Thomas had balded rapidly in the last few years, and Julien thought he looked overworked. His face had filled out as had his middle, but it looked as if there were no bones beneath the flesh.

Thomas went through the formalities of greeting his king as if he were mumbling his way through a children's prayer, and then proceeded to what was on his mind. "Roger, I'm as anxious to start an accounting of your lands as you are, but you left me in Palermo with so much unfinished business." He sounded distinctly petulant. "Since it's almost impossible to see you on business anymore, may we go over some things as long as we're both here? I have a portfolio of affairs that require the royal approval."

"Of course, of course." Roger's voice was testy, but he had enormous admiration for Thomas's skills. "Did you bring the designs for the new currency? I'm sure you'd like to have that assignment over and done with."

"I brought everything I've been working on with me," Thomas answered.

"I'm calling this new coin a ducat," Roger told the councillors. "I wanted to name it for the duchy of Apulia. Did you handle the dating as I asked?"

"Yes sir. The coin will read *AN R X*. In the tenth year of your reign. I'm afraid that's not going to sit well with Innocent."

"I didn't intend it to. It's just as well to remind him that I consider his recognition of me no more than a confirmation. Wait till he sees how I date my one-third ducat. Did you bring the drawings?"

"I have all of them right here." He held up the drawing for their inspection. It bore on the obverse side a Latin inscription surrounding a Greek cross.

"That's to please my Greek subjects," Roger said. "But look here at the reverse. I know not many of you read Arabic, but it says 'struck in the city of Palermo in the year 535 of the Hegira.' "

"Oh yes, the Church will love that one," said Julien. "I don't expect your ducats to be circulated much in the rest of Europe."

"Don't be so sure," Roger snapped. "The ducat will be a beautiful, honest coin, and I intend to make it one that can be depended on anywhere in the world. And with our trade, it will certainly be widely circulated."

They looked next at the full ducat, which was already having its first proofs struck in Brindisi. The obverse bore a likeness of Roger in full Byzantine regalia, with his son Roger in full military dress standing by his side. The reverse was more of a surprise. Earlier money had borne a likeness of St. Peter to indicate the government's vassalage to the Holy See. The new coin bore a likeness of Christ Pantocrator, the Omnipotent. Roger was delivering his message unequivocally. "Approve the proofs as soon as they're right, and start production of both coins at once. What else?"

"The Palatine Chapel. I've just a few small details to see to it when I get back. You should be using it before spring. The water clock was just installed over the entrance, and the consensus is that it is superior even to the famous one of Charlemagne's. But there is grumbling among some of your Muslim subjects about the ceiling and some of the murals."

"Really! What the Devil are *they* grumbling about? It's not a mosque."

"No, but they find it a bit too modern, and they're upset that you used Arab artists to work on it. The artists I engaged have been under the influence of the new schools in Persia, and the Muslims aren't accustomed to having representations of people, beasts, and other of God's creations executed by Muslims. They say you should have used Greek artists for your sacrileges."

"Too bad. It's my chapel and I'll employ whom I choose. They should know by now that I find orthodoxy tiresome. What about Cefalu?"

"The great mosaic of Christ Pantocrator is completed, but it will be another year or two before the church is ready for consecration. Two of Innocent's cardinals have seen it, and they've sent a report back to the pope that it will undoubtedly be the greatest work of art to commemorate his reign. That, at least, should make him happy."

"His reign indeed! Still, it wouldn't hurt to make an occasional gesture of good will towards the old man," Roger said. "I suppose I do ride him a bit hard at times. See to it he's sent the finest timber in Sicily to repair the roof of St. John Lateran. I heard it was falling around his ears. Anything else?"

"Of course. I'll need a good deal more time with you."

"Well, hurry it then." He groaned. "Oh God, I'm so tired, and I'm afraid I'm in a bad mood too. Let's continue this tomorrow. Julien, is there anything else that can't wait?"

"There are some letters that may amuse you. I have one here from Bernard, dated two months ago."

"That's definitely not on my list of priorities. Oh very well, let's have it."

Julien unrolled the letter and read: *"Far and wide the fame of your magnificence has spread over the earth; what limits are there untouched by the glory of your name?"*

"Stop it, stop it!" Roger howled. "I'm about to throw up. Just tell me what he wants."

"Well, he does go on that way for quite a while, but the only thing he asks for is a Cistercian monastery in Sicily."

"In Sicily! Oh no. Over my dead body! Still, I suppose I must do something for him. I know. Write him at once, Julien. Tell him that because we know of the Cistercian disposition towards solitude and contemplation, we're donating a parcel of land for a Cistercian monastery to be built as soon as possible . . . in Calabria. Do you think Filocastro is sufficiently remote for the Cistercian temperament, Julien?" Julien was laughing as he made some notes.

"I think Bernard must have his eye on the St. John of the Hermits you're building," Thomas said. "There's not an order in the Church that wouldn't love to have a branch in that location."

"Certainly. Right in the shadow of the royal palace, where their spies can keep their eyes on all that goes on. No, thank you. I'm still giving it to the Benedictines. Gentlemen, I beg you to leave me now. I've had enough surprises for one day."

Julien and Thomas worked harder than they ever had before, but it was more than a month later before they could think of embarking for Sicily. Julien received a new satisfaction in learning that young Duke Roger had prevailed upon his father regarding disposition of Rainulf's corpse. The body was taken from the cesspool and given a quiet Christian burial. Roger was altogether more relaxed, now that he could concentrate on the administration of a peaceful kingdom, and he recognized that he needed to assuage where he could any old bitterness his former enemies might still harbor towards him.

A new tribute, more complimentary than he could have expected, arrived in a letter from his old foe, Peter of Cluny, who had so energetically opposed him years earlier.

> *Sicily, Apulia, Calabria, before you the refuge and the robber dens of the Saracens, are now through you an abode of peace . . . they are become a magnificent kingdom, ruled by a second Solomon; would that also poor and unfortunate Tuscany, and the lands about it, might be joined to your dominion and enter the peace of your kingdom! Then they might be no more regardless of God and man; towns, villages, and the churches of God might cease to be delivered up to slaughter; pilgrims, monks, clerics, abbots, bishops, and archbishops might no longer be captured, plundered, slain by the misdoers.*

There was a cool gray fog laced with rain shrouding the harbor at Palermo when their ship drifted in, and Julien was not surprised to see that only a few officials turned out to welcome them in such unpleasant weather. The palace had been decked with banners as usual, but these were now whipped sodden and only the strings of lanterns managed to cheer their homecoming more successfully.

Julien raced through the corridors of the palace, scarcely bothering to answer the respectful greetings accorded him by the people he passed. The main hall of his apartment was ominously still. Then a door opened, and he rubbed his eyes to be sure of what he saw. His old friend and tutor Ralf was walking towards him with arms outspread.

It seemed to Julien that Ralf had become an old man in the ten years since he had last seen him. He shaved his head now, and the stark, granite features of his face were in bolder relief. He was gaunt, all skin and sinew, and his movements were sure but unhurried, deliberate.

Julien buried his face on his friend's shoulder for a moment. "Ralf! Is it really you? How? What brought you here?"

Ralf released him, but clung to his hand and kept it pressed to his chest as he spoke. "There's time for that later. Your family. They're in Furci. Julien, I'm afraid I have bad news for you."

"Claire! Quickly, tell me."

"No, Julien, Claire is fine, and so are the children. It's Adele. She died six weeks ago after bearing you a child. God has allowed the baby to live and it's well."

Julien groaned and sought out Ralf's shoulder again.

"Julien, my son. I know you too well to preach to you of God's will. But Adele left you with a fine girl. Claire has her now, and loves her as her own."

"It's so unfair. She wasn't yet fifteen."

"I know, but listen to me. Claire has learned and profited from this painful experience. I pray that you may do so too. Would it help you to know that Adele had a good death? She passed from this world with no sadness and with all her pain behind her. A Christian can ask for no more."

"No sadness! She had such a miserable life. She was just beginning to discover herself . . . to find out what life was about."

"Exactly. She did, Julien. Claire and I were with her through her delivery, and afterwards when she slipped away. I promise you there was no bitterness, no regret. She told us that she wasn't losing her life, but only making an exchange. Imagine! It was only in the last two years that she came to recognize herself as a human being. She told us that the life she lived before was only half a life. She lived as an animal in the dark for most of it. And when she had learned how truly beautiful an existence can be, she was offered the opportunity to trade her own horrible past for the life of an infant who would know love for all its life. She gave her baby to Claire and died happily. What is most wonderful is that her dying had an amazing effect on Claire."

Julien was still unable to speak, and Ralf waited a moment before he went on. "She told Claire she wanted the baby to be named Theodora for Claire's mother, and she asked me if I would be the godfather. Of course, nothing could make me happier. I wanted so much to be at your side for every christening you invited me to."

"And Claire and the children are all well?"

"Your children are the healthiest and most beautiful in all Sicily. And Claire seems utterly transformed. I think she's actually jealous of baby Theodora's wet nurse. At every chance she takes the baby to her breast and keeps it there to suck her. I've watched her at this dry nursing, and she takes on a radiance that is as lovely as anything I've ever witnessed. She's aware of it too. She told me her ideas about herself, and her feelings have been greatly changed since she took the baby."

Julien looked up sharply. Ralf stroked his head. "She's told me everything, Julien, and we both recognize how patient you've been. But don't rush it now. You must still let her take the initiative."

Despite the anguish he felt bursting inside him, Julien found himself smiling. "I never thought I'd be taking advice about women from you."

"Nor I. I know nothing about women, Julien. Like most men, I consider them a necessary evil. I speak to you of Claire as I know her, which is as a sensitive, loving human being worthy of every consideration you show her. You're a very lucky man, Julien."

"Come to Furci with me," he said impulsively. "I must see her right away. We need each other now."

"No, it won't be necessary. I sent word to her that you were due back almost a week ago, and she must be on her way now. If you tried going there, you'd surely miss her. There's something else. I hate to sound like the bearer of infinite bad tidings, but your friend Aziz lost his wife Fatima. She died a few days before Adele did, so Aziz thought it would be well for him to accompany Claire together with his son Ahmad. They'll all be back very soon. Can you put up with my poor company until they return? I know a crotchety, old bachelor is a poor exchange for your beautiful family."

Julien hugged him affectionately. "There's no man I love better. But come, you've told me nothing of yourself."

"Later, Julien. Take some wine and rest first. You no doubt want to say a prayer for Adele and be alone with your thoughts. Suppose I join you in an hour or two?"

Julien sank to his knees and prayed for Adele's peace as soon as Ralf had gone. He was dry-eyed now, and although numbed by his loss, he felt remarkably strong. He stretched out for no more than half an hour, not to sleep, but to recall deliberately as many of his moments with Adele as he could summon. When Ralf rejoined him, he was rested and composed, and anxious to hear of Ralf's experiences.

Ralf poured wine for them and began his story. "It's been an exciting life with Abelard, filled with ideas—but lately also filled with bitterness. Now that the papal schism has been resolved, Bernard is determined to crush Abelard utterly. The pressures on Abelard from Rome have been mounting, and Bernard never misses an opportunity to slander him."

"I know," Julien agreed sadly. "I listened to some Cistercians on the subject of Abelard in Salerno. The newest and most cruel twist to their argument is that Abelard's words can have no value since he is denied the kingdom of Heaven because he is without balls."

"Yes, we're familiar with the biblical source for that vile attack. It's Deuteronomy 23:1. 'He that is wounded in the stones, or hath his privy member cut off, shall not enter into the congregation of the Lord.' But if it's of any use to you in the future, there's a contradiction of that barbarism in Isaiah 56:3 and 4. 'Let not the eunuch say, "Behold I am a dry tree." For thus says the Lord: "To the eunuchs who keep my Sabbath, who choose the things that please me and hold fast my covenant, I will give in my house and within my walls a monument and a name better than sons and daughters: I will give them an everlasting name which shall not be cut off." ' So you see, once again we find that you can support both sides of an argument with the same text if you search long enough."

"Which side will our children believe, do you suppose?"

"Who knows? There is no guarantee of fairness or even intelligent choice in the decisions of history. Abelard is the superior, or at least more advanced thinker, but his adversaries have the power over him."

"I've learned one more thing from Abelard's life that I didn't get from your lessons, Ralf. It seems to me the same churchmen who find sexual expression natural and have the fewest prejudices about it are the ones who believe in peace and are also most charitable towards those who disagree with them, while Bernard and his followers, who see sex as a weapon of the Devil, are quick to demand the blood of those who oppose their ideas."

"You've already heard, then, that Bernard is expected to mount a Second Crusade?"

"It wouldn't surprise me. I can guarantee Roger will have nothing to do with this one, just as his father wouldn't support the last."

"No, the new crusade will be Bernard's next major project, just as soon as Abelard is out of the way. He's travelling through France now, working up support for his campaign to crush Abelard, just as he did when he tried to crush Anacletus. He's called a council at Sens for the express purpose of excommunicating Abelard and expelling him from France. I'm afraid Abelard will never recover from this. It was he who insisted on my leaving, or I'd still be at his side. Arnold of Brescia is still with him, and I have no doubt the Council of Sens will try to ruin them both. Arnold's already excommunicated, as you may have heard, but he continues to preach, and thousands go to hear him.

"I told Abelard that I'd see if King Roger might help his cause, but I believe it's too soon to expect him to have much influence with Innocent's clergy in the north after such a long breach between them."

"That's quite true. And there's one difficult point that may never be resolved. Roger retains the right to install his own bishops . . . the hereditary right conferred by Urban II. As a result, he refuses to dismiss the bishops who were pro-Anacletus."

"I'm beginning to like him more and more. Perhaps I'll stay on here awhile. Do your children need a tutor?"

"Oh Ralf, I'd be the happiest of men if you'd join my family. I realize more and more how much I owe you."

Ralf put a finger to Julien's lips. "I owe you far, far more. Whenever I felt the slightest doubt as to the worth of what Abelard stood for, I thought of you. You're a pure product of his ideas. Look at the world around us, Julien. Christianity hasn't conquered evil, but a belief in man can. I saw your studio, Julien, and its modesty does you credit. I was told you could have asked for much larger offices with as many assistants as you wished. I was particularly touched when I saw the motto over your desk. I'd quite forgotten it."

"You made it for me as a gift on my fourteenth birthday. I had it in my cell, but Prior Anselm made me take it down because he preferred me to gaze on something more edifying. I've always kept it with me. When you introduced me to Terence, I didn't know at the time that he was a Carthaginian before he was brought to Rome as a slave, like the Carthaginians who were among the earliest settlers of Sicily. It's no wonder the words you gave me are so very popular here. *Homo sum, nihil humani me alienum puto.* 'I am a man. Nothing concerning a man do I consider a matter of indifference to me.' It's a very Sicilian motto."

"You make me tremendously proud of you, Julien. Yes, I want very much to stay here with you. It's my turn to learn now, and I can almost feel the earth shaking beneath my feet, as if there's a new revolution in culture breeding in the soil of this island."

Julien's eyes were brimming with tears. "I'll see to it that you meet Roger tomorrow. I'm sure he'll enjoy knowing you, and he'll want to introduce you to the intellectuals of the court."

"I've already met some of them, you know, thanks to the good graces of your friend, Aziz. What a fine Christian gentleman he is."

Julien stopped him with a sly smile.

"I can see I'm going to have to change some of my speech habits," he laughed. "Anyway, Aziz introduced me to the geographer, Edrisi. What do you think of him?"

"I don't know him well yet. He arrived only recently, but he's already Roger's favorite."

"I shouldn't wonder. He collared me as soon as he heard I'd just arrived from the north and asked me dozens of questions. He's compiling a new geography and has Roger's permission to interview all travellers arriving in Sicily."

"Yes, I heard. He's dedicating his book to Roger. I believe he's to call it *The Book of Roger.* It's probably the most expensive book ever planned at this court, because he wants to accompany it with a silver planisphere over a yard wide to illustrate his theories. Roger's given him the money for it as well as his blessing."

"A planisphere. Yes, I can see why. It's a glorious project, all right, but

I wonder how many of the continent's geographers will appreciate it. He let me read his first few pages, and I was so taken with the opening lines, I sent a copy of them to Abelard. I still haven't decided yet if the man is a scientist or poet. Have you read it?"

"No, not yet, but I do know that the Arab geographers all respect him."

"How do you like this?

> *The earth is round as a sphere, but not a perfect one, and the waters adhere to its surface through a natural inertia without separating themselves. Earth and water are fixed in the celestial sphere like the yolk in an egg, and the atmosphere surrounds it on all sides and pulls it to and fro. God knows the truth of this observation.*

He stopped reading, and his eyes met Julien's in wonder.